Seeds for the Swarm

This is a work of fiction. All characters, organizations, and events portrayed in this novel are either products of the author's imagination or are reproduced as fiction.

Seeds for the Swarm

Cover art by Isip Xin
www.isipxin.com

Edited by Selena Middleton

Published by Stelliform Press
Hamilton, Ontario, Canada
www.stelliform.press

Library and Archives Canada Cataloguing in Publication
Title: Seeds for the swarm / Sim Kern.
Names: Kern, Sim, 1986- author.
Identifiers: Canadiana (print) 20220233519 | Canadiana (ebook) 20220233527 | ISBN 9781777682309 (softcover) | ISBN 9781777682316 (ebook)
Classification: LCC PZ7.1.K47 See 2022 | DDC j813/.6—dc23

For Ike

SEEDS FOR THE SWARM

Sim Kern

Stelliform Press
Hamilton, Ontario

1

The McCrackens

The morning before she went viral, Rylla woke to the sound of her mother screaming. She surged up in bed. Was mom under attack? A scrounger? Some guy she'd brought home from Lucky's? Rylla grabbed her thickest paperbook off the floor — Audubon's *Insects of North America* — and brandished it like a weapon as she crept through the trailer towards the source of the screams.

The pleated vinyl door to the bathroom was locked. "Mom?" she called in a quavering voice.

"The water smells like shit!" her mother yelled. The hissing of the shower silenced. "Check the tank!"

Rylla sagged against the wall, pressing a hand to her pounding heart. "So dramatic," she mumbled, heading into the kitchen area of the double-wide trailer, where the carpet gave way to laminate floors. She tossed the paperbook onto a stained counter and lifted the lid on the ionic recycler. Inside the tank, the water was green and stank like sewage. She reeled back, gagging.

"Wlpe down the fllter!" her mother yelled.

3

"I'm wiping, I'm wiping!" she called, pulling out the filter and squeegeeing green slime into the trash. Once reassembled, she re-started the recycler, but a red light flashed angrily, and the console read 'Error 3J-17.'

When she straightened up, Amaryllis McCracken was standing there, buck-naked, water dripping off her wrinkled skin onto the kitchen tiles.

"Mo-om!" Rylla cried, squeezing her eyes shut.

"Oh, honestly," Amaryllis huffed. "Like you've never seen your mother naked before. I know you think I'm a hideous old hag, but you might as well take a good look, because this is your future —"

"Eugh, don't say that!" Rylla groaned, heading for her corner of the trailer.

Her mother bent over the ionic recycler. "What's Error 3J-17?"

"I'll look it up," Rylla said. She flung aside the bedsheet that separated her room from the living room and fished through a pile of laundry for her Occular Generation Goggles. She slung them over her eyes and found her Gluv wadded up under a dirty sock. The wire mesh of the Gluv molded to her fingers as she pulled it on. Then a quick swipe of her hand brought up a browser, and she searched the model number for the recycler.

"This says Error 3J-17 means … 'the system has experienced a catastrophic failure. Contact the manufacturer.'"

"Oof," Amaryllis breathed. "That sounds bad."

"I think it's broke for good this time." Rylla pulled off her OGGles. No ionic recycler meant no showers, no flushing toilets, and no washing dishes for the foreseeable future. She eyed the drinking water tank above the sink, a third full. Without a recycler, there was no way their supply would last them till Distribution Day at the end of the month, even if they lived like scroungers.

"We're gonna have to buy extra water rations," her mother sighed, thinking the same thing. "But first I'm getting this stink off." She disappeared back into the bathroom, and Rylla took the moment of privacy to change out of her pajamas.

"It's too bad Tyler's not here," Amaryllis called. "That boy could fix anything. But nooo. He had to run off to Austin with what's-his-name."

"What's-*their*-name," Rylla corrected. Her mind was also on her brother as she pulled a Cicada Circus t-shirt over her head. Cicada Circus was Tyler's smash band. Three years ago, he'd moved to Austin to live with his partner, Jo, and focus on his music. Neither Rylla nor Amaryllis had forgiven him for leaving them alone with each other.

In the kitchen, her mother was scrubbing an armpit with a soapy washcloth, still naked.

"Do you have to do that *there*?"

"This is where the water is!" Amaryllis gestured at the tank. "Sheesh, how a daughter of mine turned out to be such a prude, I'll never understand."

Rylla turned her back, staring fixedly at the holowall. It was blank, except for the date, floating in glowing numerals near the ceiling — April 17th, 2075.

One week until her eighteenth birthday. Until adulthood, legally speaking.

The realization hit her like a hovertruck to the chest, but she shoved the thought to the back of her mind. Maybe if she didn't think about it, the future would never come.

She swiped her Gluv to pull up the weather. 99°F this morning, twenty percent chance of dust storms. She'd eat breakfast outside then — better enjoy these last days before summer, when she'd need a bulky cooling suit to step out the door.

"Sassy?"

Rylla bristled. Her full name was Sassparylla McCracken — an awful, redneck name. Only her mother called her "Sassy," and she hated it.

Amaryllis held the sodden washcloth towards her, a few crinkly hairs sprouted from its surface. "Here. We shouldn't waste the water —"

"Ew! We're not *that* desperate."

"— besides, you're smelling a bit ripe —"

"I showered two days ago," Rylla muttered, but she headed into the bathroom to put on some deodorant just in case. Through the wall, she heard her mother cackling with laughter.

Ignoring her, Rylla dug through her mother's cosmetics for a hairbrush and set about detangling her long, fine hair. Amaryllis entered, thankfully wearing her navy work coveralls. She pushed Rylla aside with her hip to make room at the mirror and started tracing her eyes with a thick line of royal blue, a style that hadn't been popular in a decade.

The logo on the eyeliner was *Beauxdacious of Detroit* — a Lush State brand. How many gallons of water could they buy for what it had cost?

"Why do you bother wearing makeup to work when you're just going to get covered in machine oil?" Rylla sneered.

"Some people like to look presentable for the world," Amaryllis said. She reached out and fluffed up Rylla's hair. "Why don't you let mommy dye this, or curl it, or *something*?"

Rylla snaked out from her mother's grip and pulled her hair back in her usual tight, low ponytail.

"Look at this face," her mother squeezed Rylla's cheeks together and pointed her towards the mirror. Hazel eyes, millions of freckles, skin the color of melky tea, and an extremely annoyed expression. "Put on some lipstick, and you could be pretty, you know?"

Rylla pulled her head free. "Who've I got to be pretty for?"

Amaryllis followed her into the kitchen. "Whatever happened to that sweet Miles Walker boy you used to hang around with?"

"What? When I was, like, ten?" Rylla grabbed her canteen and a cereal ration. "All he ever posts about is getting high now, and I'm pretty sure he's a scrounger." Amaryllis clucked her tongue as Rylla let the door slam behind her.

Outside the trailer, it always took a few moments for her eyes to adjust to the vast brightness. The Dust stretched in a flat plain as far as the eye could see. The only thing moving between her and the horizon was the occasional gust of wind, lifting an arcing tendril of sand.

The rooster was squawking. Rylla crunched across the gravel yard and scattered corn for the guinea fowl. Then she settled on top of the picnic table to eat, staring out at her familiar stretch of desert.

To the east, a few lone trailers clustered along the highway that led to the company town. Steam billowed from Lockburn chemical refinery, and the oil pumps dipped and reared their great black heads, silhouetted by the rising sun. To the West, a jagged spot on the horizon marked the abandoned city of New Braunfels. When she and Tyler were kids, the ghost town was their personal playground. They'd cart-raced through abandoned stores and claimed riverfront mansions as forts. But best of all was playing in the Guadalupe River.

There was nothing she loved more than standing in the Guadalupe on a spring morning, feeling the cool water flow around her ankles. It was more of a trickle than a river these days, but it was enough to keep the steep banks *alive*. Every species of plant that grew there was like a friend — *Oenothera Speciosa*, Pink Evening Primrose, whose petals looked like fairy skirts. *Gaillardia Pulchella,* with its bright red-and-yellow sunbursts, and of course, *Lupinus Texensis,* the cloudlike Bluebonnets, tempting the last bees in Texas with their perfume from a sweeter time. There were even animals down by the river — damselflies and crickets and *Argiope Arantia*, the Golden Orb Weaver spiders who stretched their massive webs from bank-to-bank at dusk.

Tyler and Rylla had always agreed, though, that the best creatures of all were *Tibesen Superba*. Whenever someone asked why his band was called *Cicada Circus,* Tyler would tell them about the Superb Green Cicadas — huge, alien-looking bugs that lived underground for years before emerging in swarms to breed in a day and then die. For their twenty-four hours in the world, they screamed so loud, you could hear the riverside chorus all the way from the trailer. "What could be more punk rock than that?" Tyler would say. Rylla still kept a shoebox full of their exoskeletons — those papery husks left behind when they took on their adult forms.

The screen door slammed, making Rylla flinch and cough up cereal. Amaryllis tossed her work bag on the table and lit a Nic-Alike cigarette, exhaling the smoke with a long, low sigh. "Do you have any idea what a new ionic recycler costs?" Her mood had changed. All the playfulness gone, voice low and icy. "I been meaning to talk to you, speaking of costs. You know what I got yesterday?"

Rylla picked at her cuticles. When Amaryllis was spoiling for a fight, it was best to say as little as possible.

"A mention, from the State Board of Education. Final notice, they said. Your birthday's next week. No more payments for keeping you in school."

Panic clawed up the back of Rylla's throat. She'd known this was coming — she'd been dreading it all year — but she'd been banking on an escape plan that had failed to materialize.

"It's past time for you to get a job, anyways," Amaryllis continued. "I know you wanted to finish school, but with a broken water recycler and no more student aid? I don't know how we're gonna get by."

"But I'm only two months from graduating!" Rylla pleaded.

"Uh-huh." Amaryllis took the last drag off her Nic-Alike, then tossed the filter. A gust of wind picked up the burning ember and sent it bouncing across the sand, spitting sparks. "Listen, I talked to Mr. Peterson, and he can get you a job in the front office. I told him you're whip-smart and too soft for machine work. It's good pay, and you can sit on a chair all day —"

Rylla knew Brock Peterson from the Water Rations Distribution Center. His head was like an old leather bag, with mean, little eyes that lingered too long.

"Brock Peterson's a creep," she muttered as stray tendrils of hair whipped around her face. The wind was really picking up.

"Brock Peterson is an old friend," Amaryllis snapped. "He got me my job after your daddy left, and now he's doing me another favor —" She fell silent, as the world around them dimmed. To the east, where the rising sun had shone moments before, the land was churning up into the sky.

"Shit," they said in unison as the dust storm swallowed the refinery.

"Get the birds!" Amaryllis called, heading for her truck to pull on its dust cover. God forbid anything mess up the paint job.

Rylla jogged towards the guinea fowl. "Shoo!" she yelled, herding them towards the coop. Obediently, the hens barreled inside, but the rooster squared off with Rylla, screeching and ruffling his feathers. Rylla chased him in a circle, the wind tugging at her clothes. The sky grew dark as twilight. Gritting her teeth, she tackled the bird. His talons gouged her forearms as she shoved him in the coop. Slamming the coop's storm-door behind him, she took off around the side of the trailer.

But the wall of sand was nearly upon her now. She pulled her OGGles onto her eyes and the neck of her t-shirt over her mouth. A second later, a wall of wind slammed into her from behind, and Rylla was swallowed in dust. Thousands of sand particles scraped along her exposed skin. They seeped through the t-shirt pressed to her face. She coughed, tasting the dust in her lungs, as she stumbled the last few yards to the trailer door. Her mother hauled her inside, slamming the door behind her.

For a few minutes, Rylla coughed and blew her nose into a dishrag, spattering it with mud. Only when she could breathe clearly did she notice how muffled everything sounded.

Digging a pinky in her ear, she dislodged a plug of sand, and instantly regretted it.

"What took you so long? Look how much dust got inside! You better not think I'm gonna clean up this mess."

Sighing, Rylla went to grab the vacuum from the closet. The lights flickered as the power in the trailer switched from solar to battery. Outside the windows, it was dark as night. Howling wind and hissing sand lashed the outer walls of the trailer. She hoped all the insects down by the river were okay. After a dust storm, the river would be muddy and sluggish for days, but somehow the insects survived. She imagined a damselfly, huddled beneath a leaf as the dust storm raged overhead, and she felt a surge of anxiety for all creatures with tissue-thin wings.

Back in the living room, Amaryllis perched on the couch, sipping koffy from a can and watching the holowall. She'd turned it to the *Actually True News* channel, and two slightly pixelated people now stood above the hologenerators just beyond the coffee table. Owned by Lockburn, *Actually True News* was her mother's favorite channel, but Tyler had always called it "brain-dissolving propaganda."

Chet Strongman was pacing through the field of the holowall, blabbing about some dam that was going to be built to his co-host, Barbie Washington. Chet had the blue eyes, sharp jawline, and rippling muscles of a white Captain America. Rylla sneered at his hologram and pulled her OGGles up over her eyes. But before she could turn them on, Amaryllis snatched them off her head.

"We're not done talking."

Rylla flicked the vacuum to the highest setting, hoping to drown out her mother and Chet.

"I got you a *good* job with Mr. Peterson. You won't find something better on your own."

"This dam is going to be a *great* thing for the people of south-central Texas," Chet told Barbie, who was nodding along with wide, surgically-enlarged doe-eyes.

"Just give me a little more time," Rylla begged. "If I graduate, I can go to college —"

"Wake up!" Amaryllis said, snapping her fingers in Rylla's face. "Tuition is what, a million dollars a year for a Lush State school? Where exactly do you think I'm hiding that kind of money?" She swept a hand around the cramped trailer. "I can't even afford enough water to get us through this month!"

"There are things called scholarships," Rylla muttered, her voice lost in the vacuum's roar.

Barbie Washington chimed in, her lavender lip gloss sparkling in the trailer's dim lights. "You mean there's all this water just *sitting* there? And the dam will send that water right to the Lockburn refinery?"

"That's right, Barbie," Chet said, "and that extra water means it will be *cheaper* to refine the oil. Cost-savings like that are good for the Lockburn Corporation. And you know what we always say: What's good for Lockburn is good for Texans!"

"Sassy, I know you wanted to finish school, but we're out of options here. I need you to start earning your keep."

But Rylla wasn't listening to her anymore.

What dam? What was Chet talking about? She flicked off the vacuum and moved closer to the holowall, heart in her throat.

"Sounds like a win-win," Barbie chirped. "And the State Senate will be voting on the dam? This afternoon?"

"That's right, Barbie," Chet said. "The *Water for Lockburn* bill is up for a vote today. So shoot your representative a mention, and tell them you support the *Guadalupe River Dam!*"

"No!" Rylla collapsed onto the couch, a hand clasped to her mouth.

Her river. They were talking about damming up *her* river.

A terrible vision of her future stretched before her. Just like her mother, she'd work ten-hour days at Lockburn and get drunk at Lucky's after her shifts. Every day would be exactly the same, and without her river, there'd be no wildflowers in spring to look forward to, no cicadas singing to her on summer afternoons. Her future looked as endless and barren as the dust.

Amaryllis either hadn't heard or didn't care about the news of the dam. "Sassy, I told Mr. Peterson you'd start work Monday."

"Why would you do that?" Rylla asked slowly, blood pounding in her ears. She stood and faced Amaryllis. "I told you, I'm not working for Lockburn. I'm not working for Brock Peterson. I'm going to finish school, go to college, and get the hell out of here!" At some point, she'd started shouting, hands clenched into fists.

Amaryllis staggered backwards. "Fine, leave," she said in a small, wounded voice. "Your brother left. Your father left. Why wouldn't you leave me too, since *apparently* it's such a hell-hole here?" Rylla's stomach twisted with guilt. "All I ever did was work hard for you kids. Did you ever go thirsty?"

Rylla buried her face in her hands. As her mother rattled on with an epic guilt trip, she felt like the walls of the trailer were closing in on her. If she stayed here, she was going to lose her mind. Or murder her mother. Either way, she had to get out.

She flung open the bedsheet to her room and swung a long, linen duster over her shoulders.

"What do you think you're doing?"

Rylla ignored her, tucking the sleeves of the duster into lightweight gloves.

"You're not going anywhere in this storm. It's thick as Louisiana mud outside." Rylla fished her respirator out of the laundry and strapped it over her mouth and nose.

Chet Strongman was talking about how the dam would clear out all the scrounger gangs who poached water from the river. Amaryllis wagged her finger at the holowall. "Hear that? Remember that guy from Fredericksburg?"

"No, mom, I don't remember 'that guy,'" Rylla muttered.

"A few months ago. His NavApp broke while he was out in a Dust Storm, remember? He wandered into a scrounger camp on accident?"

Rylla froze. She *did* remember.

"They found his body by the landfill. 'Over a hundred broken bones,' they said. I didn't even know people *had* more'n a hundred bones."

Rylla shook her head. Her mother was trying to control her, like always. Scare her into staying in the trailer. It wasn't going to work.

She slung her backpack over one shoulder and gripped the door handle.

"Sassy, we're not done here! If you go out that door, don't bother coming ba —"

Rylla flung open the door and let it slam on her mother's last word.

2

Teacher

The wind tore at Rylla's clothes and sand scraped her OGGles. She lifted a hand in front of her face but saw nothing. It was like she had been erased.

With a swipe, she loaded up the navigation app. A fuschia-colored dragon backflipped into existence in front of her. "NavAtar," Rylla said. "Show low visibility overlay." Glowing lines spiderwebbed across her vision, outlining the world the dust storm had obscured — the trailer, the picnic table, the guinea fowl coop. Looking down, she saw a glowing outline of her body.

"Take me to preset location: School."

The vibra-speakers at her temples buzzed. "There is a Dust Storm in your area. NavAtar recommends you shelter in place."

"Yeah, I know about the storm," she said. "Override."

A golden, floating compass appeared, spinning with Rylla's every movement. NavAtar turned his back to her, flew a few paces ahead, and beckoned Rylla to follow. She plodded after the dragon, shoulders pushing against the wind.

As the outline of the trailer dwindled behind, and with nothing but swirling sand ahead, Amaryllis's warning nagged at her. She couldn't get the image of that bloodied, beaten corpse out of her mind. He'd wandered into a scrounger camp in a storm just like this.

Scroungers didn't get their water from government rations — they poached it, so they stuck close to the river. They never stayed in one place too long, but Rylla knew where they liked to camp and gave those places a wide berth. When she and Tyler were kids, they'd often spotted scroungers from afar, but they'd never gotten close enough to get caught. The older she got, though, the more terrified she was of running into scroungers. They might have better things to do than chase after some kids, but if a seventeen-year-old girl, alone in a storm, wandered into their camp? The thought of what they might do to her was enough to make her look back towards home.

But then she pictured her mother, pacing back and forth, rehearsing a lecture about the joys of working for Brock Peterson. Rylla decided to take her chances with the storm.

For half an hour, she trudged West, with nothing but the holographic dragon for a guide. Sweat steamed up her OGGles, and by the time she reached the outskirts of New Braunfels, her legs ached from pushing against the wind. First, the glowing neon outline of a crumbling gas station appeared. Then a housing development, looted long ago. At last, a long, two-story brick building rose above her, the windows boarded shut.

She headed around the side of the building, where the board over the third window was held on by a few loose nails. She slipped through and pulled the board in place behind her.

Pitch-blackness. Rylla ripped the sweaty respirator from her face and took a deep breath of stale air. With a finger-swipe, cold light beamed from her OGGles, illuminating a long hallway, lined with rusting lockers ...

And a person.

Rylla froze, heart slamming in her chest. But a half-second later, she realized it was no scrounger.

"You scared me, Miss Honey," she said. As her voice echoed down the corridor, she felt silly for speaking at all. Miss Honey was plastic, a sun-bleached mannequin Tyler had once dragged here in a wagon, all the way from the department store on State Street. At the time, Rylla loved *Matilda*, a paperbook about kids who go to a real school, and Tyler had recreated Miss Honey's classroom for her as a birthday present. Pictures they had drawn with crumbling crayons still decorated the walls. Beneath a blanket of dust, Miss Honey's stuffed animal students gazed at a cracked holowall with painted eyes.

Usually, Miss Honey gave Rylla a warm feeling of nostalgia, but today the mannequin's blank stare and slightly extended arms sent a chill up her spine, and she hurried down the corridor.

Passing through a pair of double doors, she fumbled on the floor for Tyler's homemade switchboard, worrying the storm had knocked out the power line to the solar battery bank again. But a flick of a switch flooded the library in warm, colorful light. Dozens of strands of Christmas lights spread out in every direction, looping over bookcases, trailing on the floor, and swooping between the drop-tile ceiling.

Dropping into a faded yellow beanbag chair, Rylla pulled up Joinly out of habit. Her vision filled with gently drifting bubbles advertising trending holovids. Three of the bubbles pulsed red — mentions. She poked the first one, and it swelled to fill her vision. "Hey Rylla! Are you *so* addicted to the hottest new game, BabeBrawl 7?" A busty digital blonde wearing boxing gloves and a blood-soaked bikini rested her chest on the edge of the ad-bubble. Rylla waved a hand to clear the ad.

Most of her mentions came from advertising bots. She did have a few human Joinly friends, but most of them never mentioned her. Not even Miles Walker, and they used to spend hours hunting crickets together down by the Guadalupe.

Today, he'd posted a holovid of himself smoking a pipe of lolly-lolly and giving a thumbs-up as his pupils dilated. She wondered if he'd heard about the dam. If he cared.

"Run SCHOEL," she commanded. The Joinly interface vanished, and cube-shaped icons appeared around the edges of her vision. A man slowly solidified before her as his program downloaded. He had dark, piercing eyes and a jawline that could cut glass. He also had the boxy look and choppy movements of an avatar from a ten-year-old graphics engine.

"Good morning, Rylla," he purred in a mellow baritone. "Welcome back to SCHOEL, your Simulated Classroom for Holistic, Occupational, and Educational Learning."

"Good morning, Teacher," Rylla said. Teacher winked at Rylla, and she rolled her eyes. Teacher 4.1 had come out earlier this year to make SCHOEL "sexier," a misguided attempt by the Dust States Board of Education to keep teens enrolled. But kids didn't drop out because SCHOEL wasn't *sexy* enough. They dropped out because the software was terrible. If you got confused, there was no human being you could ask to explain the content another way. If you got stuck on a test, you couldn't move forward. Miles Walker and most of Rylla's friends had dropped out in the sixth grade, which was notoriously glitchy. Rich Dusties, like Lockburn executives, sent their kids to real, Lush State boarding schools, but for kids like the McCrackens, SCHOEL was the only classroom they'd ever known.

An advertising bubble popped up in front of her face. Ivy-covered brick buildings and attractive students laughing on a green lawn. Glowing text read:

```
Attend the University of Pennsylvania

   ✓ Study with Human Teachers!
   ✓ Meet your classmates in person!
   ✓ Walk to class beneath living trees!

        Click for more info
```

Oh, Rylla had clicked, and she'd seen the cost of tuition.

"You have *sixty* days left until graduation," Teacher 4.1 reminded her. "Would you like to apply for college?"

"Yeah, I would," Rylla snapped. "Only I can't afford it. And they all say, 'We're sorry,'" she mocked an official-sounding voice, "'Dust State applicants don't qualify for financial aid at this time.'"

"You seem tense," Teacher said. "Would you like to play a short de-stressing game?"

She growled at him and pulled up her grades. Holding her breath, she scanned the numbers 100, 100, 100 ... 99. Not good enough. She swiped open the SCHOEL Leaderboards — the all-time rankings of every SCHOEL student. At the top of the chart was a banner ad:

Beat The HIGH SCORE And Win A FULL SCHOLARSHIP To College!

Sponsored By Lockburn Energy Solutions

There, in 2nd place, was Sassparylla McCracken, with an all-time score of 99.96. Right above her was some jerk from California, Jae Boudreaux, who'd managed a score of 99.98. Jae Boudreaux had graduated SCHOEL last semester and was probably frolicking around the college of his dreams. For the last few months, she'd been so close to overtaking him, every 100% bringing her a fraction of a point closer. But now, according to her mother, she'd run out of time.

Amaryllis couldn't *force* her to quit SCHOEL ... could she? If Rylla refused to work at Lockburn, would mom kick her out of the trailer? Rylla's chest tightened with dread. Maybe, if she got a hundred on every assignment for the next few days, she could still win the scholarship before adulthood closed in around her.

Determined to keep working, she pulled up her assignments. She had a history quiz to take on the passage of the 29th amendment, the "Bill of Rights Qualifier" which said people had the right to the freedoms of speech and assembly *only* if they didn't interfere with economic activity. SCHOEL was supposed to disable your ability to search the OGnet, so you couldn't cheat on tests, but there were apps to get around that, and Rylla used them to breeze through the questions. *Why was the 29th amendment necessary?* Well, because large protest actions like the Climate Strike, Black Lives Matter, and Standing Rock were dangerous, disruptive to civic order, and harmful to the economy, of course!

That's not what Rylla believed, but she knew that was how SCHOEL wanted her to answer. In her heart, she felt inspired by all those people who'd crowded city streets and shouted for a better world. Especially when she learned that some of the leaders of those movements had been her age or younger. She got sucked down a net-search rabbit hole for nearly an hour when she discovered that in the early 2000's, a wave of protest movements against dams — like the one threatening the Guadalupe — led to the dismantling of over a thousand dams across the U.S. Anti-dam protests were often led by Native American tribes, fighting to restore the ecosystems that sustained their traditional ways of life. She'd had no idea that so many people had fought to protect their watersheds, and her heart swelled as she read about their victories.

Still, when she swiped back to the quiz and saw, *What did most early twentieth century protestors have in common?* she selected the correct answer, according to the state-approved study guide: *Too much time on their hands.* She got a 100% on the assignment, then checked her leaderboard stats again — no change.

Sighing, she pulled up her assignment for Civics. "Write a 2,000-word essay about a positive change you've made in your community."

Rylla snorted. What community? Should she write about doing the dishes for her mom? Picking up trash along the Guadalupe? If your only friends were insects, did they count as your "community?"

Despair churned in her gut as her thoughts returned to the dam that would doom those insects. No protest movement could stop Lockburn. She'd never heard of *anyone* protesting *anything* in Texas — at least not in her lifetime — and folks certainly wouldn't stand up to the oil corporation that employed almost everyone.

No, Lockburn was going to destroy the one good, green thing in her world, and her mother was forcing her to work for them. Everything Rylla had ever dreamed of — finishing SCHOEL, emigrating to a Lush State, going to college and studying some way to repair the ecology of the Dust — it all seemed about as likely as Lockburn giving up the oil business out of the goodness of its CEO's heart.

Tears were spilling into her OGGles, so she ripped them off her face. Sinking deeper into the beanbag chair, she gave in to the hopelessness that had been building all day and sobbed for her rapidly-disintegrating dreams.

Some part of her, though, wasn't ready to give up on the future completely. If this was to be her last-ever SCHOEL assignment, she might as well go out with a bang. The Guadalupe River *was* her "community," and maybe there was still something she could do to save it. She thought over that history quiz — all those people waving poster-papers, shouting slogans, marching on government buildings. Could she do something like that? Protect her river, like the Water Protectors at Standing Rock? Like those old-timey teenagers who started movements — Autumn Peltier, Greta Thunberg, Emma Gonzalez? If she did, would anyone care?

Chet Strongman had said the State Senate was voting on the Guadalupe Dam *this* afternoon. If she could get a ride into Austin, she might get there before the vote. And if she could make it to the Capitol building, she could do ... what, exactly?

Something. She'd do *something* to try and save her river.

She pulled her OGGles back on and called Tyler, pointing the tip of her Gluv'd finger at her face, so he could see her through the camera.

He appeared inside a bubble floating across her vision. He'd taken the call on his holowall, so Rylla could see the inside of his apartment, lined with shelves improbably crowded with potted plants. Tyler sat up in bed, blinking sleepily, his deflated mohawk flopped over one eye. On the bed beside him, Jo's broad, bare shoulders heaved with snores.

He groaned even while swiping Rylla into view. "It's my day off! Why're you waking me up?"

"I need a ride."

The State Senate

Rylla clung to Tyler's chest as the sandbike flew north across the desert. Between the wind howling in her ears and the roar of the old solar-diesel engine, conversation was impossible. Somewhere beneath the wheels wound an old highway, but it was obscured by a thick layer of sand. NavApp was the only way to chart a course through the no-man's land between New Braunfels and Austin.

As they rode, Rylla searched the OGnet to learn about the workings of the State Senate. The bill would be announced in committee, there'd be time for public commentary, and that's when she'd have a chance to speak. It wouldn't be easy to change the Senators' minds. Politicians these days were bought and sold by corporations, and Lockburn was the most powerful corp in the Dust. But hadn't she just read about activists who'd changed peoples' minds — enough to start mass movements? As she imagined herself delivering a passionate speech before the senators, fear and hope surged in her chest.

Finally, the landscape of bare rock and dust grew jagged with the ruins of abandoned homes. Hovercars and trucks crowded the road. As they neared the first checkpoint on the road to Austin, traffic slowed to a crawl. Far overhead, on a crumbling overpass, armed guards scowled in their direction. Austin was a city under siege by rival scrounger gangs, and the cops treated everyone like potential threats.

A cop examined their IDs, did a scowling double-take at Tyler's hair, then waved them through. They wound their way through neighborhoods where every tree was dead, every yard turned to dust, every house gutted for glass and wire. The vacant windows looked like eyes, the gaping doorways like mouths, faces frozen in shock at what had befallen their city.

They stopped at another checkpoint before the Congress Avenue bridge into downtown. As they sped over the dry riverbed far below, Rylla tried to imagine how massive the Colorado River must once have been. Now, not even a trickle of water was left. Wisps of dust gusted over the earth, cracked like the scales of a giant serpent.

On the far shore, tall skyscrapers penned them in, and the streets were crowded with hovercars and sandbikes. Strangers in expensive-looking clothes strolled past the storefronts along 6th street. She didn't know how Tyler got used to living in a place where there was always someone to overhear your conversations.

Just past the city wall, Rylla glimpsed a skyscraper claimed by scroungers. The bones of the building were covered in layers of graffiti — slogans like *Water is a right! Eat Water Profiteers!* and the symbols of various gangs — bison skulls, scorpions, and the crossed staff and filtration straw. Most windows had been smashed out, and campfire smoke poured from the gaping holes. One scrounger, high up, leaned against a windowframe, looking out over the city, and Rylla swore they looked right at her. Despite the blistering midday heat, a chill of fear shot up her spine, and she was grateful when Tyler rounded a corner, blocking the building from sight.

It was surprisingly easy to get through security at the Capitol building — a bored guard, a chem detector, and then they were walking up the marble steps, built when Texas was young and the land was fertile. Inside, the air smelled of mildew and dust. Cellar spider webs spanned the vaulted ceilings, and many of the lightbulbs in the wall fixtures were flickering or burnt out.

"The hallowed halls of congress," Tyler said mockingly. "What a dump."

There was no one in sight, and Rylla had no clue where to go. They took off in opposite directions, peeking in darkened offices and empty meeting rooms. Rylla started to panic that the vote would be over before they could find someone to ask for directions.

"Over here!" Tyler called from a set of impressive double doors. Rylla jogged over and heard voices from within. They slipped inside.

Like the rest of the building, this room had seen better days. Peeling wood laminate covered the walls. An aisle of faded carpet led between the rows of auditorium seats. A group of business people in black suits sat in the first row, muttering together, and two people who looked like scroungers were snoring in seats near the back. The last traces of Rylla's hope evaporated beneath the flickering fluorescent lights.

Halfway down the central aisle, Rylla dropped into a seat, and was promptly dumped on the floor. The chair was broken. Blushing, she scrambled back up, picked another seat, and sat down gingerly. A mustached security guard at the front glowered at her, like she'd fallen on purpose.

Tyler relaxed into the chair beside her. "Nice entrance," he said. She stuck her tongue out at him. Several of the suit-wearing people in the front row turned and glared.

"Who do you think it was?" Tyler whispered, nodding his head towards the business people.

Rylla looked at him quizzically.

"Who stuck those sticks up their butts?"

She snorted a laugh, but her smile quickly faded. What the hell was she doing here? Those business people weren't going to give a shit about her river.

Movement overhead caught her eye. In the gallery encircling the upper level, someone fiddled with a many-headed holographic camera. Good. At least the meeting would be broadcast. Maybe someone who cared would be out there, watching. The person caught her staring and imitated Rylla's open-mouthed gape. Rude. She stuck a tongue out at them and snapped her gaze back to the front, where the State Senators were filing into their seats behind a high, curved bench.

Tyler leaned towards Rylla and whispered, "That jacked guy in black and yellow — he represents TBC — a construction corp. And the three in black suits are Lockburn." He pointed to a young femme wearing a dress patterned in neon-blue-and-orange. "She's the senator from Omega Mart."

"How can you tell?" Rylla asked sarcastically. Neon-blue-and-orange were the colors of Omega Mart's logo. "Do you think she's contractually obligated to wear that?"

"Oh, for sure. Any time they go in public, they have to dress according to the 'brand aesthetic' of their top campaign donor. A bunch of corps even make candidates get plastic surgery to fit their brand's 'youthful image.'"

"How do you know all this?" Rylla whispered.

"Here," Tyler swiped a hand and sent an app to Rylla's OGGles — *DonorKnow*. Rylla opened the program and glowing white text appeared over the head of each senator — a list of corporate names and dollar figures in the millions and tens-of-millions.

A middle-aged man, with salt-and-pepper hair, wearing a gunmetal-colored suit had "BoCorr" as his top-listed donor. Rylla poked the name and a browser bubble appeared, linking to BoCorr's website. Weapons manufacturers.

"Why does the dude from BoCorr look so familiar?" she whispered.

Tyler waved a hand again, and a picture appeared in Rylla's vision — the same man ten-years younger, without cheek-fillers. "Oh! It's the bad guy! From that holonovela *Lágrimas del Corazón*. The one mom thought was so hot."

Tyler sighed. "You know, once upon a time, politicians were lawyers and judges and stuff, not just washed-up celebrities and influencers."

Rylla ran a face-recognition app on the other senators. The Omega Mart lady was a mukbang star, and the huge TBC guy went viral a few years back making holovids where he beat up cars with his bare hands. "Is it really worse now though?" Rylla whispered back. She thought about the history she'd read that morning — how, in 2030, Congress had responded to massive climate protests by making most forms of protest illegal. "Weren't those old-timey senators greedy and racist and awful back then too?"

The security guard bellowed, "Quiet in the chamber!" glaring at Rylla and Tyler.

Senator BoCorr spoke first, "Okay, so this is — uh, the senate infrastructure committee. I'm supposed to read this." He swiped a finger to pull something up on his OGGles. "Pursuant to State Senate Rule 8, Senators will hear from members of the public regarding the expedient allocation of funds for highways, public works ..." His voice was flat and bored, so different from his over-the-top performances on *Lágrimas del Corazón*.

One of the business people in the audience approached the podium at the front of the chamber and asked for money to repair a highway.

"Mom's gonna kill you if she finds out about this, you know," Tyler whispered. "Criticizing Lockburn? In public? She might have a brain aneurism."

Rylla chewed her thumbnail. "Yeah, well, she's already threatened to kick me out if I don't go to work for them."

"You might not be *able* to work for them if you go through with this."

Rylla grinned at the thought.

The business person finished, and Senator BoCorr called for a vote.

"Yes," said the senator from TBC. "Always yes on new construction."

"I'm a no," said Senator Omega Mart.

The senator from TBC huffed in displeasure, folding his trunk-like arms.

"What?" She curled a lip at him. "I vote how they tell me."

Senator BoCorr waved a Gluv as if scrolling through something. "My board hasn't said one way or another, so I abstain."

"We're all noes," said one of the grim-faced Lockburn senators.

"Then the noes have it," Senator BoCorr announced. The business person sagged, taking a seat. Rylla felt her resolve slipping. She wiped her clammy palms on her duster, but the linen didn't absorb the sweat. She almost missed it when BoCorr's man said, "All right, time for public comment on this 'Water for Lockburn' thing. Any of y'all here for that?" He peered at the business people up front, but they stayed seated.

Rylla jumped up and pushed past Tyler's knees, heart pounding. Senator BoCorr looked up at her, eyebrows above his OGGles raised. The walk to the podium seemed to take forever, and by the time she reached it, her legs were trembling. None of the Senators had removed their OGGles, or even turned down the opacity, so a dozen lifeless, black circles faced her. Rylla opened her mouth, but it was like all the air in the room had been sucked out. She couldn't breathe.

"What are you, like, fourteen? You gonna say something, cutie?" Senator BoCorr tipped up his OGGles and leered at her.

She wanted to run out of the room and pretend this never happened, that she'd never even heard of the dam. But that wouldn't save her river. She reminded herself she was doing this for *Tibesen Superba*. She thought of their monstrous subterranean forms, painstakingly clawing up out of the earth, emerging into sunlight, exoskeletons cracking open, glittering-green carapaces emerging into the world where they would fly, and fuck, and *scream*.

"My name is Sassparylla McCracken," she said. "And I'm urging you to vote *against* the Guadalupe River Dam."

At first, sharing her concern for the future of the watershed, her voice trembled. But as she described the plants and animals that called the Guadalupe home, she picked up speed, and her confidence grew, until the words were flowing from her like a river.

And as she spoke, it dawned on her that no one was listening. It was always hard to tell if someone wearing OGGles was listening to you. But Rylla noticed first one, then another senator whose heads were propped on their hands, mouths slack. Senator BoCorr, at least, had seemed to listen for a moment, but he'd replaced his OGGles and now was swiping at something with a Gluv.

Her fingers dug into the sides of the podium, and her words sharpened. "Look, I know that times are tough, and water is scarce. I know there's not much left to the river. But that doesn't mean we should give up on it!"

She was shouting, but if the senators noticed, they made no sign.

"Along the banks of the Guadalupe River, there is *grass* — fluffy bluesedge and purpletop and bouteloua — the only wild plants I've ever known. There are insects that live in that grass. And every day, I lay in the grass, and the grass is hope. Hope for a better world. Hope that we can bring back the past. The way the river used to be." Rylla's eyes burned, and her voice shook with emotion.

"If you build this dam, the grass will die. The insects will die. The only wildlife within a hundred miles will die! And without that grass ... my *soul* will die."

Her voice cracked. Staring at the impassable faces of the State Senators, Rylla sunk into despair. How naïve she'd been to think her words had any kind of power. That kind of hope had died with the 29th amendment.

A chime sounded, and Senator BoCorr's head snapped up. "That was a nice poem, young lady, but your time's up."

A flicker of movement caught her eye. The senator from TBC was surreptitiously punching and slapping the air beneath the table. She recognized the movements from those ads clogging up her Joinly feed. He was playing that hit hologame — BabeBrawl 7.

Rage pulsed through her blood, boiling-hot.

"Fine, sit here and play games while the world goes to hell," she shouted. "It's assholes like you who ruined this planet in the first place!" She kicked the podium. It was lighter than it appeared and flew forward — she grabbed for it — too late. It crashed down, and the top popped off like a cork.

After a moment of shocked silence, Senator BoCorr slid his OGGles up on his forehead. "Well, you're a feisty little firecracker aren't you? Why don't you come by my office, and we can discuss your concerns in more detail?" He flashed an oily smile. "But in the meantime, us grown-ups have some work to do, so off you go." He waved a hand, and the security guard lurched towards Rylla, grabbed her by the armpit, and hauled her towards the door.

4

Schlitterbahn

"Generally, you don't win people over by calling them assholes." Tyler dug into a cardboard box and handed Rylla a warm, stale beer.

"They weren't even listening!" she shouted, sitting down on the rusted metal of the high platform, dangling her legs off the edge.

"Hey, don't get mad at me." He held his hands up in submission. For as long as she could remember, Tyler had been telling her to calm down, chill out, take it easy. And for as long as she could remember, she never had. Now, as anger ebbed from her body, shame flooded in and she slumped forward, head in her hands. She had inherited these intense mood swings from their mother. It was what she hated most about herself, and what she felt most powerless to change.

Tyler sat next to her on the platform. By the time they'd gotten back to New Braunfels, the dust storm had settled. Now a nearly full moon lit the clear sky, and the ruins of Schlitterbahn cast strange, skeletal shapes across the dust. Half a century ago, Schlitterbahn — *"Slippery Road"* — had

30

been the largest waterpark in the entire world, a place where families paid to slide around on steep, man-made rivers.

"I wonder what the Comal was like back then." He squinted to make out the thin, dark line of the dried riverbed, snaking through the landscape at the edge of the park. Once, the Comal River had flowed into the Guadalupe, half a mile away. But the springs that fed the Comal had dried up decades ago, along with most of the rivers in the Dust. By the mid-'30s, a century of damming and irrigation had destroyed watersheds across the West, and climate change had brought decades of drought and mega-wildfires. Farmers scrambled to try new genetically-modded, drought-resistant crops, but they sapped the parched soils of whatever nutrients they had left. By the mid-'40s, lifeless desert spread across most of the land west of the Mississippi watershed, and people started calling these states "The Dust."

"You've never looked at the Geohistory here?" Rylla asked. Tyler shook his head. "I'll send it to you."

She slipped her OGGles over her eyes and pulled up an app. "Schlitterbahn, year 2000." The dry, moonlit landscape before her morphed into a sunny paradise. The riverbed swelled with a torrent of rushing, green water. Live oak and cottonwood trees erupted from the earth, unfurling millions of leaves that blotted out the riverbank. The strange, ruined towers all around became whole again, supporting enormous tubes of plastic, flooded with streams of crystal-clear water. A child ran past her face and launched themself into one of the tubes, only to come shooting out, moments later, into an unfathomable quantity of water far below.

With a flick of her Gluv, she sent the vision to Tyler, and her own view reverted to barren moonscape. Garbage and concrete debris filled the pool at the base of the tower. The stairs up to the platform were rusted through, so to get up here, they'd had to hoist themselves into the one intact slide and clamber up like a couple of long legged *Acanthocephala Declivises*.

She took a long drag of beer and looked over at Tyler. Tattoos of Texas insects crawled down his arms — longhorn beetles, praying mantids and emerald damselflies. His floppy mohawk fell over his OGGles. His mouth was set in a grim line. It wasn't easy to see Schlitterbahn in its prime. All that water. He sighed and pulled his OGGles down. "And now ..."

"Even this little bit will be gone." She looked towards the Guadalupe, a dark line of vegetation far in the distance. "I didn't think it was possible, but living here is going to suck even more."

"And how is our dear mother?"

"The same. I don't know. She won't shut up about me going to work at Lockburn."

"What about that one scholarship ...?" His voice trailed off as she shook her head.

They were silent for a time. Finally, Rylla forced some cheerfulness into her voice. "Enough about my shitty life — what about you? How's Jo?"

"They brought home another plant," Tyler said, scowling. Rylla laughed. Thanks to Jo, Tyler's apartment was like a tiny botanical garden. "Dragon's Tongue, this one's called. I told them, you're gonna get dragon *lips* if you keep sharing your water rations with a bunch of plants! That fool is de-hy-drate-ed!" He clapped for emphasis between each syllable. In spite of his complaints, though, she knew Tyler loved Jo all the more for their devotion to plants.

Suddenly Tyler's smile dropped. In the distance, someone *else* was laughing.

They waited in silence, hoping whoever it was would pass on by. But the voices — deep and drunk — came steadily closer.

Five figures emerged from the darkness, clambering over the rubble of an old waterslide.

Scroungers.

Their clothes were a patchwork of the most garish fabrics they could find. She assumed they were men from their deep swaggering voices and the beards all of them — except one — wore were long and matted, decorated with scraps of shiny plastic. The effect was like if a rainbow puked on a gremlin. Each carried a welded metal staff, which they used to shovel through trash heaps or beat up unlucky "consumers."

"Is that —" Tyler whispered, pointing to the one beardless scrounger.

"Miles Walker," she hissed. "I think so."

She held her breath, willing the scroungers to move on without noticing them. Right as they passed underfoot, though, the one who was wearing a crown cut from an old tire stopped. "Wait! I kella watch it again."

Someone tossed a pair of latest-gen OGGles to Tire-Crown. Scroungers refused to buy anything, but they had no qualms about *stealing* the newest gadgets. Rylla clenched the OGGles around her neck protectively.

While Tire-Crown strapped on the OGGles, two of the scroungers flopped down into the rubble filling the old pool. They looked right at home in a heap of broken concrete.

Rylla and Tyler exchanged a nervous, silent glance.

"That vid laughs!" said one of the seated scroungers with a thick black beard. He was packing a pipe with a gunky substance scooped from a plastic baggie. A loud guffaw burst from Tire-Crown, as he watched something on the OGGles. He doubled-over with laughter and slammed his staff — a fused column of melted crowbars — on the ground.

"You kella watch the remix," said Miles. Rylla rolled her eyes at the affected dialect. She remembered when he had asked her mom for cookies with a *"thank you, ma'am."*

Blackbeard put the pipe to his lips and touched it with a lighter. The bowl glowed, illuminating grease-stained features. He exhaled a cloud of smoke that blossomed into the air, drifting up to where Rylla and Tyler sat. It didn't smell like NicAlike or lollylolly, or any of the drugs their mom sometimes smoked. It was something harsher, home made at the landfill, and it made her eyes water.

Blackbeard suddenly jumped up, spread his arms wide and bellowed at the moon, "THERE IS ASS!"

The other scroungers burst into laughter. Tyler shot Rylla a puzzled look.

Tire-Crown held out a hand as the laughter died down. "W-w-wait —" he choked out, "the best part —" He ran a few steps and jumped onto a boulder of concrete, posing like a pirate captain. "Every day, I lay in the ASS, and the ASS IS HOPE!" Again, the gang dissolved into laughter. Miles wheezed so hard he looked like he would pass out. Rylla got a déjà vu feeling, like she'd heard the phrase before. Maybe she'd seen the holovid they were quoting.

The laughter died down, and Miles took a turn on the pipe. Two others started sword-fighting with their twisted metal staffs. Rylla was trying not to imagine what getting her bones smashed by one of those staffs would feel like, when she felt the sharp sting of a sneeze forming at the back of her sinuses. Her eyes watered, and she clasped a hand over her nose, shooting Tyler a desperate look. Catching her drift, he wrapped his arm around her head, smashing her face into his forearm.

The sneeze rocketed through her, but they'd stifled it enough that only a small *Snnk!* came out. She peeked over Tyler's arm at the scroungers. They hadn't noticed. Tyler relaxed and pulled his arm back, wiping her snot on his pants.

Unfortunately, the second sneeze took Rylla by surprise. Perhaps because she'd held in the first one, this one was especially powerful. The blast of mucus rang out and echoed among the skeletal ruins of the park.

Far below, five moonlit faces stared up at them.

5

Gone Viral

"I hear stray cats," growled Blackbeard. Rylla and Tyler scooted away from the edge of the platform.

"Here kitty, kitty, kitty ..." came Miles' voice, then the pounding of feet on metal.

"Good, they're on the stairs." Tyler started towards the entrance of the one intact slide, but Rylla's legs didn't want to work.

A crash splintered the air, then a scream. One of the scroungers must have fallen through a rusted stair. Laughter rang out. "How della cats climb up yon?"

"Let's go!" Tyler grabbed the roof of the plastic tube, swung his feet into the opening, and launched himself into the darkness. Rylla took a deep breath and followed, rocketing down after him. When the slide flattened out, she straightened into a crouch, ran for the moonlit opening, and leapt.

She stumbled into Tyler on landing, wrenching her right ankle. Gritting her teeth against the pain, she tensed to run.

But the scroungers already had them surrounded.

"Yulla spying on us?" growled a scrounger whose staff was topped with a hornet's nest of concertina wire.

Tyler pushed Rylla behind him. Was this it? Was she going to die at the hands of scroungers? As her heartbeat thudded in her ears, time slowed, and details crystalized. She noticed Tyler's legs trembling, the quaver in his voice. The crunch of the scroungers' boots, loud as gunshots. She could count each speck of grime on each pale hair on Miles Walker's mustache.

And looking that closely at Miles — in spite of everything she'd ever heard about scroungers being vicious, bloodthirsty, indiscriminate killers — made her fear transform into anger. She was not about to get bludgeoned to death by a kid who used to be scared of mosquito hawks.

"Fucking Miles Walker, what are you going to do, kill us?" She stepped out from behind Tyler. She was shouting again. What her mother had often prophesized was coming true — her temper was going to get her killed.

"Rylla?" Miles gaped. His grip on his giant drill-bit staff slackened, and he dropped it to his side.

"You know them?" asked Tire-Crown.

Miles nodded and started to snicker.

"Miles. Buddy." Tyler took a step forward with his open palm held out. Miles' snickers turned to giggles. His eyes were bloodshot and dilated from whatever drug they'd been smoking.

"Ay!" Tire-crown shouted, clapping at Miles. "They you kin or summa?"

Miles doubled over, laughing so hard a string of drool dangled from his lips. He pointed at Rylla. "Sh-sh-she —" he choked out.

"Oh shit." Tire-crown's eyes widened in recognition. "It's her!"

All the scroungers burst into laughter and started quoting *... something.*

"Every day, I lay in the ASS!" one shouted. Something twisted in Rylla's gut.

"Insects live in that ASS!" Her brain struggled to put together the pieces.

"The ASS is hope!"

"Without the ASS, my soul will die!"

It was her speech. The speech that had poured from her heart earlier that day, now twisted and vulgar. But how the hell had they heard it?

Tire-Crown pulled his OGGles back on and started humming and doing a crotch-thrusting dance.

Rylla's fear vanished before her need to understand what the hell was going on. She sank to a slab of concrete and pulled her own OGGles on.

"Rylla?" Tyler asked. "Let's, uh, maybe get out of here —"

"Relax," Miles said, catching his breath. "We wulla messing with y'all. We weren't gonna hurt you." He spread his arms wide. "It's good to see you, man! The McCracken kids! Been a while."

"Holovid search," Rylla commanded, turning up the volume on her vibra-speakers. Tiny bubbles filled her vision, blotting out the image of Tyler and Miles slapping each other's backs. Each bubble looped a clip of one of the most popular videos of that day. One proclaiming "12 MILLION VIEWS!" pulsed larger than the others. And flickering inside was her own face. The title read "Ass is Hope — REMIX."

Heart in her throat, she poked the bubble, and it swelled to fill her vision.

There she was, back in the Senate chamber, but now she was watching herself give testimony from high above. After a few lines of her speech, a drumbeat started up. When she got to the part where she'd said, "Along the banks of the Guadalupe River, there is grass," someone had edited out the "*gr*" sound. They'd autotuned her voice, so she sang, "There is ASS!" to a catchy melody. Music started up, and she had been vid-shopped to look like she was doing a lewd dance in the State Senate chambers. All the times she'd talked about *grass* became the lyrics of a dance song about *ass*. When the dancing Rylla sang, "There are insects in the ass," she was replaced with a guy dancing in a foam ant costume. When she sang,

"Every day, I lay in the ass," CG cockroaches bounced on a gigantic, nude butt.

The backup music fell away as she sang, "If the ass dies, my soul will die." They hadn't added any graphics here, just altered her voice to match the melody. The camera zoomed in. All the passion she had felt, fighting for what she loved, was written plainly across her face.

The song ended, but the video did not. The last shot was that moment she had kicked the podium, and the top popped off as it hit the ground, with a *sproi-oi-oing* sound effect.

"Made by Pete!" piped a squeaky voice. A dancing bobblehead appeared, with a face she recognized — the camera person from the gallery. That bored jerk had made her infamous.

As she pulled her OGGles from her face, something cold pressed into her sternum. "Need a swig?" Miles asked.

She sniffed the bottle. It smelled like it could take paint off a truck.

Tyler pulled his own OGGles down. From his cringe, she knew he'd seen the holovid.

Rylla let out a long, low groan. "I'm a laughingstock."

"You're a meme." Tyler shrugged.

"No way," Miles Walker said. "You're a LEGEND!" The other scroungers roared and thumped their staffs on the ground in agreement.

And just like that, her anger and embarrassment vanished, and she was laughing with them. She was laughing because she could see it clearly now — that *life* was a joke. The funny thing was that she'd taken it so seriously. Trying to go to college, escape the Dust, save her river from a greedy, all-powerful corporation. Hilarious. Like it or not, her life was here. After this stunt, she'd be lucky if her mom didn't kick her out, lucky if that job at Lockburn was still waiting for her. Suddenly she knew she would never log on to SCHOEL again.

She screamed her jumbled feelings at the moon, then took a fiery gulp of scrounger booze.

6

The River

An hour later, Miles, Carlito, Dante, Frog, and Ricky were Rylla's new best friends, and she'd figured out a solution to all her problems.

"Y'all, listen. LISTEN!" She clapped her hands for emphasis as she led the group downhill towards the river. "I wanna join your gang."

The guys cheered, but Tyler rolled his eyes. He hadn't drunk any of their booze and was acting like her self-appointed babysitter. She wished he would just relax. Miles' friends were harmless, and despite their beards, all were younger than Tyler.

"I'm serious!" Her words might have been slightly slurry, but she felt clear-headed. "They're always telling us scroungers are evil, but you guys are, like, *nice*. And being a scrounger seems a lot more fun that working for Lockburn."

They'd left the ancient waterpark, wandered through abandoned New Braunfels, and now picked their way down the slope to the Guadalupe River. Rylla trailed her fingers through bluesedge grass.

"The media kella make you scared of us, 'cause we live outside their rules," Miles said.

"Wait. If I join you guys, *do I kella talk like this*?" Rylla said, imitating Miles's phony accent.

Dante, the one she'd thought of as Tire-Crown, guffawed, and Miles blushed.

Down in the river basin, tall grass swished against their knees. Rylla stepped across slick green stones and sat on a flat rock jutting out of the murky water.

Miles settled on the rock next to her, while Tyler perched nearby, frowning at the pair of them. She thought she knew why — it was becoming clear that Miles was *into* her. It was sort of flattering — no one else had ever been *into* her before, but she didn't return the feeling. They'd grown up catching bugs together, so he seemed kind of like another brother.

Miles dropped the tough accent when he spoke again. "The government and the corps — they want you to *need* them for water, right? They want you working at Lockburn and grateful for their measly rations."

"But the Dust provides!" Dante roared.

"Yeah, everything you need, you can *get*," Miles continued. "People left their whole lives behind in the Exodus of '49. And for food and anything we can't loot from abandoned towns —" Miles shrugged.

"— we take," Frog said.

"You *steal*," Tyler corrected.

"Nah, nah," Ricky said, packing another pipe with goop. "That whole idea — ownership — it's just mind control, you ken?"

"They say we poach water," Dante said. "They say it's a crime. But the river's for everyone, every living thing. Now Lockburn kenna poach the whole river! So who's a thief?"

Carlito, the quietest of the Scroungers, spoke up then. "If you wanna talk about the original thieves, I mean ..." He cringed jokingly and held out a pinky and thumb to point to where Rylla and Miles sat on the rock, and where Tyler sat on the shore.

Dante burst out laughing.

"What?" Miles asked, confused. But Rylla saw it, even before Carlito began to explain. They were the three people down in that riverbed whose faces reflected the most moonlight.

"Y'all's ancestors are the ones who came here, stole this land, and fucked it all up," Carlito explained. "My mom always said we're Mexicans, from when Texas was Mexico, and even before that. If this river *belongs* to anyone, it's us Brown folk."

Dante let out a grito, which echoed off the distant water slides, and Ricky, Frog, and Carlito laughed. Rylla's cheeks burned with shame, remembering how earlier today, in the State Senate chamber, she'd thought she was the only person in the world who cared about this river. But Carlito's people had loved this river long before her ancestors even knew this continent existed. How long had McCrackens been in Texas? Had her great-great-great-grandparents killed people and stolen this land?

"We don't know much about our family history," Rylla said. "But given that our ancestors created our mother?" She shared a glance with Tyler. "They were probably monsters."

"Yeah, I wouldn't put genocide past them," Tyler said, bobbing his head. "Sorry, I guess? If that's helpful?"

"Eh," Carlito said with a shrug. "What do I do with that?"

Miles was digging a stick into the rocky riverbed. "We all grew up on this river. We all love it," he said, sounding defensive.

"We know," Dante said, and he reached out and ruffled Miles' hair. Miles pulled away like he was annoyed, but he was smiling.

Everyone fell silent then, staring into the trickling water. A few feet wide, a few inches deep, the mighty Guadalupe River still flowed across Texas, at least for tonight.

At first, the only sound was the gurgling of water slipping over rocks. Then, one by one, the insects they'd startled regained their confidence. A cricket trilled, a frog chirped, and soon a chorus of creatures filled the air with mating cries.

The thought that all this would soon be dried up and dead, like everything else in the Dust, made her feel like she was tearing apart inside. Miles Walker looped an arm around her shoulder, and she didn't pull away. Maybe she would hook up with him tonight after all. Maybe, like every other disappointing thing about her life, it was inevitable.

"Anyway, don't worry, girly," Dante growled. "They *not* kenna build that dam." The other scroungers nodded dangerously. "They kella fight *all* the clans to build it."

Could the collective might of every scrounger in Texas stop the will of Lockburn? It didn't seem likely. Rylla slipped out from under Miles's arm and waded into the cool water.

"What're you doing?" Tyler asked.

Ignoring him, she laid down, and the river embraced her, fanning out her hair, soaking her clothes to the skin. The cool water sobered her up, and despair crept back into her heart. She didn't *really* want to become a scrounger, and steal from people, and run from the police, and sleep under the stars every night. Just imagining that life felt exhausting.

A firefly flashed nearby, spoiling her night vision. She swiped at it, then realized the flashing came from her OGGles on the rock. An incoming call, probably from her mother. Would Amaryllis be worried or angry? Had she seen the *Ass is Hope* vid? Dreading a fight, Rylla sat up and slung the OGGles over her eyes.

She was in an unfamiliar place, filled with golden light. Shelves made of honey-colored wood lined the walls, crammed with paperbooks. The hologram had the best graphics she'd ever seen. If it weren't for the water flowing around her legs, she would have believed she was really there, wherever *there* was.

Across the room, two figures stood with their backs to her. "Is it working?" one asked.

Rylla could barely hear over Dante's booming laughter, so she sloshed downstream. Around a bend in the river, she sat on the bank and turned the hologram to full opacity, then pointed her Gluv'd finger at her face.

"Ah, she's behind us, Watt," said a tall, androgynous person dressed all in black. Their long, black hair was pulled into a high ponytail, bound with a golden cuff. Their clothes and accent screamed that they came from a Lush State.

The other figure turned. Rylla made a snap-assumption that this 'Watt' was a woman. She was around her mom's age, white, with blue eyes and a crown of greying curls that made her seem taller than she was. She wore a flowing suit of colorful geometric patterns and matching earrings. "This is the first time we're using a holophasic field generator," Watt said. "It lets us project the entire room into your OGGles. The graphics are supposed to be very convincing. How does it look?"

"Uh, convincing," Rylla said, careful not to slur the word. Whatever was going on here, she didn't want these fancy, Lush State people to know she was drunk.

"What have you been into?" The tall person said, gesturing to their face. Rylla reached up and touched a glob of river mud on her cheek. Of course, she must look like a swamp creature. She wiped her face clean. "Sorry, I was just, uh ... hiking, and I, uh, tripped ..."

They raised the corner of a sharp eyebrow. "You're sure about this one, Watt?"

"Have some faith, Nelson." Watt folded her arms and leaned back against the desk. "Sassparylla McCracken?"

"It's Rylla, but yeah."

"Rylla, then. I'm Professor Alexandra Watt, the Dean of Students at Wingates University, she/her. This is my colleague, Dr. Nelson Hernandez, and he's the vice-chair of our Humanity Department. We'd like to offer you an opportunity."

7

The Skimmer

One week later, on the morning of her 18th birthday, Rylla lay on the picnic table in front of her trailer, resting her head on a backpack that contained all her worldly possessions. She scanned the skies for the skimmer that was over an hour late, but the only break in the wide sky was her Gluv'd finger pointed at her face and Tyler's gently drifting call-bubble. He had just finished obnoxiously singing "Happy Birthday." Rylla smiled, but it quickly faded as another wave of anxiety washed over her.

"What if they don't come? What if they changed their minds about me?"

"They would've let you know. They wouldn't just stand you up like a bad date," he reassured her. "Hey, turn the opacity down on your OGGles. You know I hate when I can't see your eyes."

"It's bright out here," Rylla grumbled, but she swiped a finger anyways, changing the lenses of her OGGles from black to clear. She blinked as her eyes adjusted to the brightness. "What if the school isn't real? What if it's a scam?"

"You can always make good on your plan to join the scroungers," he teased. "Marry Miles Walker and have scrounger babies."

"Stop," Rylla pleaded. If Watt and Hernandez hadn't called her when they did, would she be camped out in a landfill right now? Cuddled up with Miles Walker? It gave her a dizzy feeling to think about how close she'd been to running away with him.

"His face," Tyler laughed, "when you came back from that call and just said, 'Let's go.' He couldn't believe it."

Rylla hadn't believed it either when Watt and Hernandez had offered her a full scholarship to some university she'd never even heard of. She'd been sure it was the kind of thing where you get tricked into sharing your social security number, and then you get framed for international data smuggling.

"Anyways, we've been through this, like, fifty times. The visa, remember?" Tyler asked.

"Oh yeah." Rylla dug in her pockets. "Wingates must be real. These things are impossible to get." She pulled out a card-sized booklet and ran her thumb over the embossed gold letters. "In*tra*national Visa," she read aloud, flipping open the cover.

"Show me your picture," Tyler said.

"It's truly terrible."

"It can't be that bad."

Rylla pointed her Gluv'd finger at the 3D image on the visa. Tyler burst into laughter.

They'd taken the shot that night by the river. Mud smeared her cheeks, her hair was soaking wet, and her eyes were drunkenly unfocused.

"Anyways, who cares what the picture looks like," she clutched the booklet to her chest. "I'm going to a new watershed!"

Tyler smiled, but there was hurt in his eyes, and she regretted saying it. He'd been applying for visas ever since he turned eighteen, with no luck.

"How's mom?"

"Still asleep. And still in denial." She peeked over her OGGles, searching the sky with naked eyes, as if that would make a difference. Nothing but blue. Her heart clenched with anxiety. "Argh! Where is that skimmer?"

Tyler was silent for a few beats. "Listen, my shift starts soon. I'm sorry I couldn't be there in person ..." There was a hitch in his voice, and she felt her own eyes welling up.

"I don't know when I'll be coming home again," she mumbled.

"We'll see each other soon," he said, forcing a smile. "Jo and I will be getting our visas any day now."

She knew it was a lie, but she smiled anyways.

"If you ever need anything — money —"

She shook her head. "They say I won't have to pay a dime. And there's this work/study thing I can do for spending money."

"Well, when you hang up, check your wallet app. Jo and I each sent you a little something — not much, so promise me you'll spend it on snacks and frivolous shit like that." Rylla laughed. "And promise you won't go running off to join whatever the Michigan equivalent of the scroungers is?" She laughed harder, but his face was serious.

"You have to go to work," she said finally.

"I do." He smiled. "Take care, my Officially Grown-Up sister. And happy birthday."

The bubble containing Tyler's face vanished, and Rylla pulled her OGGles down. Still no sign of the skimmer. Rylla's chest tightened with renewed anxiety, but she reminded herself of all the official links Watt had sent her that first night, to convince her the school wasn't a hoax. Only then had Rylla thought to ask *why* she was being offered the scholarship.

"It seems your 'Ass is Hope' video is quite popular among the student body," Watt said.

Rylla had felt sick. How could that video possibly be the reason for the professors' interest in her? "It's not my video," she'd mumbled.

"One of my students found the uncut footage of your speech to the Texas State Senate," Watt had said. "He shared the holovid with my class this afternoon, while we were discussing contemporary political resistance."

"Incidentally," Dr. Hernandez said. "I assume you'll be glad to know that a judge has ordered a halt on construction to the dam."

Rylla's jaw fell open in surprise. "Because of — what I —?" She pointed to her own chest.

"Oh goodness no," Hernandez said, barking a laugh.

Watt chuckled. "Not at all."

"No, nothing to do with you," Hernandez said. "The Lipan Apache tribe filed a legal suit stating that the river is sacred, and the dam will violate their right to freedom of religion."

"A local judge sided with the tribe," Watt continued. "Unfortunately, the Fifth Circuit court, which is friendly to the oil and gas corporations, is likely to overturn the ruling. Then there'll be an appeal. The legal delays will provide the tribe and various other *organized* groups time to mount additional efforts to stop the dam."

Watt had said the word *organized* like that for her benefit. Rylla's gut churned with fresh shame — and not because of that silly viral video. She'd rushed into the state senate with no plan, no allies, assuming she was the only person who cared enough to save the river she thought of as *hers*. Carlito had already shown her how self-involved it had been to think that. And she'd studied the Water Protectors in SCHOEL, just the day before! She should've known that Indigenous folk were still fighting for the water, as they had done for centuries.

Humbled, Rylla had said, "If my speech did nothing, why would you want me at your school?"

Watt had smiled kindly then. "You have a way with words, and I like your spunk. Delivering a speech like that — it's an unusual thing for a teenager from the Dust to do. Our kind of unusual."

Though she'd just met Watt, the professor's approval had made Rylla glow.

But Dr. Hernandez had been quick to cut her down to size. "Of course, we investigated your schooling. We usually don't consider SCHOEL graduates, as the curriculum is so inadequate. However, Watt believes you *might* succeed here, with remedial coursework."

He had given voice to Rylla's worst fears. The other students at Wingates had gone to real schools. How could she compete with them?

The trailer door slammed, startling Rylla out of the memory. She sat up and watched her mother striding across the yard barefoot, still wearing threadbare pajamas. The left side of her hair was flat where she'd slept on it, but the right side was puffy from a night out at Lucky's Pub.

"You're still here," her mother's voice was gravelly with sleep.

"The skimmer's late."

"Sure it is," her mother coughed. "We're out of melk. Go pick some up."

Rylla's mouth hung open. Amaryllis expected her to skip out on her ride to college for a carton of synthetic milk? "Mom — do you understand? I'm going away today."

"I thought you were *supposedly* leaving at nine."

"I was ... I am!"

"It's almost ten. They didn't come for you. Changed their minds I guess, if they were even a real school in the first place." Her mother rolled her eyes.

"So, they're late? I'm sure it's just ... traffic." She searched the empty sky again.

"Let me get this straight. You shook your ass on the OGnet, so a fancy college offered you a scholarship?" Amaryllis's voice dripped sarcasm. "You know, if you'd told me you were into that kind of thing, I could've gotten you a job at Heartbreaker's. Those girls make good money."

"I didn't *shake my ass ...*" Rylla pinched the bridge of her nose in frustration.

"Look, I'll be here. If they show up while you're at the store, I'll tell 'em to wait. Now go get mommy some melk." She smiled and held out her truck keys.

"I'm not going," Rylla hissed.

Amaryllis dropped the smile. "Sassy, I am losing my patience. We need melk, and I have to get ready for work. Now I'm asking you nicely. Don't make me get mad." She pressed the keys into Rylla's chest.

Rylla pushed her mother's hand away. "Why are you doing this? Do you want my last memory of you to be a fight?"

"I am sick of hearing about this ... this delusion!" Amaryllis yelled, sweeping a hand at the empty sky. "You're not going to college. You're not going anywhere! You're stuck here with me, so you better make the best of it. Now go get the damned melk!"

Rylla took the keys, despair spreading in her gut. When her mom laid it out like that, she realized how ridiculous it sounded. The skimmer hadn't come. The visa was probably fake. The school was all some scam.

Amaryllis turned towards the trailer with a satisfied smirk. "It's my birthday you know!" Rylla called, and Amaryllis froze. But it wasn't guilt that rooted her mother to the spot. She was squinting at something in the distance — a speck near the horizon growing steadily larger.

"That must be the skimmer!" Rylla's heart leapt.

"That's a bird," Amaryllis said.

"When have you seen a bird around here?"

"People have pets. 'Member when George Cheney's pet vulture escaped?"

"That's no vulture."

Her mother said nothing, but started smoothing down her lopsided hair. Rylla wiped clammy hands on her jeans.

The skimmer flew lower than a helicopter but higher than a hover-craft. Its beetle-black, glossy solar cells winked in the sun. A half-mile from the trailer, it dropped from the sky. Billows of dust bloomed on either side of the skimmer's wings as it landed beside their guinea fowl coop.

Something clicked, and a seamless hatch slid open. Rylla expected Professor Watt or Dr. Hernandez to step out, but instead a teenager filled the doorway — one Rylla assumed was a girl her age. She had a cheerful face, framed by a mane of bronze curly hair, light brown skin, and she was so short that the ankles and wrists of her flight suit were rolled into thick cuffs.

"Sassparylla McCracken?" the girl asked.

"It's Rylla." Shouldering her backpack, she slid off the picnic table.

"I'm the mother," Amaryllis smiled, extending a hand. She was using a weird, formal-sounding accent. The pilot raised her eyebrows nearly to her hairline at her mother's bedraggled appearance. "All these years I've made sure Rylla could focus on her education."

Rylla rolled her eyes as the pilot pumped her mother's hand respectfully.

"I'm just so proud of her, going off to — to — what's the name of your school again?"

"Wingates University," Rylla said, gritting her teeth. "I've told you like eighty times this week."

Amaryllis repeated "Wingates" under her breath.

Rylla headed for the skimmer, but Amaryllis's hand closed around her shoulder.

They wore OGGles so often, she couldn't remember the last time she'd looked directly into her mother's eyes. They were hazel, like her own, caked with crusted mascara.

"You're really leaving?"

"I've been trying to tell you that all week."

Amaryllis nodded and looked down at her bare, dirty feet. "Don't let these Yankees look down on you," she said. "You're a

Texan, and a McCracken, and you're every bit as smart as them." She grabbed Rylla in a rib-cracking hug, then kissed her on the cheek. She *never* did that anymore, at least not while she was sober. "Happy birthday, Sassy. I guess you're grown now."

She released Rylla abruptly, then walked towards her trailer and didn't look back.

Rylla had dreamed of leaving this patch of desert behind for as long as she could remember. But now, watching her mother disappear behind the slamming trailer door, she felt a surprising dash of grief, mixed in with all her relief and excitement. Swallowing the lump in her throat, she handed her bag up to the pilot and climbed aboard.

8

Dae-Dae

The interior of the skimmer looked more like the bathroom at a punk show than an official university aircraft. Stickers and graffiti took up every inch of wallspace, and the ceiling was covered in prism-marker signatures.

The pilot noticed Rylla gaping at the walls. "This skimmer was a student project, so we got to decorate it when we were done." She crawled into the cockpit and dropped into a pilot seat upholstered in hot pink synthetic fur.

"You ... built this?" Rylla asked.

"Me and, like, 100 other students. My group designed the robotics that adjust the ion streams based on feedback from the pitot tubes."

Rylla nodded, hoping it seemed like she understood.

"You can sit there." The pilot motioned to the other chair.

As Rylla climbed into the cockpit, the pilot waved her hands and flicked her fingers as if casting a spell. A small black bead was stuck to each of the girl's fingernails. Rylla recognized them as MANIs — Manual App Navigation Interfaces. She had always wanted a set of MANIs — they were so much cooler than Gluvs — but of course she'd never been able to afford them.

The pilot lowered a fist, and Rylla's stomach dropped as the craft rose into the air. A floor-to-ceiling windshield stretched before them, and the dusty trailer where she had spent her life dwindled smaller and smaller below. Part of her thought *good riddance* and couldn't wait to get as far away from here as possible, but a small, wriggling thing in her gut was terrified to leave the only home she'd ever known.

Suddenly, and without a sound, they rocketed east across the desert. The force of the acceleration pinned Rylla to the back of her seat. Holographic text streamed across the top of the windshield depicting bearings, temperature, altitude. A semi-transparent map floated in the bottom right-hand corner. The pilot conducted an invisible orchestra with glazed-over eyes. Eventually their speed leveled off, and Rylla could peel her head off the back of her chair.

"There, it's on auto-pilot." The pilot leaned back, flinging one leg over the armrest. "We have to go slow until we reach the e-mag grid. Then we'll *really* fly."

Rylla had never flown in anything before, and this was definitely the fastest her body had ever hurtled through space.

The pilot fingered a name badge stitched to her uniform. "I'm Dae-Dae, by the way, she/her," she said, confirming Rylla's guess of her pronouns. "Just say my name like the letters. D. D."

"D-D," Rylla repeated.

"I think we're the same age. You're 18, right?" Dae-Dae cocked her head to one side, furrowing her brow. "Hey, if you're gonna be sick, the bathroom's in the back."

"No, I'm —" but Rylla snapped her mouth shut. Something *was* climbing up the back of her throat, trying to get out of her, but it wasn't puke. She turned her head away, not wanting Dae-Dae to see her cry. All her life, she'd dreamed of this moment — escaping the Dust. So why did she feel so miserable?

Pressing her eyes shut, she saw her mother walking away from her, barefoot. She saw the way Tyler's face fell when she'd mentioned emigrating. She saw her river on that last night with the scroungers, reflecting the moon above. Would she ever see the Guadalupe flowing again, the dewy grass on its banks glittering in the sunrise? She wasn't off to meet her destiny — she was abandoning everything she'd ever loved.

Then again, going to Wingates might be the only way to save the river. Rylla clenched her jaw and fought off the tears. She would study hard, get a good job, and buy emigration visas for her mom and Tyler. Even Jo. Even *Miles* if he wanted one! And maybe she could learn something at this fancy Lush State school that could restore her river — maybe even all the rivers in the Dust.

"Hey, it's cool," Dae-Dae offered. "I cried too when I first started at Wingates."

Rylla cleared her throat and wiped her eyes. "When was that?"

"Twelve years ago."

"You were six when you started college?" Rylla asked incredulously.

"No, no," she laughed. "Wingates has a lower school too. I only started at the university this year." Dae-Dae folded her arms over the chair back and narrowed her eyes. "You know, you look really familiar. Have we met? Do I follow you on Joinly?"

Rylla shook her head and changed the subject before Dae-Dae realized she was the *Ass is Hope* girl. "So, uh, what do you, like, *do* at Wingates?"

"This week I've been busting my butt to finish a project," Dae-Dae flopped back into the chair. "Wanna see?"

Rylla nodded.

Dae-Dae started tracing shapes in the air with her hands, and her eyes lost focus. She must've be wearing OGLenses — all the functionality of OGGles on tiny contact lenses. Like MANIs, they were super-expensive.

Dae-Dae opened her shirt pocket, and a stream of dust flew up out of it. A blaze of green light flooded the cabin as each of the tiny particles lit up, spelling out

Hello, Rylla

Rylla gasped and the dust twirled into new shapes.

We are the Phosphorescent Integrated Remote Flying Nanobots …

They shifted again.

But you can call us PhIREFlys.

Dae-Dae beamed in the glow of the hovering letters. "Do you like them?"

"They're incredible!" Rylla breathed. "You built them yourself?"

Dae-Dae nodded and held open her front pocket. The Phireflys swarmed back inside. "Their battery life is really short — for now." She stuck a pinky into her front pocket and pulled out one speck. "Here." She brushed it into Rylla's outstretched hand. "Use an app to magnify it."

Rylla pulled her OGGles from her backpack and slung them on one-handed.

"Woah, those are old school!" Dae-Dae laughed. "They look like our nuclear lab safety goggles."

Rylla blushed in embarassment. Her OGGles were the nicest thing she owned. She opened a microscope app, then zoomed in on the nanobot 1000x. Suddenly she was looking at a monster from a sci-fi holovid. The Phirefly had six legs, double wings, and a transparent sphere protruding from its rear end. Each of its legs ended in a three-fingered nanorobotic claw.

"This is so cool! Look at that tiny proboscis!"

"I took inspiration from nature," Dae-Dae said.

"It even has eyes — can it see?"

"Sort of," Dae-Dae explained. "They're AI-equipped cam eras. Maybe someday I'll use them to spy on my enemies. Mwaha-ha," she laughed like a villain from a kid's show

Rylla pulled off her OGGles and held out her palm. Dae-Dae picked up the nanorobot with a pinky and stuck it in her shirt pocket.

"I love insects," Rylla said earnestly.

"Is that your major? Entomology?"

"I don't know," she shrugged.

"You don't even know your major?" Dae-Dae cried. Rylla shook her head.

"Well, what was your major in your high school?"

"I didn't go to high school," Rylla said miserably. "I was in SCHOEL."

Dae-Dae made a face like she'd smelled a fart. It was only there for an instant before her cheerful expression slid back into place. Rylla bit down on her lip, trying not to show how worthless the look had made her feel.

"Hey it's cool," Dae-Dae said encouragingly. "I heard a rumor that this boy in my dorm did SCHOEL. He's from the Dust States, so it could be true."

Rylla doubted it. He was probably some oil exec's kid who'd gone to a fancy boarding school.

"Okay, let's think." Dae-Dae pulled a curl straight in front of her crossed eyes, then watched it sproing back up. "You like bugs, so maybe biology is your major. Have you conducted any amateur wildlife surveys? Maybe published some research with a reputable journal?"

Rylla shook her head. "I like *learning* about insects, but no — nothing like that.

"What about math? Have you done any advanced mathematics?"

"I got perfect scores in Calculus II," she offered hopefully.

"You're only on Calculus? Then it can't be math." Dae-Dae laughed. "Do you build things? Maybe you're an engineer like me!"

Rylla shrugged. "Actually, I pretty much just read and do SCHOEL."

"So how'd you get recruited?"

Rylla sighed, figuring she might as well get it over with. She launched into her story of the past few weeks — her protest in the State Senate, the "Ass is Hope" video, and the unexpected offer from Watt and Hernandez.

Dae-Dae laughed. "So *that's* where I knew you from." She started doing cha-cha arms and singing, *"The ass is hope! The ass is hope!"* She stopped, noticing Rylla's expression. "Sorry, you're probably going to get that a lot."

"I'm getting used to it," Rylla sighed. "Although I had to delete my Joinly profile. People on the OGnet are gross."

"Ooh, I bet," Dae-Dae said. "Wait, you said Professor Watt recruited you?" She sucked air through her teeth. "I know what your major is then."

"What?"

"You're a *Humanity* major," Dae-Dae said, like it was a bad word.

"What does that mean?"

"First off," Dae-Dae jabbed a finger in Rylla's face. "Humanity majors are a bunch of snobby weirdos. They never hang out with anyone outside their major. Second, us engineers can't stand them, because if you want to build anything expensive or dangerous — fun, basically — you have to submit a proposal to the Humanity Department. For some reason, they get to decide who gets funding!" Dae-Dae shook her head in exasperation.

"But what's really weird," she leaned in and her voice dropped to a whisper. "Is sometimes a group of Humanity majors will just disappear, for weeks at a time. No one knows where they go or what they're doing."

She sat back. "Now, engineers. There's a major. We *make* shit. We built THIS," Dae-Dae slapped the hull of the skimmer for emphasis. "They make us take one Humanity class each semester. It's so annoying." She started spinning around in the chair, kicking off the hull. "Right now I'm in History of the 20th Century. All the professor wants us to do is *read* and talk, talk, talk. And they make you *write*, which is even worse."

She stopped abruptly by grabbing Rylla's armrest. "I mean, that's just my opinion. If humanity is your thing ..."

"Actually," Rylla smiled, "talking about history sounds kind of fun." She thought about all her lonely hours studying in the abandoned library, with no one to talk to but Teacher 4.1.

"Ugh, then you *must* be a Humanity major." Dae-Dae made a gagging face. "It's okay, we can still be friends. Just promise not to get snobby and stop hanging out with us science-y types."

"It's a promise." Rylla stretched out a hand, and Dae-Dae slapped it.

Friends, Dae-Dae had said. Rylla hadn't had many of those in her life — Jo, Tyler if you could count your brother, Miles, and a few other Lockburn brats she'd played with as kids. This whole ride, Rylla had thought Dae-Dae was looking down on her for her clunky OGGles and crappy schooling, but maybe it was just that Dae-Dae had never met anyone like Rylla before. Rylla had certainly never met anyone like Dae-Dae, and she hoped that everyone at Wingates would prove just as friendly.

9

Welcome to Wingates

"Look!" Rylla pointed out the windshield, as a clump of green whizzed by. "Trees!"

"We're getting close to Louisiana," Dae-Dae said.

Rylla pressed her nose to the windshield. Grassland turned to brackish prairie as they reached the submerged Gulf Coast, with clouds of tree-tops tracing winding bayous. Soon they were flying above the flooded city of Houston.

A traffic jam of boats crowded the channels of brown water filling the city streets. Walkways wove between clumps of skyscrapers downtown, and beyond, a labyrinth of pipes, scaffolding, and steaming vats stretched towards the glittering ocean at the horizon.

"Petrochemical refineries," Dae-Dae sneered. "Can you believe these things are still in business?"

"My mom works for an oil refinery," Rylla said. "Practically everyone I know does."

The skimmer passed a tower belching flame and greasy, black smoke. "Well not to offend you or anything, but oil is such a dirty fuel. I don't understand why our species can't give up the habit."

"Trust me, I'm not offended," Rylla said. "No one hates those refineries more than me."

A few minutes later, a snaking line of gray appeared ahead on the horizon.

"That's the Wall, isn't it?" Rylla's voice caught in her throat. During the Exodus of 2049, as soil turned to sand all across the West, the Lush States along the Mississippi and Missouri watersheds had built the Wall, from Louisiana up through Montana, "to ensure safe and orderly emigration."

A grid of white tents lined the wall from horizon to horizon. "Emigrant City," she whispered under her breath. Emigrant City was the last stop for desperate Dusties. Most of its residents would die there, waiting for a visa that would never come. All her life, Amaryllis had threatened her with that place. *If you don't learn some responsibility, you'll wind up whoring yourself for a sip of water in Emigrant City.*

"Are you ready?" Dae-Dae asked.

"Ready for what?

"Ready to get the hell out of the Dust?"

"Don't we have to go through border control or something?"

"This is a Wingates skimmer." Dae-Dae grinned wolfishly. "And Wingates has *connections*." Dae-Dae extended her MANI-studded hands, operating controls only she could see, and the skimmer swung towards the north and blasted forward. This time, the force of acceleration glued Rylla's cheek to her seat and she strained to breathe. Finally, the engines leveled off. The green land blurred past so fast she could barely make out any landmarks.

"Louisiana has an electro-magnetic highway grid — all the Lush States do. We can go *way* faster on e-mags."

Dae-Dae stretched and crossed her legs on the seat. She flicked a finger and smash music flooded the cabin.

"Is this 'Endtimes Endochrines?'" Rylla shouted over the rapid-fire drums.

"No way — you listen to smash?"

It turned out they liked a lot of the same bands. Dae-Dae had never heard of Cicada Circus, though, so Rylla sent her some of Tyler's best tracks. Dae-Dae played them over the skimmer's speakers and called them "very clean."

Arkansas, Missouri, and Illinois whizzed past as Dae-Dae peppered Rylla with questions about life in the Dust States. She was fascinated by the mechanics of ionic recyclers and how water rationing worked. Weirdly, she was especially curious about Rylla's family.

"Your mom is cold as wet helium, no offense," Dae-Dae joked. "If my mom isn't going to see me for a while, she sobs. Even when I go on these long flights, she worries."

"Actually, that was as warm and fuzzy as mom ever gets," Rylla said. "Sober, that is."

"My family is so boring compared to yours," Dae-Dae said. But Rylla disagreed. The more she heard about it, the more she thought Dae-Dae's life sounded magical. Her father had grown up in Nigeria, before he was recruited to Wingates. There, he fell in love with a New-New Yorker concentrating in Astrophysics. Both of them were now physics professors at Wingates. "Maybe you'll take a class from one of them," Dae-Dae said. "Professor Ogunaike and Professor Rosenbaum."

Rylla hoped not — physics was one of her worst subjects in SCHOEL.

"They're mostly great, except that they don't approve of me majoring in engineering. They think it's not a 'pure' science."

"What would they've done if you'd been a Humanity major?"

Dae-Dae snorted. "Probably disown me!"

The skimmer slowed. "That's the autopilot off — we just crossed into Michigan." Dae-Dae's eyes glazed over as she focused on steering the shuttle. "Ten more minutes, and we'll be home."

A brick of anxiety lodged in Rylla's chest at the prospect of seeing her new "home." At this slower speed, she could make out the landscape below. "So many trees," she breathed in awe.

"Yeah, but it's nothing like what it used to be. The Great Lakes are drying up. Just like everywhere else ..." Dae-Dae's voice trailed off.

The land below looked plenty lush to Rylla. They passed over a wall manned with guards, then the forest beneath them ended and a meadow of tall, swaying grasses and flowers stretched ahead. Giant geodesic domes protruded from the landscape — their triangular glass faces blazing in the sunlight. Each dome was surrounded by rings of circular hills, as though they were giant water droplets that had just hit the land, causing ripples in the earth.

"Most of the school is underground," Dae-Dae explained. She flicked her hand and the craft dropped suddenly. Now Rylla could see long rows of windows set into the grass-covered corridors and classrooms she'd mistaken for hills.

Dae-Dae eased the skimmer into a large, square opening in one of the landscaped mounds. Darkness swallowed them, and green splotches obscured Rylla's vision as her eyes adjusted to the gloom of the aircraft hanger. With a jolt, the skimmer came to a halt.

"Welcome to Wingates," Dae-Dae said, beaming, as they stepped out into the cavernous hangar. Nearby, a group of students in yellow shirts swarmed over the bones of another half-finished skimmer.

"So, we're actually a little late," Dae-Dae said. "But if I run, I can still make it to Quantum Mechanics. Do you mind finding the admin building yourself? I'm supposed to walk you there, but it's easy to get to."

Not waiting for an answer, she pointed to a corridor on the far wall. "Go through there, cut through the Cloud Forest to Ward 6, then follow the signs to 'Administration.' Got it?"

Rylla was repeating the directions under her breath when Dae-Dae took off running in the opposite direction. "If I'm late, all the good ionoscopes will be taken," she called over her shoulder, then burst through a double-doorway and disappeared.

Some of the students working on the new skimmer had paused to stare at Rylla. Hitching her backpack up, she strode to the far door, hoping she looked like she belonged.

The doorway led to an arched corridor bustling with people and conversation. Sunlight streamed through high windows. A sign overhead told her she was in Ward 5 – Engineering. As she passed open classroom doorways, she saw students crowding around holographic schematics of rockets and soldering together tangles of wires. In one room, a pre-pubescent boy unleashed a cannon of blue fire onto a mannequin covered in a gelatinous raincoat. The mannequin's head melted, but the torso remained unscathed.

The students crowding the halls wore uniforms of the same canvas material as Dae-Dae's flight suit, but their shirts were all different colors. Rylla felt self-conscious in her dusty T-shirt and jeans, and after four nervous hours in the skimmer, she *stank*. The students of Wingates, by contrast, were the cleanest people she'd ever seen, most of them with hairstyles she'd only ever seen in holovids. Overhearing bits of their conversations made Rylla doubt she could ever fit in here.

"I needed the four millimeter coaxial cable, but all he had was a six, so I —"

"Right, but if you account for the plasticity of those chemical bonds —"

"We found a polymerate that just might do the trick!"

Most of the students were too absorbed in their own conversations to notice her. But as she neared a branch in the corridor, a group of preteen students blocked her way. They were staring and whispering, and she swore she heard the words "ass" and "hope."

A kid with a thick, black braid strode towards her. Rylla froze like a startled animal, hoping if she stayed still, the girl would pass on by.

"Hey, settle a bet," the tween said loudly. Her friends snickered. She was a head shorter than Rylla, but had the confidence of a scrounger gang-leader. "Aren't you from that holovid —"

Panicking, Rylla bolted. She shouldered past the preteens and kept moving until she reached a set of vacuum-sealed steel doors. She ducked through, and the steel doors hissed shut behind her. Alone in an anteroom, relief flooded through her, followed by shame. If she was going to live around other people, she couldn't keep running away from them. Or her reputation. Dae-Dae had accepted her, maybe everyone else would too.

Taking a steadying breath, she headed for the inner set of doors. As they slid open, a cool mist enveloped her body, and she stepped onto spongy moss, gaping in awe at the astonishing lushness all around her. Colorful tropical plants crowded the path and vine-laden trees rose overhead. Beyond the canopy of leaves, geometric angles broke up the sky. This must be the 'Cloud Forest' Dae-Dae had mentioned, growing inside one of those huge geodesic domes.

As she moved through this slice of jungle, lizards scuttled underfoot. Her breath caught as a massive blue morpho butterfly fluttered across her path to rest on a flower. She'd seen them in books, of course, but never dreamed of examining one in real life. Rounding a bend, she came face-to-face with a long-limbed mammal, hanging from a vine by three long claws. It blinked at her, ever-so-slowly, tilting its head to one side in curiosity.

"I know what you are," she whispered reverently. "But you're supposed to be extinct."

She stared at the sloth for a long time, losing herself in the black orbs of its eyes. Her heartbeat slowed, and a smile crept over her face. If there was a place for an extinct three-toed sloth at Wingates, maybe there was a place for a desert-dwelling creature like her too.

A voice on the path behind startled her. "Today we'll be checking the Ambrosia Beetles. Locate your specimens and determine what they're eating, and what's eating *them*. Log your findings —"

Through a gap in the trees, she glimpsed a pack of students in dark green shirts. Though she wished she could join in their research, she hurried off, dutifully following Dae-Dae's instructions until she reached the administration building.

Hours of placement testing later, Rylla dragged herself down a corridor lined with doors, five stories underground. "501, 503 ..." At the administration building, she'd been quizzed on math and science. The questions started off easy, but got harder and harder until they might as well have been written in Elvish. Now, she felt ignorant as a brick, had a pounding headache, and was desperately hoping for a nap.

"... 511 ... 513!" A thumping bass line leaked from the other side of the door. She hadn't counted on having a roommate. Shifting the bundle in her arms, she smoothed down her hair, suddenly nervous. She hoped her roommate would be nice, someone like Dae-Dae.

Taking a steadying breath, she knocked.

E-scape music blasted out as a giant flung open the door — a woman, Rylla assumed from her femme dress and curvy figure. She was probably about seven feet tall, filling the doorway in part thanks to huge platform boots. Her hair was hot pink at the crown of her head, then purple, then indigo, and finally black at the tips that hung about her ribcage. She had some of the whitest skin Rylla had ever seen — made brighter in contrast with thick black eyeliner and fuschia lipstick. She looked over Rylla's head, her eyes focused on something on her OGlenses.

"What do you want?" the giant asked.

"Uh ... I think I live here?"

The giant slumped against the door frame. "Oh. Right. The roommate. They sent a mention about that." She leaned to one side so Rylla could enter. "Come in, I guess."

The room was much more cramped than Amaryllis's double-wide trailer. Along each wall stood a desk, a wardrobe, and a bed, with only a four-foot-wide corridor between them. The far wall framed a floor-to-ceiling holowall, currently showing a feed of the surface meadows of Wingates.

"Bathroom's through there."

In the bathroom, Rylla tried the sink faucet, and a shocking quantity of clean water shot out. She quickly turned it off and opened a frosted glass door, poking her head in a rounded chamber, like a giant egg.

"When are we allowed to shower?"

"Uh ... whenever you want?"

"Whenever we want?" Rylla repeated in an astonished whisper.

"What, are you a Dusty or something?" her roommate asked mockingly.

"Actually, yeah."

The giant blinked, and her eyes *focused* on Rylla for the first time. "Hey, I know you. You're that 'Ass is Hope' girl!"

Blushing, Rylla pushed past her roommate into the main room.

"Don't worry, I won't call you that." She dropped into her chair and started applying mascara.

Rylla looked for a seat, but there was stuff covering her side of the room. Her desk was buried beneath paperbooks and dishes crusted with dried-up noodles. Her wardrobe was packed with the giant's clothes, and her bed was serving as a shoe closet. "You can just dump that stuff on the floor. I'll clean it tomorrow." Rylla gathered up an armful of shoes with six-inch soles.

"So what *should* I call you?" her roommate asked.

"Rylla," she said, dumping the shoes on the floor. "Rylla McCracken."

"I'm Magenta. *Just* Magenta. I don't use a patriarchal surname, and I'm nonbinary — pronouns they/them," they said, painting a line of silver underneath each eye.

"Got it," Rylla said, making a mental note to use 'they' and 'them' for Magenta from then on. After Jo, Magenta was only the second nonbinary person Rylla had ever met. Unfortunately, there were still a lot of transphobic people in Texas. Based on what she'd gleaned from vids and social media, the Dust was about a century behind the Lush states in terms of social consciousness. And because just about everyone Rylla had ever known was cis, she'd grown up with the habit of making snap-judgments about peoples' pronouns. Now that she was in a Lush state, she'd have to be more careful not to assume folks' genders on sight.

She scooped up another armful of shoes off her bed. "I'm a 'she,' sorry, should've said that earlier."

"I'd help clean, but I'm heading into Chicago." Magenta brushed makeup from their hands and spun around in their desk chair. "We're going to see this e-scape band play at the Metro." They pointed at the ceiling, where throbbing, epic melodies blasted from the speakers. "Aren't they so clean?"

"Uh, very clean," Rylla agreed, dropping on her now-clear mattress.

Magenta pulled off their uniform shirt, exposing their bare chest. Rylla blushed and looked at the floor.

"Oh, are you uncomfortable with nudity?" Magenta asked. Rylla kept her eyes glued to their platform boots as they crossed to the wardrobe. "Fear of the human body is a kyriarchal construct, you know." They pulled something from their closet that looked like a black, wrinkled-up plastic bag.

Rylla forced herself to hold Magenta's gaze and prove she wasn't "afraid" of anything.

Magenta pulled the bag-like thing over their shoulders, pushed a button near their shoulder, and it inflated, becoming a structured military-like jacket. The buttons were tiny holoscreens showing fluffy baby chicks nuzzling each other.

"Gotta go. Doors open at six." Magenta waved a MANI'd hand, and the music silenced. Then they vanished through the door.

It was a relief to be alone again, but for a moment Rylla had hoped Magenta might invite her along to Chicago. She'd always dreamed of visiting the richest city in the world.

Oh well, she thought, looking down at her shabby t-shirt. *I wouldn't have had anything to wear, anyways.*

10

The Grove

Rylla untied the hemp string securing the bundle she'd received at registration. Tucked into the folded stack of uniforms and unbelievably soft bed linens was a small black case. Inside lay a set of MANIs and OGlenses of her own. She grinned. At least no one would laugh at her nuclear lab safety OGGles anymore.

She would never forget that first shower. Showers back home — algae-stinking water trickling from a rusty spigot — didn't deserve to share a name with that glorious experience. As soon as she closed herself inside the egg-like stall, twin streams of crystal-clear, steaming hot water shot out from the showerheads above, enveloping her entire body in a warm embrace. She massaged shampoo into her scalp, feeling years of grit and dust streaming away. Watching so much water swirl down the drain made her feel instinctively guilty, even though the registrar had explained that 99.9% of water at Wingates was recycled on-site.

Her Wingates uniform was comfortable   sturdy but soft cotton, with deep pockets in the pants. Cuffing her sleeves in the mirror, she took a long look at herself. The bright red uniform shirt brought out her sunburned cheeks, peeling nose, and cracked lips. Back home, she had rarely given a thought to her appearance. Now, she found herself wishing she had some of Magenta's style.

She spent the next twenty minutes jabbing her OGLenses at her eyeballs, trying to get them in. Then, one-by-one, she stuck each tiny, black MANI to her fingernails, right next to the cuticle. She wiggled her fingers — her hands now looked like they belonged to the richest influencers on the holonet. Two clear beads — her microvibe speakers — went behind the tragus of each ear. These and the MANIs should stay stuck on for a month or two, but she dreaded having to take out her OGLenses each night and put them in again every morning.

A red dot glowed in the left corner of her vision. When she pushed it with her MANI-dotted finger, a great horned owl appeared, blinking wide, orange eyes. He introduced himself as Winifred, her guide to the Wingates Academic Portal.

An owl for an academic avatar? That was way too cliché. Rylla poked a wrench icon that led her to "settings," swiped through a bestiary of options, and morphed Winifred into a terrifying, five-foot-tall Shoebill, *Balaeniceps Rex*. The extinct bird at the foot of her bed clacked its impressive bill and ruffled gray feathers. "Hmmm, Winifred doesn't suit you any-more," she said, renaming him "Kyle." She selected a soothing baritone voice for the audio output.

"That's better. Load up Joinly for me, Kyle," Rylla said.

"Sorry, but I cannot comply," Kyle crooned. "For security reasons, social media sites are banned on Wingates campus."

Rylla felt a moment of bottomless panic. No Joinly? No mentions? How did people survive? But then she thought about all the lewd threats and insulting mentions she'd gotten since *Ass is Hope* went viral. Maybe it was best to stay off social media for a while.

Her stomach grumbled angrily, reminding her that she hadn't eaten since leaving Texas. "Okay, Kyle. Where can I get some food?"

Kyle trotted down the corridor ahead of her on dinosaur-like legs, his hologram phasing in and out of the bodies of students she passed. Outside the windows, the sun had nearly set, painting the meadows gold and red in the dying light. Dozens of students were bunched up ahead, waiting to pass into another geodesic dome. The sign above the doors read "The Grove."

"You've arrived at the dining facility for college and graduate students," Kyle said and vanished.

Now alone with a crowd of folks her age, she weirdly missed the company of the huge digital bird. She half-expected someone to point and start singing *Ass is Hope*, but no one noticed her in her Wingates uniform. Grateful for the anonymity, she followed the press of students into another anteroom. When the door ahead opened, Rylla's breath caught in her throat.

A carpet of thick moss dotted with flowers spread before her. Students ate and talked at large, round tables beneath the massive oak trees that ringed the meadow. Globes of light hovered among their gnarled branches, where jewel-colored birds perched, singing in uncanny harmony. Were these more de-extincted birds? She didn't recognize the species.

The most beautiful place she'd ever known in the Dust was the Guadalupe, wreathed in morning mist, but that was a sparse kind of beauty, all wiry grass and rocks and a trickle of water. The lushness of the Grove made her head spin, like so much life in one place should be physically impossible.

A student bumped into Rylla from behind, and she realized she was blocking the line. Tearing her eyes from the angelic birds, she followed other students through a gap in the trees. Through the massive trunks, she emerged into a place that was a cross between a cafeteria and a forest. She grabbed a tray, plate, and silverware, all made from the same honey-colored bamboo. She didn't recognize any of the brightly-colored foods on offer, so she took a little bit of everything. There was a drinks fountain, where students could take as much as they wanted, so she greedily filled three large cups with ice water.

In the dining area, the tables were packed with students talking and laughing. Shyness froze her in place as she scanned the nearby tables for empty seats. *Just pick somewhere and sit!* The registrar had explained that the colors of the uniforms signified a students' major, and while most of the tables were a jumble of colors, at one table, all the students wore red shirts, like hers. Humanity majors. She made up her mind to sit there, but as she approached, a few of them started whispering together, and she thought she heard someone humming *Ass is Hope*. Taking a sharp turn, she headed for the far end of the Grove, where she sat down at a blessedly empty table. She could always make friends tomorrow.

Everything on Rylla's plate smelled delicious, but the food looked so strange. She jabbed a tree-like thing with her fork. Back home, all their food came packed in ration bags, but this "broccoli" was a plant, picked right out of the dirt. Biting into it made her feel almost like a cave-person. It was earthy and rubbery, but she liked it. Tyler probably wouldn't have taken a bite — he was such a picky eater — but Jo shared her love of trying new foods. She wished they were here to eat with her and share these gorgeous little green spheres that popped when you bit into them.

She caught someone watching her as she ate, with a pair of eyes like two black ball-bearings. Clinging to the nearest tree trunk was a red-and-black striped squirrel. Odd coloration for a prey animal. What kind of biome would favor such a garish adaptation? Its puffy, flame-colored tail twitched.

"Staking out my food, huh?" she asked the small mammal. "Well I'm eating all of this!" She stuck another forkful of the orange stick-things in her mouth.

A hand smacked into her shoulder, almost making her choke. "Talking to squirrels? Not very social, are we?"

Turning, she saw a grinning, familiar face under a mane of curly bronze hair.

"Dae-Dae!"

Dae-Dae set down her tray and turned to the two students behind her. "Rylla was my passenger today. She's from *Texas* and she did *SCHOEL*." Dae-Dae said these things like they were fascinating secrets. "And she doesn't want to hear any *Ass is Hope* jokes, so be nice."

Next to Dae-Dae stood a very tall person with tan skin and jet-black hair pulled back in a lazy bun. "Theo Reyes, he," he said, sliding into the seat next to her. She hadn't met many people her age, but she suspected that by any standards, Theo was terribly handsome.

"I'm Azam, she," said the other student with a slight accent. She was fat and beautiful, with long eyelashes and full lips painted a turquoise hue that exactly matched the silk hijab draped loosely around her hair.

Theo began drumming the table with his MANI-studded fingers. Typing. His eyes stared unfocused past them, breaking off occasionally to shovel in a bite of food.

"Don't mind him," Dae-Dae said, waving at Theo. "He's working on a research proposal."

All three of them wore gold uniform shirts. "So you're all engineers?" Rylla asked. Dae-Dae nodded. "Does that mean y'all take classes together?"

"*Y'all.*" Theo smiled, still typing. "That's cute, Tex."

Dae-Dae shot him a *be nice* look. "Not really," she said, answering Rylla's question. "Our concentrations are too different." Rylla must have looked confused, because she explained. "My concentration is nanocybernetic engineering. Tiny robots, basically."

"And I'm a chemical engineer," Azam said. "Working on depolymerization reagents." She laughed at the puzzled look on Rylla's face. "How do I explain this?"

"It's like recycling with chemicals," Dae-Dae offered. "Take a landfill full of plastic trash, dump Azam's reagents on it, and all you're left with is pure, organic materials."

"That's the idea," Azam sighed. "But for now, manufacturing the reagents is too costly to be useful in real-world contexts."

Theo slammed a hand on the table. "Bacteria!" he cried. "I'm telling you — bioengineer microbes to deliver your reagents. Bacteria that'll eat plastic and crap out carbon."

Dae-Dae rolled her eyes. "Bioengineering is your answer to everything."

"What do you expect? I'm a bioengineer," Theo said, turning his green eyes on Rylla. She knew exactly what bioengineering was, but Theo mistook her look of open-mouthed horror for confusion. "Think of me as an artist," he explained, leaning forward. "DNA is my paint, and my canvas is life itself. Basically, I play God."

"Well, your head's big enough," Azam said, and she and Dae-Dae laughed.

Rylla didn't see anything funny about "playing God" with DNA, having lived all her life in a wasteland made from bio-engineering's unintended consequences. "Bioengineers helped *create* the Dust." Her voice shook with barely-restrained anger. "Soy3 was a mod!"

Soy3 had been a crop designed to survive the wild climate fluctuations of the midcentury West. It had been bio-engineered to release a chemical that would protect soy plants from white mold that bloomed in the wake of flash floods. But the fungicide worked *too* well. The first crop destroyed essential microbes and microrrhiza in the soil across the Western states — turning rich farmland to dust in a single growing season. After that wildfire season ended, nothing could regrow in the poisoned earth, and the desert spread.

"That was in the 2040s." Theo waved his hand dismissively. "That was the Wild West of bioengineering. You wouldn't believe the amount of red tape we deal with these days. We've got the Humanity department and the FDA breathing down our necks, making sure we don't develop the next Ebolike."

"Well good," Rylla said. "You *should* be careful. Messing with DNA is ... unpredictable."

"That's what I always say," Dae-Dae exclaimed. "Best to stick with good old-fashioned robots. You want to clean up pollution, Azam?" Dae-Dae bounced on the heel she was sitting on. "Program robots to deliver your reagents. Easy as Math," she said, snapping her fingers.

At that moment, a *boom!* rent the air, and an ear-splitting siren rang out. The ground shook violently, then fell away, and they were sinking into the earth. Rylla screamed, clutching the table. The noise had sounded like a pipeline explosion. Had there been some terrible industrial accident in one of the labs? Were they falling into a sinkhole? Dae-Dae was shouting something, but her voice was lost in the din of shrieking metal.

Past the treetops, giant steel plates slid over the geodome, swallowing the sky. They slammed shut, plunging the Grove into darkness. Then ultraviolet lights blazed on, casting everything in a ghostly hue, and all was quiet and still.

A squirrel that had fallen into the middle of their table hopped up, bounded once onto the grassy floor, and skittered up a tree.

Theo was chuckling. "You screamed," he said to Rylla. "Actually *screamed.*"

"Oh shut up, Theo," Dae-Dae said. "You remember your first drill?"

"Hey, I was six years old."

"He wet his pants!" Dae-Dae said, and she and Azam burst into laughter.

"That was a drill?" Rylla gasped, pressing a hand to her pounding heart.

"A cataclysm drill," Dae-Dae explained. "We have them once a month or so. In case of an apocalyptic event, the whole school is designed to sink underground. Right now, we're fifty feet below the surface."

Rylla looked at the metal plates above the trees and tried not to think about being buried alive.

"Don't worry," Dae-Dae said. "This is the safest place on earth. Wingates can withstand a nuclear holocaust."

"As long as the nuclear winter allows enough light to reach our solar fields," Theo added.

"That's a big *if*," Azam said. Her lipstick glowed ghostly in the eerie lighting.

"Anyways, I don't think it'll be nuclear weapons that sends us underground," Theo said. "It'll be trillions of tons of bacteria farts."

Rylla snorted a laugh, but no one else joined in.

"I'm serious. Every year, the ocean currents are slowing," he said. "When they finally stop, the seas will become a stinking bog. And all that bacteria will produce enough methane to poison the world's atmosphere."

"An anoxic event," Azam nodded solemnly.

"But don't worry, it'll only last half a million years." Theo smiled ironically. "That is, unless we can *bioengineer* organisms to reverse it." He grinned, and everyone rolled their eyes.

"I think disease will get us," Dae-Dae said, sticking out her tongue at Theo. "One of your bioengineered bacteria, gone wild."

"Being underground wouldn't do much good then," Azam said. "If even one person got sick —"

"This place would be a death trap," Dae-Dae finished.

"Personally, I think we're going to cook," Azam said. "Surface temperatures keep rising, deserts are spreading ... eventually, the heat will send us underground."

Rylla listened in stunned silence. They were *joking* about the end of the world, sounding almost like they wanted their predictions to come true. She had her own idea, but was nervous about voicing it. It wasn't exactly scientific.

"What if," she began cautiously, "it's just *other people* who send us underground? There's so much here that people want. Water, for starters." She held up one of her three glasses of water. "If this school was in the Dust, y'all'd need an army to protect it from scroungers."

"I never thought of that." Azam frowned. "Simple greed and violence."

"Not greed — necessity. When people get thirsty enough, they'll do *anything* for a drink of water," Rylla said.

Theo stared at her unnervingly. "She's a Humanity major, all right."

Another boom rang out, but this time Rylla didn't scream. The Grove shuddered and began to rise to the surface. "Drill's over," Dae-Dae said. "Back to the world of the living."

11

Ward 7

When the school emerged topside, Theo did not resume work on his proposal. Instead, he tried to convince Rylla that her lifelong hatred of bioengineering was unfounded. He explained that most of the Habitats on campus, like the Cloud Forest, were de-extinction projects, but the Grove was an *experimental* ecosystem. Here, every plant and animal had been bioengineered. That explained the uncannily melodic birdsong and brightly-colored squirrels.

"See these oak trees? You'd probably think they're what? 100, 200 hundred years old?" He leaned in dramatically. "They're *fifteen*. Their DNA was spliced with bamboo to make them fast-growing. And they produce enough oxygen to keep everyone in this room breathing if we're forced underground."

He grinned at her and looked pointedly at her plate. "And are you enjoying your meal?"

She nodded warily, afraid of what was coming.

"All of our food crops have been modded to require less water, provide more nutritional value, and be naturally resistant to pests and disease."

Rylla set down her fork, suddenly losing her appetite.

78

"That table's getting up," he pointed to some nearby students who were pushing back chairs. "Watch what happens."

In the branches above the table, squirrels and birds were congregating. The instant the last student stepped away, all the animals swarmed down. The birds pecked at crumbs. The squirrels licked the plates clean. In moments, not a crumb was left. "No food waste."

When every plate was spotless, the animals dashed off towards the farthest corner of the Grove, vanishing between two tree trunks. A drone rolled up to the table, swept all the cleaned dishes and plates into its gaping maw, then trundled towards the cafeteria.

"What's back there?" Rylla asked, pointing to the space where the animals had disappeared.

"The shitting corner!" Dae-Dae said.

"The world's most efficient composting system," Theo said. "But yeah, basically, the shitting corner. They didn't want the animals crapping all over your food, so they go back there. Then some brilliantly designed arthropods eat the larger animals' waste, fertilize the soil, and keep the whole system going. Look!" He scooped up something from the grass. "A rainbow beetle." It was the size of his knuckle, with wing casings striped in all the colors of the spectrum.

"It's like a neon *Lucanus Elaphus*," Rylla said breathlessly. Her loathing for mods couldn't quite overcome the thrill of seeing such a brilliant insect.

Theo's eyebrows shot up. "Very good! It *is* a stag beetle mod. Are you sure you're a Humanity major?"

She blushed. "I just know Texas insects."

The rainbow beetle snapped giant mandibles. "It may look fierce, but they're not strong enough to bite human flesh. That's one of our rules — our mods can do no harm to humans." To prove his point, he poked the beetle's jaws. The beetle squirmed and snapped.

Theo yelped and shook his hand, sending the bug flying.

"So much for 'do no harm,'" Dae-Dae laughed.

"Maybe it's, 'do no harm, except to fools who are totally asking for it,'" Azam said.

"Wait, look." He held up his finger triumphantly. "No blood. Just a pinch, see? There may be a few kinks to work out, but you have to admit," he leaned back and held out his arms, "our Grove is something special."

Now that the sun had set, the globes in the trees blazed brighter. Tucked between the leaves, the eyes of forest creatures twinkled overhead.

"I do — I *did* think it was beautiful," Rylla said. "But that was before I knew these were all mods." Harmonizing birds and frolicking squirrels might be adorable, but knowing they were bioengineered, she wasn't sure they ought to exist.

Rylla and the engineers were one of the last groups of students to leave the Grove. Strolling down the corridors of Ward 4, Dae-Dae skipped ahead, and Azam walked arm-in-arm with Rylla, grilling her about life in the Dust States. Outside the windows, the sun was sinking low over the meadows of Wingates. At the junction with the Chemistry wing, Azam broke off.

"I have to check my polystyrene samples," she said, "so this is where I split."

"Me too. Got a test running in the cryo lab." Dae-Dae turned to Rylla. "Can you find your way back to your dorm?"

"I'll walk her," Theo said. Dae-Dae arched an eyebrow meaningfully at him. "What? I'm heading back anyways to work on my proposal."

Rylla was perfectly capable of getting herself back to her room, but she didn't protest the friendly offer. Dae-Dae and Azam waved goodnight and headed off arm-in-arm, glancing back at Rylla. Something was going on here.

"Come on," Theo said. "Let's take the Jet Stream. It's the quickest way to get between Wards." He led her down a stairwell.

They emerged onto a wide subterranean platform. Beyond the edge, five tunnel openings yawned, each perfectly round and glistening with a black, oily substance.

Kyle the shoebill reappeared, startling Rylla before she remembered the giant bird was her academic avatar. Clacking his football-sized bill, he asked Rylla if she wanted to call a Jet Stream pod. Before she could respond, Theo flicked a wrist and ordered one for them.

As they waited, Theo slouched next to her on the platform, loose strands of hair falling into his eyes. His silence was making her nervous, and she racked her brains for something to ask him. "So ... you and Dae-Dae have been friends a long time?"

"Ever since my first day at Wingates. We had math together, and she had to help me with long division." He rolled his eyes. "She still throws that in my face."

"Are your parents professors too?"

He laughed. "No. I am a local, though. Started out at a public school a few miles from here. My kindergarten teacher thought I was a sociopath, so they sent me for psychological testing." He tapped a finger against his skull. "Figured out I'm just a genius."

"A kindergarten sociopath?" Rylla laughed nervously. "Why'd she think that?"

"I may or may not have replaced my teacher's koffy creamer with pure sodium." His hands made an exploding motion, and he mouthed *Boom!* "Oh, don't look so horrified — she wasn't seriously hurt. And I'd warned her to give it a rest with that insipid *Rainbow Fish* book."

Before Rylla could respond, the elevators behind them opened, and five people in military dress uniforms stepped out. In the lead was a pale, middle aged person with a thickly muscled neck, a large bust, and black hair pulled back in a severe bun. Their eyes swept over Rylla with as much interest as they'd give to ants beneath their feet.

A gust of wind blasted the platform, and a white pill-shaped capsule shot out of the far-right tunnel. It stopped at the edge of the platform, hovering in mid-air. The pod door slid open, and without a glance at them, the military personnel boarded.

"Hey!" Rylla whispered. "Wasn't that *our* pod?"

Theo just scowled. "That's the third time I've seen the army snooping around this week. It's like they've moved in or something."

The pod sped into the far-left tunnel. A moment later, another pod appeared, and a group of brown-shirted students got off. Theo gestured for Rylla to enter after them.

The pod bounced slightly on its magnetic field as she climbed aboard. Even though there were a dozen empty seats, Theo sat directly next to her, which made her anxious. She wasn't used to being so close to people. As the capsule door slid noiselessly shut, claustrophobia gripped her chest. "So, uh —" she forced her voice to sound nonchalant "— what's the army doing here anyways?"

"I wish I knew," he said.

"We should follow them and find out," she said — joking, of course, but Theo's face lit up with mischief.

"We *should*. I like your style, Tex."

"Wait, I was kidding —"

But Theo's MANI-studded fingers were already drumming on his knees. The holoscreen at the front of the pod filled with code.

"What are you doing?"

"I've been at Wingates a long time," he said with a smile. "I may have figured out how to do some *light* hacking into its internal operations systems." The holoscreen filled with data that was incomprehensible to Rylla, but Theo peered at it closely.

"Okay, here's the pod log. It came from Ward 3 and headed to —" Theo frowned. "But that doesn't make any sense."

"What?"

"This has to be a mistake. Hang on." The code reappeared, and his fingers flew again, typing furiously. "If I delete their log, I can trick the system into thinking *this* is the pod they were in. Then I'll rerun the protocol, and it should take us where they went."

Rylla suddenly pictured Professor Watt looking very angry. "Is this allowed? Are we going to get in trouble?"

He grinned wolfishly. "Would it be so bad to get in trouble with me?"

His words sent something electric shooting through her, chasing away the responsible part of her mind. She *was* dying to know what the army was doing here, and she didn't want to let Theo down — not when he was gazing at her so intensely. She didn't know the rules of Wingates — whether being an accessory to "light hacking" could get her expelled — but Theo had gone here nearly all his life. He must know what he was doing.

"Okay," she breathed. "Let's do it."

Theo waved his hand and the burst of speed pushed her back in the seat. After a few moments, they took a hard right turn, then her stomach lurched as the pod hurtled deeper underground.

"Fascinating," Theo said. "I never knew this tunnel was here."

Rylla's ears popped with the pressure change and the pod stopped suddenly, like it'd slammed into a wall. They were thrown out of their seats. Red lights bathed the cabin, and a siren blared.

"Uh-oh." Theo got to his knees. The pod doors slid open into the middle of a pitch-black tunnel.

A voice in Rylla's microvibe speakers announced, "THIS IS A RESTRICTED AREA. YOUR GENETIC CODE IS NOT AUTHORIZED."

"Shit!" Theo typed furiously.

"SENTINEL HAS BEEN DISPATCHED TO YOUR LOCATION. REMAIN STILL WITH YOUR HANDS IN THE AIR."

Heart hammering, Rylla stretched her hands above her head. "Theo? What's Sentinel?"

"I'm trying to get us out of here before we find out," he said. "But the system's locked. Hang on —"

She pictured a gun-wielding drone speeding down the tunnel towards them, and her arms trembled overhead with fear.

"There!" Theo flicked his hand, the door slid shut, and the pod shot back the way they'd come, throwing Rylla against the wall.

As they climbed out of the pod in the Ward 6 station, Theo muttered, "Walk normally," which made doing that twice as hard. Rylla kept expecting someone to yell "freeze!" or feel a gunshot in her back. She had to concentrate to make it across the platform and into the stairwell without breaking into a run. Theo didn't say another word until they burst through the doors into the meadows outside.

After they'd gone a few paces down the path, he looked over his shoulder, then visibly sagged. He let out a long breath. "Okay, I'm pretty sure we're in the clear."

"Pretty sure?" Rylla's voice came out shrill.

"I was able to wipe our DNA signatures and make it look like a pod malfunction." He interlaced his fingers and stretched his arms overhead. "That was wild, huh Tex?"

"I need you to explain what just happened," she said in a trembling voice. His nonchalance made her want to throttle him.

"What just happened?" He sounded giddy. "What just happened was we found Ward 7!" He laughed, grabbing her by the shoulders. "Ward 7 is real!"

"Ward 7?"

"A secret lab block, deep underground, where professors and their top graduate students work on the really dangerous, classified research." He skipped a step and turned back to Rylla, eyes bright with excitement. "There's rumors about it, but I never knew where it was." He chewed a thumbnail. "Man, I hope my proposal gets me access."

She couldn't believe that he was acting so cavalier. "What would have happened if 'Sentinel' got to us?" she demanded. "What kind of 'dangerous research' are you talking about? What the hell kind of school *is* this?"

"Woah, chill," he laughed, holding up his hands. "Look, I've been at Wingates a long time. If we'd been caught, the worst thing that would've happened would've been a lecture from Professor Watt." He smirked. "As for what kind of school this is? Trust me, whatever research they're doing down in Ward 7, I guarantee it's all good stuff, *for the benefit of humankind,*" he said, quoting the school motto.

Rylla narrowed her eyes. "Then why is the army visiting Ward 7?"

"Now that's a good question." He tapped his lips with a finger. "Maybe they're trying to steal our research, so they can weaponize it against the Siberians."

It all sounded so outrageous — like the plot of a holo-thriller — but after what they'd just been through, Rylla couldn't help wondering if he was right.

They took the winding path through the meadows to reach her dorm, Theo rattling off all the rumors he'd heard about the dangerous, futuristic tech being developed in Ward 7. With the sun setting, Rylla was distracted by how chilly — actually *chilly* — it was, and in April! When they finally reached the prairie-covered topside entrance to her dorm, she was shivering, but didn't feel like heading underground just yet. The air was too crisp, what they'd gone through was too unbelievable, and she wanted to linger under the wide open sky, hugging her arms to her chest. Theo made no move to leave, either. He stood there *staring* at her, from between long, dark lashes.

"Well, that was ... intense," she said to break the silence.

"It was! And not all bad, right? You have to admit you had a little fun?"

"Ehhhh," her voice trailed off. She wasn't sure. She'd been truly terrified for her life, but according to Theo, they'd never been in any real danger. Now, her blood was charged with adrenaline, and thinking of all they'd gotten away with — she couldn't help grinning.

"I knew it! Well, I'll spy on the U.S. army with you any-time, Tex." Theo smiled down at her. Something was *definitely* happening here, and it sent her into a panic.

"Okay, good night," she squeaked, turning to fling open the glass door into the artificial hillside.

As she repeatedly pushed the elevator call button, she heard Theo chuckling as the door swung shut behind her. "Good night, Tex."

Relieved that Magenta wasn't around, Rylla fell face-first onto her bed, giving in to her jumbled feelings. Theo was a bio-engineer, and awfully arrogant, and she *should* hate him for it. On the other hand, he was very tall.

He liked her, right? She didn't have any experience, but she'd seen plenty of romance holofims. As they'd said good-night — that *look* he'd given her! She was pretty sure that was flirting. But doubts rushed in: she'd insulted his major, and she'd even shouted at him. He probably thought she was some backwards, anti-science redneck. Was that why he kept calling her "Tex?"

To distract herself, she powered up her OGlenses and found two messages waiting for her. Her heart swelled to see

Tyler's familiar face floating at the foot of her bunk. He wanted to know all about school and told her to call him tomorrow after his shift.

The second message was from her mother. Amaryllis was halfway through removing her makeup when she recorded the vid, so one eye was black-and-pink with eyeshadow, while the other was pale, wrinkled flesh. She said she didn't have no money to be sending, so Rylla was going to have to fend for herself, don't even *bother* asking.

"Nice," Rylla muttered. "Real comforting, mom."

She couldn't believe that just that morning she'd hugged her mother and her whole life goodbye. Visions from the day crowded her mind, like scenes from a nightmare — Emigrant City and the Wall, the cataclysm drill, army officers, and the dark tunnel to Ward 7. She'd met Dae-Dae, Azam, and Magenta, and she wondered if any of them would become her friends. Most of all, though, she thought about Theo, with his crooked grin. Theo calling her "Tex" as he backed away. All these images were connected, somehow, like threads in an intricate pattern. If she could just zoom out far enough, the strands would form a picture, something terribly important. But whatever it was, she fell asleep before it came into focus.

12

New Here

Rylla was so excited to get to class the next morning, she could barely choke down her breakfast in the Grove. All her life, she'd wanted to go to a real school. Today, for the first time, she'd have teachers: not plastic mannequins, not pixels — live, human teachers. They'd be wise and patient. They'd encourage her and help her learn what she needed to know to save the Dust, or at least bring her family out of it. And she'd have classmates, other 18-year-olds she'd spend late nights studying with before finals, like in her favorite academia animes.

But when she walked into her first class of the morning, Discrete Math 101, her heart sank. There had to be some mistake.

A middle-aged teacher approached and introduced herself as Professor Nagle, she. "You're the new student?"

"I — I think I'm in the wrong place," Rylla stammered.

The professor raised an eyebrow. Her eyes glazed over.

"Sassparylla McCracken? I'm looking at your math placement scores right now, and trust me, you're in the right place."

"But ..."

"New Humanity majors often have to take introductory math courses." She smiled sympathetically. "You can sit with that group over there. Rhonda's closest to your age. She's nearly twelve!"

Rylla's cheeks burned the color of her shirt as she crossed the room to the low, round table. With horror, she recognized the officious-looking preteen with the thick, black braid.

"Hey, you're that lady who ran away from me yesterday!" Rhonda said. "I was just gonna say you look like you're from that *A-S-S is Hope* video." She whispered the letters of the cuss word, and the other students giggled. Some looked about seven years old.

Rylla lowered herself into a child-sized chair, bumping her knees on the bottom of the table. "I *am* that lady," she said miserably.

She expected the kids to make fun of her, but Rhonda just said, "Whoa, clean!" Then Professor Nagle called the class to attention and assigned them problems to work on with their groups. The children chattered in incomprehensible math jargon. Trying desperately to keep up, Rylla copied their notes on her holoslate.

At the end of class, Professor Nagle approached her again. "Looks like you're a bit lost." She smiled, swiping a hand in Rylla's direction. "I'm assigning a chapter that should help." At the edges of Rylla's vision, icons appeared. A stack of books labeled "Library" glowed, and a number one appeared within its borders. "And some problem sets." The Nightwork icon — a moon and pen crossed — illuminated with a number three.

Her next class, Climate Modeling, was all the way across campus in Ward 4. She headed towards the Jet Stream, but Kyle appeared, narrowed his orange eyes at her, and told her the Jet Stream was reserved for faculty during passing periods. She followed the trotting shoebill across campus on foot.

Dr. Pupala was already closing the door as she arrived.

"McCracken?" The professor frowned. "Cutting it close."

"Sorry!" she cringed, squeezing into the room.

The entire class watched her, but at least the students looked a bit older — fourteen or fifteen. The chairs were thankfully adult-sized, but instead of desks, a black, conical device sat at each student's feet.

"What are you waiting for?" Professor Pupala asked the students. "Get to work." The room blazed with light as glowing planets appeared in the air beyond each student's knees. Some of the planets were blue and green, like old-timey Earth. Some were brown and dead. Some looked like Venus, with thick, milky clouds obscuring the surface. Under the students' rapidly typing and gesturing hands, the planets shifted and morphed.

Rylla chose a seat in the back, and Professor Pupala came to her side and introduced himself. Her first impression had been that he was much older than her, but up close and illuminated by the glowing planets, he looked like he could be in his late twenties. Only his scowl and receding hairline made him seem like a crotchety old man.

"There are two assignments in this class," he said. "First, create an accurate model of Earth's climate. Then, use your model to figure out how to reverse climate change."

"Oh, that's all?" she joked. "I just have to create the world, then save it?"

"Is that a problem?" He did not crack a smile.

She shook her head. "No problem. When do I turn it in?"

"When it's finished."

A student leaned across the aisle and whispered, "You're new here, huh? We don't have due dates. You just stay in a class until you finish the work."

Professor Pupala, ignoring the interruption, tapped something out with his MANIs. "I'm sending you a chapter on climate regulation and the latest IPCC report. You'll need to internalize both to complete the assignment. If you need help, ask *her*." He pointed at the student who'd whispered before. Then he returned to the front of the room and sat down at a hologram of a complicated chemical reaction.

Rylla's Library icon pulsed with the number 5. Kyle appeared at her shoulder and asked if she'd like to download "Climate Modeling Application XZ7.0."

"Yes, download," she said aloud.

Heads all over the classroom whipped in her direction, and several students held a finger to their lips. The helpful girl leaned in again. "Voice commands are ... *not clean.* Breaks peoples' concentration. Use your MANIs instead."

Rylla blushed and gave the girl a thumbs-up.

Once the modeling App was installed, a "Create New Planet" button floated in the air above her holo-generator. When she pressed it, an interface opened up, asking Rylla for the planet's mass and surface area. After a quick OGnet search, she plugged in the right numbers, and a perfectly smooth sphere popped into existence. Now the app wanted the elemental composition of the planet, the size of the tectonic plates, schematics of the ocean floor ... this first assignment was going to take a very long time.

Towards the end of class, Professor Pupala took a lap around the room, commenting on everyone's work. He stopped at one student's station and the cloudy-looking Earth hovering there. He shook his head and growled, "Think! What lives *in* the ocean?"

"Fish and ... stuff?"

"ALGAE!" Professor Pupala roared. "It's only the largest carbon sink on Earth!" He raised his voice, addressing the class as a whole. "I'm assigning all of you a study on the role of algae in climate regulation. Read it tonight, and I better not see ANY algaeless oceans tomorrow!" Rylla's Library icon glowed again.

The helpful girl flinched when the professor approached. "I know it's wrong! The planet's an iceball, but I can't figure out why."

"Look up 'albedo.'" He rubbed a hand over his face in frustration. "And account for it!"

Finally, Professor Pupala stopped at Rylla's planet. She had just gotten the shape of North America recognizable and was feeling rather proud of it.

"Why are you *drawing* continents before you've created a magnetic field? This isn't art class!" Several students giggled. Rylla wilted. "Read this and this." The Library glowed, now showing a number 10. "And I expect to see your Earth *in orbit* around a sun by the end of class tomorrow!" He smoothed a flyaway strand of his combover. "Class dismissed!"

As they stepped into the corridor, Rylla sidled up to the helpful girl from earlier. "Is he always like that?" she asked.

She nodded.

"What's his deal?"

The girl shrugged. "If you studied climate all day, wouldn't you be depressed?"

✸

Rylla had a late lunch hour, so the Grove was practically empty when she got there. She sat down to eat alone and, figuring she'd get a start on her nightwork, pulled up the first of her many assigned readings.

Albertson's *An Introduction to Climate Science* was over three hundred pages long.

She groaned and laid her head in her hands. Today had gone nothing like it was supposed to. Being the oldest person in all her classes was humiliating, and she was totally lost to boot. The amount of homework she'd gotten already made her want to run screaming back to the Dust. Still, she forced herself to take a bite of food and started reading chapter one, page one, of the textbook.

Her afternoon Humanity seminar was again all the way across campus in Ward 1. Passing through each ward, she started to figure out the different majors. In the geology department, students wore brown shirts, studied rock samples and manipulated holographic images of tectonic plates. In aerospace, students wore black and peered at holographic star charts. And in the arts building, students wore purple and manipulated digital art on hologenerators.

Finally, she passed through a set of double doors into the dazzling afternoon sun over the Quad. On the long, rectangular lawn, clumps of students were lounging in the grass, chatting or typing with their MANIs. A group of three were tossing something invisible to each other — probably a holographic disc. Rylla took her time walking beneath the dappled shade of sprawling oaks, her heart swelling with gratitude. She vowed to never complain about life here, not as long as she got to walk to class beneath *real* trees.

Unlike most of the subterranean school, the buildings surrounding the quad were old-fashioned, above-ground stone structures, though each sat on a metal platform designed to sink below-ground in a "cataclysm drill." The five-story Humanity building sat at the furthest end of campus. Pushing through the heavy oak doors, her breath caught in her throat. A wide staircase of honey-colored wood spiralled upward, landing at each of five balconies. Hundreds of shelves wrapped around the rotunda, bearing tens of thousands of paperbooks — far more than the paltry collection in her abandoned school library back home. She took a deep breath of the smell of aging paper. So *this* was where she belonged at Wingates.

Her classroom was on the fifth floor, overlooking the campus. Two other students sat at a round table, and Rylla sagged with relief to see that they were actually her age.

One student, typing with MANIs on the table, had amber-brown skin and a waterfall of dark brown hair cascading down a ramrod-straight back, mouth twisted to one side in concentration. Across the table sat a masculine student with stubble dusting a square jaw, a golden complexion, sharply pointed eyes, and a wave of blue black hair that crested on his forehead.

A familiar voice startled her. "You're in my seminar *too*?" Magenta dropped into the seat next to Rylla. Their messy bun was a riot of purple-pink colors, and they still had smears of last-night's makeup crusted around their eyes.

Before she could respond, Professor Watt appeared in the archway, wearing another brightly-patterned suit of fuscia and grey fractals. She closed the door behind her. "I see our newest member has arrived. You all remember Rylla McCracken, of the Guadalupe River Dam protest?"

"We liked your speech," said the black-haired guy, and Rylla swelled with pride. It was nice to be known for her protest, for once, and not the video making fun of it.

"*Loved* that remix, though." Magenta said. They started humming, "Ass is Hope," bobbing their head, and Rylla deflated. Watt shot Magenta a look, and they stopped.

"Welcome to your Humanity seminar, Rylla." Watt walked slowly around the table. "Like all Wingates students, you four will work as a team to conduct research. And as our name suggests, the subject of that research is *humanity*." She spread her hands wide. "Unlike science majors, your research methods will not always be so straightforward. Humanity is unpredictable, illogical ... *messy*. Sometimes your research will need to be messy as well."

The other students chuckled knowingly.

"These three have been working together for a few months already, and we think you'll be a good fourth for them," she told Rylla. "You all complement each other's strengths and compensate for each other's weaknesses. Never forget that — what makes you different, makes you strong." She cast a meaningful look at all of them. "Unlike in your other classes, where peers may come and go, you four will study together as a team for the duration of your undergraduate degree. Now, I'll let you introduce yourselves. I take it you already know your roommate, Magenta?"

Magenta tipped two fingers off their brow.

"Ynez Espinoza, she, from New-New York," said the typing woman.

"I'm from the Dust like you," said the one who'd smiled. "Los Angeles." Then he gave his name, and Rylla's heart stopped. It was a name she knew. The only person to beat her GPA in the history of SCHOEL, the guy who'd stood in the way of her dreams for so long — he was Jae Boudreaux.

13

Watershed Rights

"We're going to dive right in, Rylla," Watt said. "If you want to listen for today, that's fine. But by our next class, I expect you to come prepared to discuss."

Ynez presented on some bill before Congress called the Watershed Rights Act, flicking her MANIs to project data on the hologenerators set into the center of the table. Rylla's mind swam with so many questions for Jae that she didn't realize she wasn't paying attention until a discussion began.

"Do you think it will pass?" Jae asked.

"Most likely," Ynez answered. "The Dust States don't have enough votes to stop it."

"President Kraft could still veto," Magenta pointed out.

"Why would he?" Ynez asked. "He doesn't need the Dust States to get re-elected."

"Wait," Rylla broke in. Everyone's eyes swung to her. "What does this have to do with the Dust States?"

"This bill that's in Congress? It would let Lush States stop sending their water to the Dust," Ynez explained slowly, like Rylla was a kid.

Every month, Rylla's mother drove to the Water Rations Distribution Center and brought home tanks of drinking water, each tank stamped with a U.S. Flag. She'd never thought much about it before, but obviously all that water had been pumped out of a Lush state.

"So if the Lush States don't have to share —" Her heart dropped into her stomach. Tyler, her mother, everyone she'd ever known would lose their drinking water. "They can't let people go thirsty, can they?" she demanded.

"The Lush States are framing this as a state's-rights issue," Ynez explained. "They want the *right* to sell their water. Or not. And they want to set the prices."

"The Lush States are already so rich," Jae said with a scowl. "But they still want to squeeze every last penny from the Dust."

"So if the bill passes, people in the Dust will have to *pay* for water rations?" Rylla asked.

"Exactly," Ynez said. "The Lush States say they're tired of giving 'handouts' to Dusties."

"Now, don't bite my head off," Magenta said, holding a hand towards Jae. "But I see where they're coming from. Every watershed is drying up. What if there's just not enough water for everyone?"

"What are you saying?" Rylla's voice shook with anger. "You want to let millions of Dusties die?"

Magenta frowned and raised their shoulders. "It sounds like Dusties can still *buy* water, and if they don't like that, they can emigrate to a Lush State."

Rylla and Jae scoffed simultaneously.

"You have no idea what it's like in the Dust, Magenta," Jae said. "We have *nothing*. If water rations are cut, only the rich will be able to afford it. Rylla's right — thousands will die of thirst, all so the Lush States can turn a profit." He spat the last word.

"And you have no idea how hard it is to emigrate," Rylla said. "My brother's been trying to get a visa for three years! It's impossible to get out of the Dust unless you're rich."

Magenta started to reply, but then pressed their lips together, momentarily stunned.

"Maybe it would help to make this a thought experiment," Ynez said conciliatorily. "Let's say there are twenty people on a desert island, but only enough drinking water to keep ten of them alive until they're rescued. What do you do?"

"You make a hard decision," Magenta said authoritatively. "I get that this is very personal for the two of you." They glanced at Jae and Rylla. "But if you can't choose ten people to save, everyone dies."

Rylla hated that Magenta had a point. "So how do you choose?" she demanded.

Professor Watt interrupted. "Not how *do* you choose. How *should* you choose who gets the water?"

Jae pointed at Magenta. "Apparently they think whoever's richest gets to *buy* the water."

"Don't speak for me," Magenta snapped. "I said no such thing, and you know I despise plutocracy. I was just saying I can see where the Lush State leaders are coming from."

Watt spoke again. "As Humanity majors, we are educating you to be leaders, and sometimes leaders must make hard decisions. So I'll ask again, how *should* you decide which ten people get the water?"

"Honestly?" Magenta said, sticking out their chin. "I'm with the Lush States. If you're the one in charge of the water, you pick the ten people you care about. You protect your own."

Watt turned to Jae, who covered his face with his hands. "I don't know," he groaned. "It's not a decision that should be made lightly. If I were in that situation ... I like to think I'd give up my share for someone else."

Across the table, Magenta rolled their eyes.

Ynez leaned forward, stacking her palms on the table. "The only fair thing to do is make it completely random. Use a lottery to decide who is saved."

Now everyone looked to Rylla, who felt on the verge of crying from listening to her classmates casually discuss the impending doom of her homeland as if it was a logic puzzle. She wasn't sure what she was going to say until the words poured out. "I don't accept that we can only save ten people. I — I'd build an ionic recycler out of coconuts or something. I would find a way to save everyone."

"You'd kill everyone in the process," Magenta muttered.

Professor Watt had nodded after each student's answer, not indicating approval or disapproval. "As Jae pointed out, this is not a question to be taken lightly. I pushed you to give a response today, but please continue to meditate on your answer."

For the rest of class, Rylla struggled to concentrate. Would this Watershed Rights Act pass? What would happen to Tyler, Jo, and her mother if it did? It made her sick to think that the fate of her family would be decided by a bunch of greedy Lush State politicians.

Jae gave her a sad smile, and she knew he was thinking the same thing.

✳

Hours passed in heated discussion — politics and philosophy, history and sociology — leaving her mind a jumble. When she finally stepped from the Humanity building, the sun was low in the sky, casting long shadows across the quad. The tossing treetops of the oaks filled up all the worried spaces inside her, and she took a circuitous route back to the Grove, so she could gawk all she liked at the dragonflies flitting above the meadows.

At dinner, she found Dae-Dae and Azam sitting together. "Did you really find Ward 7 yesterday?" Dae-Dae asked as she sat down. "Or was Theo just pulling our legs?"

Rylla nodded and described their subterranean adventure from the night before. Dae-Dae squealed when she got to the part about Sentinel. "That's so scary! What do you think it was?"

"I don't know," Rylla said. "Some kind of security system? Theo said he didn't think it would've hurt us."

"Yeah, no." Dae-Dae frowned. "They wouldn't hurt a student." But she didn't sound as confident as Theo had.

Rylla described her first day of classes, and Azam assured her that feeling old and ignorant was normal for a new Wingates student. Dae-Dae wanted to hear about Rylla's Humanity seminar.

"You just talked?" she asked, sounding disappointed. "Three whole hours? Just talking?"

Azam chuckled. "Your major is so secretive, we figured you were up to something far more sinister."

"Maybe she won't tell us what they're really up to because she's already sworn to secrecy!" Dae-Dae said.

"Aw, you guessed it," Rylla said sarcastically. "There was a blood oath and secret passwords and everything."

"I knew it!" Dae-Dae pounded the table and they all laughed.

Rylla's laugh faltered as she spotted Theo walking towards them from across the Grove. Her heart started racing — probably because she was eager to grill him more about what might be happening in Ward 7. But Theo just gave a head-nod to Dae-Dae and walked past, without even acknowledging Rylla. Two tables away, he slid into a seat next to a gorgeous person with blue-black skin, high cheekbones, and a shock of short neon-green hair. The two were soon engrossed in conversation, their heads practically touching.

Rylla's stomach lurched. She'd only met Theo twenty-four hours ago, so how could she already feel thrown off because he'd gone to sit with someone else? An extremely attractive someone else? It was a bummer they hadn't gotten to talk more about Ward 7, that was all. She forced herself to eat, though suddenly she didn't feel very hungry.

Back in her dorm room, Rylla pulled up her climate reading and flicked through a few pages but couldn't concentrate. Her mind kept returning to the Watershed Rights Act. She searched the OGnet for news about it but couldn't find any new information.

"Kyle," she said, and even though she was expecting him, she startled when the massive bird suddenly appeared, its fearsome orange eyes inches from her own. "When am I going to get used to that?"

"When are you going to get used to what?" Kyle asked.

"Never mind. I should probably turn you into a bunny or something. Anyways, I need you to help me call a number outside the school."

A few seconds later, the sight of Tyler's face, drifting across the wall in a call-bubble, made her heart swell.

"My favorite sister!" Tyler cried.

"Your only sister."

"Still my favorite. Tell me everything! How's school? What's life like in a Lush State?"

The words poured out of Rylla. She described that first shower, the sloth, the Grove and its dirt-grown foods. Only Tyler could understand how overwhelming all this lushness was. How it made her feel guilty and angry and grateful all at the same time.

Jo appeared, wrapping their arms around Tyler's shoulders. "Ryllita! Look at my newest friend." They held up a plant that looked like a cactus crossed with a buttercup. "Kalanchoe.

Isn't it the prettiest thing you ever saw?" Tyler groaned and Rylla chuckled. Past their shoulder, a riot of green covered every surface of the apartment.

"How many plants do you have now?" Rylla asked.

"Different species? Thirty-seven. Different plants? I don't know, hundreds …"

"It takes an hour to water them all," Tyler grumbled. Jo gave a wave and floated out of view. Tyler might complain about Jo's plants, but he smiled sweetly, watching them go.

"Speaking of water, listen. In one of my classes, they were talking about this new law that might pass. The 'Watershed Rights Act.'"

"That's so random," Tyler said. "We played a show last night and guess who was there? Miles Walker! And he was going on and on about the same thing —"

"It could mean the end of water rations for the Dust States."

Tyler nodded gravely. "That's what Miles was saying. He told us to stock up on black market drinkables. Said he had a connection for industrial-grade water recyclers. I didn't believe him, to be honest. He was cosmically high on tam."

"Tyler, I think you should listen to him! If you can stock up on water, do it."

"You know I've been saving up for a bribe to get visas. I'd rather get us the hell out of here before they cut our rations."

There was a long silence. Rylla chewed her lip. "Promise me you'll look into it."

"I will." He mustered a strained smile. "Don't worry about me, okay? Just focus on school. I'll talk to Miles again. He's … *connected*."

They agreed to talk soon, and the bubble containing Tyler's face popped.

Forcing her worries to the back of her mind, Rylla started in on her math homework, working out the problems in the air with a MANI'd finger. By midnight, her brain was throbbing and her eyelids drooping. But just as she drifted off to sleep,

Kyle appeared, making her half-jump out of her skin. "You have an incoming call from Amaryllis McCracken," he crooned. "Do you wish to answer?"

Rylla punched the settings icon first and shrunk Kyle down to the size of a pigeon. He preened some feathers while perched on her knee, looking downright cute.

"Still awaiting response," Kyle said. His voice came out higher-pitched, sounding almost annoyed about the change. "Do you wish to answer?"

Talking to her mother was the last thing Rylla felt like doing, but guilt tugged at her. The least she could do was warn Amaryllis about the Watershed Rights Act.

Her mother's face burst into view, hair blown out huge, makeup painted on thick, like she was on her way to Lucky's. "You look terrible."

"Nice to see you too, mom," Rylla said.

"They feeding you enough?"

"I'm just tired. It's been a long day."

"Well honey, it shows. No offense. Where's this school at, anyways?"

"Michigan, I've told you —"

Her mom whistled. "Michigan, that's a *really* Lush State. Guess you ain't never coming home now you've made it big."

"Made it *big*? It's college, not — you know what, never mind. Listen, I heard about something in class today —"

"Be nice to all those rich kids, you hear? Even if they treat you like dirt, you smile back and compliment their outfit. In this life, you never know who you're gonna need."

"Mom, listen! There's a bill in Congress — the Watershed Rights Act. If it passes, they're gonna stop water rations to the Dust!"

"Honey, the news didn't say anything about that."

Rylla tried not to roll her eyes. "Just — if you can stock up on water rations, do it, okay?"

"Sassy, I'm sure if it was something I needed to worry about, Chet Strongman would've mentioned it. Now I gotta go, but remember what I said about being nice to those Lushies. I know you think your mom's a brainless redneck, but I've been around this world longer'n you, and I know some things."

"I don't think that about you," Rylla muttered, but she couldn't tell if Amaryllis heard her before the call-bubble popped.

Maybe Chet Strongman was right, and the Watershed Rights Act was nothing for Amaryllis to worry about. But when had he ever been right before?

14

What the Floorbot Heard

For the rest of the week, it was all Rylla could do to make it to class and try not to drown in nightwork. On Tuesdays, she had evolutionary biology and neuropsychosociology in a huge lecture hall with Dr. Hernandez, the long-haired man who'd recruited her alongside Watt.

After dinner, she was supposed to meet her work/study supervisor in the Humanity building. She'd been assigned "sanitation," so as she trekked across the quad, she was dreading an evening of scrubbing toilets.

A guy in a rumpled, grey uniform shirt greeted her outside the Humanity building. Hoshiko was a graduate student, and he could use some *personal* sanitation, she thought. Dandruff dusted the mop of shaggy hair that hung in front of his acne-scarred face. His sleeves were cuffed to his elbows, and one of his forearms was tattooed in Russian words.

He led her inside. "So you'll be cleaning this," he waved a hand at the entire five stories.

"You're joking." She gazed up at the hundreds of book-shelves lining the walls, the dozens of empty classrooms and offices. "That'll take all night!"

105

Hoshiko shrugged. "I'll get you a broom."

"A broom?" Rylla cried. "You don't even have a vacuum?"

He met her stare for a moment, then burst into laughter. "Sorry, I had to. A *broom!*" he wiped his eyes with a knuckle. "Ah, that was a good one. Undergrads are so gullible."

"You mean I don't have to clean all this?" Rylla sagged with relief.

"No, you do. Well, not *you*. What is this, the dark ages? Come on, I'll show you the drone closet."

It turned out the job of sanitation worker was more supervising a fleet of robots than scrubbing toilets — there was a drone for that. Small, cube-shaped drones polished the floors, dog-sized spider-looking drones dusted the bookcases, and hovering mosquito-like drones cleaned the windows and light fixtures. From time to time, they'd return to Rylla for a refill of their cleaning solutions. Besides that, her job was to rescue them if they got stuck in a corner or a book fell on them. Hoshiko sent her an app that showed each drone's location and alerted her if anything went wrong.

"Other than that, chill, do nightwork, whatever." Hoshiko shrugged. "Just make sure they all get back to their charging stations." As he walked out, she heard him imitating her: "*You don't even have a vacuum?*"

Rylla found an empty office with a comfy couch and dove into research for her first neuropsychosociology essay. Dr. Hernandez had assigned them readings on the history of experimental utopian societies. She was thoroughly engrossed in reading about Shakertown, when a red light flashed across her vision. A holovid popped up, showing Floorbot 17-C bouncing off a locked door on the fourth floor. That was odd — the other drones had been able to enter locked rooms.

While she was riding the elevator up to the fourth floor, the door blocking Floorbot 17-C suddenly opened. Through the drone's camera, she saw a pair of polished black boots. Someone in a camouflaged uniform squatted down, and Rylla recognized the pale, stern face and muscled neck. It was the army person she'd seen in the Jet Stream with Theo.

Rylla turned on Floorbot 17-C's microphone.

"— just a cleaning drone."

"Good, let it in," said a familiar voice. "I saw some ants in here yesterday." The drone zoomed into the office, and the hem of Professor Watt's colorful pantsuit appeared.

The elevator doors slid open, but Rylla ducked out of sight and flicked her MANIs to send it back to the first floor. She felt a little guilty for eavesdropping on Watt, but way more curious to find out what the hell the army was doing at Wingates.

Rylla cranked up the volume on her microvibe speakers.

"Like I was saying," the army person hissed, "the Joint Chiefs of Staff have —"

"Are you sure I can't tempt you, General?" Watt interrupted, clearly chewing a mouthful of food. "I ordered from Luigi's. *Real* cheese. Sometimes I can't take that rabbit food they serve in the Grove —"

"— The Joint Chiefs of Staff have ordered you to give me *full* access." The general raised her voice. "To all Wingates research."

"And you have it!" Watt said, exasperated. "You've peered into every lab. You've toured Ward 7 multiple times. Are you disappointed you didn't find what you were looking for? No chemical weapons? No nuclear warheads?"

A slam made Rylla jump — someone must've pounded the desk. "It's not your engineers I'm worried about," the general snarled. "I want to know why I saw one of your Humanity majors standing behind the Siberian Emperor at a press conference last week. And why do I keep running into them at the Gray House?" The voice dropped low and dangerous. "And I want to know *exactly* what the Manifest is."

There was a long pause where Rylla couldn't hear anything over the floorbot's whirring motor. She accessed its settings and slowed it down, hoping it wouldn't finish vacuuming the room before she figured out what these two were talking about.

"Yes, I know about the Manifest." The general sounded triumphant.

Watt chuckled. "Oh, you military types — for all your supposed bravery, you never fail to jump at your own shadows." She clapped slowly. "Congratulations, you got me. You intercepted The Manifest. It's a *thought experiment*, Dorne. A grad student's assignment, nothing more."

"Don't play me for a fool," Dorne said.

"As for my students, haunting halls of power around the world — they're there to *learn*. Ever heard of an internship?"

"To the Siberian empire?" Dorne thundered.

"Yes, *especially* with them. Our Humanity majors are groomed to lead. So much the better if they understand our — as you would call them — *enemies*."

Watt's feet pushed back from the desk as she stood up. "Now let *me* make something clear. You're new to this post, so I understand your zeal. But if you interfere with the day-to-day operations of this school, or if you continue to hack my secure communication with students, I will have to inform the Board, and they will not be pleased."

Dorne scoffed. "Pleasing those dinosaurs is your job, not mine."

"If I'm not mistaken, a number of Board members are friendly with those Joint Chiefs of Staff you mentioned. They vacation together in the Canadian Rockies, I believe."

"Is that supposed to be a threat?"

"Just a fact," Watt crossed to the door. "I'm a teacher, General Dorne. I believe in learning all the facts ... and acting accordingly."

Having completed its job, Floorbot 17-C zoomed out of the open doorway, and Rylla lost audio of the conversation. Frantically, she switched between feeds of the other cleaning drones on the fourth floor, but none were in audio range. She was as eager as Dorne to learn what this "Manifest" was. And why *were* Wingates students shadowing the Siberian emperor? The general had seemed defensive and nervous, while Watt had seemed calm — and *in control*. Was Rylla's professor really more powerful than an army general?

Suddenly the elevator lurched and began to rise. Shit. General Dorne must have called it. Panic surged through Rylla's veins. Keep it together — Dorne had no way of knowing she'd been eavesdropping. As the doors slid open, Rylla tried to arrange her face into an innocent expression.

General Dorne glowered at her, and Rylla staggered back as the general stepped inside.

"McCracken! Are you here to see me?" Watt asked from her office doorway.

"Uh, yeah," Rylla stammered, gladly fleeing from the the fuming general.

"And what brings my newest student to my doorstep?" Watt asked, closing the office door behind her. Rylla recognized the cluttered, paperbook-filed room from the night she'd been recruited to Wingates. She racked her brain for some pretense for being there.

"I — uh — well — "

"Let me stop you there." Watt stuck a forkful of take-out pasta in her mouth and spoke out of one side. "I encourage curiosity in my students. Curiosity is essential to your success here." She swallowed. "However, I do not tolerate being spied on." Her face fell, all trace of a smile vanishing. Rylla's heartbeat pounded in her ears. Watt knew she'd been spying. How was that possible?

The professor's eyes glazed over, and her MANIs flew over the surface of her desk. "You should know that any professor can access any student's OGnet activity at any time." Rylla blushed and looked down at her feet. "So stay curious, Rylla, about everyone and everything else. But if you ever eavesdrop on me again, you'll be done at Wingates. Do you understand?"

"I'm so sorry," Rylla breathed, wishing she could sink into the floor.

"It's in your best interest to forget what you heard tonight," Watt said, picking up the dish of pasta once more. "At least for the time being. And I'm sure this goes without saying — but do not breathe a word of this to anyone." Watt's eyes flashed dangerously. "I'll hear it if you do."

15

Secrets

Rylla had little practice keeping secrets. In the Dust, what did she have to gossip about? "Did you hear the scuttlebutt, mom, that the *Tibesen Superba* are swarming?"

Now she'd stumbled upon a mystery of global importance, and she'd been forbidden to tell a soul. Throughout the rest of that week, she was practically sweating with the effort of keeping it to herself. But she didn't dare breathe a word, for fear that Watt was listening.

Even if she could talk to someone, away from Watt's surveillance, she didn't know who she could trust. Dae-Dae and Azam might not appreciate her dragging them into her trouble with Watt. And while Theo seemed to enjoy breaking the rules, every time she saw him in the Grove that week, he was locked in conversation with the gorgeous green-haired person. Azam and Dae-Dae never mentioned Theo's absence, and Rylla didn't want to bring it up and risk them thinking she was obsessed with him or something.

On Friday morning, she headed towards the West Gymnasium in Wingates-issued workout clothes. The P.E. class was her last of the week, and she was desperate to get it over with, even though her only weekend plans were to make a dent in her ever-growing mountain of nightwork.

When she got to the gym, Jae Boudreaux was leaning against the front doors, and Rylla felt a sudden urge to confess everything to him. Being the only two Dusties here, maybe they could have each other's backs. Watt was Jae's teacher too, and he would probably want to know about their professor's strange dealings with army generals. Maybe he knew what the Humanity department was up to in the Grey House and the Siberian empire. On the other hand, she barely knew the guy — Jae might go running straight to Watt if she confided in him.

"You here for Alpinism and Orienteering?" he asked, slicking his black hair back.

Had he been waiting for *her?* "Yeah, it was the only P.E. credit that wasn't full. What even is this class?"

"Wildernesss sports. Alpinism is mountain climbing. Orienteering is basically running through the woods, with just a paper-map and compass to find your way."

Rylla snorted. "That's silly, why not just use a NavApp?"

"Maybe you find yourself stuck in the wild without OGLenses? Maybe because it's a challenge? And it's fun?"

"Okay, okay." She held her hands up in surrender. "So where's the teacher?"

"You're looking at him."

She blushed as he explained that he was some kind of internationally renowned wilderness trekker, and teaching this elective was his work/study assignment. Rylla felt bad about calling his sport "silly." If she was going to make him her confidante, they were not off to a great start.

He led her through the maze-like gym, past an Olympic pool, ice rink, and a boxing ring, where a flash of pink hair caught her eye. Magenta was wailing on a man twice their size, fists blurring as they pounded into him. Rylla made a mental note never to piss off her roommate.

The rock-climbing gym took up the entire fourth sub-floor, with fifty-foot-high walls that students moved along like spiders. Jae ducked into an office and re-emerged with a pair of climbing shoes. As Rylla laced into them, he addressed a group of students and sent them off in pairs to start climbing.

"So who's my partner?" she asked.

"I am."

"Lucky me, I get teacher." She smiled, but Jae didn't return it.

"Safety is the most important thing at all times when climbing." His tone was all-business, and he launched into a twenty-minute lecture on proper climbing harness maintenance and belay technique. Finally she was allowed to strap into the harness.

He stepped close to check the fit of her harness, and she got the same claustrophobic feeling she'd had in the Jet Stream pod with Theo. She wasn't used to being so physically close to *anyone*. Satisfied, he cleared his throat and stepped back. "So, uh, let's talk tying in. Knots are a matter of life-and-death," he said, launching into another twenty-minute lecture on the history of knots.

After nearly an hour of lecturing, he let her actually *climb*. She quickly ascended the first few handholds, but when she glanced down, she reeled at how high she was. Her arms were already trembling, but she forced herself to find the next handhold. Ten feet higher, she got stuck. All her weight was in her arms, and if she loosened her grip, she would fall.

"Stand up," Jae called from below. "Use your legs."

Her feet were bent at awkward angles, on tiny footholds. "I can't!" she called.

"You can!" he shouted. "Stand up!"

She gritted her teeth, hating him in that moment. He'd promised she could trust the rope, trust *him* to break her fall, but her brain didn't quite believe it. Pushing down with her right leg, she inched higher up the wall. Tentatively, she reached her right hand up for the next-highest hold, but her fingers had no grip strength left. They slipped, and with a terrible lurch, she was falling.

The harness snapped tight around her legs as it caught her. She dangled from the top rope, twirling slowly. Below her, Jae was laughing.

"I told you I couldn't do it!"

"You know this is the kiddie route? We use it to teach the lower school students," Jae teased her. "Have you ever exercised in your life?"

The truth was she hadn't. Not unless hiking through dust storms counted. But she just made a face at him in response. Her plan to befriend Jae and tell him all about Watt's secret conversation was quickly evaporating.

He lowered her, and as soon as her feet touched the ground, she started unclipping from the harness.

"What are you doing?" he asked. "You're going again."

"I can't do it!"

"You're going to try. Over and over. Until you get to the top."

Her muscles still burned from the last ascent, but there was no way she was going to quit and give him more ammunition to make fun of her. She faced the wall again and grabbed the first handhold. He made her try again and again, until her arms were jelly. By the end of class, she'd given up any idea of confiding in Jae Boudreaux. Instead, she was wishing for Magenta's boxing skills and fantasizing about punching him in the face.

After lunch, Azam and Dae-Dae invited Rylla to hang out with them. They had the whole afternoon and evening to themselves. Maybe they'd go to a party? Or head into Detroit for a smash show? She could use a beer after this *very* long first week.

But "hanging out" for the engineers turned out to mean doing nightwork together in the chemical engineering lab. A labyrinth of humming aluminum vats and pipes, the chem lab was like the intestines of a giant robot. Dae-Dae perched atop a steel drum, and her eyes glazed over as she set to work on coding her Phireflys' AI. Azam busied herself with a machine that looked like a microwave with a perm made of wires. Sighing, Rylla pulled up her report on fossilized birds for evolutionary bio and started tapping away.

Her brain felt like mud though, and after twenty minutes of rewriting the same paragraph, she couldn't take it anymore. "I'm so bored, y'all. It's Friday night! What do you do around here for fun?" She cleared the essay from her vision and her jaw dropped as she tried to make sense of what she was seeing. The right side of Dae-Dae's hair was *moving*. Tendrils of hair lifted into the air of their own accord and were weaving themselves together into tight braids.

"Do you like my new 'do?" Dae-Dae asked, posing with her fist under her chin. Azam looked up and laughed. Rylla's jaw hung open. "It's the Phireflys! I programmed them to braid my hair."

When Rylla squinted, she could just make out a swarm of grey specks grasping the end of each strand of Dae-Dae's dancing hair. "That's so cool!"

"See? We're fun! Nanorobotic programming is fun!" Dae-Dae laughed. "But you're right. We should go to the arena after dinner."

"I'm about ready for a break." Azam stretched her arms behind her head. "But I have to run a test first. Want to see?" Rylla nodded, and Azam crossed to a bin that Rylla had mistaken for a trash can.

"This sample should do." Azam used a pair of tongs to pick out a plastic chip bag. She shook it to dislodge some crumbs, then placed the bag in the microwave-looking-thing. "Remember when you asked me what depolymerization reagants were?" She pressed some buttons, and a grid of white lasers swept over the bag.

"The sensors are analyzing the chemical composition of the plastic to determine how to break it down," Azam explained.

The machine roared, made a clicking sound, then hissed. The bag vanished.

"Where'd it go?" Rylla cried.

"The recycler generated a series of reagents that broke down the polymer molecules."

Azam opened the door. A fine black powder was all that was left where the bag had been moments before. "Carbon," she said, swiping the soot with a gloved finger. "While it's part of a plastic molecule, it can't biodegrade — it's trapped. But with this process, we can free the carbon." She pointed to the tubes snaking out of the Chemical Recycler. "And the nitrogen, oxygen, and hydrogen atoms get sucked into those tanks up there."

Azam led them around the back of the machine, where more tubing descended into a sheer black box. Dae-Dae followed, Medusa-like — the Phireflys starting on braiding the middle third of her hair.

"And here's a bio-printer." Azam's MANIs whirred in midair. "We can use the elements we just released, along with a few stored macronutrients, and —"

The printer vibrated, made a mechanical ripping sound, then *dinged.* Azam opened the door and retrieved a small black sphere. She placed it in Rylla's palm.

"*That* is a lotus flower seed."

Rylla gaped. "You turned that bag ... into a seed?"

Azam nodded, eyes dancing with pride.

"That's amazing!" Rylla cried. She was starting to see why her friends were so obsessed with their work. "It's like magic! You could clean up all the garbage in the world with this!"

"If only it was that easy," Azam sighed, folding her arms and leaning against the table. "That one little test took up an obscene amount of energy. It's too energy-inefficient to use on a large scale."

Dae-Dae leaned in, and Rylla ducked out of the way of her twirling tendrils. "What's the biggest energy draw?"

"Synthesizing the compounds," Azam said.

"Can you share your specs with me?" Dae-Dae asked. "There's something I want to look into — ouch!" Dae-Dae flinched, her hand flying to her scalp.

"What happened?" Azam asked.

Dae-Dae's eyes glazed over, and her fingers flew, typing midair. The half-finished braid started jerking wildly. "Ow, ow, owwww!" she yelped. The Phireflys were tugging and tangling her strands. "I can't turn them off!"

"What should we do?" Rylla asked.

"Get them off me!" Dae-Dae cried, still typing furiously.

Azam grabbed a strand of Dae-Dae's hair and swiped it free of nanobots. But the Phireflys she knocked off kept coming back for more, so Rylla clapped them like mosquitos and stomped the ones that fell to the floor.

By the time the Phireflys lay motionless, Dae-Dae looked like half her head had gotten caught in a skimmer engine.

"My babies," Dae-Dae moaned, kneeling on the ground to collect the smashed bots into her cupped hand.

Rylla cringed. Maybe stomping them had been a bit much. "I'm so sorry —"

"No, no, it's my fault. I should have programed a kill-switch," Dae-Dae poured the damaged bots into her front pocket.

"What happened?" Azam asked.

"It's their crappy batteries. Some ran out of power and returned to the charging pouch," she patted her front pocket. "But the rest kept going, and because of the mismatch, they started making knots in my hair." She touched a hand gingerly to her scalp. "From there, things ... spiraled." She pulled a wide-tooth comb out of her pants pocket and started picking at her hair.

After a minute of tugging, she sighed in frustration. "I need help with this."

Azam took a step forward, holding her hand out for the comb, but Dae-Dae snatched it to her chest. "Are you kidding? You think I'm gonna trust you straight-haired girls with my curls?"

"Fair enough," Azam said, tucking a strand of razor-straight hair beneath her lemon-yellow hijab.

"I saw Tavia down the hall. I'll text her to come over." Dae-Dae's MANIs flew.

A few moments later, the door behind them hissed open and Rylla heard an explosion of laughter. Turning, Rylla's heartrate spiked. Tavia was the neon-haired, supermodel-looking person who'd been stuck to Theo's hip the last few days.

"What did you do to yourself?" Tavia laughed as she sat Dae-Dae down at a work surface and began picking gingerly at the massive knot on her head.

Dae-Dae explained about the Phireflys. "You're so good with hair!" she whined. "Can you fix it?"

Tavia dug into her shoulder-bag. "Lucky for you, I've got some leave-in conditioner on me." She poured a glob of goo onto Dae-Dae's hair and started massaging it in.

Tavia noticed Rylla for the first time and smiled in recognition. "Hey, I know you. You're that *Ass is Hope* girl."

Rylla's cheeks burned. How long would it be before people forgot that vid?

"Theo told me you'd started here."

Rylla's stomach churned at the thought of them talking about her. "Yeah, uh, I think I've seen you, like, around with him?" She tried to sound casual as she asked the question that'd been plaguing her all week. "Are y'all dating or something?"

Tavia snorted. "Gross, no. I'm just helping him with his research proposal. He needed help from a biocyberneticist."

"Wait, why'd you say 'gross?'" Rylla asked cautiously.

"He's an undergrad!" Tavia said, wrinkling her nose. "I'm a graduate student. He's, like, a baby to me."

Hope sparked in Rylla's chest and she smiled.

"Besides, who could ever put up with his ego?"

Azam and Dae-Dae laughed. "He'd always be talking about how much more important his research was than yours," Azam said.

"When you kissed, he'd lecture you on the fascinating properties of the bacteria in human saliva," Dae-Dae added, giggling.

"Why're you asking about him anyways?" Tavia turned a sharp gaze on Rylla.

Her cheeks burned. "Nothing ... I just, I saw you together is all."

"Ooh," Dae-Dae crooned. "Are you blushing?"

"You like him?" Azam cried incredulously.

"What — no, I —"

"You do. You like Theo." Tavia smirked.

Rylla hid her burning face in her hands and wished she could disappear.

"Aww, it's okay," Azam said. "He's not that bad."

Tavia snorted.

"What? He's gotten better lately ... maybe. You have to understand we've known him for years. He's like a brother to us. A very annoying brother."

Rylla peered over her fingers. "You don't think I'm a loser for liking him?"

"He's certainly handsome," Azam said, sticking out her yellow-painted bottom lip. "I can see the appeal."

"And so have half the people at this school," Tavia muttered.

"What Tavia means," Azam explained, "is that Theo is very, uh, sexually ... *motivated?* So if you want to sleep with him, he'll probably be up for it."

Dae-Dae made a gagging sound.

"What? No, I didn't —" Rylla stammered, blushing crimson.

Tavia arched an eyebrow. "You've never had sex, have you?"

Was it that obvious? "There weren't a lot of opportunities back home." Rylla said. "I've never even kissed anyone."

"Well, if you want to give it a try, I'm sure Theo would oblige," Tavia said.

Azam looked concerned. "Oh, but Rylla, I don't want you to get hurt. If you're looking for any kind of relationship —"

"Theo's probably not capable of it," Dae-Dae finished.

"Hey, y'all are getting ahead of me," Rylla said, trying to sound unconcerned. "I just thought he was kind of cute, all right?"

"We'll find you someone else," Azam said, patting her arm. "There are so many people at Wingates. People whose egos aren't the approximate size of the sun."

"Are y'all dating anyone?" Rylla asked.

Azam explained that she'd had a serious girlfriend who'd graduated the year before. They'd broken up when she'd moved to Tokyo to build carbon reclamation towers.

"Partners are a distraction," Dae-Dae said. "My Phireflys are all the company I need."

"I'm seeing a few people right now," Tavia said with a satisfied smile. She had finished detangling Dae-Dae's hair and combed through the oiled-up ringlets with her fingers. "Do you want me to braid this?"

"Nah, I'm hungry. Let's just go eat," Dae-Dae said, patting her curls — sleek, lustrous spirals once more. "And then we'll take Rylla to the arena! You'll see — we're not just researching-nightworking-robots."

As they left the lab together, Rylla thought about who might be joining them in the Grove, and her stomach twisted into knots. "Hey, if we see Theo, promise me —"

"Your secret's safe with us," Azam said, but Dae-Dae and Tavia were grinning way too hard for Rylla to trust them.

16

The Arena

"Hey, Tex," Theo said, dropping into the empty seat next to Rylla. Dae-Dae winked, and Rylla shot her a pleading look.

"Did you finish your research proposal?" Tavia asked.

"I did," Theo tipped back in his chair, hands behind his head. "For better or worse, it's off to committee."

"What committee?" Rylla asked, eager to keep the conversation off her.

"The Research Funding Committee," Dae-Dae explained. "The head of each department sits on it, although Watt gets the final say. They look at all the senior research proposals and decide who gets the cash," she said rubbing her fingers together.

"You're a senior?" Rylla asked Theo. "I thought we were all the same age? Well, except Tavia."

"We are, I just work more quickly than some," Theo said, shooting Dae-Dae a taunting grin. She stuck a tongue out at him. "I'll graduate with my Bachelor's degree this year. *If* my senior research gets funded."

Rylla asked Theo what his proposal was about, but he said it was bad luck to discuss a proposal before it was funded. Dae-

121

Dae told Theo about the Phirefly debacle and had everyone laughing. Soon, though, the conversation turned scientific, and Rylla struggled to understand it.

"It's a power problem. If I increase battery size, the Phireflys will be too heavy to fly."

"So ditch the battery," Tavia said. "Use direct current."

"Solar power?" Dae-Dae asked. "I've considered that, but the solar cells I'd need would make them too bulky to fly."

"You need a better solar cell," Theo mused, rubbing his jaw.

"I've run the specs using latest-gen models. A better solar cell doesn't exist."

"Oh, but it does." Theo's eyes lit up. "Chlorophyll!"

"Chlorophyll?" Rylla asked. "Like the green stuff in plants?"

"That 'green stuff' uses some tricky quantum mechanics to turn photons into freed electrons and store them in glucose. It's the world's most perfect battery." Theo beamed.

"Okay, how does that help me?" Dae-Dae asked.

He drummed on the table excitedly. "The Teacher's Assistant in my Photonics class — he's working on artificial glucose metabolization!" Rylla must have looked lost, because Theo turned to explain. "Basically, he's powering machines with mod plant cells!"

Azam chuckled and shook her head. "I knew it. Your answer to everything is bioengineering."

"That's because it usually *is*."

Dae-Dae looked thoughtful. "How far along is his research?"

"You'll have to ask him."

"Nanobots powered by plant cells ..."

"Not nanobots," Tavia said, leaning forward. "If you're incorporating living tissue, we're talking about nano-cyborgs."

"Nanoborgs!" Dae-Dae grinned. "I need to meet this guy!" A moment later, though, her face fell. "Wait, we promised Rylla a trip to the arena. She thinks we never stop working."

"That's okay —" Rylla began.

"The arena, huh?" Theo's eyes glazed as he started typing. "I'll see if he wants in."

An hour later, the five of them stepped out of the Jet Stream into a dimly lit hallway, lined with numbered doors. Theo's friend waved them over. As they approached, Rylla fought to keep a neutral expression on her face. It seemed rude to reveal the horror she felt, seeing evidence of suffering all over the man's body. His hands, face, and scalp were covered in large swaths of synthetic skin. The back of his uniform shirt bulged along his spine and she could see a cybernetic collar encircling his neck — evidence of a prosthetic exo-spine.

"Hello," the man waved jovially at the approaching group. His movements, controlled by the exo-spine, were abrupt and precise. "I'm Yevgeniy Rozhdestvenskij." He spoke with a thick Russian accent. "But most people call me Jenny."

A refugee with a Russian accent, burns all over his body... Rylla wondered if he'd survived the Taiga Megafires, or maybe the Third Siberian war.

"And you — do you *prefer* Jenny?" Dae-Dae asked cautiously. Rylla nodded, glad Dae-Dae had asked. Jenny was usually a femme name, and Yevgeniy seemed like a burly, cis dude.

He shrugged. "When I was in refugee hospital, my parents would visit and call me Zhenya — like a nickname for Yevgeniy. The British kids thought they were saying Jenny. And the name stuck." He seemed to embrace the nickname, but Rylla still felt bad that he'd had to change his name because English speakers couldn't or wouldn't wrap their tongues around it.

He smiled, turning to Rylla. "And you — you're the *Ass is Hope!*"

"I *don't* want to keep that nickname," Rylla said. "Please call me Rylla. And can I call you — is it Zhenya?" she asked, hoping she'd pronounced it correctly.

"Yes, you said it right!" He beamed. "Nice to meet you, Reella." He rubbed his hands together. "So, what sim are we playing?"

"One of the comp-sci majors dropped a new installment of *Castle of Mystery*," Theo said.

"Oooh, I love puzzles!" Dae-Dae clapped. She turned to Zhenya as they filed through the doorway. "So I hear you're into chlorophyll! What got you into that field?"

"I started in cyberprosthetics, for obvious reasons." He let out another booming laugh. "I was trying to build a better blood-powered sweat gland, but in quantum photosynthetics, I fell in love with chlorophyll! I knew if I could just find a way to mod thylakoid receptors ..."

Rattling off bio-jargon, Zhenya led them into a booth that looked over a huge circular room covered in fine, grey sand. The others headed towards the back wall, where jumpsuits studded with e-mags hung from a rack. "So what is a *sim* exactly?" Rylla asked Theo, as he climbed into one of the jumpsuits.

"Imagine a hologame, where you can *touch* the holograms."

"How's that possible?"

"You'll see." He grinned, sweeping his hair back into a knot.

Theo waved his MANIs, and the arena below was bathed in red light as lasers divided the room into four quadrants. In the quadrant closest to them, the gray sand began to vibrate, then mold itself into solid shapes — arcing stairwells, spindly towers, ramps and slides and platforms that seemed suspended in the air.

As the arena transformed, Dae-Dae and Zhenya were still loudly chattering away about thylakoid receptors. Theo must've noticed Rylla's astonishment, because he came over and explained in a low voice, "As we move through the level, the 3-D printer will stay one step ahead of us, preparing the next area in the game." He pointed over her shoulder to the newly-sculpted arena. "We'll be moving in a circle down here, but it won't feel like that."

They followed the others onto a freight elevator that took them to the floor of the arena. As soon as Rylla's foot stepped off the lift, the grey forms around her exploded into brilliant color.

They were standing at the edge of an island floating above a turbulent ocean. Arching stone bridges connected their island to others floating nearby, and waterfalls spilled from the edges of the islands, plunging thousands of feet to the sea. In the center of the island stood a castle, which looked ... *wrong* somehow.

"Why does that castle make my brain hurt?" she asked, cocking her head and squinting.

"Impossible geometry," Theo explained. "Optical illusions. See, there's a Penrose staircase." He nodding towards a looping stairwell that seemed to lead to the front doors of the castle, only it didn't. "And an Escher waterfall," Theo said, pointing to where water spilled from a high scaffold into the moat, powering a waterwheel. But when Rylla stared at it too long, the flow switched directions. "And a Reutersvard window," Theo added. Through the opening in the castle wall, a walkway was visible that defied all laws of the universe.

Dae-Dae had skipped ahead and was trying out the Penrose staircase. After several minutes of climbing, though, she kept coming back to where she'd started. "There's got to be a switch or something," she called, out of breath.

They fanned out to explore the courtyard. Theo stomped on loose cobblestones. Azam and Tavia felt the walls of the castle for hidden secrets. Rylla searched for something that might help solve the puzzle, but mostly she had to concentrate on not tripping over her own feet in the mind-bending landscape.

"I found it!" Zhenya cried. He spun a statue that looked like a triangle, and it morphed into a cube. At the same time, the stairwell ahead of Dae-Dae split in two, and one of the branches led to the massive brass doors of the castle.

"I think this sim might make me nauseous," Rylla said, following the others up the stairs.

Theo grinned. "Wait until the gravity changes."

She didn't have to wait long. In the massive entryway of the castle, there were three open doorways — up by the ceiling. This time, Tavia found the switch that rotated the room. The whole chamber tilted on its axis, the floor becoming the walls. Rylla was sliding — screaming — and then falling as the ceiling became the floor. She closed her eyes, expecting her legs to shatter on hard stone any moment. But just before she smashed into the floor, she was caught mid-air, as if by a giant hand, then gently lowered to the floor.

"And that's why we wear e-mag suits," Theo chuckled.

"First time in a sim?" Zhenya asked. Rylla nodded sheepishly.

"Three doorways," Theo said, stroking his jaw. "We should split up. Zhenya and Dae-Dae, you stick together, so you can talk chlorophyll." Dae-Dae and Zhenya headed into the left-hand door, still engrossed in their conversation.

"Azam and Tavia, why don't you two take that door," Theo nodded towards the doorway directly ahead. "And Rylla and I will go to the right," he grinned. Rylla's breath caught in her throat at the thought of being alone with him.

Azam cocked her head to one side. "Is that what we should do, Theo?"

"Yes, Theo," Tavia cocked her head to the other side. "Is that how you'd like this to go?"

"What?" Theo asked innocently. Tavia and Azam looked at each other, then Rylla, then burst into laughter, heading for the middle doorway.

"Have fun, you two!" Azam called, as they disappeared into the corridor. Rylla felt like running after them. They'd all but given away her crush on Theo.

"Come on," Theo said, heading for the right-hand doorway.

As soon as they'd both stepped over the threshold, the floor spiraled away into a slide. Rylla yelped as they shot down through pitch-darkness and tumbled out in a heap of limbs. Rylla scrambled up immediately, heart hammering in her chest, looking everywhere but at Theo.

They'd landed in a round, deep dungeon. A tiny opening, high overhead, let in just enough light to see cobwebbed skeletons and straw littering the floor. Just graphics, Rylla reminded herself. There was nothing underfoot *really* but the grey plastic of the arena.

Theo pressed a hand against the sheer, stone walls. "No handholds," he said. "It's an oubliette — a dungeon with no exit. We might have to wait for the others to throw us a rope or something.

Rylla's stomach knotted up — whether from claustrophobia or being alone with Theo, she wasn't sure. To busy herself, she desperately felt along the walls. Surely, there had to be a hidden switch somewhere. Theo sank to a cross-legged seat. "So, Tex, have you done any more sleuthing since our trip to Ward 7?"

Rylla froze. In the excitement of the last few hours, she'd actually forgotten about the conversation between General Dorne and Watt. Now, the burning desire to tell someone returned. Wasn't this what she'd wanted all week, the chance to talk to Theo alone? But she remembered Watt's threat — professors were always listening in. *You'll be done at Wingates.*

"What is it?" Theo pushed himself up off the floor. "You know something! Tell me."

He crossed the dungeon towards her, and with each step her heart beat faster. She was afraid of spilling Watt's secrets. She was afraid she couldn't be trusted with him. He stood over her and gazed down with those dark eyes and long lashes. Her resolve melted.

"The professors — they can see everything we search, right? Hear everything we say?"

"Tex!" He laughed. "Don't tell me you haven't installed ProfBlock?"

"ProfBlock?"

His MANIs flew mid-air. "Just accept this ..."

Kyle appeared mid-air, glaring at Theo with his now tiny but still murderous orange eyes. "User Theo Reyes wants to access your operating system controls. Do you trust this user to make changes?"

Did she trust Theo? It was a question that probably warranted more reflection, but he was leaning closer now, waiting for her answer, and her brain was feeling fuzzy, and her skin was blooming with heat, and before she could think it through, the word slipped out — "Sure."

The oubliette disappeared, and strings of incomprehensible code obscured her vision. Theo was deleting, adding, altering her operating system code, lightning fast. An irrational terror gripped her that he was actually reprogramming her brain. But it was just her OGLenses, she reminded herself, just plastic discs and OGnet settings.

A few moments later, the code cleared from her view, and she could see Theo again, grinning down at her.

"There. Now we can talk. You've got the latest patch."

"What did you do?"

"There's an ongoing battle at Wingates between the professors' surveillance system and ProfBlock," he said. "A few dedicated, noble comp sci majors update ProfBlock constantly. It sends wholesome, bogus data to the professors, making it look like you never do anything but your assigned nightwork. Try it out — next time you're in class, pull up some really disgusting porn. The professor won't have a clue."

"No thanks," Rylla said, blushing at the suggestion. But relief spread in her chest — all week, she'd imagined Professor Watt spying on her every conversation and OGnet search. "You're sure it works? They can't overhear us? Like, if I were to tell you a secret, something that might get me expelled —"

"If a professor checks on us, they'll hear you and me having a very boring, bot-generated conversation about the weather." He folded his arms and smiled wickedly. "Now what is this secret that could get you expelled?"

She chewed her lip, feeling torn. Could she trust Theo and ProfBlock? And even if ProfBlock did work, was she willing to betray Watt? The professor had recruited her, believed in her, and had given her a second chance after catching her spying. Rylla was lucky to be at Wingates, and if she had any sense, she would't do anything to jeopardize that.

But Theo grabbed her hand, his palm warm against her cold fingers, sending fire coursing through her veins. "I'm dying here, Rylla." Suddenly his closeness wasn't claustrophobic, but thrilling, and she didn't want it to end.

"All right, all right." She grinned, relaxing into her desire to confide in him. "So I was doing my work/study in the Humanity building, when this floorbot ..." Rylla gestured as she spoke, tracing the movements of the cleaning drone. Theo's eyes never left her face.

17

The Proposal

When Rylla finished telling Theo about the confrontation between Watt and Dorne, he let out a long whistle. "Well done, Tex! I *knew* your department did more than just write papers." He rubbed his stubble. "Sending operatives to the Siberian empire? I wonder what they're up to —"

Rylla kicked the digital straw littering the floor. "I can't stop wondering what this *Manifest* is. It got me thinking about 'Manifest Destiny,' which was, like, this awful, racist idea from colonial times that white people were *supposed* to conquer the continent? I'd hate to think the Manifest has something to do with that? Or maybe it's like a *ship's* manifest — like a list of people on board a boat. So maybe it's a list — but for what?" Rylla pinched the bridge of her nose. "You should have heard the general talking though. Whatever the Manifest is, it freaked her out."

"Good for Watt. For not letting that general push her around." He chuckled, leaning one hand against the wall. "I'm not surprised that the Board of Wingates can pull strings with the military's top brass."

"Who are they?"

"The Board?" He looked up to the oubliette's opening high above. "Just a bunch of rich, old people who donate the money to run this place. You know Wingates was founded by a couple of billionaires, right?"

Rylla shook her head.

"Back in '49 — during the Exodus — these two rich people figured humanity's best chance for survival was to bring together all the genius kids in the world. Throw a bunch of money at us and hope we figure out how to save them."

The way he'd said it made the Board sound selfish, but still, pride surged in her chest. She was *part* of Wingates, part of a school tasked with saving the world.

"Next time you have work/study, let me know," Theo said. "If you can get me into Watt's office, I can put an app on her holowall that'll let us spy on her."

"No way!" Rylla cried. "You'll get us expelled."

"You're too scared of Professors. If they haven't expelled me by now, after all the stunts I pulled in my lower-school days? Trust me, this is nothing." He raised an eyebrow mischievously. "I think they're scared of what I'd do left to my own devices."

"Okay, Mr. Evil Genius, maybe they won't expel *you*, but Watt said that's what she'd do to me. I'm new here. I can't risk getting sent home to the Dust."

"Don't you want to find out what the Manifest is?"

"I want to do my work, graduate, and get my family out of the Dust," she said, ticking each goal off on her fingers.

"You're no fun." He said it jokingly, but it hurt more than she'd like to admit. Abruptly, he stood and turned to study the walls of the oubliette. After a few moments of running his hands over them, he stepped back. "What if I do this ..."

He leaned back and placed one foot flat against the wall. As soon as his heel touched down, the room tilted ninety degrees. Rylla fell to the wall — now the floor — in a heap. The oubliette had become a long tunnel. Theo moved towards the bright opening at the far end without glancing back. As Rylla hurried to follow, she wondered if he'd known how to escape all along.

They emerged onto another floating island where Azam, Zhenya, Dae-Dae, and Tavia waited for them, sitting cross-legged in a sunny meadow.

"Took you long enough!" Dae-Dae cried, hopping up to greet them.

They played *Castle of Mystery* until midnight, staying together as a group from then on. Theo suddenly had ears only for Dae-Dae and Zhenya, and Rylla didn't understand anything they were saying about porphyrin rings and cyanobacteria.

Doubt and guilt roiled in her gut. She shouldn't have told Theo about the Manifest. He was a troublemaker, and Dusties couldn't afford to get in trouble. But it was like he'd cast a spell on her when they were trapped in the oubliette together. Now he wouldn't even meet her eyes. She tried to focus on the game, laughing along with Azam and Tavia's jokes, but her heart wasn't in it. She was relieved when they finally switched off the sim, finding themselves back in an arena of gray plastic forms.

Waiting for Humanity seminar to start the following Monday, Rylla half-expected Watt to storm in shouting and throw her out of school for telling Theo about the Manifest. ProfBlock must have worked, though, because the professor just smiled and asked Rylla how her first week had gone. She answered vaguely, trying to look innocent.

Watt clapped her hands and said, "I have a research proposal for you today."

Jae, Magenta, and Ynez looked up eagerly.

"As head of the Humanity department," Watt told Rylla. "I chair the committee that decides whether or not to fund student research proposals."

Rylla nodded, grateful that for once she knew how things worked around here. Dae-Dae had already explained this to her.

"Humanity majors study literature, philosophy, and social sciences to acquire something that can't be obtained through scientific research — *wisdom*. Sometimes, students propose research that is ethically ... interesting. And I sometimes share these proposals with students as a kind of exercise. To see what you make of them."

"You're going to let *us* decide whether or not to fund this research?" Rylla asked.

"The final decision will rest with me and the other department heads, but I'll consider your thoughts seriously." Watt turned to Rylla, her expression stern. "And you are not to discuss what you see outside this room. Students invest a lot of time and energy into their research. I'd hate to deal with the bruised feelings that would result if you gossiped about these proposals."

Rylla shifted in her seat and nodded in understanding.

Watt dimmed the lights with a swipe of her MANIs, and Rylla fervently hoped that this research proposal came from some random student she'd never met.

No such luck. Watt swiped her hand again, and a life-size, holographic Theo appeared, standing beside the conference table. Rylla tried to keep her expression neutral, but the sight of his hologram unnerved her.

"Imagine, if you will, that an alien species discovered a 1972 Ford Mustang," hologram-Theo said. Behind him, big-eyed, green-skinned aliens appeared, examining an antique car. "Bear with me. Imagine this species has never developed a motorized vehicle. Their top minds study the car. They learn how to drive it." The holographic aliens started joyriding around the room. "They learn to repair it." The aliens tinkered under the hood of the car. "To modify it." The aliens spray-painted the car blue. "And even clone it." The aliens built a twin to the first car. "But they never stray far from the original blueprint. They lack the imagination to build, say, a hoverbus or a motorcycle."

Magenta, Jae, and Ynez snickered and looked at each other with raised eyebrows. So far, the proposal seemed silly. Rylla cringed internally for Theo. Where was this going?

The aliens vanished and holo-Theo spread his hands. "This analogy illustrates the history of bioengineering to the present day. Like those aliens, we've only tinkered with existing life forms. We make faster-growing trees and desert-growing potatoes. We've used gene therapy to eliminate diseases. But until now, we've lacked the imagination to bio-engineer something entirely new."

"I'm proposing the establishment of a new field of research — Radical Bioinvention. Bioinventers will design *new* life forms." The room suddenly filled with an alien menagerie of flying, crawling, glowing, many-limbed beings. "And for our first project, I propose we bioinvent a creature that will capture the imagination of donors and result in a steady stream of funding for future projects. A creature out of our storybooks, both familiar and strange, beloved and feared. I propose to bioinvent —" Theo paused and licked his lips before pronouncing the final word. "— dragons."

Holographic flames flooded the room. Winged, scaled monsters soared through the walls. Rylla's jaw dropped, and the other students howled with laughter. She felt nauseous — and not just from the frenzy of swooping monsters. This proposal was so ridiculous, so obviously a bad idea that she regretted ever trusting Theo's judgment.

The dragons vanished, and Theo raised his arms and opened his palms, as if inviting his audience to question him. "You may be asking — how is this even possible?"

"Uh, yeah," Jae said, and everyone but Rylla laughed.

"For our genetic template, we start with the DNA of the extinct *Quetzalcoatlus Northropi*, the largest known pterosaur." A bird-like dinosaur with an extremely long neck appeared beside him. "We add in phenotypical variants of Komodo Dragons and Armadillo Lizards." The pterosaur's beak morphed into a blunt snout and strong jaws. Its scales grew large and serrated, and its tail elongated, making it look like a fairytale creature.

"But what makes a dragon a *dragon*, is the fire-breathing mechanism, of course."

"Of course," Magenta echoed mockingly.

"And this is where the bioinvention gets really exciting." The dragon hologram split in half, exposing its internal organs. "We can modify the lymph nodes here to produce a fireproof gel to coat the larynx. This venom sac" — he touched a leathery pouch nestled above the stomach — "secretes an enzyme, which, combined with stomach acid, yields explosive results." The pouchy thing pulsed, and a jet of fire shot up the tube and out of the dragon's maw.

"You may be asking — why start with such a challenging project? Why not bioinvent, say, a unicorn?" Theo interlaced his fingers into a fist. "But anyone can stick a horn on a horse. The greater the challenge we take on, the more we will learn about gene expression in the process. And we *must* gain this understanding, if we have any hope of saving our world."

A turning model of planet earth appeared behind him. "If we can bioinvent a dragon, there's no limit to what we can do. We can bioinvent flora to withstand megafires. Animals to survive acidifying oceans. Forests that'll grow in the Dust." Green spread across the vast brown continents of the earth, blue rivers unfurled across her home state, and a lump lodged in the back of Rylla's throat.

"With bioinvention, we won't just re-create the world that was — we'll create entirely new ecosystems. The only limit to life in the solar system will be the boundaries of our imaginations." His eyes were wide, as if he was in the grip of religious ecstasy.

Holo-Theo and all his graphics vanished. Rylla's mind reeled in the sudden darkness.

Jae spoke first. "Dragons? Is he serious, professor?"

"Tell me what you think," Watt said, face neutral.

"You were right that this raises *a lot* of ethical questions," Ynez said.

Jae scoffed. "I don't understand why we're even entertaining the idea."

Rylla had to agree. "Just imagine the havoc those things could wreak on a fragile ecosystem." She shuddered. "Starting wildfires? Eating everything in sight?"

"I can hear the headlines now." Ynez imitated a news anchor. "ESCAPED MOD MONSTER DEVOURS FAMILY OF FOUR."

"Is the science even plausible?" Jae asked.

"DNA printing has been available for decades, so theoretically, yes," Ynez answered. "You could design a creature that has never before existed, print an embryo, and gestate it in a synthetic womb."

"I'm still not convinced he can do it," Jae said. "Say he prints this 'dragon" — what's the likelihood the fire-breathing mechanism even works?"

"Eesh, good point," Magenta said. "Imagine a bunch of aborted-Frankenstein-looking pterodactyls wandering the grounds of Wingates, leaking fire into their own guts and begging for death."

Jae chuckled darkly.

"If you ask me, we shouldn't be messing around with DNA, period." Rylla said firmly. "Look at what happened with Soy3 in the Dust States." She felt guilty, like she was betraying Theo, but her loyalty to the Dust went much deeper than her feelings for him.

"You sound like a primitivist," Magenta said. "You think we should stop bioengineering altogether?"

"Yeah I do," she said, turning to Magenta. "Wait — what's a primitivist?"

"Primitivists believe all technology is inherently bad. It's a movement that's becoming increasingly popular, especially in Europe," Ynez said, sounding like a dictionary app.

"Then yeah, I'm a primitivist." Rylla said. "Modern technology caused climate change!"

"How can you go to a school like Wingates and think all technology is bad?" Magenta asked, flabbergasted. "You're surrounded by the most cutting-edge tech on earth."

Again, Rylla felt like she was betraying Dae-Dae, Azam, and Theo. She liked her new friends but had a bad feeling their research would do more harm than good. She didn't share their faith that technology would save the world.

"You don't understand," she began. "Because you're not from the Dust —"

"Hey, I'm from California," Jae cut in, holding up both hands. "And I'm no primitivist. Technology alone isn't to blame for what's happened to Earth. Humans are."

"But we never could have done the kind of damage we have without modern technology!" Rylla cried. "Nuclear waste, climate change, deforestation —"

"We haven't studied primitivism this year, have we?" Professor Watt interrupted, tapping her lips with a finger. "As Ynez said, the philosophy is rapidly gaining popularity."

"It's a ridiculous philosophy!" Magenta smoothed back their hair in frustration. "Humanity is not going to go back to to riding around on donkeys and shitting in ditches!"

"Even if it *is* ridiculous, that doesn't mean it's not worth studying," Ynez pointed out. "After all, we're studying humanity here, and humans are often ridiculous."

"Rylla doesn't seem to think primitivism is ridiculous," Watt said.

Rylla blushed as everyone stared at her. "So what if I don't?"

"I think a field trip is in order," Watt said.

Jae grinned. Magenta sighed. Ynez's eyes glazed over, and her MANIs drummed the table — already researching something.

"What's a field trip?" Rylla asked.

"Real-world research," Jae said. "We'll join a primitivist community. Learn as much as we can about how people live, what drives them, how their society functions —"

"So observe them?" Rylla asked. "Like anthropologists?"

"Not exactly," Watt explained. "We want you to become part of the fabric of their society. Remember, Humanity majors are training to become leaders. Field trips can be a chance to ... *experiment* ... with leadership. You will, however, make an effort to fit in." She shot a look at Magenta.

Rylla wondered about those students General Dorne had mentioned — shadowing the Siberian emperor, living at the Gray House. Were they on "field trips" too? What type of leadership were they *experimenting* with? And what would it mean for the world? She studied Watt's face, wondering what kind of person the professor was. Her eyes appeared kind, with laugh lines at the creases, but her jaw was set in steel.

"I've found several primitivist collectives we could join," Ynez announced, her eyes refocusing. She flicked a hand, and a dense holographic jungle filled the room. A single file of people walked around them, wearing nothing but scraps of woven fibers over their genitalia. They could have been an Indigenous tribe, except that most of the walkers had the light skin of Western Europeans. "PaleoComm," Ynez said. "They're primitivist purists. They live a hunter-gatherer lifestyle in a fragment of the old Amazon Rainforest."

"Oh, please let's don't," Magenta groaned. "I am not into loincloths."

"And they're *super* problematic," Jae said. "Appropriating Indigenous culture, invading their territory — I don't want to be part of that."

"The next group is in Las Vegas." The jungle was replaced by an all-too-familiar scene. Heaps of holographic trash appeared around them, raked by wind-swept dust. In their midst stood people wearing motley-colored outfits, each of them carrying a large, menacing-looking staff. "They're called scroungers —"

"No," Rylla and Jae said in unison. They looked at each other.

"Scroungers are violent, dangerous —" Jae began.

"Not the ones I've hung out with," Rylla interrupted. Magenta raised their eyebrows at her, surprised that Rylla had *hung out* with scroungers. Rylla shrugged. "The ones I know are more like stoned teenagers."

"Well, they're primitivists," Ynez said. "They don't believe in buying any new tech —"

"They may not buy it," Rylla said, remembering Miles's latest-gen OGGles, "but they steal it. They're not primitivists they're — they're —"

"Pirates," Jae said. She nodded in agreement.

"I'm not into living in garbage either," Magenta said. "So can we see what's behind door number three?"

Ynez flicked a hand. "Okay, how about this." Snow-capped mountains appeared around the edges of the room, a green valley spread across the floor, and in the middle of the seminar table sat a quaint village.

"It's called Camelot," Ynez explained. "High in the French Alps. A town of several hundred primitivists living a medieval lifestyle."

"I know a little Cajun French, but not enough to get by," Jae said.

"Actually, their official language is English. The land is owned by a British billionaire," Ynez said.

Inside the village, people in roughspun clothes walked down cobblestone streets. Some even rode horses. Rylla's pulse quickened with excitement. Camelot looked ripped straight from the covers of her favorite fantasy paperbooks.

"This *is* more what I had in mind, professor, in terms of primitivism," Rylla said. "And it seems ... *nice?*"

Magenta nodded. "If you're going to convince people to give up technology, you at least have to give them an appealing alternative. Scroungers and those Paleo-whatevers — their lives are just *not* appealing."

Watt stood up and gripped the back of her chair. "Part of me thinks you should join PaleoComm. Problematic or not, they're the strictest Primitivists."

Magenta groaned, throwing their head back in despair.

"But since this is Rylla's first field trip, I'll let her decide."

"Camelot!" She grinned, as an armor-plated knight on horseback trotted into view just past her fingertips. "Definitely, Camelot."

Never, in all those years curled up with a paperbook, had she ever imagined it would be possible to step into the past — into a simpler, lusher time.

Jae turned to Rylla and winked. "Time for you to find out what being a Humanity major is *really* about."

She smiled, but his words sent a chill up her spine. Were they really just going to Camelot to "study primitivism," or were there secrets to being a Humanity major she had yet to find out?

18

A Peaceful Protest

Rylla called Tyler as soon as she got back to her dorm, dying to tell him about her upcoming trip to Camelot. But seeing Tyler's stricken face, she knew something was terribly wrong.

"That bill? The Watershed Rights Act? It passed Congress today, and they say President Kraft is going to sign it. Rylla, they'll cut off our water rations!"

She felt sickened with guilt. She'd completely forgotten the vote was today. "What did Miles say? Can he get you a better recycler?"

Tyler shook his head. "Apparently, the rich Dusties knew this was coming. The price for recyclers has skyrocketed. No way we can afford one now." He fingered the leaf of a vine tumbling over the dresser behind him. "I haven't talked to Jo about it yet. They have to understand ... there's no way we can keep all these plants if we lose our water rations."

Jo would be crushed if their beloved houseplants died, but human lives were on the line. "Forget the plants. I'm worried about the two of you. What's going to happen? They're not gonna let Dusties go thirsty?"

"The law won't go into effect for a month, and then they'll start charging us for rations."

"And what about the people who can't afford it?"

Tyler shrugged. "Miles says a bunch of people are gonna, like, protest? I don't know much about it, but Jo wants to go."

"Nothing illegal?" Rylla asked, worried what Miles might drag her brother into.

"Don't worry, it's supposed to be totally peaceful. Families and stuff."

Rylla frowned. The 29th amendment had made even "totally peaceful" rallies illegal, if they threatened any business's profits.

※

After he ended the call, Rylla flicked the holowall through the major news channels. None of the anchors even mentioned the Watershed Rights Act. They just covered the usual — crimes committed by Dusty emigrants, celebrity gossip, and ads for the latest tech.

Rylla felt a new appreciation for Ynez Espinoza's research skills. Clearly, Ynez hadn't found out about the Watershed Rights Act watching these newscasts.

At breakfast the next morning, Theo showed up to their table scowling, tossing his tray on the table like he was mad at it.

"Your proposal?" Dae-Dae asked cautiously.

"I don't want to talk about it."

Theo had no way of knowing that Rylla had seen and voted against his proposal, but he sure acted like he did. There was no "Hey Tex" today. In fact, he didn't look at her once through-out the meal.

Azam must have noticed, because on their way out of the Grove, she took Rylla aside. "I'm sure it's nothing personal," she whispered kindly. "He probably has a chip on his shoulder against the whole Humanity department right now. Give it a few days."

A few days passed, though, and Theo continued to ignore her.

He was a self-involved jerk, she told herself. He was an egomaniacal scientist who wanted to bioinvent *dragons*, so why did she care what he thought of her? She wanted to quit thinking about him altogether and focus on her work. But every time his eyes skated over her, it hurt like a punch to the gut.

🪲

Over the next few weeks, Rylla set out to prove that she belonged at Wingates. She worked extra problem sets for discrete math. In evolutionary bio, she was getting the hang of carbon-dating bone shards. In climate science, she set her Earth in orbit and filled her oceans with water, though she couldn't get the currents to work. Still, she felt pleased with her progress, until Professor Pupala asked if she'd ever heard of a little thing called "salt?" Warily, she nodded.

"Then why are your oceans full of *fresh* water?"

Biting a lip to keep from screaming, she set about adding salt to her oceans.

The worst part of her week by far was **Alpinism &** Orienteering with Jae. The next Friday, he made the class run laps through the woods beyond Wingates. As much as she loved spiders, she didn't enjoy catching their webs full in her face as she ran. And after each lap, when they returned to the soccer field, Jae sent them a quadratic equation to solve on their OGlenses.

"Even the simple math needed to navigate the wild is challenging when you're out of breath," he explained.

143

After her third mile-long lap, she fell to her knees on the soccer field and puked into the grass. She collapsed on her back. Colored spots clouded her vision as she struggled to slow her breathing.

"Get up," Jae said, kicking her shoe. "Push your limits."

She wanted to tell him to stick his *limits* up his ass but couldn't spare the breath.

Later, in the shower, she watched the dirty water swirling down the drain, hating the bottomless feeling of being constantly behind. Despite the hours of nightwork she'd put in reading climate studies, Professor Pupala thought she was an ignoramus. She still needed the twelve-year-old's help in discrete math. Maybe *that* was why Theo hated her. Maybe he'd figured out that she just didn't belong here.

As soon as she put her OGlenses back in, though, all thoughts for herself vanished. A missed call from Tyler. He'd left a message.

The vid was shot from Tyler's viewpoint. It was dark. He was running. Screams rang out all around, bangs and sickening, wet thuds — the unmistakable sounds of violence. When he looked back over his shoulder, she saw the Capitol building behind him and throngs of fleeing people.

"Rylla —" His words came in spurts between pants. "Wanted — let you know — got out of there, before —"

A siren screamed along the street, and she didn't hear the next few words.

"— can't find Jo — supposed to —"

Someone shouted Tyler's name and his vision swung left. A scrounger in a long duster, OGGles, and a black handkerchief covering their face beckoned to her brother from an open doorway. She recognized the movements of the figure — it had to be Miles Walker.

Tyler followed Miles through the building and into a back alley. Miles dropped to a knee and grabbed a crowbar from his backpack, then used it to lever open a manhole cover leading down to the sewers.

"Rylla, I want you to know —"

"Are you on a call? Cut the vid!" Miles yelled.

"I gotta go," Tyler panted. "I'm okay. And Jo — I have to believe they're okay too. I'll call as soon as I can."

The vid ended. Silence rang in Rylla's ears.

She tried calling Tyler back, but he was disconnected from the OGnet. Pulling up a browser, she searched for news of the protest.

None of the pundits used the word "protestors," instead calling them "rioters," "scroungers," and even "terrorists." A view from a helicopter showed a platoon of soldiers in urban warfare fatigues, closing in on the crowd in front of the capitol building.

"What caused the riot?" asked a bubbly, blonde newcaster.

"Tonya, these Dusties are violent people. They expect handouts from the government. When you draw the line and say, 'No, you can't have things for free,' they throw a tantrum." A clip of a scrounger punching a policeman in riot gear played on a loop behind him.

"Dusties may be lazy and uneducated," said a new talking head, wearing glasses and a bowtie. "And have the highest rates of poverty and crime in the nation, but they are still *Americans*. Don't we have some obligation to take care of them?"

Rylla snarled. She wanted to stuff that bowtie down his throat.

"It's not our fault they destroyed their watersheds!" The first pundit shouted back. "I've got a message for Dusties. 'Get off your butts, get a job, and *pay* if you want our water!'"

Rylla swatted away the newscast, shaking with rage. The anchors were acting like it was the Dusties' fault they didn't have water. But Rylla and Tyler were born a decade after Texas turned into a wasteland. Did they deserve to suffer just because of where they were born?

Rylla took stock of what she knew. Tyler had said the protest would be peaceful, but the cops had responded with violence. In the chaos, Tyler had gotten separated from Jo. She felt nauseous picturing Jo's skull cracking under a police nightstick or getting trampled by a fleeing crowd. Sweet Jo, who sang to their plants and French-braided Rylla's hair while they watched holofilms. Now Jo was god-knows-where, and Tyler was hiding out with Miles's gang. She hoped they would keep him safe.

Rylla's gaze caught on a final headline, twisting the knife of dread in her chest. *Fifth Circuit Court Overturns Lipan Apache Tribe v. Lockburn — Governor Orders Dam Construction to begin Tomorrow.*

She had no clue how to help her brother or Jo or even the river she loved. She had never felt so powerless in her life.

The next day in Humanity seminar, Rylla raised her hand to speak first.

"Professor Watt? I'd like to change our field trip. I think we should go to the scroungers instead of Camelot after all."

"No way!" Magenta cried.

Watt gave Rylla a sad smile. "You've heard about the Austin riots I take it?"

"Someone I know is missing," she said in a shaky voice. "They might be with scroungers."

Jae shot her a sympathetic frown.

"I wish I could grant your request," Watt said. "Embedding with scroungers during this time of civil unrest would be an invaluable learning experience."

"So why can't we go?"

"Because as of last night, scroungers have been classified as terrorist groups by the U.S. Government," she said. "Wingates has a lot of clout, but with the army breathing down our necks right now, even *I* can't get away with sending my students to train with terrorists."

"They're not terrorists!" Rylla cried. "They're teenagers! They're not trying to overthrow the government or anything."

"It's not up to me," Watt said, showing her hands in helplessness. Rylla searched the professor's face for signs of a lie. Watt had sent students to embed with the Siberian emperor — was embedding with scroungers really worse? Or did Watt have some other motive for keeping Rylla away from the Dust?

19

Camelot

The morning of the field trip, Rylla rubbed sleep from her eyes beneath the glaring lights of the aircraft hangar. Anxiety for Tyler and Jo had fueled her insomnia last night, intermingled with dread of a month in close quarters with her classmates. Jae was insufferably bossy, and Magenta and Ynez still talked to her like she was a child. But maybe this would be a good chance to get closer to them, earn their trust. Maybe they knew something about the "Manifest" or Watt's other secrets.

As sunlight broke through the open hangar bay, Professor Watt arrived with their pilot.

"Right," Watt said, clapping her hands. "You're off to study the primitivists. I'll expect a 10,000-word defense or critique of primitivist philosophy, due a week after your return. So keep detailed notes."

She turned her gaze on Rylla. "This is your first field trip, and we chose it because of your faith in primitivism. But faith tends to get in the way of research. Don't go looking for what you *want* to see. Look courageously."

It was good advice, and Rylla would try to "look courageously," whether she was investigating primitivists, or her fellow Humanity majors, or Watt herself.

Rylla had never flown in a jet before, and she spent the first few hours of the flight with her nose glued to the window, marveling at the puffy cumulous clouds passing beneath the plane, tracking the contours of the green half of the continent with a GPS overlay. When they reached the Atlantic, the ocean filled the horizon. The unfathomable quantity of water made her dizzy, and she got up to stretch her legs.

The other three students were gathered around a table that folded down out of the wall, playing a slapping game with paper-cards Magenta had brought.

"Doesn't jet fuel emit a whole lot of carbon?" Rylla asked them, dropping into an empty seat next to Jae. The thought had been nagging her the whole flight. "Isn't Wingates supposed to be trying to *stop* climate change?"

Magenta laid down a king and Ynez slapped it, claiming a big pile of cards. "I guess they figure these educational trips are worth the carbon cost." She shrugged, shuffling the new stack of cards into her hand.

"But why?" Rylla said. "So we can go to Camelot and write a paper? Isn't there more to this trip?"

"What do you mean?" Magenta asked. They'd dyed their hair jet-black and braided it over one shoulder, maybe in an attempt to fit in with the primitivists.

"Well, I've heard rumors that Humanity majors go on, like —" Rylla leaned forward, dropping her voice lower "— *secret missions* for Watt?"

"Shit," Magenta cursed, exchanging a knowing look with Ynez and Jae. "She knows about the secret missions."

"But she's not supposed to know yet!" Ynez whispered urgently, suppressing a smile. "She's not *ready* —"

"She'll figure it out eventually."

"What?" Rylla asked eagerly. "You can tell me!"

"They're just messing with you," Jae said, rolling his eyes.

"Yeah, no, yeah!" Magenta pointed at Jae. "He's right. We're just messing with you."

"Totally," Ynez said, snapping down an ace of hearts. "There's no secret mission."

Rylla dropped the subject and asked the others to teach her the game, which passed the hours over the Atlantic in a flurry of fast-paced competition. She kept losing her cards to the more experienced players, and her mind wandered to their earlier conversation. Ynez and Magenta had been messing with her, right? Unless there *was* a secret mission, and Jae was covering for them. No, that was too paranoid. But then she thought of Watt's threats to General Dorne, and how Watt had been so elusive with Rylla in their last conversation. *Was* it paranoid to think there was more to this field trip than researching an essay?

✳

They disembarked from the jet on a strip of runway outside a small French village ringed by snow-capped mountains. It was midday on this side of the planet, and crickets trilled in the heat. At the edge of the airfield, a man out of the middle ages waved them over and introduced himself.

Alastair Canterbury was a white guy with a British accent, and even more freckles than Rylla. He wore a roughspun linen tunic over his broad shoulders, and tied his long brass-brown hair back with a strip of leather.

With a roar, the private jet took off behind their group. Alastair flinched until the ship had vanished into the upper atmosphere.

"Loud," he laughed nervously. "I'm not used to it anymore. We don't allow vehicles like that inside the borders of Camelot, so we'll be hiking in from here." He raised an eyebrow. "I trust you haven't brought any electronics?"

Hyper-aware of the small cloth pouch hidden inside her bra, Rylla nodded, flashing an innocent smile. They were supposed to leave their OGLenses and MANIs back at Wingates, but how could she? What if Tyler tried to get in touch while she was on this trip?

"We're eager to leave such things behind," Ynez said earnestly, and Alastair visibly relaxed.

He led them up a switch-back trail into the mountains. Delicate alpine flowers clung to mossy boulders, and streams of snowmelt crossed their path. Rylla would have liked to stop and search for local insect life, but she was too busy panting for air as she pushed her burning legs up the unrelenting slope. The others had to keep stopping and waiting for her to catch up. "You know this is going to reflect badly on your Alpinism and Orienteering grade," Jae said, as she sat on a boulder at the top of a ridge, panting. Saving her breath, she flicked him the middle finger in reply.

After nearly an hour of hiking, the forest ended in a sheer face of cement that stretched as far as the eye could see in either direction. Whorls of barbed wire lined the top of the twenty-foot wall, where a guard trained a large gun in their direction.

"That doesn't look like medieval weapons technology to me," Magenta muttered.

Alastair frowned. "The lands beyond, our resources — there are people who would try to take these things by force. We don't like guns, but until the world embraces primitivism, they're necessary to protect our way of life."

Magenta looked skeptical but said nothing while the massive steel portcullis raised. As they passed beneath its jagged teeth, the back of Rylla's neck prickled. Walls were supposed to make you feel safe, but they always made her feel caged instead.

"Before we go further, you'll need to change out of those synthetic fabrics." Alastair led them down a stone corridor into a room lined with racks of clothing. "You'll have to wear one of these loaners for now, until the tailor can make you something custom." On one wall was a sign — "Lords" — where pants and tunics hung. On the opposite wall under the sign "Ladies," were skirts, blouses, and dresses arranged by color.

"I knew we'd have to deal with this cisgender binary bullshit," Magenta said, snatching a few things from the Lords' and the Ladies' sides. Rylla chose a long green dress made of linen, with vines embroidered up the sleeves. In the fitting room, she twirled experimentally in front of a full-length mirror. Why had people stopped wearing long dresses? They were so swooshy and comfortable, and she looked like she could be Eowyn or Cimorene — her favorite fantasy heroines.

"That color brings out your eyes," Ynez said.

"Uh, thanks," Rylla said, taken off-guard by the rare compliment. "That sky-blue color's really pretty on you too."

"Oof!" Ynez gasped as Magenta pulled the laces of her bodice. "It's tight!"

"But look at your tits." Magenta grinned.

Ynez laughed. "Look at yours!"

Magenta had also laced into a flame-red bodice, but instead of full skirts, they wore black pants slung low on their hips.

Jae chuckled from where he was changing in the corner with his back to them. He'd chosen a Robin Hood look — green sleeveless tunic, brown roughspun pants, and knee-high leather boots.

"Don't you all look smashing," Alastair said, when they rejoined him outside the fitting room. "Now before we enter

Camelot, we must go over the laws of our land." He pulled a long roll of parchment from his tunic. He explained that everyone had to contribute to the community, working at least thirty hours a week. They didn't get paid, exactly, but got free food, lodgings, and other necessities. If they worked more than the required thirty hours, they'd earn "Lyons" — coins they could trade for luxury goods.

"There's no engaging in fisticuffs, unless both parties consent to a duel. No killing, even in the course of a duel. No stealing. And of course, no witchcraft." Alastair grinned wryly.

"Witchcraft?" Ynez quirked an eyebrow.

"That's what we call electronics, synthetic materials, using the OGnet. Some of us take the 'medieval lingo' a bit too seriously, if you ask me."

Magenta snorted, folding their arms. "And what happens if we break one of these rules?"

"There's a council that settles disputes and rules violations."

The cloth bag, still tucked inside Rylla's clothes, burned against her skin. What kind of medieval punishment would be in store for her if she was caught with her OGLenses?

Alastair led them through another set of wooden doors into a blaze of sunlight. Emerald pasture rolled towards lush forests, farmland, and the village of Camelot far below. The valley, surrounded by snow-capped mountains, sprawled under a sapphire blue sky — a blue that made Rylla realize that even on the clearest days, the skies of her childhood had always been hazy with dust. She'd had no idea the world could be *this* beautiful.

A few puffy, white mammals lazily chomped clover nearby. "Are those *sheep*?" Her voice came out in a high-pitched squeal. "Can I pet them? Will they bite?"

Alastair laughed and approached one of the animals, burying his hands in its thick coat. "Come on, then."

Tentatively, she brushed her palm over the sheep's wool. It was coarser than it looked and left a sheen of oil on her hands.

She rubbed the lanolin between her fingertips and squatted down to look the sheep in the eye. It continued chomping on grass, blinking its long eyelashes, uninterested in her presence. She watched the working of its jaw muscles, noted the delicate cleft in its hooves. Sheep were magical creatures out of storybooks, and she wanted to remember every detail of the encounter.

"Are you finished?" Magenta asked, interrupting her study.

Ynez snorted a laugh.

"Give her a break," Jae said, shooting Ynez a look. "She's probably never seen a large land mammal before."

"Just a few dogs and cats," Rylla admitted. "And half of those were probably robotic."

"Would you like to meet my horse?" Alastair asked, meeting Rylla's eyes for the first time. She nodded excitedly. "I think we can squeeze that in at the end of the tour." He shot her a half-wink.

As soon as he'd strode a few paces downhill, Magenta whispered, "Wanna meet my horse?" in a fake British accent, and they and Ynez burst into snickers. Rylla blushed, not sure if they were mocking Alastair or her.

Alastair led them through the dappled orchards and rolling farmland, into the cobbled streets of Camelot. He pointed out the tailor, the laundry, and the bathhouse. In the central square was a fountain that provided the town with clean water. Across from it rose the keep — a large hall where the village ate communal meals together.

At the schoolhouse, they snuck into a classroom and watched a group of children sitting around a woman reading a story. The children's eyes went wide as the teacher read about goats and trolls. Rylla bit her lip to conceal her emotion. These weren't mannequins and stuffed animals — they were real kids, in a real school, with a real-live human teacher — everything she'd longed for as a child. When Alastair signaled that they should go, she didn't want to leave.

On the outskirts of the village, they came to the tallest structure in Camelot, a stadium that rose above the trees. Alastair led them through wooden stands of seating to the edge of a packed dirt ring, where armored men were readying lances or trotting about on horses.

Knights. More than anything else she'd seen that day, the knights made Rylla feel like she'd stepped into a fairy tale.

"We have a tournament next week." Alastair glanced at Rylla. "I'm a knight too, you know. Not just a tour guide."

"So besides jabbing each other with pointy sticks," Magenta interrupted, "what do knights *do* exactly?"

"Our tournaments provide entertainment — good for morale." Alastair said. "We also take shifts guarding the wall. And the rest of the time, we hunt."

"Hunt?" Rylla clasped her mouth in horror. "As in you kill? *Wild animals*? To *eat*?" With each question her voice climbed to a higher pitch. She thought of the gentle sheep she'd just encountered — was it too being raised for slaughter?

"We have to hunt," he explained. "The woods around Camelot are filled with deer and boar, but the wolves and bears that used to keep them in check are long extinct. It doesn't give me any joy to kill, but we have to keep the ecosystem in balance. And besides," Alastair grinned, "meat is *so* delicious."

Rylla felt sick. She wasn't so sure she could eat a dead wild animal.

"See that fellow?" He pointed to a pale, black-haired knight hoisting a lance. "That's Logan, the Penndragon of Camelot."

"The *Penndragon*?" Jae repeated quizzically.

"Our leader. He heads the council and deals with the outside world — taxes and whatnot."

"What's 'whatnot' exactly?" Jae asked.

"And how'd he become Penndragon?" Ynez added.

"Is that an elected position?" Magenta piled on.

Rylla glared at her classmates. They were acting more like a bunch of investigative reporters than eager converts to primitivism. "We just want to learn everything we can," Rylla said, trying to cover for them.

Alastair laughed good-naturedly. "How about I answer your questions on the way to the stables?"

As they headed through the pastureland south of town, Alastair explained that Logan had been one of the founders of Camelot, and he'd won every Penndragon election since by a landslide. Jae, Ynez, and Magenta peppered him with questions about the political workings of Camelot — how the council was elected, and how citizens' rights were protected. For the first half of the tour, they'd all seemed bored. Why were they suddenly so curious about Camelot's politics? Could their interest be connected to some secret mission that Watt had entrusted only to the three of them?

Alastair led them through the complex of barns, where he called the dozens of young women tending to the livestock "milkmaids." There were no men in sight. Like Magenta had guessed, the people of Camelot seemed to stick closely to archaic binary gender roles.

Finally, Alastair took them out to a horse pasture. He whistled with two fingers, and a magnificent dark brown horse ran towards them.

"Meet Jezebel," he said, as the horse pushed her muzzle into his shoulder. He scratched her forelocks tenderly. "She's the finest steed in Camelot."

"Arabian?" Magenta asked and Alastair nodded. "She's beautiful," they said, grudgingly offering their most positive comment all day.

"She's gorgeous!" Rylla exclaimed, clasping her hands under her chin.

"You want to pet her?"

Rylla grinned assent and stretched out her hand, but Jezebel bucked her nose and snorted. Rylla snatched her hand back reflexively. Jezebel was, after all, a giant animal with very large teeth.

"It's okay, she won't bite," Alastair said. He stroked Jezebel's nose, and motioned for Rylla to do the same.

"It's so soft!" she cried. Alastair smiled.

Rylla launched into a torrent of questions. How old is Jezebel? "Seven." What does she eat? "Grass of course, but oats for a treat." Is it a lot of work to take care of her? "Not really." Do you ever braid her hair?

Alastair burst out laughing at the last one. "I could teach you to ride, if you'd like?" he offered.

"Ahh!" Rylla cried in excitement. "Really? I've always wanted to ride a horse!" She stared into Alastair's eyes, noticing for the first time that they were the same blue-green as *lupensis* leaves.

Magenta groaned.

"Hate to interrupt," Jae said, "but is this the end of the tour? Can we go now?"

How were they not freaking out about the chance to ride real live horses? As a kid, Rylla had dreamed of just getting to *see* one someday. But Magenta had guessed Jezebel's breed, so maybe they'd grown up around horses. Maybe large mammals were nothing special to folks from Lush states.

"Uh, right." Alastair rubbed the back of his neck. Like Rylla, he seemed to have forgotten the other three were there. "I should show you to your lodgings."

He took them back to the outskirts of town to a large tent with four cots inside. "Just until some rooms are available," he said apologetically. "We're growing fast, and we're a bit short on housing."

From his satchel, he passed out a slip of parchment to each of them and produced some reed pens and a bottle of ink. "Write down a few jobs you've seen today that interest you. I can't promise a match, but we do try to give our citizens work that suits them."

When they handed the slips back, he turned to Magenta. "You just put 'Knight.'"

"That's right." Magenta straightened to their full height and stared down at him — he was maybe half an inch shorter.

"I'm uh … I'm so sorry, I should've explained. We don't have any female knights."

"Good thing I'm not female," they said, smiling tightly.

He frowned for a moment, then seemed to understand. "Right, I should say — the knights are all men."

"Looks like that's about to change," Magenta said.

To his credit, Alastair smiled good-naturedly. "Got it. I'll pass this on to Logan." He spoke more softly to Rylla, "And we'll work out that riding lesson later."

As he disappeared through the tent flap, Magenta said, "Riding lessons, huh?" and Ynez burst into laughter.

"Tease me all you want," Rylla muttered. "I'm going to get to ride a horse, and that's awesome."

"Sure." Magenta wiped away a tear of laughter. "I'm just saying that's not all he wants you to ride."

Rylla's cheeks burned. She thought over the day, realizing that Alastair *had* mostly talked to her, but she'd assumed that was because the others had shown so little interest in the tour. It didn't mean he wanted her for —

She shook her head to banish the thought. Magenta was just messing with her again. Alastair was going to teach her to ride a *horse*, and that was all.

Magenta collapsed on a cot and slipped an OGlens case out of their pocket. Jae and Ynez followed suit, withdrawing contraband tech from their clothing.

"Wait, y'all brought them too?" Rylla fished her OGLens case out of her dress.

"And here I thought you were an earnest little primitivist!" Magenta beamed in approval. "Smuggling in forbidden technology? I didn't think you had it in you."

"I had to," she said, staring at the dirt floor. Her fear for Tyler, lurking at the back of her mind all the time, suddenly swelled and made her voice catch in her throat. "I have to know what's going on in the Dust."

"Of course," Ynez said in a small, earnest voice. She twisted her mouth to one side, like maybe she felt guilty about all the teasing.

Rylla swiped each OGLens out of its cleansing fluid and popped them in. Checking her messages, she found no word from Tyler. She cleared her vision with a swipe of her hand and turned back to Ynez. "Can I ask something? Where did you read about the Watershed Rights Act? Like, how do you find out what's *really* going on in the world?"

Ynez crossed to Rylla's cot and sat down. "Can we interface? It'll be easier to show you."

Rylla nodded and Ynez waved her MANIs so she and Rylla were seeing the same thing.

"The government and the corps control the media on the OGnet. So to find news they don't want you to hear, you have to access the Dark Net. It's hosted on illegal servers all over the world," Ynez explained. "But be careful. It's called 'Dark' for a reason. The worst things you can imagine — no, probably much worse things — are on here."

She showed Rylla how to access independent news agencies that reported on the Dust States. Ynez bookmarked some legit sites she trusted and warned Rylla that there were plenty of misinfo-factories on the Dark Net, run by trolls who got their kicks spreading deepfake holovids. Left to her own devices, Rylla flicked through the "legit" vids and articles that now clouded her vision.

Long Lines For Water Rations

Price Gougers Go Unpunished

Blast Stalls Dam Construction At Lockburn

Blood pounded in her ears as she tapped this last one. An explosion had destroyed the foundations of the Guadalupe River Dam, halting construction. Lockburn management claimed the blast was an accident, but an anonymous source said scroungers were responsible.

Had scroungers really blown up the dam? She thought of Miles Walker expertly disappearing into a sewer. If Miles was involved, didn't that make him a terrorist? But then again, no one had been hurt. Miles would've said Lockburn were the real terrorists for destroying the river that people relied on.

News on the Dark Net was totally different from OGnet sites. The bloggers didn't hate Dusties, for one, and they were critical of the government and the oil corps. Rylla read everything she could find, heart filling with anxiety. When Ynez shook her shoulder, saying it was time for dinner, it took Rylla a moment to remember where she was — dressed in a gown, in a tent in the French Alps. Pretending she lived in another era, a world away from her family.

20

Riding Lessons

A din of conversation greeted them as they mounted the stairs to the keep. Most of the benches in the long hall were already full, but they found some empty seats near the back. Cheers erupted as cooks emerged from the kitchen, arms laden with platters that smelled incredible.

After filling her plate with a little of everything, Rylla bit cautiously into a hunk of something white and soft. Salty, fatty goodness flooded her tastebuds. "What *is* this?"

"What, the cheese?" Ynez replied.

"Cheese?" The white blob looked nothing like the neon yellow cheez packets that came in rations. She took another bite. "I love cheese," Rylla said earnestly.

Jao, seated across from her, laughed. "It is really good."

"Why don't we have cheese at Win —"

"Shhhh!" Ynez hissed. Rylla clamped her mouth closed. In her cheese-induced-euphoria she'd forgotten that they were strictly forbidden from mentioning where they were from.

"And what are these pink squishy bits?" Rylla asked, poking the things mixed in with the stewed leaves. "They're so good!"

"Bacon, I think," Jae said.

Rylla looked at him quizzically. The word meant nothing to her.

"Pig meat? Boar, probably."

Rylla's stomach bottomed out. She had never eaten real meat before — just the flavorless, grey, lab-grown stuff.

"First time eating wild meat?" Jae asked.

Rylla nodded, gulping down her revulsion.

"Look, the way I figure it is — we're here. They already killed the poor animal. No reason for its death to go to waste, right?" He chomped another bite of the stewed-leaves-with-bacon.

"I guess so," she paused with her fork hovering above the greens, wrestling with the ethics of eating sentient mammals. Her heart ached with the *wrongness* of it. But then she remembered Alastair's explanation about "balancing the ecosystem." And Jae had a point — the deed was already done. She decided to take another bite and — shit, the knight had been right. Meat was *so* good.

A raucous din erupted as folks stomped the floor and slammed empty tankards on their tables. Logan "The Penndragon" stood on a table, striking his stein with a knife.

"Camelotians!" he thundered as the keep fell silent. "A few announcements before we adjourn for the evening. We have some new recruits to our fair village! Please make them welcome as they get accustomed to our ways." Again the room broke out in applause, this time directed at their group. Rylla raised a hand awkwardly in acknowledgement. Ynez and Jae nodded, smiling, and Magenta bowed with a flourish.

When the applause died down, Logan added, "We're also welcoming back one of our own. Maisie and her son Adrian returned to us this afternoon."

Heads swiveled in the direction of a red-headed woman holding a curly-haired toddler in her lap. The applause faded into a few weak claps and a sustained whispering that seemed to continue as the feasting resumed. Maisie stared ahead with a defiant tilt to her chin, not meeting anyone's eyes.

"Interesting," Ynez said, wiping her lips with a napkin. "I wonder what that's about."

The next morning, Alastair arrived with the dawn at the entrance to their tent flaps. "I've received your work assignments from Logan. Rylla, you got your first pick — you'll be helping out at the schoolhouse."

Rylla clenched a fist in excitement.

"Ynez, you can head to the dairy. Jae, you can join the carpenters — they meet at the north end of town. You have experience with construction?" Jae nodded. "Good man."

Finally he turned to Magenta and cringed. "You're not going to like this."

"What?" they asked, raising a sharp eyebrow.

"Logan said — well, the knights are sort of ... full up? He's not looking to train anyone new right now, but if you wait a few months —"

Magenta snatched the parchment out of Alastair's hand. "Dishwasher?!"

"It's just — you didn't put anything else, and that's where we need another worker the most. If you don't like it, I'm sure we can talk to Logan."

"Oh, I'm gonna talk to Logan." They flung open the tent flap and stormed off in the direction of the stadium.

"I wouldn't try to stop them," Ynez said.

"They tend to do what they want." Jae patted Alastair roughly on the shoulder before heading for the north of town.

At the schoolhouse, Rylla was assigned to help Miss Farraday, the teacher for the five- and six-year-olds. She was a stout, pale woman in her mid-fifties, with greying red hair pulled into a bun at the nape of her neck. Her classroom was furnished with chalk slates, wooden toys, and a few shelves of handwritten books, bound with pasteboard covers. Rylla was surprised to learn that students only attended school until age 10, after which they apprenticed to one of the jobs in town. There was no advanced education for Camelotians.

Miss Farraday was both warm and strict, funny and no-nonsense. When she wanted the students' attention, she'd ring a bell, and they'd freeze in place. After a few hours, she asked Rylla to watch the class so she could visit the latrine. Rylla was excited to try out her teaching skills, but as soon as Miss Farraday left, Alexis and Madeline started fighting over a doll, each pulling on one end until the knit head popped off. Then some of the boys started kicking the head around the room like a soccer ball — doll stuffing flying out — which made the girls shriek in protest. Rylla rang the bell to get their attention, but everyone ignored her. She rang it again and shouted for them to settle down, but she might as well have been a ghost. By the time Miss Farraday returned, Rylla was trying to separate the two kids wrestling on the floor, while another was eating chalk, and a third stood on a table, chucking scissors across the room.

Miss Farraday rang the bell, and the students froze.

"Why do they listen to you and not me?" Rylla asked.

"Because you're afraid they won't." Miss Farraday tapped the side of her nose. "And they can smell fear."

By the time school let out for the afternoon, Rylla felt more exhausted than after one of Jae's workouts. Back at the tent she collapsed onto her cot and napped until late afternoon.

✸

When she dragged herself to the center of town for dinner, the square was bustling. On the steps of the keep, a group of musicians played folk songs on violin, lute, recorder, and handdrum. Jae talked with some Camelotian Council members they had met on Alastair's tour. Ynez sat on the lip of the fountain, bouncing a red-headed toddler on her knee and laughing with a group of women — including Maisie, who'd received such a cold welcome the night before. Close by, a circle of knights joked in booming voices, casting glances over at the women by the fountain. In the midst of the group of muscular men, Magenta guffawed and clapped Logan on the back.

In a single day, her classmates had somehow positioned themselves at the heart of Camelotian society. Were they just naturally popular? Or were they purposefully getting close to key people — was this part of their secret mission from Watt?

Movement in the corner of her eye caught Rylla's attention, and she turned to see Alastair trotting over.

"Where've you been?" he asked, bounding up to her.

"Asleep." Rylla gestured towards the men. "What's going on? Is Magenta a knight now?"

Alastair shook his head with a broad smile. "I think so. Sh — *They* just showed up at training this morning. Logan told them to clear off, but they wouldn't go, copied everything we were doing. He said, 'Fine, you want to be a knight? Keep up with us.' And he put us through our paces!" Alastair laughed. "We've never done a workout like that. 10-mile run, with 30-pound packs, followed by pole-arm drills and sparring. A lot of us were dying, but she's — sorry!" He winced, looking around furtively. "*They're* incredible! Left us in the dust." He shook his head in Magenta's direction. "But at the end of the day, Logan said they still couldn't join because 'We didn't have any armor that fit *girls*.'"

Rylla sucked in a sharp breath.

"Yeah," Alastair said, drawing out the word with a grimace. "That did not go well. Magenta decked him right in the eye!"

Rylla gaped at Magenta and Logan, who now had their arms slung across each others' shoulders, singing along to an old pirate shanty. The skin along Logan's left cheek was a constellation of burst blood vessels.

"They scrapped for a while, and eventually Logan pinned them. But they got in a few good hits." The song ended and Magenta and Logan huzzahed together. "After their fight, Logan said, 'You're not going to leave me alone until I let you be a knight, are you?' And now, apparently, they're fast friends." Alastair shrugged, bewildered.

"I bet Magenta let him win," Rylla said smugly. Magenta might not be her favorite person, but she couldn't help feeling proud of them for literally kicking patriarchy's ass.

"I wouldn't be surprised," Alastair chuckled, turning towards the keep where the kitchen staff had just thrown open the doors. The crowd gathered on the steps began moving inside. "So about that riding lesson," Alastair said. "You free after dinner?"

"Oh, uh — yeah, of course!" Rylla stammered, trying to sound casual. She wished Magenta hadn't teased her about Alastair's interest in her. Now the idea was in her head, making her stomach go all fluttery. This was purely about getting to ride a *horse*, which was an awesome, old-timey thing to do, and she might never get another chance at it.

As he saddled the horses after dinner, Alastair was quieter than he'd been as tour guide the day before. Rylla couldn't help but imagine how Jae would act in the same situation. *So here's the entire history of saddles, starting with the Ancient Mesopotamians.* She didn't need a lecture, but she wished Alastair would talk a little more, because the silence made her nervous. At least he didn't seem shy or bored. Every time their eyes met, he'd smile warmly. Maybe this was just how chilled-out primitivist dudes were — they didn't need to fill the air with pointless talking. Not like the tech-addicted masses.

He saddled an older horse for her to ride, explaining that Vega was one of their calmest mounts, good for a beginner. Vega had once been all-black apart from the white starburst on his nose, but now grey fur speckled his neck and powerful legs. She stared into Vega's huge eyes, searching out the deep, animal intelligence there. Rubbing the long plane of his nose, she slowed her breathing, trying to psychically convey that she was a friend, and if it was okay with him, she'd rather not be kicked, or thrown out of the saddle, or have her fingers bitten off. He nuzzled her shoulder, which was slightly terrifying, but Alastair said that meant Vega liked her.

Rylla hooked her foot in Vega's stirrup and hoisted on the pommel like Alastair had done, but it took three or four tries before she finally splayed herself across Vega's back and struggled to a seat.

"If you're ready, just give him a squeeze with your knees," Alastair said. Rylla squeezed, and Vega fell into step beside Alastair's Jezebel. Once she got used to it, the rocking motion of the horse's haunches was relaxing, and she allowed herself to look around and appreciate the beauty of the last rays of sun frosting the pasture around them in pink and gold.

But after ten minutes or so, the silence between them became unbearable. Rylla racked her brains for something to say, and finally managed, "So, uh, what brought you to Camelot?"

Alastair was quiet for a few of his horse's paces. "My parents died when I was sixteen."

"Oh god, I'm so sorry," she breathed, regretting the question. She'd meant to start up some small-talk, not uncover his most painful memories.

"It was the burning of southern England," Alastair said, reaching forward to pat Jezebel's neck. "The fires came up too fast. They tried to take shelter in our fish pond, but there was too much smoke in the air. They fell unconscious and drowned."

"How terrible," Rylla whispered.

"I was at a club in Tokyo when it happened, partying. I partied a lot back then." He fell silent for a few paces. "They were very rich, and after they died, I inherited their money, which was, uh, *not* good for me." He chewed his bottom lip. "Here I was this lost, grief-stricken kid who could buy up the world, but nothing made me happy. One morning, I woke up in a hospital after nearly overdosing on lolly and booze and who knows what else. And when I checked Joinly, I saw an ad asking if I was looking for "meaning" and a "simpler life." The vid was of Camelot, and I realized that if I didn't make a big change — come to a place like this — I was going to get myself killed. That was five years ago."

"I'm so sorry," she said again, even though she knew that apologies were useless when it came to grief. "It's not exactly the same, but I know a little about what it's like to lose a parent." Rylla's words came slowly — she'd never told anyone what had happened to her dad. Amaryllis and Tyler avoided ever mentioning his name. And so it took time to find the words that would turn that massive, scarred-over hurt into a story. "My dad got a visa to work in Louisiana when I was three. He was supposed to be gone a few months, make a bunch of money, then come back to us. But he never did." She rarely thought of her dad anymore, but now the few memories she had of him crashed over her. Tattooed arms throwing her into the air. Scruffy, bearded bedtime kisses that tickled her face. The way her mom cried on the couch for a year after he was gone.

"Your own father left you?" He turned to look at her in outrage. "How could anyone do that?"

Rylla shrugged and they walked on in silence, each wondering about the other's inscrutable grief. After a while, they crested a ridge, and the slope evened out, revealing a wide, flat pasture.

Alastair pulled Jezebel's reigns to a halt. "I was supposed to be teaching you to ride, wasn't I?" He shook his head a bit and smiled. "How about going a little faster?"

Rylla was feeling like a bit of a natural. Between the fantasy books she'd read as a kid, and imitating Alastair's movements, she'd gotten the hang of this riding thing pretty quickly. "Let's do it," she said with confidence.

As instructed, she squeezed Vega with her knees — twice this time — and the horse took off in a burst of speed that she was wholly unprepared for. After just a few paces, she dropped the reigns and was hunched over the pommel, holding on for dear life, feeling like her skeleton was about to bounce right out of her skin.

"Whoa, whoa," Alastair called, pulling ahead and stretching out a hand towards Vega. Her horse stamped to a halt. "Uh ... good try."

"Was it? Because it felt *terrible*," she said. "My butt's gonna hurt for a week."

Alastair laughed. "Next time try to sit up straight and move *with* him, rather than locking up. And, you know, try not to drop the reins."

✱

Later, after they'd brushed down the horses and stabled them, Alastair offered to walk Rylla back to her tent. As they were descending the slope into town, a small mammal burst across their path and leapt onto a boulder. Glowing eyes peered at them through the dusk. Pointed ears, sharp snout — a fox.

The thrill of the sighting quickened her pulse. "I've never seen a wild mammalian carnivore before," she whispered, reflexively touching Alastair's wrist to keep him still. A moment later the fox bounded off the boulder and disappeared into the forest. "It's so cute — but I thought they'd be bigger!"

"It's good luck," Alastair said, staring down at Rylla's hand on his arm. She snatched it back in embarrassment. "You know, the fox is on my coat of arms."

Rylla massaged her hand where it had touched him. "If I were a knight, I'd want a cicada on my coat of arms. *Tibesen Superba.*"

"An insect?" Alastair crinkled his forehead at her, bemused. "You're so unusual, Rylla. So excited about everything. It's like the whole world's new to you."

"Well, it kind of *is*. I grew up in the Dust, so all this — trees, mountains, horses, freaking foxes! It's all like ... like something out of a paperbook."

Alastair stared towards the jagged horizon, where the last purple glow of the sun was fading behind silhouetted peaks. "I can't tell you how totally, unbearably *bored* of the world I was before I came here."

"Seriously?" Rylla asked, knitting her brows together. "You had all this money, you could travel anywhere — go see the lushest places left on earth — and you were *bored* of it?" Heat bloomed in her chest and a sudden anger coursed through her veins. "To be honest, Alastair, that kind of pisses me off. That *sucks*." She started down the switchback path to the village.

"It does. It completely does," Alastair called, jogging after her. "But I don't feel that way since I came to Camelot." He caught her wrist in his hand, and now she was staring down at *his* hand on *her* arm, and she didn't pull away. "I especially don't feel that way when I'm with you."

Rylla looked into those blue-green eyes and felt like she was on a jet doing barrel-rolls. Shit, Magenta had been right. He was going to kiss her, wasn't he? It was terrifying, and also she couldn't wait, but what if her breath stank? And what if *his* breath stank? Did they brush their teeth in Camelot? What if she did it wrong, and did she even like him? It'd be good to get her first kiss over with, but she'd been pissed off at him a second ago —

Before she could sort out her feelings, Alastair stepped closer, bowing his head to hers. Their lips met, and for once in her life, her mind shut the hell up.

She kissed him back. He tasted good, like ale and wild mint. He wrapped his arms around the small of her back, and she melted into his chest. In the forest nearby, a chorus of frogs sang for their mates. His lips were so soft, and his tongue grazing hers made a fire bloom low in her belly. A small, annoying part of her mind yelled, *This is a bad idea! You're supposed to be* studying *these people, not* kissing *them! You have to leave in a month, remember?* But the voice was drowned out by the heat coursing through her, and all she wanted was to stay inside that kiss forever.

"So, did you screw him?"

That was how Magenta greeted her when she ducked back inside their tent. Jae and Ynez were already stretched out on their bunks, lost in the OGnet. Magenta sat on their cot, a derisive half-smile on their face.

"No — wha — Not that it's any of your business!" Rylla stammered.

"I'm just curious," Magenta said, holding up their hands in mock surrender.

"Did — did you screw Logan?" Rylla shot back.

"What, that dinosaur?" Magenta snorted, flopping onto their back. "Nah, I'm not sleeping with any of those knights. Wouldn't give them the satisfaction. In their primitivist little minds, they'd think it meant they'd conquered me or something."

Ynez laughed, sitting up cross-legged on her cot. "So you're staying celibate on this trip? That'll be a first."

"Hey, I never said anything about the ladies of Camelot," Magenta said, leaning towards her with a wink.

"Can you be a little quieter?" Jae snapped.

Magenta tsk-tsked. "So sad. It's the 2070s, and cis men are still uncomfortable with a frank discussion of sexuality that doesn't involve them."

"That's not what I meant," Jae mumbled, rubbing his temples. "I'm trying to hear the news. There's other things going on in the world, you know?"

At his words, a wave of guilt crashed over Rylla. She hadn't spared a thought for her missing brother all day. She'd been so tired from teaching, and then entranced on the sunset ride with Alastair. As quickly as her trembling hands allowed, she slipped in her lenses and scoured the Dark Net for news from the Dust.

Officials had confirmed traces of homemade explosives at the site of the Lockburn dam, and a scrounger gang called Scorpion Nation was claiming responsibility for the attack. Rylla prodded a bubble to watch a vid they'd released. The figure wore a plastic skeleton mask, voice scrambled as they railed against the government. Rylla studied the speaker's gestures. Was that slight head waggle familiar? She replayed the video seven times, before telling herself she was being paranoid. It was ridiculous to think that Tyler had anything to do with the bombing.

That night, she lay awake, at first worrying about Tyler. But after a while, her mind drifted to Alastair, and she relived every moment of their ride together. She kept wondering if she'd said the right things, and what Alastair thought of her, and if she'd been good at kissing. It took her forever to get to sleep, so when she woke up in the pre-dawn gloom, she figured it was just insomnia.

But a rustling sound came from across the tent, and she peered through the darkness. Jae was sliding into the backpack he'd carried into Camelot, wearing his forbidden "synthetic" clothes. He eased out of the tent flap silently. What the hell was he up to? It was a sobering reminder that she was *not* here to play damsel-and-knight, but as a Humanity major of Wingates university. Was Jae heading off to fulfill some secret mission from Watt?

Halfway through breakfast at the keep, Jae reappeared wearing his Robin Hood getup.

"Where were you this morning?" Rylla asked, trying to sound casual.

"Just went for a workout," he said, sliding into the bench across from her. "Got to stay in shape. You should join me sometime."

"You're not my P.E. teacher here," she scowled, tucking into a pile of fluffy yellow eggs. "And if you were running, why'd you bring your pack? And wear your regular clothes?"

"Uh-oh, Jae, watch out," Magenta said, pointing a fork at him. "She's onto you."

"Onto what?" he asked, reaching for a pitcher of water.

"The *secret mission*, remember?" Magenta said, winking.

"Shhhhh!" Ynez hissed, pressing a finger to her lips dramatically.

"Oh, right. The mission." Jae turned back to Rylla. "They're still messing with you, you know."

"I know," Rylla said, but she watched Jae closely, and could swear he'd squirmed when she's asked about this morning. There was more to his disappearance than a workout. She was sure of it.

21

The Night of the Joust

Two weeks later, Rylla was checking a stack of chalk slates full of spelling tests, counting down the last hour of the day. Poor little Madeline couldn't spell for crap, and Rylla felt a stab of regret, marking nearly every word wrong. Across the room, Madeline was arguing with some of the boys, hands on her hips. Ever since Magenta had joined the knights, Madeline had refused to wear skirts, much to her mother's chagrin. Anker's test was next — every word perfect and neatly lettered. The towheaded Danish boy crouched alone in a corner, building an elaborate city out of blocks.

"Miss Reella!" cried an excited voice at her shoulder. Guillaume, the blacksmith's son, held his clasped hands under her nose. "Look what I found in the garden!" he breathed in a thick, French accent.

Grateful for the excuse, Rylla abandoned the stack of slates. "Show me outside — remember how Miss Farraday freaked last time?"

Pushing through the door to the gardens, Rylla and Guillaume emerged into the crisp mountain air. She sat on the sun-warmed stoop beside Guillaume, who slowly opened his tiny hands, dirt crusted under his fingernails, revealing an emerald-green insect inside.

"Beautiful," Rylla exclaimed.

"We call them *sauterelles*," Guillaume said. "What is it in English?"

"Grasshopper," Rylla said.

"I heard it singing in the grass — that's how I found it."

"Not singing — stridulating!" Rylla said. "They make that sound by rubbing their hind legs against their forewings."

Guillaume attempted to pronounce *stridulating,* but had a hard time wrapping his tongue around it. "I wonder what it is called in French?"

"I wish I could look it up for you" Rylla sighed. "Or the name of this species. I can't tell you the Latin for any of the insects here. Now if we were back in Texas — there, I know them all by heart."

Guillaume often asked Rylla questions about his scientific discoveries that she couldn't answer — not without her OGlenses. He was a born naturalist, always helping in the garden so he could escape the confines of the classroom. Of course, he was Rylla's favorite student. She'd tried to teach him some general principles of biology, but they were starting from square one. Before he met Rylla, Guillaume had never heard the words "evolution" or "adaptation."

"I see you two are investigating creepy-crawlies again," Miss Farraday said disapprovingly from the doorway behind them. "How about you read a story to the class, Miss Rylla?"

Rylla and Guillaume exchanged a guilty look and followed the teacher inside.

An hour later, Rylla burst out of the schoolhouse, hurrying first to her tent for a change of clothes, then to the communal bathhouse so she could wash up before dinner. Because *after* the meal came the best part of every day — her riding lesson with Alastair.

She'd learned to keep her seat while cantering and trotting, and that night he even led her to try some jumps over fallen logs in the northern pasture. Jumping was surprisingly easy, as long as you approached each obstacle with confidence. And she had started to feel as at home in Vega's saddle as she did in Alastair's arms. After an hour or so of riding, they let the horses graze at the crest of the ridge. And as the sun set over the valley below, they walked and kissed and shared their life stories.

Rylla dreaded returning to the tent, which always punctured the bubble of her dream-like days with cold, hard reality. That night, as she scoured the Dark Net for news of the Scorpion Nation, her heart filled with anxiety for her still-unreachable brother. She did her best to block out the other's conversation. As usual, they were complaining about Camelot. They were so *bored* here. Magenta missed the soda fountains in the Grove. Ynez missed wearing OGlenses all day — always having information at her fingertips. And Jae'd give anything to play a sim at the arena. They didn't seem to notice all the good things — like startling a herd of deer on your walk to breakfast. Or seeing everyone's eyes all the time and knowing they were looking at you, not some OGnet site. Rylla thought they hadn't given Camelot a chance.

But there *were* some things they complained about that bothered Rylla too. Ynez had gotten close to Maisie and learned why she'd received that cold welcome the first night. Maisie's son Adrian had asthma, and she'd left Camelot to get him treated at a hospital during a bad attack. Now Maisie kept a plastic rescue inhaler for Adrian, and for this, half the town shunned her for "witchcraft." Ynez said a lot of people quietly supported Maisie and thought there should be exceptions to primitivism, especially when it came to medicine, but they were too afraid to speak up.

Magenta's complaints about Logan and the knights also got under Rylla's skin. They said that Logan was always calling the knights "girls" to motivate them, and their workouts were filled with lewd, sexist jokes. Ynez added that she'd heard "whisper network" rumors about Logan. Other milkmaids had warned her not to find herself alone with him, and never to get drunk at his house.

The following morning, Magenta put up a parchment poster in the keep:

KNIGHT'S COMBAT TRAINING

EVERY DAY. EAST PASTURE. HOUR BEFORE DINNER.

<u>ALL</u> ARE WELCOME!

GET FIT. KICK ASS.

On the first day, only three women showed up — Maisie among them. But the next day, they brought along a few of their friends. These friends brought a few more, and after a week, nearly thirty people — mostly women — were working out with Magenta. The clacking of their wooden practice swords rang throughout the town in the late afternoons. And by their fourth week at Camelot, "Magenta's knights," as folks had started calling them, wore swords at their hips all day long. There was a crackle in the keep now, in the looks passed between Logan's knights and Magenta's.

Meanwhile, Maisie's group of reformers had started passing out hand-written parchments, calling for medical exemptions to primitivism. Some people pocketed them, some tossed them in the nearest fireplace with disgust.

It felt eerily like Ynez and Magenta were *trying* to tear Camelot apart at the seams. Maybe Watt really had sent them here on a "secret mission" to destroy Camelot from within. And maybe the reason Rylla wasn't included was that she actually *believed* in primitivism.

But then she'd remember Jae's eye rolls and shove the thought to the back of her mind. It was getting crowded back there, what with her fears for her missing brother, and the reality that they'd leave Camelot soon. Whenever she thought of saying goodbye to Alastair, it felt like the oxygen was being sucked from her lungs. So she thought about it as little as possible over the next few weeks, until she couldn't deny it anymore — until the night of the Jousting Tournament.

She sat in the stands beside Ynez and Maisie, surrounded by Magenta's knights. As night fell, hundreds of torches around the stadium were lit, and the band played blood-boiling songs — fast drums and trumpeting that whipped the crowd to a frenzy. Rylla held her breath as Alastair readied his steed for his first bout.

He won the first tilt, slamming his lance into his opponent's shoulder. For the second tilt, a familiar figure trotted into the ring. Magenta shook their long hair out of their face and jammed a helmet on their head. Their powerful black horse shimmied its feet, but they checked it expertly with their knees. *Of course* Magenta rode like they'd been born in the saddle.

As they bore down on Alastair, Rylla clenched her hands together. He brought down his lance, but too late — Magenta's weapon slammed into his chest first, knocking him into the dirt. Alastair's body lay still. There was a terrible dent in the engraved fox on his breastplate.

"No!" Rylla reached a hand towards his prone body and time stood still —

But only for a moment, and then Alastair was up and waving good-naturedly to the crowd. Rylla collapsed back into her seat, and Magenta's knights burst into cheers.

It was time for the last bout, and Magenta was up against the undefeated champion, Camelot's fearless leader — Logan.

"I hope they kick his ass," Ynez whispered.

Rylla nodded, biting her lip in anticipation. She wasn't sure if it was school pride, her dislike of Logan, or real affection for Magenta, but she badly wanted to see them knock Logan off his saddle. The two knights squared off on either end of the stadium. Then their horses were charging, lances seeking out their enemies. There was a crash, and for a moment Rylla couldn't tell what had happened. But Logan was leaning to one side, barely hanging onto his horse, while Magenta sat upright, a jagged lance tip pointed at the sky. The front of Logan's armor was deeply gouged — the tip of Magenta's lance had shattered against his breastplate. Magenta waved to the crowd, and the stands exploded in cheers. "Magenta! Magenta!" called all the women of Camelot. Logan dismounted, tore off his helmet, and kicked it.

By the time the chanting died down, though, he'd regained his charm. "We shall toast the victor at my house!" He shouted into the stands, with forced cheeriness. "I challenge you all to drink up my entire cellar of mead!"

The crowd dispersed, but Rylla lingered near the stadium entrance for Alastair. Finally, he bounded out, catching her around the waist. "Not bad, eh? I won the first match and lost to the victor!" There was no bitterness in him at losing to Magenta.

They walked hand-in-hand to the center of town, where Logan's family lived in a three-story house off the main square. The front doors were flung open, spilling light and music into the street. By the hearth, the band played a cover of a popular smash song on fife, lute, and drums, and in an open space, couples were dancing.

As soon as they pushed their way inside, Logan slapped Alastair on the back and congratulated him on the joust. They dove into a technical conversation of tilting angles and lance maintenance, which thoroughly bored Rylla, so she watched the dancers instead. Magenta led a golden-haired milkmaid around the dance floor — spinning and dipping her with the same confident grace they'd used to check their stallion in the joust.

She felt a tapping on her arm. Jae Boudreaux was nudging her with a bottle of mead.

"Having fun?" he shouted over the din.

Rylla took a swig from the bottle, the honeyed wine quickly spreading its warmth throughout her body. "More fun now," she said with a smile.

Jae leaned forward to whisper into Rylla's ear. "Check out Logan's face."

Logan was also watching Magenta and the blonde dancer. His brow furrowed, and his eyes sparked with intensity — rage, jealousy, lust? A mix of all three?

The hair on the back of Rylla's neck stood up. "Should we be worried about them? Logan seems like he might be ... *bad news.*"

Jae nodded. "I know what you mean. But if anyone can handle themselves —"

"— it's Magenta," Rylla finished.

Snaking arms grabbed her from behind. "What are you two talking about?" Alastair asked. He smiled at Jae, friendly enough, but gripped Rylla possessively. "Let's dance!" he said, twirling Rylla around by the hips.

"I don't know how," she said, going stiff with panic.

"The girl's part is easy," he said, "You just follow me."

Before she knew it, they were in the middle of the dance floor, and he was pulling her in by the waist.

"Go like this, with your feet," he said, shifting from foot to foot. She copied the motion. "Good!" he grinned. "That's all there is to it, just faster!" Then he took off. He was right — her part was easy. The pressure of his hips and arms guided her. All she had to do was keep up and not trip. When he flung her away, she was spinning out of control, but then he caught her by the fingertips and twirled her back in. He slung an arm around her waist and dipped her back, so her head nearly grazed the floor. He pulled her close again, lifted her in the air with surprising ease and brought her down gently for a kiss. After a few songs, it was like all her thoughts and fears had been whirled away. She was just a body, hurtling through space. Sweat and flesh and a pair of eyes lost in his.

When the party broke up a few hours later, they stepped out into the cool night, and Alastair started towards her tent as usual. But she tugged him the other way.

"Actually, I'm walking *you* home tonight," she said, making a sudden, rash decision.

Alastair raised an eyebrow. "Is that so?"

"That's so." She danced off in the direction of his house. "There's all manner of foxes and bears and *beasties* out. You need protecting."

Alastair jogged to catch up. "And you're going to protect me?"

"Yup. In fact," she grinned wickedly, "I better walk you all the way to your bed. Just to be safe."

"Are you sure?" he asked, his voice serious.

The thought of going up to his room was slightly terrifying, but she was sick of being teased for her innocence around sex — Magenta and Ynez, even Tavia and Azam had given her crap for it. And the attraction she felt for Alastair had grown to a steady blaze over the past few weeks. Their chaste kissing-sessions always left her unsatisfied, tossing on her cot at night, wishing for privacy. Her sudden decisiveness might have something to do with the wine in her belly, but maybe what she'd needed was a little liquid courage.

"Yes, I'm sure," she said, pecking him on the cheek. "Now come on."

When they got to his room, Alastair rushed inside ahead of her, kicking some laundry into a pile in the corner. "Sorry about the mess." The room smelled like sweat and feet, but she didn't mind — it was a good reminder that he was human. She was human. No need to be nervous about this, right?

Then he kicked the door shut behind him, and they were kissing deeply, crashing onto his narrow bed. Rylla buried her fingers in the thick waves of his hair. He ripped the laces from her dress and pulled it over her head with a dexterity that made her wonder how many times he'd done that before. She tugged at his shirt, and he lifted his torso from the mattress so she could pull it off. His tightly muscled chest and abdomen were dusted in thousands of freckles, and she kissed them hungrily, moving lower and lower. She had never done this before, but she was trusting that it would come to her as easily as dancing.

But just as she had reached the drawstring of his rough-spun pants, an evil thought popped into her mind.

Three days left.

Three days until this dream was over. She would leave Camelot, leave Alastair — probably forever. Suddenly, her throat felt like it was closing up and her eyes burned with tears. She sat back on the bed, hiding her face in her hands so he wouldn't see.

"What —?" he asked. "Hey — hey, what's the matter?" He sat up beside her, pulling her hands from her face.

"It's —" The words caught in her throat. "I can't tell you. But you deserve to know before we —"

"You can tell me anything, Rylla." He tucked a strand of hair behind her ear. She was in imminent danger of an ugly, snotty cry. "We don't have to do anything if you don't want to."

"No, it's not that." She wiped her face with her arm. "I want to. It's just ... I like you so much, and —"

"I like you so much too! No, you know what? Fuck that." He rested his forehead against hers. "I don't just like you. I — I've never felt this way about anyone before. I *love* you."

She broke into sobs.

"Ahhh, what's wrong?" he asked, grabbing her hands. "Please tell me."

She took a few deep breaths. *Could* she tell him something? About all this being a *field trip*? She had been sworn to secrecy, but in this moment, burning for Alastair on his bed, she couldn't care less about Professor Watt and Wingates. Alastair might hate her for deceiving him. But if she was honest, maybe there was hope for the two of them. Maybe they

could do a long-distance thing? He'd said he *loved* her. And —
well, what else could it be? This all-consuming feeling? Wanting to touch him and be with him every second of every day?
She must love him too. And didn't love conquer all? Isn't that
what every novel and holofilm had promised her?

"Can you keep a secret?" she asked. He nodded with
chivalrous solemnity.

They talked for hours. She told him everything — from
playing as a girl along the banks of the Guadalupe, to her dis-
astrous State Senate protest and the Ass is Hope video, and
finally her time at Wingates. She lay in his arms, and he traced
circles on her stomach as she talked. She even told him her
suspicions about her classmates' "secret mission."

"— I don't know, maybe it's paranoid to think they're
messing with Camelot *on purpose*, but they certainly seem to
hate it here. And yeah, they have some good points. I think
Maisie's kid should have his medicine! And I think Logan's an
asshole — sorry —"

"No, he is," Alastair agreed.

"But there's a lot of good here too, and I wish we could
stay, and make it better. I wish I could stay with you," she
groaned, tears threatening again.

"So why don't you?"

"What — stay? I can't, I — it's just a field trip."

"But you said you love it here. You're happier here, with
me."

Rylla sat up again, staring out the open window at the
mountains reflecting moonlight. "I do love it here. But I have a
scholarship. And Wingates is a *really* good school."

"You don't need a college degree to live in Camelot," he
said, stroking the long line of her back.

She shook her head in frustration. "I can't just move to
France!"

"Why not?" He smiled with maddening simplicity.

She gaped, scrambling to remember her reasons. "Well,
because of my family, for one."

"What about them?"

"I have to help them! If I stay in college, then I can get a job in a Lush State — I can get them emigration visas out of the Dust."

"They can move here too."

Rylla scoffed. "Right, because it's so much easier to get a European visa."

"I can get them one," he said, matter-of-factly.

Rylla laughed, but his face was serious.

"I'm a hundred-billionaire, remember?" He laughed. "Trust me, I can make it happen. I just need to make a call."

Was he serious? Life in Camelot, with her brother at her side would be a dream come true. Of course, her mother would have to come too, but maybe she wouldn't want to live *in* Camelot, but in some neighboring country. Rylla could visit on holidays.

But something was holding her back from accepting Alastair's offer. Azam, Dae-Dae, and Theo would never understand her decision, and they'd certainly never leave their research behind for this primitivist life. And there was something else — something about being a student. She liked going to school, and she couldn't quite imagine living somewhere they didn't even teach kids basic evolutionary theory.

But life in the Dust was becoming more and more treacherous, and Alastair was offering her family a way out. In the face of that reality, her desire to keep studying seemed too selfish to mention. And wasn't living in Camelot a way of changing the world? Surely, if everyone embraced primitivism, the planet wouldn't be in such bad shape.

"Let me take care of you," he pleaded, kissing her shoulder, "and your family. Then will you stay?"

Rylla sank her fingers into his hair and pulled him in for a kiss.

"Is that a yes?"

She nodded.

Their bodies did the talking for the rest of the night. Alastair was gentle and voracious, reverent and ravenous. She didn't know if she was being worshiped or devoured, but she didn't care. He took his time, letting her ache for him build, until all doubt and fear disappeared and there was nothing left of her but an all-consuming hunger. And when he finally pushed himself inside her, she shattered.

22

Unraveling

Rylla could have spent all day in Alastair's arms — kissing, making plans, and memorizing the curves of his lean muscles. But when half the day had passed, they reluctantly parted ways. Alastair headed to the council offices, where there were OGGles he could use to call his "fixer," the guy who'd arrange the visas. Meanwhile, she needed to tell her family the plan. Hopefully Amaryllis knew how to get ahold of Tyler by now.

Back at the tent, as soon as she ducked through the flap, Magenta whistled and slow-clapped. Rylla stopped short — not because of the teasing, but because she'd have to tell her classmates about her plan.

"What's wrong?" Magenta said, dropping their smile. "What'd he do to you?"

"Nothing — it's not that." Rylla dropped onto her cot. "But I do have to tell you something." She took a deep breath, staring at her clasped hands. "I'm not going back to Wingates."

"What?" Jae, Magenta, and Ynez all shouted at once.

"I'm staying here. With Alastair."

Magenta made a disgusted noise. Ynez sighed and shook her head, and Jae stared at the ceiling of the tent like he couldn't bear to look at her.

"I don't even know where to start," Magenta spat. "Wingates is the best university in the country, and you're going to throw that away to play medieval *house* with a guy you've known a month?"

"He can get my family out of the Dust," Rylla said sternly.

"If you finish your degree at Wingates," Ynez said, "you won't need a man to help you. You can help your family yourself."

"But things back home are bad *now*," Rylla said. "My family might not be able to wait until I graduate."

"Look, I get that," Jae turned to face her. "You know I do. But talk to Professor Watt. Maybe she can do something to help your family."

"It's not just about my family." Rylla said, exasperated. "It's also — I love him, okay?"

They groaned and shouted at once. How could she know that? After only a month? Magenta called her "a pathetic child who'd surrendered agency to the first man to smile at her."

"It's not just about Alastair either!" Rylla wrapped her arms over her head. "I *believe* in what they're doing here. Laugh all you want, but I still believe in primitivism. Y'all are always complaining about the bad stuff, but there's a lot of good here too!"

"Good enough to make up for the fact that Maisie's kid can't have medicine? Or that a kid died last year of an *ear infection?*" Ynez asked.

"Wake up!" Magenta said, snapping their fingers in her face. "This place isn't primitive, it's a fantasy! The Middle Ages were a brutal, violent time, when your life expectancy was, like, thirty-five, and it was a toss-up whether you'd die of the plague or get murdered by a pillaging army. Is that what you want? Does that sound like a fun place to live?"

Ynez shook her head in disgust. "She likes it so much because she fits in here. She's white and straight and cis and abled and —"

"Hey, I'm not totally white! My mom says my dad was half —"

Ynez's raised eyebrow silenced her.

"Okay, fine, I'm white," Rylla mumbled. "But I'm *not* straight."

"You're dating a literal knight in shining armor," Magenta said derisively. "I can't imagine anything straighter than that. Ynez is right. You fit into their fantasy. Whereas we —"

"— are constantly *othered.*" Jae nodded. "Do you know how many times a day someone asks me some shit like 'What part of *the Orient* are you from?'"

"Yeah, and that knight William asked if I was 'spicy as my mom's salsa,'" Ynez said.

"And me — well, no one says shit to my face," Magenta smirked, "but I know that behind my back, they're all misgendering me and making disgusting jokes."

"I'm sorry." Rylla's gut roiled with shame. "I — I didn't know all that."

"You didn't *notice* it," Ynez corrected.

"I didn't, and I'm sorry. But you never gave Camelot a chance!" Rylla sucked in a deep breath as she gathered the courage to put it all out in the open — the secret fears she'd harbored all month long. It was time for them to come clean with her. "I've figured it out, so y'all can stop pretending. There *is* a secret mission, isn't there? You're trying to destroy Camelot from the inside — that's why Watt sent us here! Because primitivism is a threat to everything Wingates stands for!"

Magenta pressed their hands together and shook them in Rylla's face. "What. The actual fuck. Are you talking about?"

"That's why you started your knights' group — to destabilize Camelot! And Ynez, you're trying to get people to abandon primitivism. And you —" Rylla rounded on Jae.

"Well, I don't know what you've been up to, but I've seen you sneaking out before dawn, and I know it's *something.*"

Ynez shook her head. "You think I befriended Maisie for a 'secret mission?' It never occurred to you that maybe I just think kids shouldn't die from lacking basic medical care?"

"And I didn't start training women to fight to 'destabilize Camelot.' I mean, okay, I knew it would piss Logan off, and that *was* pretty funny." Magenta laughed. "But maybe I just thought the women around here would find it fucking empowering. You ever think of that?" They waved a hand in disgust. "You know what — do what you want. Stay here with loverboy. At least I'll get my dorm room back."

Jae knelt in front of Rylla. She was cradling her head in her hands, feeling dizzy with the growing sense that she'd misunderstood everything, badly.

"Do you really still believe in primitivism?" he asked.

She nodded, mumbling uncertainly. "I do. All that high-tech stuff at Wingates — nanobots and bioengineered mods — we wouldn't need it if we hadn't made such a mess of the planet in the first place. If we just lived *simply.*"

"Life has never been simple," he sighed. "You want to know where I've been going in the mornings?"

She nodded, and he asked her to put in her OGlenses so he could show her something. As soon as she'd popped in the contacts, a bubble appeared, asking if she'd accept a holovid from Jae Boudreaux.

"When I sneak out of the tent in the morning, I leave Camelot. I climb over the eastern wall, at a spot that's out of sight of the guard towers. At first, I was just looking for some good bouldering cliffs in the area. But then I found this."

Rylla swiped open the file, and the tent disappeared. She was on a slope that could be Camelot, except that all around stretched a sea of severed tree stumps. A forest had been clear-cut here, and now only long grasses stirred in the wind. The holovid jostled as Jae walked towards a creek winding down the clear-cut slope. Unlike the clear snowmelt streams that trickled through Camelot, the water here was cloudy and brown.

"What am I seeing?" Rylla asked, dread creeping into her gut.

"All the houses in Camelot, the keep, the stadium — where do you think that lumber came from? They leveled this forest to build Camelot. And the water running south of Camelot goes past the latrines and the dairy — it's full of untreated sewage."

"Come to think of it, there *isn't* a water treatment facility here, is there?" Ynez mused.

"No, that would spoil the view," Magenta muttered.

"Skip ahead about twenty minutes," Jae said. Rylla swiped her hand to fast-forward, until the scene of clear-cut forest changed to an abandoned alpine village, where ivy grew through shattered windows and weeds pushed up through cracked pavement.

"That's Larmes de la Montagne, a village south of here — well, used to be. After Camelot moved in, folks there started coming down with dysentery, because of the polluted water. A couple of kids died. There was a big protest at the walls of Camelot, but then a few protestors *disappeared*. There was an investigation — Logan went to court — but the charges were suddenly dropped, and the government ordered the people of Larmes de la Montagne to evacuate. I had to dig deep to find this stuff out, because someone's scrubbed the story off the OGnet."

"Turns out Camelot isn't as self-sustaining as it pretends to be. The gardens don't produce enough food, so once a month, the guards smuggle in food shipments from mega-farms. And they've stopped clear-cutting the forest around here, but now they're buying lumber from poorer countries."

"How are they paying for it all?" Magenta asked.

"Logan and all the founders were billionaires, remember? They advertise Camelot exclusively to the super-rich, then hit them up for massive dues. There's a trust for Camelot that's invested in the global stock market and owns real estate all over Europe. Turns out, Camelot doesn't exist apart from the modern world. It's just a place for rich people to pretend they're living an old-timey, eco-friendly lifestyle. It's a *resort*."

Rylla swiped to clear her vision with a shaking hand. Less than an hour ago, she had curled against Alastair's chest, feeling like all her earthly problems were solved. But now? How could she spend her life here, knowing the fantasy of Camelot was built on lies?

Her voice trembled with uncertainty when she spoke again. "Thank you for showing me this. I'm glad I know it, but I — I still have to talk to my family." Her mom and brother were still caught between a scrounger army and the police. Would they be able to get water this week, or the next? What if accepting Alastair's offer was a matter of life and death for them?

"Of course," Jae said, heading for the tent flap. "Let's give her some privacy." Magenta shot her a 'you-are-so-hopeless' look, while Ynez frowned at her pityingly, and they followed him out of the tent.

Rylla called Tyler first, but as usual, he wasn't signed in to the OGNet. She called her mom next, and Amaryllis McCracken's face appeared inside a call-bubble.

"Well, it's my long-lost daughter. To what do I owe the pleasure?"

"Hey mom."

"Do you see this?" Her mother pointed her Gluv'd finger, showing Rylla a long line of their old neighbors wearing bulky cooling suits and carrying parasols to keep the harsh summer sun off their heads. The line stretched for blocks down Main Street. "This is what I'm doing on my day off."

"What's going on?"

"I'm waiting in line to buy water rations. Can you believe that?"

"That's what I told you about, mom! That's the new law — the Watershed Rights Act."

"It's not the buying I mind so much, but this line is ridiculous! We've never had to wait so long for rations before. They need to get more folks working up there," she craned her neck in the direction of the post office, where rations were being distributed.

"But mom, you shouldn't have to buy water! Water is a *right*, a basic human right."

"Oh honey, nothing on this earth is free," Amaryllis said, taking a step forward in line.

"Our water used to be!"

"Yeah, and between free water and food stamps, that's why you got so many —" Amaryllis dropped her voice to a conspiratorial grumble "— good-for-nothings, sitting on their ass playing holoporns all day instead of getting a job. It's a good thing, if you ask me, charging for water. People 'round here need a kick in the ass."

"People will die without water!" Rylla shouted.

Amaryllis shushed her. "You are embarrassing me. I'm not gonna argue with my bleeding-heart daughter here, for the whole town to see!"

Rylla took a deep, calming breath. "What if I said you won't have to deal with those lines anymore?"

Her mother just snorted.

"I've made a — a friend here. He says he can get you and Tyler European visas."

Her mother burst out laughing.

"I'm serious, mom! You can live anywhere in Europe with those visas!"

"That's sweet." Amaryllis wiped a laugh-tear from her eye. "But you might as well give tap shoes to a fish. I'm not moving to *Europe*." She fanned her face like a debutante. "My life is here. All my friends are here. My job —"

"But mom, it's the Dust. It sucks."

"Well, I know that's how you feel. That's no big secret." Amaryllis rolled her eyes. "But I've lived here my whole life. The Dust is my *home*."

Rylla was stunned. She'd never imagined her mother wouldn't jump at the first chance to leave the Dust States.

"I don't think you'll have much luck getting Tyler to leave either. These days, he's all *Dust States Rights* and *People of the Dust Unite!*"

"Wait — you've seen Tyler?" Rylla exclaimed. "I haven't heard from him in weeks!"

"He came by a few days ago — asking for money to bail his boyfriend out of jail."

"Jo's still in jail? Are they okay?"

"I don't care for his new friends. Brought that boy around you used to hang out with. What's his name — Milo? Mikey?"

"Miles Walker?"

"That's it. He's some kind of punk now. Anyhow, I told him if his boyfriend's in jail, it's probably for good reason. If he wants bail, he needs to work for it. And that's when he started ranting. Said I'd fallen for — what was it? 'Capitalist Hegemonic Brainwashing.'" She laughed. "You kids think your big words make you so smart."

Rylla frowned. "You really wouldn't use a visa, even if I could get you one?"

"When I'm only five years from retirement? Are you kidding? Look, honey, it's nearly my turn in line. I gotta go," Amaryllis said, even though she was still half a block from the post office. The call bubble vanished.

Rylla sat back on the cot, thoughts swimming. Had Tyler really gotten so swept up in scrounger ideals that he'd refuse to leave the Dust? And if Amaryllis wouldn't immigrate either, what was the point of Rylla staying in Camelot? For Alastair? Was he alone enough reason to give up her scholarship?

She started replaying every moment they'd spent together in her mind, suddenly doubting his every word and gesture. She'd been so wrong about Camelot, her classmates, and the "secret mission" she'd imagined for them. What if she'd been wrong about Alastair too? He'd never taken advantage of her or been the least bit unkind. But had he lied to her? Did he know about the clear-cut forests, and Logan's 'reputation,' and those kids who'd died in Larmes de la Montagne? Did he not care, or was he — like Rylla — too caught up in the fantasy to see the truth? Before she threw away her life at Wingates, she needed to find out.

23

Savior

In the central square, Rylla couldn't find Alastair in the crowd that had gathered to watch Maisie. The fire-haired woman was standing on the lip of the fountain, giving an impassioned speech about medical rights. Magenta's knights stood around the perimeter of the crowd, hands on their sword hilts, facing off against Logan and his knights. Finally, Rylla spotted Alastair near the doors of the keep, watching the scene by the fountain with folded arms. Rylla waved until she caught his attention and met him at the bottom of the steps.

"I should get back," he said. "Logan's worried something's happening."

"We need to talk," Rylla said, grabbing him by the arm.

He asked what was wrong, but allowed himself to be led down a quiet side-street. Rylla glanced around to be sure they were alone.

"Docs the name *Larmes de la Montagne* mean anything to you?"

Alastair shook his head.

Searching his face, Rylla saw only confusion. She didn't *think* he was lying. "It's a village to the south, poisoned by

Camelot's sewage run-off. Did you know that?" Breathless questions tumbled out of her. "Did you know about the food shipments? Or the lumber? Did you know the girls say Logan's a rapist? And that he maybe, like, murdered some protestors —"

"Whoa, whoa, slow down." Alastair held up his hands. "Where's all this coming from?"

As she poured forth everything her classmates had revealed in a breathless rush, a bemused smile spread across Alastair's face.

"Look, I've known Logan for three years now. Sure, he can be an asshole, but he's a good guy at heart — he and Alice are happily married, with three kids! There's no way these rumors are true. And yes, I know about the food shipments, but that's a temporary thing, because Camelot's population is growing faster than our farms. And this stuff about the French town — that sounds like a conspiracy theory. Jae said he learned about it on Dark Net sites, right? You can't trust what you find there."

"But I *saw* it," she said, grabbing his hand with conviction.

"You saw a holovid. Don't you know holovids can be faked?"

"Of course I do," she said, annoyed at the patronizing tone of his voice. She'd *told* him about the faked Ass is Hope video that had scrambled her life.

"You told me this 'Watt' person sent your friends here to destroy Camelot from within, right?" Alastair asked. "So, what if Jae faked that vid to convince you to turn on us too?"

"No, but ..." Rylla clutched her head. "Wait, *does* that make sense?" Her mind was spinning.

"Look, I made some calls, and I should be able to get your family's visas by the end of the week."

Rylla moaned. "They don't even want them. Or I don't know — maybe Tyler and Jo do, but I can't get in touch with them."

Alastair stiffened. "But you — *you're* still planning on staying, aren't you?"

Rylla opened her mouth to respond, but the words stuck in her throat.

"Are you staying or not?" He demanded, eyes boring into her.

"I —" Rylla held his gaze but couldn't seem to finish the sentence. She didn't know what to do or who to believe.

The heat in Alastair's eyes turned cold. "I have to get back," he said, his jaw set in steel.

"Wait —" Rylla touched his arm, but he shrugged off her hand. She followed him out of the alley, into the square, where the crowd was roaring.

"— and that is why I am calling for a new council election and announcing that I will run for Penndragon!" Maisie shouted triumphantly.

Her supporters cheered, their heads swiveling towards Logan and his knights.

Logan boomed his answer over the swell of concerned voices. "Fine! There's an election scheduled for October, just like every year. You can try your best then." He smiled mirthlessly.

"No!" shouted someone in the crowd. "Elections now!" called someone else, and the chant was taken up by a dozen voices.

"Under my leadership," Maisie boomed, raising a fist in the air, "we will live our primitivist lifestyle — growing our own food, making our own goods — but we will also have access to common-sense, life-saving medicine!"

"Huzzah!" someone cried, and the chorus echoed around the square. Some of those on the side-lines were booing though, or shouting about "slippery slopes," and "witchcraft!"

"How can you call yourself a primitivist," Logan roared, "when you give it up as soon as it becomes inconvenient?"

Maisie bared her teeth at him. "My son's life is not *inconvenient*. And furthermore, in my Camelot, anyone who so desires can become a knight!"

Logan broke into guffaws — looked around at his fellow knights expectantly — and then they were roaring in laughter too. All except Alastair, who scowled at thin air, oblivious to what was going on. He refused to meet Rylla's eye.

"And if everyone's a knight, who's going to do the dishes? Or work the laundry?" Logan taunted. "Already this little sword-fighting club of yours," he snarled at Magenta, "is pulling workers away from their responsibilities."

"Easy," Maisie said with a smirk. "All knights have to take a shift doing the dishes, and the washing, and all the other work you look down on. Who here would like to see Logan elbows-deep in our dirty washwater?"

The crowd erupted in laughter and applause. Logan blushed purple.

"Enough!" he bellowed. "Enough of these disruptions. Everyone will get back to their regular work assignments. And from now on, only *official* knights are allowed to carry swords. I order you all to disarm."

One of Magenta's knights — a girl of about fifteen with short, choppy hair — stepped forward. "Come and take it," she growled, unsheathing her weapon.

The hissing of steel rang across the square as all Magenta's knights — and then Logan's — drew their weapons. Then it was deathly silent, like no one even dared to breathe.

"STOP!"

Rylla was as astonished as the people around her to realize that the cry had ripped from her own lungs. But now that people were staring at her, she had to try and stop this before blood was shed. She pushed her way through the crowd.

"What are you doing?" Someone grabbed her arm — Magenta.

Rylla wrenched out of their grip.

A few more steps and she broke into the empty space between the tips of the knights' drawn swords. All eyes were on her. Jae, Magenta, and Ynez clustered together near the keep. Ynez held a finger to her lips. Jae was swiping his hand at neck-height — whether to mean 'they're gonna kill you' or 'cut it out' she couldn't be sure. But she wasn't going to shut up and let Camelot tear itself apart.

"I — I know I'm new here," she began tentatively, "but I love Camelot, and I hate to see you fighting. We should be working together, not trying to kill each other!" There was some mumbled assent from the group.

"Logan," she turned to face Camelot's leader. "Maisie's demands for a medical clinic seem pretty reasonable. And you *already* bend the rules of primitivism, don't you? Because you're secretly bringing in mass-produced food and lumber."

The crowd erupted in cries of surprise. A broad man in a stained apron cried, "It's true! They bring in a shipment of food every few weeks."

"That's just a temporary measure," Logan growled through clenched teeth.

As the whispering in the crowd grew to cries of outrage, Alastair grabbed Logan's shoulder, whispering something in the Penndragon's ear. What the hell was he saying? His gaze flicked to Rylla, and her heart clenched. As Logan listened, his eyes went wide, and he dispatched one of his knights, who took off running. Rylla tried to catch Alastair's eye, but he wouldn't look at her.

"Alastair Canterbury has informed me," Logan sneered, "that his little girlfriend here is a *spy.*" The crowd muttered in confusion. "She and her friends were sent here by the United States government on a mission — to destroy Camelot, to stop primitivism from threatening their decadent way of life!"

A hundred voices cried in outrage. The crowd shoved Jae, Magenta, and Ynez into the open space surrounding Rylla. "Is it true?" asked the girl who had first drawn her sword. Magenta shook their head, lips pressed in a line of rage.

Glaring at Rylla, Ynez pinched the bridge of her nose. "You had to be a fucking savior, didn't you?" she muttered.

Rylla iced-over with shock. How could Alastair have betrayed her like that? As if nothing they'd been through the past month mattered? She took a deep breath to stave off panic — maybe she could still salvage this, save Camelot, save her family, even save her and Alastair. She'd had enough with secrets and lies — it was time for the truth.

"We're not spies, we're students!" she yelled. "We're here to *study* primitivism, not destroy it!" The crowd rumbled with skeptical voices. "And what we learned is — well, this place is so beautiful, in so many ways." Her eyes stung as she stared at Alastair. "And the people are so beautiful."

"That's good," Ynez whispered. "Go with that. Butter them up."

"But there are serious problems here in Camelot, that *they* don't want you to know about." Rylla pointed at the knights on the stairs of the keep.

"No, no, no," Ynez hissed. Rylla ignored her.

"Like how Camelot has been clear-cutting the forests to the south and poisoning the watershed for miles around!"

"Lies!" Logan roared.

"And *you* —" Rylla turned on him, though her knees trembled. "Maisie's right — you're not fit to lead this community. What did you do to those protestors from Larmes de la Montagne, huh? And why do all the women in town say *'Don't get drunk around Logan,' 'Don't be alone with Logan'*?"

Something in the crowd snapped then. Cries of "Whoa!" and "Hang on!" and "Logan's a good man!" erupted from every corner of the square. It was not the reaction she'd expected. People were rallying to Logan's defense, instead of turning on him. She searched for Maisie near the fountain, hoping for support, but the woman had disappeared.

On the steps of the keep, the dispatched knight ran up to Logan, carrying something.

Jae's backpack. Rylla's blood ran cold.

"We have proof!" Logan shouted triumphantly, thrusting the backpack high. "Proof that these four are spies." He unzipped the pack and started pulling objects out, holding them aloft for the crowd to see — Jae's OGLens cases and MANIs, the synthetic clothes he'd worn in. But the object that elicited cries of horror from the crowd was a sinister-looking robotic claw that snapped open and shut as Logan held it high.

Ynez and Magenta glared at Jae, who shrugged. "What? It's a hydraulic grappling hook! For climbing. You expected me to come to the French-friggin-Alps and *not* bring a hydraulic grappling hook?"

Someone cried "Witchcraft!" and the word echoed through the square as others took up the chant. All the knights now — even Magenta's group — shifted their stance so their weapons were pointed at Rylla and her friends. The two groups had found a common enemy.

"This is not good," Jae whispered.

"I can't believe you told your boyfriend about Wingates," Ynez said. "The first rule of field trips is you don't tell anyone it's a field trip!"

"Remind me, Rylla," Magenta said in a furious whisper, "what did they do to witches in the Middle Ages?"

As if on cue, someone shouted, "Burn them!"

They were joking, right? They couldn't be serious. But then more and more voices took up the cry. "Burn them! Burn the witches!"

Logan shouted for the council members to join him on the steps of the keep. A group of people gathered there, huddled in conversation. Rylla was heartened to see Miss Farraday among the council members. Surely Miss Farraday wouldn't let them set her on fire? Not in front of the children.

"The council has ruled," Logan roared, "that they are to be punished as witches, in accordance with our laws!"

"No!" Rylla screamed. The nearest knights sheathed their weapons and grabbed her and the others with rough hands.

"Don't you fucking touch me!" Magenta shouted, already swinging. They landed a few punches before they were overwhelmed by three knights. Ynez and Jae were both diplomatically trying to talk their way out of this — offering bribes, threats, explaining how well-connected Wingates was. People would come for them!

"What are you going to do to us?" Rylla demanded, but none of the knights would answer as they dragged her through the square. Other men came bearing long posts and erected them near the fountain. They held back laughter as Rylla squirmed in their grip, like her terror was hilarious. Little Anker from school was sitting up on his father's shoulders, grinning as she was lashed to one of the posts. With a sinking feeling of doom, she realized that people were so much more vicious than she'd ever given them credit for.

She struggled against the ropes binding her wrists behind the post. "Stop! Please!" she cried, trying not to imagine how it would feel to burn alive. She searched the crowd for Alastair — surely he'd rush to her rescue any moment now — but he was nowhere to be seen.

Two burly knights carried something heavy through the crowd — an oaken barrel — and dropped it at Rylla's feet. With a heave on a crowbar, one of them cracked open the lid, and a sadistic cheer rose from the crowd. What the hell was that thick, black substance inside? A cruelly grinning woman grabbed a paintbrush and plunged it into the sludge. She reared back with the brush — Rylla flinched — and globs of ropey ooze splattered her face. The acrid smell of pine tar filled her nostrils. Cackling with malicious glee, the villagers took turns splattering Rylla and her friends with pine tar. Rylla struggled hopelessly against the ropes, tasting the tar in her mouth. Why were they being tarred — for fuel? To make sure they burned faster?

"Please, stop! We didn't mean any harm!" Rylla sobbed with panic, but laughter drowned out her cries for mercy. From the corners of her eyes, she could make out Jae and Ynez trying to persuade their tormentors with as little luck, while Magenta gnashed their teeth and threatened horrific acts of revenge on anyone who got close. The band struck up a rousing tune, and bottles of mead were passed around. The kitchen staff brought food from the keep, and some of the young folk started dancing a reel.

Then a great roar went up, and the people parted again. This was it, wasn't it? Someone was bringing a torch. Holy hell, how had she ever thought time-traveling to the Middle Ages was a good idea? She sobbed for all the things she was going to miss — crickets and the Guadalupe River, Tyler and Dae-Dae, horses and cheese, and kissing and sex! Which she'd only gotten to do once, but it had been an awful lot of fun. Pain shot through her at the memory. She'd trusted Alastair so completely, and he'd turned her over to this bloodthirsty crowd.

Finally, a stout, weathered woman — one of Camelot's cooks — emerged from the crowd grinning from ear-to-ear. She was carrying — not a torch — but a long butcher's knife and a stuffed burlap sack.

Expecting the end, Rylla flinched as the cook raised her knife overhead —

— and plunged it into the sack, tearing the burlap. A cloud of white fluff exploded outwards.

Feathers. Chicken feathers rained down around Rylla, sticking to every inch of the tar coating her skin and clothes.

Rylla's sobs of fear turned to cries of relief. "This — I've read about this! Tarring and feathering. You're tarring-and-feathering us, aren't you?" she shouted, giggling hysterically. "You're not going to burn us?"

"No, we're not going to burn you, child," the woman with the sack laughed. "We're primitivists, not animals!"

The vengeful party in the square lasted for hours. Finally the four of them were trudged through the town at sword-point, until a knight shoved Rylla and her friends to the forest floor, just outside the gate where they'd first entered. The earth shuddered, as the portcullis slammed shut behind their backs. High on the wall above, Logan held a torch aloft and announced that they were exiled, never to return. A cheer went up from behind the wall, and then the laughter of the very drunk crowd of Camelotians dwindled into the night.

Three feathery, oozing chicken-demons stared at Rylla, the moonlight glinting off their feathers and the whites of their enraged eyes.

Rylla sighed, unsticking herself from the leaf-littered ground. "Y'all. I am so, so sorry."

It was a long, sticky, miserable trudge back into the village where they'd first landed. Jae led them through the shadowy forest, and Rylla had to admit she was glad for his orienteering skills. When they reached the town, they managed to convince a terrified villager that they weren't actually mountain-devils and borrowed a set of OGGles to call for a jet back to Wingates. The pilot unfurled tarps for them to sit on for the plane ride home. Finally, they endured a humiliating trudge across campus, hounded by whispers and stares.

Her classmates were too furious to speak to her the entire, day-long journey home. But when they finally got back to their dorm, Magenta gestured for Rylla to shower first. Rylla scrubbed her skin until every speck of pine tar vanished, but she couldn't get the goo out of her hair. The tar had dried it together like matted carpet that wouldn't come clean no matter how much shampoo or conditioner she rubbed into it.

When the shower finally shut off automatically, she heard a loud buzzing from the other side of the bathroom door. Wrapping a towel around her, she opened the door and found Magenta reclined in their chair, pushing clippers through their tarry hair. As Rylla stepped into the common room, the last hunk of their three-foot-long hair fell to the floor in a sticky clump. Magenta ran a hand over their newly-bald scalp, noticed Rylla, and held out the clippers.

It was a dare. Or maybe a chance for penance. Rylla crossed the room slowly and took the clippers in one hand. She liked how heavy they felt. She clicked them on.

"Fuck it," she said, and she pushed the clippers into the matted hair above her right temple.

"Fuck what?" Magenta asked with a raised eyebrow.

"Fuck Camelot," she said. The first chunk of Rylla's hair separated gummily from her scalp.

Magenta nodded with approval.

"Fuck their fake fucking primitivism!"

"Yes," Magenta said, slow-clapping.

"Fuck Logan, who's a rapist and maybe a murderer?"

"YES."

Rylla started in on the second half of her head. A huge chunk of hair swung loose from her scalp. "And fuck boys who say they love you and then accuse you of witchcraft!"

"Huzzah!" Magenta cried.

"And fuck you, Magenta! You're always so mean to me! I'm sorry I got assigned to be your roommate. I'm sorry I'm not as cool as you, okay? I'm just like … figuring shit out, so give me a break!"

Magenta frowned. "That's fair," they said, holding Rylla's gaze.

Rylla shaved the last bit of hair, and the whole wadded mess fell with a wet thunk to the floor.

Her head felt so light. She rolled her neck experimentally, the air cool against her scalp.

Magenta reached up and tousled Rylla's fuzzy head. "It looks good."

"I don't give a FUCK how it looks," she shouted. Magenta looked momentarily stunned, then burst into laughter. Rylla joined in, but after a while, she wasn't laughing anymore. Tears streaked her face. She collapsed on her bed and curled up in a ball.

"Oh honey," Magenta sighed, sitting on the edge of the bed. "You're not the first person to lose their head over some weak-ass flirt, you know?"

"He said he loved me," Rylla snuffled.

"I know." Magenta patted her arm stiffly.

"He duped me."

"He *was* pretty cute," Magenta conceded.

"He was!" Rylla wailed. The memory of Alastair's body was so vivid — the curves of his shoulder muscles, his freckled abs. If she squeezed her eyes tight, it was like he was right there in the room with her.

"To his credit, I think he knew they wouldn't hurt us."

"Yeah, but he picked them over me. He picked *Logan* over me." Magenta rubbed her arm. Even though Rylla had never felt pain like this — like her heart was cracking open — she could feel something inside herself hardening. It was like Magenta's spirit was flowing into her, making her stronger.

It wasn't just Alastair who'd broken her heart. She had *believed* in Camelot and primitivism, and so she'd ignored the lies and corruption beneath Camelot's perfect pastoral surface. She never wanted to feel duped like that again.

And suddenly, all her questions about Wingates resurfaced with burning urgency. Why was Watt bossing around generals and spying on the Siberian Empire? What was the "Manifest," and what were they developing in Ward 7? Like Camelot, there was a lot to love about this school, but her gut told her that dangerous secrets lurked beneath the surface. She needed to figure out what exactly she was part of here.

And there was only person she could trust to help her find out.

24

A Ruse

Sitting in Climate Science the next morning, Rylla had the uncanny sensation that the last few weeks had been a dream. Pulling up her climate model, she set to work balancing the ocean's chemical makeup, determined to put Alastair out of her mind, and to earn her place at Wingates. She was sick of feeling ignorant all the time, of being wrong about so many things.

By the end of that first morning, her planet was starting to look like Earth, and Pupala even grunted his approval at the end of class. In Discrete Math, the new nine and ten-year-olds who'd joined the class while she was on the field trip asked *her* to check *their* answers.

Watt had cancelled their afternoon seminar so they could work on their 10,000-word essays on primitivism. Hunkered in her dorm, Rylla drafted a scathing critique of Camelot — typing so furiously her fingers hurt from pounding the desktop.

At dinner that night, Dae-Dae and Azam waved to Rylla excitedly from across the Grove. Each swept her up in a hug, and even Theo gave a smiling nod. It seemed her shunning was over.

Good, because she needed to talk to him.

But his first words only reminded her what an asshole he was. "What happened to you?" he asked, pointing to his scalp.

"It looks very clean," Dae-Dae said, sticking her tongue out at Theo.

Rylla ran a hand over her buzzcut. "I just needed a change."

"Nah, something happened to you. Girls only shave their heads when they get dumped by a boy or something."

Azam, Rylla, and Dae-Dae scoffed at the same time. "That is so sexist!" Azam said. "Cis men always think women's hair has something to do with *them*."

"Ignore him," Dae-Dae turned to Rylla. As she spoke, her fork levitated, scooped up some rice, and hovered unsteadily in the air before her, like it was wielded by an invisible toddler. Looking closely, Rylla could see tiny gray specks dusting the surface of the handle.

"Are those your Phireflys?" Rylla asked excitedly.

"Yup," Dae-Dae said, leaning forward to take a bite from the hovering fork. "I was able to use Zhenya's research to power them with chlorophyll generators. They're a lot more powerful now. But I'm still working on the glucosite batteries." She held her hand over the fork, casting it into shadow. After half a second, it dropped. "Block their light source and they lose power — but I'm working on it." Dae Dae swiped her MANIs and the fork levitated again, clumsily scooping another clump of rice. "Anyway — how was France?"

"Kind of a shit show," Rylla admitted. She briefly described her trip to Camelot, leaving out any mention of Alastair. She didn't want to prove Theo right about her haircut. Her friends found the story of her getting tarred and feathered a lot funnier than it had felt to live through it.

"Primitivists are so silly," Dae-Dae said, shaking her head.

"I bet you're happy to be back in civilization," Azam said. "I can't imagine going a month without a holowall."

"Well, there are *some* things I'll miss about Camelot," Rylla said. *Kissing Alastair* popped into her mind, but she shoved the thought away. "Have y'all ever had cheese? *Real* cheese?"

Azam and Theo shook their heads no, but Dae-Dae nodded. "There's a place in Detroit where you can get pizza with real cheese. My parents took me when I was little."

"It's so good right?" Rylla said.

Dae-Dae mm-hmmed, catching another hovering bite of food in the air.

"Why don't they ever serve cheese at Wingates?"

Theo laughed, "From cows? No way."

"All the food at Wingates has to be sustainable," Azam explained.

"And dairy cows are *way* not sustainable," Dae-Dae nodded. "They should be illegal."

"They sort-of are," Azam said. "There are international treaties limiting cows-per-capita, but all the countries cheat, because rich people will pay anything for beef and cheese."

"I can understand why," Rylla said, her mouth salivating at the memory of the fatty, salty goodness. "If I had the means, I might violate some international treaties for a bite of cheese."

The others laughed, but Theo scratched his dark stubble thoughtfully. "So we need to make it impossible to cheat. Control cattle populations remotely ..."

"Uh-oh, I know that look," Dae-Dae said. "Now Theo's gonna make the cow super-virus that mutates and kills us all!" She and Azam mimed dying horribly and slumped on the table.

Theo rolled his eyes at them. "It's good to have you back, Tex," he said, winking.

"It's *Rylla*," she said flatly.

"Okay, Rylla." He blinked slowly. "And for real, I like the hair."

At the compliment, an annoyingly giddy feeling spread in her chest, but she squashed it dead. She was *not* going to lose her head over some guy again — especially not over an arrogant jerk like Theo. But she *was* going to use him to find out what the Manifest was and what was being researched in the bowels of Ward 7. And so, as their group left the Grove, she stuck by Theo's side until Azam and Dae-Dae split off to their respective labs.

"So, Rylla," Theo said, leaning in close and dropping his voice. "Are you going to follow me all the way to the bio-engineering ward? Or are you hoping for another wild jet stream ride?" He winked.

"Funny you mention that." She swiped a MANI to pull up her OGlens settings and checked that ProfBlock was turned on. It was, but still she dropped her voice to a whisper. "Remember when you, uh, wanted to spy on a certain professor?"

A slow smile spread across Theo's face.

"I'm in."

As midnight approached, Rylla paced nervously in front of the Humanity building, waiting for Theo to appear. She'd used the cleaning drones to triple-check that no one was inside, but she still had a bad feeling about this. Even the wind-tossed crowns of the oaks seemed sinister, bowing their heads together in conspiracy.

When she spotted Theo loping across the quad, anxiety tightened in her chest. Theo, on the other hand, smiled laconically as he bounded up the steps, two at a time.

"Ready for this?" he asked, sounding like they were going to play a sim in the arena, not risk expulsion, or worse. She had a horrible inkling of what Watt might be capable of doing to anyone who crossed her.

"Ready for what, exactly? You haven't told me the plan."

"Simple. You use the cleaning drones to get us into Watt's office. I slip inside, access the control panel on her holowall, and add a bit of code that'll let us listen in on her calls."

"Oh, that's all? And how are we gonna explain why we went in there? ProfBlock won't make us disappear off security cameras, will it?"

"Rylla, have some faith. You think I can't loop a security video feed?" Theo shook his head at her. "But now that you mention it — maybe we should have some kind of alibi. We need a ruse in case a security guard glances at the live feed from Watt's office. Don't worry!" He held his hands up to Rylla's horrified look. "I don't think that's likely. The Humanity building is not a high-security part of the school ... but just in case."

"So what's this 'ruse' going to be?" she asked, glancing over her shoulder.

"I have an idea," he said, grinning mysteriously. "Just follow my lead."

He bounded up the stairs to the front doors, and she chased after. "Why can't you just tell me —"

As soon as she'd followed him through the front doors, he caught her around the waist, spun her so her back was to the wall, and brought his face *very* close to hers.

"Because it's more fun to *show* you," he said, speaking softly beside her neck, hot breath caressing the curves of her throat. Her heart slammed against her ribcage, and it had nothing to do with her fear of Watt. "If someone looks at the security feed right now, they'll just see two hormonal teenagers, looking for a private place to —"

"Ohhh," she breathed. "Right. The ruse."

Just a few days ago, she'd allowed herself to get this close to Alastair, and he'd betrayed her. Theo knew nothing about that — he couldn't know this little "ruse" was a painful reminder of that heartbreak. Still, part of her wanted to shove Theo off and slap him for his audacity. Another part of her threatened to break down sobbing. And her body — which didn't seem to care *who* was in front of her — ached to grab him by the hips and pull him closer.

But the thought of giving into any of those desires was mortifying. This flirting meant nothing to Theo. It was a game to him — he was trying to shock her, or maybe make her fall head-over-heels for him. If she let herself *feel* anything, he would win. There was no way in hell she'd give him the satisfaction. She would prove she could be just as phony and ruthless as he was. Smiling saccharinely, she said, "Shall we head upstairs then?"

If anyone was going to catch feelings here, it'd be him.

Theo grabbed her hand, backing away, and led her towards the elevator, swiping a hand to call it.

"Rylla, my darling, I simply cannot live without carnal knowledge of you for another moment." His smile was earnest but his voice sarcastic.

"Yes, tee-hee," she said, matching his tone. "Let us abscond to a secluded location to engage in this *carnal knowledge.*" She couldn't help snorting with laughter at the term. Theo raised an eyebrow like, *keep it together*. The elevator dinged, the doors opened, and he backed her inside with his hips.

She looped her arms behind his neck and tilted her head to one side.

"You're a good actress," he whispered, peering down at her. "I mean, you're even *blushing*. You should win an award or something."

Her blush spread from her cheekbones to her chest. Her body might betray how unnerved she was feeling, but she wouldn't let him know he was getting to her. As the doors opened on the fourth floor, she placed a hand on his chest and pushed him backwards, maneuvering him towards the door to Watt's office. "And what award would that be?"

"How about 'Best Supporting Actress in a Brilliant Ruse?'"

"*Supporting* actress!" she shoved him playfully, knocking him back into Watt's door. She pulled up her cleaning drone app and called a drone to their location. As the door slid open ahead of a zooming FloorBot, Theo grabbed her wrists and pulled her inside.

"What? You think you're the *star* of this show?" he asked, his head inclined towards the holowall — their target.

"That's right." Rylla grabbed the front of his shirt and pulled him towards her, turning so her back was against the mesh of the holowall.

With both hands on either side of her head, he purred, "Showtime, starlet."

This close to Theo, Rylla couldn't help but breathe him in. His scent was cleaner and more delicate than Alastair's had been, but it made her dizzy all the same. She lost track of what they were doing, fire spread through her veins, and now her body moved of its own accord. Her neck arched, her lips parted, and she was stretching on tiptoe up to kiss him —

— but then, with a *click*, the holowall's control panel snapped open. His MANIs drummed beside her head, his eyes glazed over.

Right. He was doing what they'd come there for — installing spyware.

She sank back on her heels, and an empty, windswept feeling rushed over her. Alastair's face flashed before her eyes. *He'd* actually cared about her. He'd said he loved her. What she wouldn't give to —

No. Alastair had betrayed her, she reminded herself, smothering the emotion.

"Done!" Theo whispered, his eyes focusing on her once more. "Let's get out of here." He grabbed her hand, and the lonely feeling evaporated, replaced by the thrill of having pulled-one-over on Professor Watt. Rylla had to bite her lip to keep from breaking into hysterics as they stole out of the room. It didn't help the roiling emotions in her chest that Theo kept his fingers entwined with hers until they burst through the double doors to the outside.

Beneath the swaying oak trees, the gravity of what they'd done settled on Rylla's shoulders like a mantle.

"Did we get away with it?"

Theo shrugged. "Seems like it. So far, at least. But it's always possible Watt could discover my little patch on her holowall."

Rylla's stomach churned at the prospect. "So now we — what? Spy on Watt 24-7 or something?"

"Nah, I'm too busy for that," Theo said with a chuckle. "I set an algorithm to listen for key words — Manifest, Ward 7, Sentinel. Now we wait for Watt to make an *interesting* call."

25

X-Day

Rylla was a nervous wreck the next day, unable to concentrate in her classes, expecting a furious call from Watt, demanding to know why she'd been canoodling in her office. But Theo's hack of the security feeds must've worked, because the week passed without incident. Every time she passed Theo in the halls, she'd arch an eyebrow, and he'd shake his head. No *interesting calls* yet.

Rylla's anxiety only got worse at night, and so she buried her fears in studying. She wrote a paper for Neuropsychosociology on *Gotterdammerungangst* — the unique depression people felt as a result of living in a dying world. In Evolutionary Biology, she was carbon-dating bone shards like a pro. She even swallowed her complaints and pushed her muscles to their limit in Alpinism and Orienteering, as a way of apologizing to Jae for getting him tarred and feathered. And every night after choking down a few bites of dinner, she would head to the Climate Modeling lab to work on her model of Earth. She added the world's cities and set billions of humans to algorithmically-determined behaviors. On Friday, Professor Pupala checked her calculations one last time.

"I suppose your Earth is accurate enough," he said. "For an entry-level class."

"Thanks?" Rylla said.

"Go ahead and run your X-day calculation."

She looked at him quizzically.

He sighed and flicked his MANIs to access the "Advanced" menu of her modeling App — controls she hadn't messed with. "Here we go," he said, swiping a finger.

Time kicked in on her planet Earth. Green places shrank and deserts spread. Temperature readings climbed higher and higher. The sliver of white at the poles melted, and the edges of the continents sank further underwater. The oceans turned sickly green, then deep blue-black. All the while, the human population plummeted from billions, to millions, to a few thousand — and finally to zero. Clouds thinned, thinned again, and vanished. Then all was still. Every bit of land on her planet was the color of dust.

"417 years," Pupala said. "That's generous. Most models put X-Day between 200 and 400 years."

"X-day?" Rylla asked.

Professor Pupala looked incredulous. "Haven't you finished the reading? Extinction Day is *it*. The end. The day the last macroflora dies. You might still find some bacterial life in the deep ocean, but that's it. If humans are still on that," he said, pointing to her model, "they'll have to be in some kind of bunker underground. Might as well be living on Mars — and remember, we don't *have* the technology to sustain life on Mars."

A lump rose in Rylla's throat. "And this — this is definitely going to happen? A few centuries from now?"

"Your X-Day was calculated based on the model of Earth you've built. Assuming your inputs are correct, X-Day will occur in 417 years."

"So how do we stop it?" Rylla asked.

"No, *you* tell *me* that." Professor Pupala pinched the bridge of his nose. "That's the second half of this assignment.

Your X-Day calculation is based on everything staying the same — humans don't change their behaviors. Now you start playing with the variables. Figure out what we need to do to prevent X-Day."

"Save the world," Rylla said. "Got it."

For the rest of that week, Rylla spent her spare time in the Climate Lab, determined to push back X-Day. She stopped the burning of all fossil fuels, then re-ran the calculation, but X-Day moved back only 50 years. Even if humans stopped burning oil, permafrost kept melting and deserts kept spreading. White ice turned to dark water, absorbing more heat from the sun; the oceans acidified, absorbing less carbon — it was a positive feedback cycle she couldn't break.

On a whim, she decided to re-create the primitivist lifestyle at Camelot on a global scale. She removed power stations globally, setting all humans to using wood-burning stoves for heating and cooking. She ended global transportation systems, making all agriculture local. Then she allowed for one cow per three people — roughly the human-to-livestock ratio in Camelot.

When she ran her X-Day calculation again, forests fell as lumber was harvested, and all those cows overgrazed the remaining wilderness, turning it to desert. Her X-Day calculation jumped to just 237 years from the present day.

Here, then, was proof that primitivism — at least Camelot's brand of it — wouldn't save them. Human technology had wrecked the climate, and human technology would have to fix it. She'd expected to feel satisfaction, but the sight of the dead planet turning before her gave her no pleasure. Instead, a choking feeling of *Gotterdammerungangst* clawed up her throat.

At lunch that day, Rylla picked at her food. She couldn't eat, couldn't concentrate on the engineers' conversation. Azam asked if something was wrong, and Rylla told them what had happened in Climate Modeling.

"You really didn't know about X-Day?" Dae-Dae cried. "I've known about it since — since I can remember!"

"Not everyone has scientists for parents," Azam pointed out.

"I knew on some level," Rylla said. "Growing up in the Dust, you figure out that the world is not —" She pushed peas around with her fork, swallowing the lump in her throat. "— not *doing okay*. But something about calculating it — 417 years until the end of all life on Earth? It's so final."

"400 years is generous," Theo mused. "I built a very aggressive model. Put X-Day around 150 years."

"I don't think you're helping," Azam said, narrowing her eyes at him.

Rylla's food tasted like dust in her mouth. "How do you deal?" she asked them. "How do you get up each morning knowing we're headed for extinction?"

"That's *why* we get up each morning," Azam said. "We're all trying to invent some nanoborg, or chemical, or bacteria that will help push back X-Day."

"Speaking of which, here's something to cheer you up." Dae-Dae's eyes glazed over and her MANIs flew across the tabletop. "I integrated Azam's chemical recycling tech with the Phireflys and taught them to do this ..." She pulled a wadded-up plastic bag of Choklit Crisps from her back pocket and placed it on the table.

Dae-Dae tapped something out with her MANIs, then flourished her hands at the bag like a wizard casting a spell. A greyish-green haze of Phireflys flew from her front pocket onto the bag. The edges of the bag began to curl, then vanish into nothingness. In moments, only a small pile of black soot remained in its place.

"Whoa," Rylla breathed. "It's just like Azam's chemical recycler!"

"Yeah, but way more efficient," Azam said, beaming at Dae-Dae.

"Once I figure out how to scale these puppies, we can dissolve the world's plastic waste like that." Dae-Dae snapped her fingers.

"That's amazing!" Rylla's mind spun with the possibilities. Would Dae-Dae's Phireflys be able to transform landfills? Clean up the Great Pacific Garbage Continent?

"It's very impressi —" Theo broke off, staring the table, which appeared to be melting. "Hey Dae, you want to turn them off now?"

The Phireflys were eating a rapidly-spreading hole in the middle of the table. "Uh-oh," Dae-Dae said. "They shouldn't be doing that."

The hole spread towards Rylla, and her cafeteria tray fell through the middle of the table into the grass, where it too started to dissolve into black powder. She scooted back her chair, not wanting to find out what would happen if the Phireflys touched her.

"Turn them off!" Theo shouted.

"I'm trying!" Dae-Dae cried, MANIs whirring.

A memory flashed through Rylla's mind — Dae-Dae shading the Phireflys with her hand, and them falling dead. "Light!" she yelled. "We have to cut off their light!"

Dae-Dae smacked her head. "Duh! We've got to shade them with —" she looked around desperately.

Theo picked up his lunch tray and smacked it down onto the Phireflys devouring the tabletop. Rylla did the same with hers, then grabbed another from a kid eating a sandwich at a nearby table. After a few frenzied moments of tray-slamming and people crying in outrage as their trays were snatched, the ring of spreading destruction was covered in trays, and the Grove fell silent.

Dae-Dae lifted the corner of a tray, peeked underneath, and sagged with relief. The Phireflys had stopped inches from the edge of the table. The four table legs were connected by only a thin ring of plastic.

A crowd of a hundred students had gathered around them, craning their necks to see what was happening.

"Did you get them all?" Azam asked breathlessly.

Theo stomped on a clump of Phireflys eating away at a napkin.

"I — I think so — " Dae-Dae stammered.

Tavia pushed her way through the throng of onlookers. "What happened here?" She demanded, scanning the edge of the crowd. "Whose research is this?"

Dae-Dae and Azam sheepishly raised their hands. Dae-Dae explained that her nanobots had gotten carried away — must have been something wrong with her AI coding, probably just an unclosed parenthesis — no big deal.

Tavia shook her head. "Sorry, Dae, I think this *is* a big deal." Her eyes glazed over for a moment and she spoke to someone on her OGLenses. When her gaze refocused, she said, "Watt wants to see you in her office." Then she turned to face the crowd of onlooking students. "All right, dinner's over. Everyone out!"

Rylla and Theo tried to hang back with their friends, but Tavia pointed them towards the exit. By the time they reached the door, a half-dozen professors had appeared, talking in hushed tones to Dae-Dae and Azam. One was using a fork to peer under a lunch tray.

"Are they in trouble?" Rylla asked.

"Nah, you'd be surprised how often engineers nearly destroy the school." Theo laughed. "But I bet they have to work in Ward 7 after this." He chewed his thumbnail. "*Lucky*."

She headed back to her dorm room on auto-pilot, too charged with adrenaline to notice her surroundings. She forgot about her afternoon Evolutionary Bio class until she collapsed onto her bed. Panicking, she sent the professor a mention — lying that she was too sick to make it to class. In a way, it was true — she couldn't concentrate. She put on one of her favorite holo-animes to calm down, but couldn't follow the plot. Her thoughts kept returning to the Phireflys. Would they have eaten her alive if they'd touched her? And since they clearly belonged in Ward 7, what *else* was being developed down there? And if Dae-Dae and Azam started working in Ward 7, would they become a part of Watt's secret plans?

And where the hell was Tyler? And why hadn't he called?

She checked Dark Net sites for news out of the Dust but found nothing new. She skipped dinner, hitting up the vending machine instead for a few bags of cheez puffs.

Magenta's voice startled Rylla just as she'd settled back into scrolling the Dark Net for news of her brother.

"This is pathetic."

Rylla turned down the opacity on her lenses to find her roommate towering over her bed. "What?" she said, mouth stuffed with cheez puffs.

"Ever since we got back from Camelot, you've been holed up in this room every night." Magenta crossed to their wardrobe and pulled on a top that looked like it was made of liquid gold. "I get that we all have nightwork but this —" They gestured to the anime on the holowall, the cheez powder on Rylla's shirt. "This is not healthy. This is moping. You need to go out."

"You can't kick me out of my own room!" Rylla said angrily, spraying a cloud of cheez powder.

"Not *get* out. *Go* out. Like ... have some fun? Night on the town?"

Rylla froze mid-chew. Was Magenta finally inviting her along to — wherever it was they went at night?

"With you?" She swallowed.

Magenta nodded.

"Where?"

"Detroit."

Rylla sat up. As a girl, she had dreamed of visiting one of the rich, swanky Lake Cities.

"Will there be beers?" Rylla asked, a slow smile spreading across her face. "I could go for a beer. Or some scrounger hooch, for that matter," she muttered.

"Of course, but you have to let me dress you, okay? That," they gestured to Rylla's food-dusted uniform, "is not going to cut it."

26

The Velvet Underground

Magenta dressed Rylla in one of their jumpsuits — sleeveless, with lenticular nebulas swirling across her legs. They painted her buzzed hair in glittery black goop and lined her eyes with iridescent makeup. Her reflection in the holowall looked unrecognizably fierce.

"You have your own hovercar?" Rylla gaped as Magenta climbed into the sleek vehicle parked in Wingates' student parking structure.

"My family's rich," Magenta said. "Like disgustingly, crimes-against-humanity-level rich. My dad makes your boy Alastair look like a peasant. I hate his guts, of course."

"Right." Rylla climbed into the passenger seat. "Still — nice to have a car."

"The way I see it, my purpose in life is to destroy his power and redistribute his wealth," Magenta said. They waved a hand and the consoles glowed. The vehicle lifted off the ground. "But yeah," they said with a grudging smirk. "It's nice to have a car. And he pays my tuition."

"Tuition?"

"I'm not like you and Jae and Ynez, okay?" they snapped. "I wasn't chosen by Watt, because I'm a genius or whatever. I'm a Patron student. *Daddy* pays my way." Their voice dripped with loathing. "He's on the Board of Wingates."

Magenta waved to set the autopilot and sat back with folded arms as the car maneuvered itself onto the electro-magnetic highway. E-scape music blasted from the speakers, so there was no way to talk. Magenta had gotten so defensive about being a "patron" student, like they were actually *insecure* about being rich. For all their confidence, maybe Magenta was also worried about whether or not they "belonged" at Wingates.

As they reached the glittering downtown district, Rylla pressed her nose against the windows of the hovercar. Water-falls poured from the bustling walkways connecting crystalline skyscrapers, and hanging gardens spilled from every level of the many-tiered city. Rylla was mesmerized and appalled by the ostentatious lushness.

Soon they'd left the bright lights behind, driving through an industrial area along the lakefront, lined with shuttered warehouses. They turned down an alleyway, plunged under-ground into a derelict parking structure, and stopped next to a few abandoned wrecks. Magenta got out, and Rylla followed nervously.

"Aren't you worried about your car?" The cherry-red luxury machine looked out of place, to say the least. Magenta waved a hand, and the car transformed into a rusted-out heap. In the dim light, the security hologram was very convincing.

"You want a crystal before we go in?" Magenta asked, pulling from their jacket a small bag of what looked like pink rock candy.

Tam. Rylla knew what it looked like, though she'd never tried it. Half of Amaryllis's paychecks used to go towards those little pink rocks, money she should have saved for new water recyclers, or visas, or college tuition. On tam, her mom was always fake-lovey-dovey, bringing home disgusting guys from Lucky's she'd never talk to in the light of day.

"No thanks," Rylla said, her voice more bitter than she'd intended.

Magenta shrugged and placed a chunk of tam on their tongue. After a moment they sighed contentedly, then hid the bag away in the folds of their clothes. Following them deeper into the parking garage, Rylla fought a creeping feeling that coming here had been a mistake.

Magenta stopped at a filthy steel door and knocked. The door swung outwards, and a huge, bearded person filled the space, towering over even Magenta. They were covered in color-shifting tattoos, and every facial feature was studded with metal spikes. Rylla shifted closer to Magenta, barely resisting the urge to duck behind them.

"Ayyy, Magenta! Long time no see!" The bouncer cracked a wide, friendly grin. "Who's the new partner? I think I spooked them."

"Just a friend," Magenta said. "Are we late?"

"Nah, everyone's just getting started."

Magenta led her past the guard, up a stairwell, and into an open area that was probably once a factory. But the cavernous space had been carved up into hundreds of little rooms by half-walls made of collections of *things*. There was a wall made of dirty, old teddy-bears, a wall of pink high heeled shoes, and a wall of broken brass instruments. Suspended walkways criss-crossed overhead, lined with thousands of ferns and hanging plants, fed by a welded-together, hodgepodge irrigation system.

"Welcome to the Velvet Underground," Magenta said.

The place was teeming with the trendiest-looking people Rylla had ever seen. Many of them, like the bouncer, had color-changing tattoos. Their hair was dyed all colors, and some didn't have hair at all, but extensions of living moss or vines sprouting from their scalps. Some people dressed like scroungers in handmade clothes quilted with scraps from a dozen decades. Others had carefully curated vintage outfits, looking like they stepped out of the 1890s or 2030s. Still others wore the type of high-tech clothing Magenta preferred.

People lounged on the mismatched furniture packed into every nook and cranny, talking, laughing, doing tam and lolly-lolly, drinking. Others painted on massive canvases, or hunks of concrete, or each other's bodies. Performers were making music with guitars or vintage synthesizers, or dancing on long silk ropes suspended from the rafters. Magenta wound their way through the chaos, and Rylla followed wide-eyed in their wake.

Everywhere they went, people stopped Magenta.

"Magenta! I'm such a big fan."

"I've been following you for years!"

"Will you take a holovid with me?" Magenta looped their arm around the teen, smiled, and held up three fingers like the prongs of a fork — the hand sign that meant 'eat the rich.'

Finally, Magenta led Rylla up a staircase to the gangway above the factory floor. They headed into the former factory overseer's office — now a lounge overlooking the Underground. Rylla sank onto a green velvet couch beside them.

"So what *are* you?" she shouted over the music. "Some kind of celebrity?"

They shrugged. "I guess you could call me a ... style guru? A cultural icon?"

"What does that even mean?"

"If I feature an artist on Joinly, they'll blow up. That's why everyone here kisses my ass." Magenta stared into space, then bobbed their head in greeting as a group of their friends approached. Someone sat down next to Rylla with vinelike hair extensions, black tattoos snaking up their arms, and a ring piercing their full, bottom lip. They had such symmetrical features that it was mesmerizing to watch them speak.

"Did you go to my high school? You look *so* familiar." The person purred, in a voice thick with vocal fry. They probably recognized Rylla from the *Ass is Hope* video, but with her shaved head and Magenta's makeover, she must've looked too different to place.

"I don't think so. I grew up in Texas."

"No way! You're a *real* Dusty? That is so cool. Most of the people who claim to be Dusties around here are just gentrifying trash."

"Gentrifying trash?" Rylla asked.

The lip ring'd person explained how during the Exodus of '49, a ton of rich white people moved from the Dust to Detroit, buying up property, taking over Black neighborhoods and pushing Black residents out of the city center. To this day, the glittering downtown was inhabited by rich, white, trust-fund kids whose parents had fled from the West Coast. Waving a long, elegant hand, they admitted that they were descended from Beverly Hills climate refugees. "But now my politics are super radical, eat-the-rich, smash white supremacy, all that shit," they said.

Rylla hadn't caught their name or pronouns, but at this point they'd been talking for half an hour, and it seemed rude to ask.

A tiny monstrous bird appeared in the corner of Rylla's vision, and it took her half a second to realize this wasn't some art piece — it was Kyle. "You have an incoming call from an unfamiliar number. Do you wish to accept?"

It was probably a bot or a scammer, but there was a sliver of a chance that the call was someone else, someone who *couldn't* use their usual number — someone like her brother. She searched the lounge for somewhere to talk, ducking into a bathroom, where the music was marginally softer, and answered the call.

Tyler's face appeared in a call bubble. "Tyler! It's so good to see you " But her voice faltered as she took in his appearance. He was too thin. Stubble covered his cheekbones. His skin was sunburnt, peeling, and coated with a film of dust. His mohawk had grown out into a shaggy mop, and he was dressed in rags. If she didn't know him, she would have assumed on sight that he was a scrounger.

He said something she couldn't hear, so she pressed her microvibe speakers.

"What?!"

"I can't talk long," he repeated.

"How — how are you? Where have you been?"

"Jo is dead."

The world spun and dropped away, and she collapsed to the filthy tile floor. "Oh no, no," she breathed, choking on the words. "Not Jo."

Tyler clenched his jaw and spoke matter-of-factly. "They were at Travis County Jail, and the power went out in their wing. No AC. There was a heat wave, and —" His voice cracked, his eyes welled. "— it was like an oven in there."

Rylla couldn't speak. Tears streamed down her face.

"The bastard guards just sat in their air-conditioned office and watched them die." Tyler's face was a picture of rage. "We're not going to take it anymore. This — this is a breaking point."

"Who's 'we?' Tyler?" Rylla asked, pushing herself up. "What are you going to do?"

"I can't answer those questions. Not on a call."

"Don't do anything dangerous!"

"Life in the Dust *is* dangerous, Rylla. Or maybe you've forgotten that in your fancy, lush life?" His words felt like a slap. Suddenly she remembered she was wearing Magenta's makeup and clothes. She realized what she must look like to him — a spoiled, Lushie party girl.

"Tyler, I just — I need you to be okay," she pleaded.

Tyler stared up at the ceiling of wherever-he-was. "Maybe I needed you! Maybe Jo did. But you left. You weren't here when —" His jaw clenched and his eyes turned to stone. "Never mind. Get back to your party. I have to go. It only takes a few minutes for their algorithm to find me."

"What algorithm? Who's *they*? I want to help with — whatever you're going through."

"You can't help because you're not *here*." Tyler scowled. "I only called because of Jo. Because I thought you should know."

Her brother's face vanished, and she was left staring at a stained, sticker-covered toilet.

She walked unsteadily back to the couches where Magenta was talking with their friends. How could Jo be dead? And did Tyler really blame her for it? She desperately wished she could teleport back to Wingates, to the quiet comfort of her room. But to get there, she'd have to tell Magenta what was going on, and she was terrified that if she opened her mouth, the storm of grief inside her would come pouring out and never stop.

So she sat back down amid a burst of their laughter, now sounding hollow and far-away. The person with the lip ring smiled at Rylla and held out a little baggie of pink crystals.

Tam made you feel better. That's why people did it. No matter what was going on, tam could *always* make you feel better. And Rylla needed something to help her feel better right now — just until she got back to campus. A little chemical glue to keep her from cracking into pieces, right here, in front of all these strangers.

She took a crystal.

Magenta watched her with an arched eyebrow as the tam melted, sugary-sweet on her tongue. For a few breaths, she felt nothing, and then every tight muscle in her body unspooled. Colors intensified. The make-up of the lip-ring person started pulsing, and she could see the blood flowing beneath their alabaster skin. Part of her still knew that Jo was dead, but it was like she had fast-forwarded through all that crying and grief to arrive at acceptance. Suddenly all she could think about was what it would feel like to kiss someone with her newly heightened senses. As if reading her mind, lip ring leaned towards her, and then their faces melted together. Surprisingly, the lip ring wasn't cold.

Time skipped forward an hour or so. She must have decided to leave the lounge, because she was back on the floor of the Velvet Underground, wandering. Art that had made little sense to her earlier now vibrated with meaning. In a room walled with wooden rolling pins, a couple of performance artists rubbed peanut butter on each others' faces, and she *got* it. In another room, two muscular men braided plastic flowers into each others' hair, while a hyper-femme woman stomped around them in metal shoes, screaming in their faces. Rylla cried at that one. The men with the plastic flowers reminded her of Jo.

Another skip. She was in a restaurant eating pizza with real cheese with Magenta and their friends. Rylla's tongue was too thick with pizza to talk, and her ears were too full of buzzing cicadas to follow the conversation.

Skip. She was back in her bunk at Wingates. Even though she was laying still, the room tilted violently. She kept telling Kyle to turn off the room's spinning, but the tiny shoebill kept saying he, "did not understand the request."

Skip. Hanging over the toilet, vomiting. The pizza tasted much worse coming up.

Skip. Someone shaking her. Rylla groaned and cracked an eye to find Magenta standing over her.

"Lemme sleep," she mumbled.

"It's three in the afternoon," they said, "and we've got Watt's class in ten minutes."

27

The Second Proposal

Somehow Rylla oozed out of bed, pulled on a uniform shirt, and stumbled after Magenta into the elevator to topside. But the mid-afternoon light proved too much for her, and as soon as they burst through the outer doors, Rylla promptly puked into a bush.

"Ugh, I can't watch this. You took a *big* crystal for your first time." Magenta pulled something from their pocket. It was a tiny baggie of tam, with just a few crystals at the bottom. "A little hair of the dog should get you through the rest of the day." They pinched the bag to crush the remaining crystals, then dipped a pinky in. "Swipe a little bit inside your cheek. It'll be enough to stop the puking but won't get you high."

Rylla reached for the bag, but Magenta snatched it back. "A. Little. Bit," they repeated.

"Don't worry." Rylla belched, and it nearly made her hurl again. "I won't get addicted. I don't want to feel like this ever again."

Magenta handed over the bag, and as soon as Rylla had swiped a few grains of tam inside her cheek, the knots in her stomach unclenched and the pounding in her head subsided — enough for her to pick herself up off the ground.

But her mind was still scattered — as if her memories were spread out over the grounds of Wingates, and she had to find them one by one. With dread, she remembered that this was their first seminar since Camelot. Surely, Watt would yell at her for getting them tarred, feathered, and exiled. Her heart hitched again as she remembered that this would also be her first time facing Watt since she and Theo had hacked the professor's holowall. What if the professor had been waiting for this class to confront Rylla about her spying?

As she stepped inside the cool air of the Humanity building, another memory slid into place. Someone had been angry with her last night. Tyler. Tyler had said she'd abandoned her family. Tyler had told her that Jo was dead.

The spiraling, bookcase-lined stairwell started to spin then, and a panicked, desperate feeling came over Rylla. She ducked into the bathroom and locked herself in a stall. Bile rose up the back of her throat, and tears threatened to overwhelm her. There was no way she could make it through class feeling like this.

Then she remembered the baggy in her pocket. Maybe one swipe hadn't been enough. One more couldn't hurt, right? She slipped a pinky in and swiped the dust on the inside of her cheek. Instantly, her stomach unclenched and her heart rate slowed. She was starting to understand why her mother had paid so much for this stuff.

🪲

"I see the primitivists made an impression on you," Professor Watt said, raising her eyebrows at Magenta and Rylla's bald heads. "I've read your essays."

Rylla flinched, expecting to be scolded.

"— and I was impressed. Well done all."

Jae, Ynez, and Magenta looked as stunned as Rylla felt. Hadn't getting tarred and feathered had been a colossal screw-up?

Watt grilled them about their time in Camelot. Ynez explained how she had situated herself at the dairy — the social hub of Camelot — and encouraged Maisie to stand up for herself. Magenta chuckled as they described how they'd destabilized Logan's authority by defying Camelot's binary gender roles. And Jae recounted his discovery of Camelot's ecological crimes. Rylla, still feeling out of it, didn't participate until Watt turned to her.

She braced herself for a lecture, but Watt asked, "Why did you request a job as a teacher?"

Rylla shrugged. "I never got to go to a real school. I guess I wanted to see what I'd missed."

"And what did you learn, as a teacher?"

Remembering her miserable attempts to get the five-year-olds to pay attention to her, Rylla said, "Teaching is really, really *hard*." Then she recalled Miss Farraday's advice. "Oh, and kids can smell fear."

Magenta snorted a laugh and rolled their eyes.

"Those are good lessons for a teacher to learn," Watt said. "And believe it or not, teaching —" she shot Magenta a stern look "— is a powerful form of leadership." Watt turned back to Rylla. "I particularly liked this quote from your essay." She swiped a hand, sending some text up onto the holowall.

Camelotians' faith in primitivism prevents them from perceiving the devastation they cause. This faith is vital because it gives them a sense of control over X-Day. Thus, the growing popularity of primitivism may be viewed as a response to Gotterdammerungangst.

"I'm impressed with you, Rylla, for keeping an open mind. You had faith in primitivism, but when presented with contradictory evidence, you adjusted those beliefs. That's more than many people are capable of." Rylla blushed at the professor's rare compliment.

"I also share this quote because it suggests to me a future line of inquiry. You refer to Gotterdammerungangst. I believe you're studying this "doomsday depression" with Professor Hernandez?"

Rylla nodded.

"You correctly identified that Gotterdammerungangst motivates many types of human behavior in these times. So, what are some other ways people cope with Gotterdammerungangst?"

Watt looked around expectantly, but was met with a long silence.

"That's hard to answer," Ynez began. "Because we all know about X-Day, right? Isn't everyone depressed about it?"

"Some people pretend it isn't happening," Jae said. "Where I'm from, there are shut-ins who spend all day in hologames and get everything by drone-delivery. Some of them go years without stepping outside, because they can't face the sight of the Dust."

"Drugs." Magenta said, and Rylla felt like the bag of tam was burning a hole in her pocket. "A lot of people use drugs to deal with Gotterdammerungangst." Rylla cleared her throat nervously.

"— Or religion," Ynez said. "There hasn't been such a boom in cults since the 1970's."

Watt clapped her hands together. "It sounds like you have some ideas to start with. Do some research. Next class, I want to hear some well-developed theories about other ways Gotterdammerungangst motivates human behavior."

Magenta pushed back their chair as if to stand, but Watt held out a hand. "I haven't dismissed you yet. A bioengineer we've heard from before has put forth another research proposal. I'm curious what you'll make of it."

"The dragon guy again?" Magenta sat back down. "This should be good."

Watt waved her MANIs, the lights dimmed, and for the second time, a holographic image of Theo appeared in Rylla's seminar room. This time, Rylla hoped he'd come up with something more reasonable than bioengineered dragons.

"Cows," he said flatly, and a black-and-white Holstein winked into existence beside him.

Magenta snorted in amusement.

"A staple of human agriculture since ancient times. Currently, there are 1.9 billion cows on planet Earth." Theo broke off as the cow lifted its tail and dropped a plop of shit right in the middle of the conference table. "And every one of them does *that*." The cow burped. "And that." The cow blasted out a long, wet fart. "And *that*." Everyone else was laughing, but Rylla blushed with embarrassment for Theo. Where was he going with this?

Theo crouched down over the holographic cow turd. "All these *emissions* release methane — up to 100 million metric tons of it every year. And methane is a greenhouse gas four times more powerful than carbon dioxide."

He straightened up. "Many governments have pledged to reduce cattle populations to fight the climate crisis, but few countries hold up their end of the deal."

The holographic ground fell away, and then they were looking down, as if from a skimmer, over a jungle being cleared by tractors and fire. "Forests are still being cut down for use as cow pastures — often turning to Dust after a few short years."

Theo straightened and turned one hand palm up. "Where politics has failed to solve this problem, science can succeed — with this 'Retroviral Implantation Device.'" A white cube appeared, hovering above his upturned hand. "Thanks to advances in nanotechnology, this machine, the size of a mere speck of dust —" The cube shrank until it vanished from sight. "— can be cheaply and easily embedded beneath a cow's skin."

A herd of cattle appeared around the room. Magenta scooted their chair to one side to avoid being stuck in a cow's holographic haunches.

"Once a cow is injected with RID, farmers will see all kinds of benefits. RID can be activated to print retroviral gene therapy to combat cancers and viral diseases that are becoming more prevalent as the environment deteriorates. Farmers will rush to adopt this one-size-fits-all miracle device for keeping their cattle populations healthy." Theo smiled like a saint, arms spread wide. "And we at Wingates will make the implants available through one of our charitable organizations — to every farmer in the world."

He dropped his arms with a self-satisified smirk. "And once the global cattle population is seeded with RID, we — Wingates bioengineers — will gain total genetic control over every cow on earth. If host countries follow their agricultural treaties — great! No need to interfere. But if anyone starts exceeding their livestock limits, we can trigger the RID devices inside each animal to induce sterilization." Theo snapped his fingers, and one by-one, the cows winked into non-existence. "No more calves. No more procreation. Soon, the country's cattle population will be extinct."

The field disappeared, leaving Theo's hologram alone in the middle of the room.

"Bioengineered population controls have been used in the past to great success. As early as the 2020s, billions of bioengineered mosquitos were released across the Americas to sterilize the disease-carrying *Aedis Aegypti*, and eventually, we wiped out dengue fever and zika as a result. But when genetic population controls have been considered on mammals, science has balked."

Jae nodded as if to say, *No shit*.

"But our goal isn't the extinction of the world's cattle but a precise, drastic reduction. Until now, the available genetic engineering technologies couldn't deliver that level of precision control. But with RID, we can remotely alter the DNA of every live, adult cow on earth. As far as farmers are concerned, RID will keep their cattle happy and healthy — until they try to break the law and exceed their livestock limits. Then —" Theo snapped his fingers. "We do what we must to protect the planet."

From there on out, Theo rattled on in bioengineer technobabble Rylla couldn't understand. Her interest did catch as he was thanking his collaborators on the design proposal, naming Tavia Jones, Dae-Dae Ogunaike-Rosenbaum, and Azam Tehrani.

Rylla felt a little hurt that her friends had been in on this proposal and none of them had mentioned it to her. Maybe Theo had thought that even *talking* about it to a Humanity major would jinx his chances. But at least this time, Theo's idea had been useful. She wondered if he'd gotten the idea for RID from her — from that time she said she'd "violate international treaties' for a bite of cheese."

After the presentation ended, Jae spoke first. "That's a hard pass right?"

Ynez nodded, but Magenta furrowed their brow.

"I have to be honest that I didn't catch all that," they said. "What *is* this RID-doohickey, exactly?"

"It's an implant, right?" Rylla said, feeling proud to have caught more than Magenta for once. "So a medical device — like a pacemaker, or an exo-spine — only it's a tiny implant, that sits beneath the cow's skin."

"But why was he talking about viruses? I thought bio-engineering viruses was illegal?"

"*Retro*viruses," Ynez clarified. "Retroviral gene therapy has been used since the early 2000s to fight disease — even in humans. It's a common cancer treatment today. The science of using retroviruses to alter an adult organism's genes isn't new or groundbreaking."

"Okay, so then what's so special about RID?" Magenta asked.

"Retroviral gene therapies are costly, and you have to go into a hospital to get them," Ynez said. "Not really worthwhile to use on the world's cows."

"Right," Rylla said. "But he's saying that now — because of nanotechnology — we can make an implant you stick in a cow, and then it can print these retroviral gene therapies whenever you want."

"So basically a gene-scrambling device?" Magenta asked, eyebrows raised.

"Exactly," Jae said, running his hands through his hair. "Which is why it's an obviously terrible idea! It doesn't take a genius to realize this could have all kinds of terrifying applications — on *humans!*"

"Consider this," Watt said, "if RID could sterilize every cow on earth, Professor Pupala says that *alone* could push back X-Day by five hundred years."

Magenta whistled. Everyone was thoughtful for a few hushed moments.

"I'm still with Jae." Ynez said. "An implant that can be triggered remotely to change an animal's DNA? That technology shouldn't exist."

"I don't trust dragon-boy to bioengineer viruses —" Magenta began.

"*Retro*viruses," Ynez corrected again.

"Whatever. I still don't trust him."

"Now *y'all* sound like primitivists," Rylla said quietly.

Jae rounded on her. "Don't tell me you think RID is a good idea?"

"I don't know," she said, raising her hands defensively. The last time Jae, Ynez, and Magenta had glared at her like this, she'd gotten them all tarred and feathered. She didn't want to look ignorant in front of them again, but she wasn't going to lie about what she thought. "All I'm saying is — food is *powerful*. When I'm around cheese, my body is like *GIMME THAT CHEESE*. When I ate meat in Camelot, I knew it was wrong, but — ugh ..." She dropped her cheek to her palm and smiled dreamily. "It was just so good. I didn't care."

"And your point is?" Magenta asked.

"My point is I think Theo's right. People won't stop eating meat on their own, at least not enough of them to prevent X-Day. Politicians aren't doing any good either. So maybe scientists *should* take a more direct approach. Wipe out all the cows if they have to. If it'll give us another couple centuries of life on Earth? How is this even a question?" She folded her arms and scowled at the table, hardly believing the words that had come out of her mouth. Just a month ago, she'd been a budding primitivist. Now she was defending a DNA-scrambling implant.

"And that's *really* what you think?" Jae asked, looking at her with derision.

"Yes."

"And you're not letting your *feelings* for Theo Reyes influence your judgment?" he taunted.

Rylla scoffed in outraged confusion — what did Jae know about her feelings for Theo?

"Jae, what are you insinuating, exactly?" Professor Watt asked, frowning.

"They eat together — every meal in the Grove," Jae said, unwilling to meet Rylla's eyes. "So they have some kind of relationship —"

"He's a *friend*," Rylla said, shooting eye-daggers at Jae. "But that has nothing to do with how I feel about this project. Didn't I vote against his last proposal? And y'all made fun of me for being a primitivist! Well maybe my mind has expanded, all right? Isn't that what you wanted? Professor Pupala says this can push back X-Day by *centuries*. Isn't that the point of this whole school? Isn't that everything?"

Ynez pursed her lips and looked away. Jae shook his head, exasperated. Chewing their lip, Magenta muttered, "I still don't think we should let dragon boy work on viruses — retro or not."

Watt clapped once to grab their attention. "You've all made good points." She rubbed her hands together. "However, the research committee took the same stance as Rylla."

The others cried out in surprise. Rylla gaped at the professor in disbelief. She'd disagreed with everyone and been *right?*

"The applications for RID are too exciting not to explore. Besides livestock controls, RID can be used to target invasive animal populations that are destroying ecosystems. It may have therapeutic use in combating cancers in whales and genetic diseases in other wild species that are too close to extinction to have a healthy gene pool. And so, Mr. Reyes will be developing his Retroviral Implantation Device. Although, I assure you, he'll do so under the *strictest* supervision this school can offer."

Rylla had a hunch that meant he'd be working in Ward 7. Theo was going to be thrilled.

28

The Board

When Rylla got back to her dorm, the "hair of the dog" tam had worn off, and she felt like a wrung-out rag. Her muscles ached like she'd run for miles, her head was pounding, and she could barely keep her eyes open. Finally, she had some privacy to mourn for Jo, but no tears came. She knew Jo was dead in an abstract way, but her heart felt empty.

She decided to check the Dark Net news about the Dust, hoping to find some information about the prison deaths. But all the headlines were dominated by another story.

"Dust Liberation Army" Delivers Ultimatum to President Kraft

Dust Liberation Army Claims Responsibility for Raids on Water Storage Facility.

Thousands of Weapons Stolen from Military Base: DLA Suspected

Scrounger gangs from all over the Dust States had banded together, calling themselves the Dust Liberation Army. The DLA was demanding open borders with the Lush States, free water, and 50 50 representation in Congress. In San Antonio, soldiers on a military base had defected to the DLA and stolen a bunch of weapons. Now the DLA was playing Robin Hood, hijacking water trucks and distributing the rations for free. Local police were outgunned, so President Kraft had called in the National Guard to protect water shipments. More than one journalist wondered whether the Dust and Lush States were headed for civil war.

After her last harsh exchange with Tyler, Rylla had a sinking feeling that her brother was involved.

A knock sounded on the door. Without looking away from the article she was reading, she swiped a hand to unlock it, assuming Dae-Dae or Azam were paying a visit.

But a deeper voice said, "I've got something for you."

Rylla shook her head to clear the browser window and found Theo standing over her. Theo was in her room.

"The algorithm caught something interesting last night. You've got to see this," he said, eyes sparkling.

"Watt's holowall?"

He held a finger to his lips. "Shhh — hang on a sec." He pressed a hand to the holowall, and code streamed across the holographic surface. His MANIs blurred as blocks of text shifted over the screen. After a few moments, he turned to her and tsk-tsked. "You didn't have ProfBlock installed on your holowall? What were you thinking?"

She shrugged, hoping she hadn't said anything compromising in her dorm over the last few months. "You seem like you're in a good mood," she said.

"You haven't heard!" He grinned. "My research proposal was fully funded!"

"No kidding," she said, trying to look surprised. "Congratulations."

"Even better — I'll be working in Ward 7."

Rylla forced her eyebrows up, as if this was news to her. "So now that you've got access, are you gonna tell me what Sentinel is?"

"Of course — if I find out. From what I can tell, even once you have access to Ward 7, security there is tightly controlled.

It's not like I can just pop into everyone else's labs and be like, 'hey whatcha working on?'"

Rylla wondered how much tam she'd have to take to feel as giddy as he seemed right now. "So, are you gonna tell me why you're here?" she asked.

"Right!" He dropped down next to her on the bed. Noticing the Choklit Crisp crumbs next to his hand, Rylla wished she'd washed her sheets more often. "Watt made a phone call to some of the Wingates Board members last night, and — well, you should see it." He typed something, and the holowall glowed to life.

The vid captured a conference call between Watt and three people. At first glance, all three looked young and pretty — like they could be in holofilms — but after a moment, she saw there was something *off* about them. Their pale skin was too smooth. Their hair lay too perfectly. And their movements were too abrupt and precise. Suddenly she knew who they reminded her of — Theo's friend, Zhenya. But unlike him, their synth skin wasn't in patches, but covering their entire bodies, and she had a hunch it wasn't just their spines that were cybernetic.

"What the hell are they?" she asked. "Robots? Cyborgs?"

Theo laughed. "No, no — they're just ancient. Kaylee Jaxx, there on the left, she was a pop star in the 2030's. She's eighty now. Tom Waltrip, the guy in the middle, he's in is seventies. And Sergei on the end is a hundred and ten. Their bodies are mostly synth by now — but listen, their voices give them away."

As if on cue, Kaylee growled, "Can we get started?" Her skin might have looked twenty-one, but she had a gravelly voice, and an old-timey accent. "I've got a facial tensioning at five."

"Thank you for joining," Watt said. "I have the updated budget projections for our third quarter." Something in her voice was strange, and it took Rylla a second to realize the professor sounded *nervous*. Watt launched into an explanation of the school's financials — seventeen million dollars going to this department, twenty million going to that.

"Is this it?" she whispered to Theo after a few minutes, feeling bored and disappointed. "I assumed Wingates was spending a ton of money —"

"Just wait," he said.

Rylla studied the board members. Her mother had been a fan of Kaylee Jaxx as a kid, and Rylla had seen some of her old music vids. But now her face looked distorted, like a playdough sculpture of her younger self. She dressed like a teenager, with hot pink moss-extensions and one of those fuzzy sweatshirts that pulsed in time with her heartbeat.

Tom Waltrip, the Chairman of the Board, had plastic-surgeried himself to look middle-aged, with a perfect stripe of gray hair at each temple. He wore a simple suit, which probably cost more than Rylla's hometown. The mahogany bookcase behind him was filled with ancient paper-books bound in what looked like animal skin.

Sergei, the hundred-ten-year-old treasurer, wore a simple black t-shirt stretched over massive — and probably synthetic — biceps. When he spoke, his jacked-up muscles clashed grotesquely with his trembling, feeble voice.

They were wrapping up the conversation, and Rylla was starting to wonder what the hell Theo had found interesting about this call, when Tom Waltrip asked, "Incidentally, Alexandra, how's my daughter doing?"

Theo nudged Rylla, as if to say *This is it.*

"Your *child* is doing well," Watt paused. "They're getting closer to understanding the necessity of the Manifest. But we're still building an ethical framework."

Rylla shot Theo a confused look, and he just shrugged.

On the holovid, Kaylee Jaxx sighed with annoyance. "Why do we have to wait for this 'framework?'" She traced air quotes. "Just tell them what's up and be done with it."

"We've gone over this, Vice-Chair," Watt said. "If students determine the necessity of the Manifest *on their own*, they're far more likely to accept it. Must I remind you that students who've rejected our plans have caused ... *difficulties*?"

Something in Watt's tone sent a chill up Rylla's spine.

"I'm not questioning your methods," Tom Waltrip said. "But is there any chance she'll 'get it' by Thanksgiving? Her mother would love to have Mary home for the holidays."

"I can't give you an exact timeline," Watt said, clearly irritated. "And I don't see why you expect knowledge of the Manifest to repair your relationship with your child."

Tom waved a hand dismissively. "Once she 'gets it,' she'll understand I'm not the monster she thinks I am. Can't you hurry it up?"

Rylla noticed the difference in the pronouns Tom and Watt were using — *she* and *they*. It was like how she always had to correct Amaryllis over Jo's pronouns.

"Introducing students to the Manifest is a delicate process," Watt said. "They have to understand the science and sociology and firmly grasp cataclysm ethics. Be patient. Thanks to the addition of the Texan, your child's seminar is now complete. They're all coming along, though I expect the two Dusties will have the hardest time accepting the Manifest."

Rylla clutched Theo's arm. Was she "the Texan?" That would make her and Jae the "two Dusties." And that meant this "Mary" was — Magenta?

Kaylee Jaxx made a disgusted noise. "I don't see why we have to use Dusties at all."

"We've been over this, Jaxx. Honestly, sometimes I think you're more senile than me," Sergei said, in his trembling voice. "There are critical assets in the Dust. We'll need ambassadors to secure them."

Kaylee snorted. "What could the Dust possibly have that we need?"

"I really must stop you there," Watt interrupted. "We can never assume these long-distance calls are secure. I will update you on the details of our top-security projects *in person* at our next Board meeting."

Sergei tilted his head. "Is General Dorne still being a pest then?"

"No," Watt said. "She understands what's at stake, and I don't think she'll make trouble anymore. But we never know who might be listening in — Siberians, Saudis ..."

"Your own students," Theo whispered.

The call ended, and the dorm room was suddenly dim without the glow of the holowall. Rylla stared at Magenta's bed as her vision adjusted — Magenta, her roommate, offspring of the Chairman of the Board of Wingates.

"What the hell is the Manifest?" Rylla breathed. Theo was staring down at her hand — still clutching his arm, like it was the one steady thing in a world whirling uncontrollably. Embarrassed, she let go and folded her arms tightly. "Watt's using me. I'm supposed to be an 'ambassador' and 'secure critical assets' in the Dust. What does that *mean?*"

"I have no idea," he said. "But we're going to find out."

He smiled at her then, and she felt a rush of gratitude. Jo was dead, Tyler hated her, and Watt was part of some sinister club of rich geezers. But at least Theo was on her side. Brilliant, boy-genius Theo. Here, on her bed. And as she held his gaze, something electric charged the air. Either lightning was about to arc between them, or he was going to —

He shot up and paced the room. "We need to find out more about this Manifest. There's got to be data on it stored on the Humanity department's servers, but I don't know where they're kept, and my hacking skills probably aren't good enough to crack them. We need a comp sci major we can trust."

At that moment, the door hissed open and Magenta strode in. When they saw Theo, they froze in shock, then winked at Rylla.

"Don't mind me," they said, grabbing a paperbook off their bed. "Didn't realize you had a friend over."

"No, it's not like that —" Rylla blushed. Theo arched an eyebrow at her. His MANIs blurred against his hip, and a text from him popped up in her vision.

Tom Waltrip's kid might have answers. Can we trust them?

Rylla considered it. Magenta might be rude, inconsiderate, and slightly terrifying, but they were also the most honest person Rylla had ever met. Like Theo had said, they might have answers. And she had a hunch Magenta wouldn't mind taking some risks to uncover the truth.

"Do you have ProfBlock on your OGlenses?" Rylla asked.

Magenta shot her a withering look. "Of course."

"Let's say, hypothetically, that Theo and I had uncovered a creepy conspiracy between Professor Watt and your dad. Would you want in on it?"

Magenta grinned wider than Rylla had ever seen. "Oh, hell yes."

They caught Magenta up on their spying and let them watch the holovid of the board meeting. Magenta growled every time their dad misgendered them.

"I'm starting to see why you thought Watt sent us on some 'secret mission' to Camelot," Magenta said as the vid ended.

"Right?" Rylla cried, feeling a delicious satisfaction.

"But I don't have a clue what this 'Manifest' is. I know lots of Humanity majors, though. I'll try to ask around without drawing attention."

"See if you can find out where the Humanity department's servers are kept," Theo said.

"Servers?"

"The physical machines that store our OGnet data. If we can hack into them, I have a hunch we'll find out more about this Manifest."

"Should we ask Ynez?" Rylla suggested. "She's so good at research ... it's like she can find out anything. Maybe she can hack the servers?

"Are you kidding?" Magenta blurted. "She's such a goody two-shoes — she'd snitch to Watt in a second. And Jae's a golden boy too, so don't go telling him."

Theo shook his head. "Even *I* can't crack a Wingates server. We'll need a real hacker."

As she struggled to fall asleep that night, Rylla's brain wouldn't shut off. What if Watt got past ProfBlock and knew what she, Theo, and Magenta were up to? What if this Manifest was something seriously evil? What if Watt was brainwashing her to be part of her nefarious plans?

She longed for the simplicity of her old life, of smash band concerts with Tyler and Jo. With vivid clarity, she remembered a night they'd stayed up late watching Kung Fu flatvids. She was maybe twelve or thirteen years old. Jo and Tyler had fallen asleep, cuddled on the couch, and she'd gotten the feeling that the two of them were her *real* parents — the loving, competent caregivers she'd never had. It was the safest and happiest she could ever remember feeling.

Now, Jo was gone. She tossed and turned, tortured by grief and worries. Everyone at Wingates had their own agenda, and there was no one here she could trust. Her brother was lost to her — and probably involved with a rebellion that would get him killed. Her thoughts grew darker and darker, until the world and everything in it seemed full of despair.

And then she remembered the baggie Magenta had given her, with the power to make her feel instantly better. Fishing it out of her uniform shirt on the floor, she dug inside and swiped a bit of tam inside her cheek. A few glittering moments later, she finally fell asleep.

29

Dead Water

All the next week, it rained. When the first thunderstorm hit, Rylla stood out in the meadows beneath the emptying clouds until her clothes were soaked through, in awe of what the sky was capable of. She had never experienced anything like it back home, where the showers that fell once or twice a year were brief cloudbursts that immediately evaporated. After a few days though, the rain began to feel oppressive. In the ground-level classrooms, rain drumming on the solar mesh rooftops was as incessant and repetitive as the questions running through her mind. *What's Watt up to? What is the Manifest? Is Tyler in the DLA? Can I trust anyone?*

She'd used tam a few more times, sneaking a hit between classes when she couldn't relax enough to think straight. When she swiped the last grains of glittering dust from inside the baggie, she felt mingled relief and regret. It scared her how quickly she'd come to rely on the stuff to keep her mood steady. Better it's gone, she thought, chucking the baggie in the trash and promising herself she'd never eat another crystal.

Humanity seminar had always been her favorite part of the week — the one class where she didn't feel like an ignoramus. But during their next seminar, she couldn't look at Magenta, because she was worried she'd somehow give away their secret. She felt too guilty to look at Jae and Ynez, knowing she was keeping a massive conspiracy from them. And looking at Watt, she had to fight the urge to shout, *Tell me what the Manifest is! What 'assets' are you using me to 'secure' in the Dust?*

Strained by the performance, Rylla was dying to get out of class when time was up, but Watt had one last announcement. "It's time to decide on your next field trip. You don't have to go to the French Alps to learn about humanity. We'll stick close to home this time, exploring how people stave off Gotterdammerungangst here in Detroit. So," she clapped her hands, "start researching different communities. In two weeks, you'll present on where we should embed, and I'll choose the best proposal."

Rylla caught Magenta's eye and they shared a questioning look. Why did Watt want them staying in Detroit? How would this prepare them to learn about the Manifest?

※

On Saturday, Rylla was headed to the Humanity building for her work/study, when she got a message from her supervisor, Hoshiko. The entire sanitation crew was to meet on the West Lawn for a "special assignment."

A dozen students she'd never met stood around awkwardly, as Hoshiko pulled up in a hovervan. "Hop in," he said out the window. "We're going to Crystal Lake. The chemistry department wants groundwater samples."

"Crystal Lake? Isn't that dead water?" someone demanded. Rylla's breath caught in her throat. Dead water sites were radioactive — too polluted to use for tens of thousands of years.

"Don't worry," Hoshiko said in a patronizing voice. "You won't be collecting samples with your *bare hands.*" The students laughed nervously. "If we're in and out in two hours, we'll get less than 5 millisieverts of radiation. That's like half a CT scan." As the students reluctantly piled into the back of the van, Hoshiko grumbled as if to himself, "Though the kid's got a point. Patron students would never have to do this."

Rylla took the seat behind Hoshiko's. "What do you mean?" she asked as he set the vehicle's auto-pilot. "About patrons?" She remembered Magenta explaining that they were a patron — someone whose parents paid for their kid to attend Wingates.

"Patron students don't have to do work/study," Hoshiko sneered. "But us scholarship kids? Send us into the nuclear meltdown! Who cares? What's a few millisieverts to us poor folk?"

"We're going to a nuclear meltdown?"

"An old one," Hoshiko said. "Thirty years ago, a storage tank cracked at a nuclear reactor on Crystal Lake, leaked a bunch of radioactive fuel. It's been a dead water site ever since." He climbed into the back of the van. "Get dressed," he said, opening a storage compartment filled with HazMat suits.

Rylla took one of the heavy suits off its hook and climbed into it. "This feels like it's made of lead."

"It is," Hoshiko explained. "Lead fibers, ion-repulsing magnets. They're a pain to work in, but they'll save you from sprouting a bunch of tumors."

She double-checked the seals on her gloves.

The van slowed as they reached a row of towering pylons stretching to the horizon on either side of the road. Rusting signs were bolted to each one — the symbol for radiation, a skull, and warnings in ten languages. The pylons emitted an ominous hum.

"What are those things?"

"Giant e-mags," Hoshiko said. "The magnetic field underground here is strong enough to stop your heart. Water holds a magnetic charge, so the pylons are supposed to keep the contaminated groundwater from leaking into the land around the lake, but it still *sort of* does." He shrugged. "That's why Wingates has a closed water system." He raised his voice to address everyone. "We're about to enter the containment field. Helmets on."

He sent them all a dosimeter app — a meter appeared in the upper-right-hand corner of her vision, with three colors — green, yellow, and red.

"Make sure the needle stays in the green," Hoshiko said ominously.

They unloaded their drones in a cracked asphalt parking lot. A cement boat ramp led down, not to the edge of a lake, but straight into the side of a hill covered in scraggly grass. Husks of dead trees stood all around the edges of the hill, obscuring the remains of old houses — a wall choked with ivy, a chimney standing in the midst of blackened rubble.

"Where's the lake?" Rylla asked. Her voice came out tinny through the helmet's speaker.

"Down there." Hoshiko pointed beneath the base of the hill. "The lake was so radioactive that they covered it with cement. And then, since this place was already uninhabitable, they dumped a bunch of trash on top."

"So, basically Crystal Lake is a hill of toxic garbage?" she asked in horror.

"Yep, and it's real weird under there. A mixed-up goo of battery acids, heavy metals, plastics, all melted together in a radioactive stew. The chemistry department's trying to figure out how to clean it, or at least do a better job containing it."

"I heard even a drop on your finger would kill you," someone said. Rylla looked down at her gloved hands, and her stomach twisted into knots.

None of them were to step foot on Crystal Lake, as sinkholes had been known to suck unsuspecting deer to their doom. Instead, Hazbot drones would collect their samples in heavy, lead canisters.

Hoshiko paired them off and sent Rylla and her partner to collect soil samples along the eastern shore. With each step she took towards the barren hill, the needle of her dosimeter crept closer towards the yellow. The lifeless limbs of the dead forest clawed at the overcast sky pressing on their heads.

Unloading the lead canisters, hooking them to the HazBot, and reloading them was sweaty work. Soon the ledi-glass visor of Rylla's helmet steamed up. She could barely see, and her clothes were drenched in sweat.

I'm cooking inside this suit, she thought —

And then she remembered Jo. Literally cooked alive in an overheated prison cell. Dizzying grief flooded through her, and she stumbled, landing on the cracked soil.

"You okay?" Her partner's voice sounded far away, but maybe that was just the helmet.

"Yeah," she said, getting to her feet. "I think —" she tried to take a deep, steadying breath, but she couldn't pull in any air. She tried again, sucking in a long breath, but her lungs wouldn't fill. "Something's wrong," she wheezed. "Something's wrong with my oxygen supply!"

"Stay here. I'll get Hoshiko."

"No!" she gasped, terrified of being left alone beside the radioactive hill. "No, I — I have to get out of here." She took off stumbling in a beeline back to the hovervan. Her partner shouted at her to wait.

She tripped over a tree root and fell, hard, to the forest's floor. She got up, pawing at her suit to check for tears. Brightly-colored spots clouded her vision. She ran up the ramp into the van and collapsed onto her knees.

If she took her helmet off, she'd breathe in airborne radioactive particles. If she kept it on, she was going to suffocate. She could already feel consciousness slipping away. Her hands scrambled at the seal on the front of the helmet.

Two hands clamped her wrists. "What the fuck do you think you're doing?" Hoshiko shouted. "You have a death wish or something?"

"I ... can't ... breathe," she choked out.

"Yes. You can."

"No ... I ... can't!" Tears and bright spots blotted out Hoshiko's face. She was heartbeats away from losing consciousness.

"You can!" he said firmly. He twiddled his fingers before her face. "I'm hacking into your vital signs, okay? Look at that. You're HYPERventilating. Too much oxygen in your blood, not too little. Just calm down. Breathe slower."

Tears streaming down her face, Rylla forced herself to take a long, slow breath. Then another. "T — too *much* oxygen?" she stammered. "So there's nothing wrong with my air supply?"

"There's nothing wrong," he said. "You're just panicking."

The spots cleared from Rylla's vision as her breathing slowed. A crowd of students had gathered outside the van, and Hoshiko ordered them back to work. Then he sat back on his heels, watching her breathing return to normal.

"Did you really hack my vital signs?" she asked.

He snorted a laugh. "No, I just said that because I know what a panic attack looks like. These suits are pretty claustrophobic, huh?"

She tilted a head to one side. "Okay, but *could* you hack someone's vital signs? Is that even a thing?"

He leaned back against the wall of the van. "Yeah, sure. OGlenses collect biometric data, and I could code a spyware program to transmit that info. But it would take more than a few seconds. Then I'd have to get it installed on your OGLenses — which would mean either you giving me access to your settings, or hacking your account." His eyes glazed over and his MANIs blurred with typing.

"Hey! Cut it out!" Rylla cried, as her vision clouded with code. Kyle appeared, stretching his gray wings to the sky in warning, saying that an external user was attempting to access her settings. Did she authorize this user?

"No!" she shouted.

Pixelated slices of Kyle's wings glitched in and out of existence. Then her vision cleared and Hoshiko was laughing, squatting on the van's floor in front of her.

"You have ProfBlock installed," he said. "That's good for keeping out professors, but bad for keeping out *me,* because I wrote the latest patch. Another five minutes, and I'd've had full access to your OGlenses, settings, data —" He held up his hands to Rylla's scowl. "Don't worry, I'm not gonna do it. But you should really beef up your OGnet security."

Rylla tried to stand, but the world tilted wildly, and she thought better of it. "What would've happened if my oxygen supply *had* broken?"

He shrugged. "Good thing it didn't, huh?" He shook his head at the HazMat-clad students loading up lead canisters on the shore of Crystal Lake. "Patron kids would never get sent out here. They treat us scholarships like our lives are disposable."

Hadn't Theo said they needed a comp sci major? A skilled hacker who could crack into the Humanity department servers? Hoshiko was both, and he clearly had a bone to pick with Wingates.

She tapped out a text to Theo and Magenta.

I think I've found our hacker.

30

The Sunken Tanker

When she got back to the dorm, Rylla still felt shaky from her panic attack at Crystal Lake. As she sat down at the edge of her bed, Kyle appeared on her knee and announced an incoming call from her mother. She hadn't talked to Amaryllis since their fight in Camelot, but mom might have news about Tyler. Bracing herself, Rylla expanded the call bubble.

Amaryllis was shouting as soon as her face materialized. "He did it, Sassy, your goddamn brother. I know it's him. They call him a terrorist. They're right! A murderer to boot."

"What? — Mom — MOM! I don't know what you're talking about."

"The explosion!" Amaryllis shouted.

Rylla pulled up a browser and searched Dust State news. Every site was dominated with headlines about a bombing. At the Lockburn refinery.

12 Dead. Dozens injured. Dust Liberation Army claims responsibility for the blast.

Rylla skimmed the reports, heart in her throat, as her mother railed against Tyler, wishing he'd never been born. Rylla opened a holovid of the explosion — a massive fireball, shooting a mile into the sky. The oil fields were still burning, blackening the sky over New Braunfels.

"Well, is it him? Is it Tyler?" Amaryllis demanded. "Is he part of this *DLA*?"

Rylla shook her head. "I don't know ..." But she had a sick feeling in her gut. Tyler had seemed so changed and so very angry the last time they'd talked.

"I got a pink mention from Lockburn. Twenty-five years working for them, and they've fired me! What the hell am I supposed to do now?"

"Mom, I'm so sorry."

"Can you still get me that visa to France? I got no desire to be a frog, but I don't know how I'm gonna pay for rations without a job."

"I can't, Mom." Sudden tears stung her eyes. "I screwed that up. I'm so sorry."

"Course you did." Amaryllis rolled her eyes. "What'd I tell you about being nice to everyone? Especially those rich kids?" She shot Rylla a withering look. "Well, don't worry about me. Your mom'll survive this somehow. I always do." She stared into space. When she spoke again, her voice trembled. "He could've killed me, Sassy. He had no way of knowing I wasn't on shift." Her voice cracked, and she fell silent. Then she shook her head, and her tone abruptly hardened. "Study hard, you hear me? Get you a good job and buckets of money, so you don't end up like your mother."

Rylla opened her mouth to say something comforting, but the bubble containing her mom's face vanished.

For long minutes she sat frozen, staring at a crack in the tile floor. Could it be true? Could Tyler have carried out this bombing? Certainly, he'd always hated Lockburn, more than ever since they started damming up the river. But the people killed in the explosion weren't the executives who decided to build the dam. They were workers, like her mother. Neighbors they'd known all their lives. Was it possible Tyler was so far gone that he saw them as the enemy? Or did their lives not matter to him anymore?

Rylla ached to talk to him. To have her big brother assure her that he wasn't a bomber, and everything was going to be okay. But she had no way to reach him. Now her mother was out of work, with no way to pay for water rations, and Rylla was powerless to help either of them.

The anxious feeling she'd gotten by the shore of Crystal Lake tightened like a band across her chest.

The door hissed, and Magenta entered, back from dinner. "You want to go out again tonight?" they asked, stripping off their uniform shirt. "Some smash bands are playing the sunken oil tanker. You can tell me about this hacker you found."

"I — I can't," Rylla stammered. "I've got to start on that research for Watt."

"This *is* research!" Magenta said. "We're supposed to investigate different communities in Detroit, right? So let's go investigate. You want to get to know people? Don't read about them on your OGlenses. Party with them."

It had been so easy to lose herself in the performances at the Velvet Underground — especially with a beer in one hand and a crystal on her tongue. Rylla had promised herself not to do any more tam. And she wouldn't, but the beer might be nice. And the thought of spending all night in the dorm, freaking out about who Tyler may or may not have bombed, made her want to jump out of her skin.

So she borrowed some of Magenta's clothes again, and they headed into the city. This time they drove straight to Lake Erie, then under it, through a tunnel to a sunken ship, sealed off and pumped full of air. The Sunken Tanker groaned under the weight of the water around it, and the interior walls were rusty and covered in ancient barnacles. Rylla tried not to think about what would happen if the ship sprung a leak.

She had a beer, and then another, but the alcohol didn't settle the anxiety crawling in her veins. She tried dancing with

Magenta and some of their cool Detroit friends, but she felt awkward and miserable. Coming here had been a mistake.

But then the lip-ring person appeared — the one she'd made out with at the Velvet Underground. Rylla wanted to find out what their name and pronouns were, but couldn't ask without revealing she'd forgotten — or never known? — what they were. And when they offered Rylla a crystal of tam, it seemed rude not to accept. She put the crystal on her tongue, and within moments, her worries evaporated and all that mattered was the music vibrating in her bones.

Rylla danced with Lip-ring for a bit, but they wandered off, and she was okay with that. She talked and danced with plenty of strange people, but strangest of all was an ageless person with a shaved-bald head. Everyone else was dressed to impress with clean makeup and elaborate clothes, but the bald person wore patched, brown robes. They smiled up at the smash band on stage, swaying to the music.

"You look so happy," Rylla shouted over the music. "Whatever drug you're on, I want some!"

The person laughed, the skin at the corners of their eyes crinkling, revealing they were much older than Rylla had guessed. "I'm not *on* anything," they said, luminously. "Nothing but the Way of the Waste."

The person was a Wastrel. Rylla had heard of the religion before, but it wasn't popular in the Dust. The nun introduced herself as "Sister Fun Guy," which made Rylla burst into giggles. Sister Fun Guy didn't seem to mind.

The rest of the night blurred together — dances, drinks, and hits of tam melting on her tongue. When consciousness returned, she was back in her dorm, lying in bed as the room whirled around her, trying to remember what she'd talked about with Sister Fun Guy. It had all seemed vitally important at the time. But like trying to remember the details of a dream, her memories on tam slipped through her fingers the moment she sobered up.

Waking the next morning, her head screamed, her stomach lurched, and she only had ten minutes until her first class. As she peeled off the sweat-drenched glitter-pants she'd fallen asleep in, she felt a lump in the pocket — a baggie of tam she'd somehow acquired the night before. She considered dumping it in the toilet, but that seemed wasteful. So she stuck it in the pocket of her uniform shirt before heading out the door.

With every step she took towards the climate lab, dread rooted in her chest. The light streaming through the windows felt sharp and cold, and every passing student had something sinister lurking behind their eyes. Did they know about the Manifest? Did they work in Ward 7? Was everyone at Wingates part of Watt's conspiracy, working towards some evil plan that only *she* was oblivious to?

By the time she reached Ward 4, her blood was pumping so hard, it felt like it would burst from her veins. She ducked into an empty classroom and leaned against the wall. Unconsciously, her hand found its way to her pocket.

This terrible feeling was probably just because she'd taken too much tam last night. She needed a teeny bit more — what had Magenta called it? "Hair of the dog?" Enough to take the sharp edges off the world. There was no way she could face Professor Pupala with nerves like this.

So she crushed a bit and swiped it inside her cheek. A moment later, her chest unclenched and her headache dissolved. As she stepped out into the glittering light of the corridor, she realized Wingates wasn't evil — how could a place so beautiful be evil? And Watt must have a good explanation for everything, and Tyler couldn't be a terrorist — and what could be so wrong about taking a bit of tam now and then to remind herself that the world was excellent?

For the next few weeks, Rylla swiped some tam every time she felt another panic attack coming on. When her stash ran low, she'd ask Magenta to take another trip to Detroit. Magenta asked her once, warily, if she was using tam. "It can be dangerous you know — very addictive stuff. And too many crystals can kill you." But Rylla assured them she was only using a teensy bit to sleep at night.

One night, she met up with Magenta and Theo in Hoshiko's dorm room — a single he got all to himself. The desk was cluttered with four monitors, a jumble of humming electronics, and tangles of wires. The walls were plastered with vintage propaganda posters from various Communist regimes — all stern faces in red, black, and gold — and his bookshelf was filled with yellowed paperbooks of leftist theory.

Rylla was sitting on the edge of his bed, bouncing a knee furiously and waiting for their meeting to end so she could get back to her dorm, where she'd left her baggie. A nagging voice at the back of her mind said, *"You're doing it more and more. This isn't good. Remember what it was like when mom got hooked on this shit?"* But she shook her head to chase those thoughts away.

"I found out where the Humanity department server is stored," Magenta said. "Just had to post a pic with a weaselly PhD candidate to get the info. He wanted to make his ex jealous." Magenta shook their head ruefully.

"Where?" Theo asked from where he leaned against the wall.

"Hold on, I wrote it down," Magenta's eyes blurred and they swiped something mid-air. "In the 'clean room' on the fifth subfloor of Ward 3."

"That's not good," Hoshiko said, folding his arms over the back of his desk chair. "The fifth subfloor of Ward 3 has some of the tightest security on campus. That's where they keep all the hardware for the school's power regulation and environmental controls."

"What's a clean room?" Rylla asked.

"Exactly what it sounds like," Hoshiko explained. "A totally sterile environment, to protect all the most important electronic systems at Wingates. They're pretty uptight about letting even a single mote of *dust* in there. Needless to say, getting in will be a challenge.*"*

"If we *can* get you inside, will you be able to hack the server?" Theo asked.

Hoshiko grinned. "So, funny story. The senior faculty — they haven't understood my code, not *really,* since I was in the lower school. But they know it's on another level than anything they can come up with. They've been stealing my work for years, using my protocols on every critical system in the school, even though they don't understand half of what's in it. And that half they don't understand? It's like ... you could call them trap-doors, ones only I can use. For things like ProfBlock. We can't let the professors have too much power over students, now can we?"

"Certainly not," Rylla said, glancing up at a holo-poster of Vladimir Lenin pointing towards the future, his coattails flapping in a digital breeze. "So you're saying you can hack it?"

"Probably. The problem will be getting *inside* the clean room. Only tenured professors have access to that subfloor. And once I'm there, I can't just march up to the servers and start messing with them. We'll need some kind of cover."

"Like what?" Rylla asked.

Theo, pacing by the holowall, stopped suddenly. "Chaos," he said, with a slow smile. "Lots and lots of chaos."

31

The Clean Room

Rylla's heart raced as the clock in the corner of her vision ticked closer to 8:37 PM. That was when Professor Tuan Amari, department head of computer science, usually crossed the first-floor atrium after his office hours ended. Rylla sprawled at one of the tables that lined the edges of the atrium, pretending to do nightwork like the other dozen students still working this late in the evening. In reality, she was double-checking the feeds of all the cleaning drones on this floor and trying to stave off another panic attack. By the end of the night, they'd either have Watt's top-secret data files in their possession, or they'd be expelled.

Or — if Theo was wrong about the murder hornets — they'd be dead.

Hoshiko had transferred Rylla's work-study assignment from the Humanity building to Ward 3, so she could carry out her part of the plan. Three hover-drones scrubbed the darkened glass dome of the atrium, strategically close to the ventilation ducts they used to travel between sub-floors. Two vacuuming floorbots spun near the elevator, where Professor Amari was soon to emerge, and a floor-waxer was whirling in

slippery circles near the entrance to the western corridor —
where Theo was set to appear.

8:34. A *slam!* nearly made her jump out of her skin, but
the sound was just a student at a nearby table closing an old
paperbook. There was no way she could focus like she needed
to if her nerves were this jumpy. She crushed a bit of tam and
swiped it inside her cheek — choosing a spot that wasn't raw
from overuse. Within moments, her breathing slowed, her
head cleared, and panic dissolved into excitement.

At 8:35, right on cue, Magenta strode into the atrium
through the eastern corridor, loudly talking with two
Humanity majors Rylla didn't know.

Late the night before, as they'd run through the details of
their plan one last time, Magenta had wanted an alibi for being
in the atrium. "Just in case there are questions," they'd said. "I
want witnesses on my side. I'll invite some friends to play a
sim at the arena, and we'll cut through Ward 3 on the way
there."

"But you know what'll happen to your friends, right?"
Theo had said. Magenta had shrugged, and their apathy sent a
chill down Rylla's spine. She had no doubt Magenta would put
her in harm's way too if it meant achieving their goals.

Theo had laughed and said, "Brutal."

8:36. A minute early, the elevator doors slid open, revealing Hoshiko and a slight, middle-aged man wearing a lab coat.
Hoshiko was Professor Amari's TA — and it had been his job to
ensure the professor got to the atrium on time.

Rylla's MANIs flew as she texted Theo — *Go*.

But Theo didn't appear, and Professor Amari was crossing
the atrium too fast. Maybe Theo had gotten hung up securing
the murder hornets for transport? Magenta's friends were
nearly at the far doors, so they dropped to one knee to tighten
a shoelace. Hoshiko laid a hand on the professor's arm to ask
him something — also stalling. But where the hell was Theo?

Rylla's heart clenched — were they going to fail before
they even got started? If Professor Amari left the building,

their plan was shot. But then the western doors burst open, and Theo, whistling casually, pushed a cart laden with a dark crate into the atrium. The crate was dotted with tiny airholes, plastered with warning labels, and buzzing ominously.

Rylla sniffed the skin of her arm, reassured by the faint, chemical stink. Theo had promised that the pheromone lotion would keep the hornets from attacking their group. Praying he was right, Rylla's MANIs flew, and she uploaded the program Hoshiko had coded into the cleaning drone control app. A moment later, the drones all around the room started jerking, sparking, and emitting horrible metallic squeals. Students looked up from their studies at the short-circuiting machines. Rylla could still control the drones, but what mattered was they *looked* like their AI had been corrupted by a virus. Hoshiko had assured her that later, when the drones were investigated, that's what their logs would show — a crudely programmed virus which would appear to be some amateur hacker's prank.

Rylla took control of the erratically-zooming floor waxer near Theo, cranked its speed to max, and smashed it into his cart. The cart tipped over, spilling the crate, and the latch securing the lid — which Theo had made sure was faulty — popped open. The buzzing swelled to a roar, as a cloud of darkness rose from the crate into the air. Someone screamed.

Rylla didn't need to pretend to act frightened. She dove under the table and covered her head with her arms as the first of the huge black-and-yellow hornets tore past. Everyone in the atrium was screaming and running and swiping at their heads. Murder hornet stings weren't usually fatal, but they *were* one of the most painful sensations on Earth. "And we've made them a bit more painful — for riot control purposes," Theo had explained during one of their planning sessions. "Oh, don't look at me like that. It's an effective, bloodless defense system if the school is ever attacked by a mob. And we've altered their DNA to inhibit an anaphylactic response, so they can't *kill* anyone."

But as students shrieked and fled from the swarm of enraged hornets, Rylla was having a hard time believing Theo's assurances. Professor Amari lay slumped against Hoshiko, his face already blooming with distended, purple welts.

As planned, Theo and Magenta were acting out a rehearsed scene for the benefit of the security cameras.

"What are these things?" Magenta cried, swatting at their head.

"Mod hornets!" Theo cried back. "Their sting can't kill you, but it hurts like hell."

He pulled out two aerosol cans from the back of the over-turned crate. "Catch!" he said, tossing one to Magenta. "This should calm them down."

Magenta ran to the panicked people who hadn't escaped the atrium, now howling in agony on the floor, and doused them in pheromone spray. "Let's get you out of here!" they cried. "Follow me!" Their job was to take charge amid the panic, make sure everyone evacuated safely. Meanwhile Theo crossed to Hoshiko and Professor Amari, acting out another planned scene. First, Theo would explain that to subdue the wasps, they needed to lower the temperature to a hibernation-inducing 50 degrees. Then Hoshiko would say that the environmental controls for Ward 3 were in the clean room on the fifth subfloor, but as a lowly grad student, he didn't have access to that floor! Professor Amari mumbled something, hopefully offering them the use of his biometrics. They'd need his palm-print to gain access to the clean room.

Rylla yelped as something touched the back of her neck, but it was just a hand, dragging her out from under the table. "What the hell are you doing?" Magenta hissed in Rylla's ear. "Why aren't the ducts open? The elevators?"

"Fuck," Rylla said. Everything was happening so fast — it'd been just minutes since the cart tipped over — and watching the chaos unfold, she'd forgotten her crucial part in the plan. Her MANIs flew, and she sent a hover drone — still jerking and sparking — zooming for the nearest clump of hornets. She dove it in and out of the swarm, harassing them until bugs were crawling all over it, trying to sting the plastic hull to death. Then she sent the drone zooming for the nearest ventilation duct, which the drones used to move between floors. On her video feed, she watched the drone, pursued by hornets, burst into a robotics lab on the first subfloor. The students within screamed and abandoned their stations.

She sent her other drones to do the same — leading packs of hornets into the corridors beyond and into the elevator.

During their last planning session, Rylla had voiced a nagging worry — by letting the hornets spread throughout the school, wouldn't some of them get outside? What if they established a colony outdoors and wrecked the ecosystem? But Theo had assured her that these mod hornets were sterile and died after 24 hours outside their crate.

As the elevator doors slid shut on a swarm of hornets chasing a Floorbot, she ran for her friends, hunched over.

What was her line? Oh yeah — "I don't know what's wrong with the cleaning drones! They've gone haywire! And they're leading the hornets down to the subfloors!"

"I'll take care of the people up here," Magenta said on cue. "You get everyone below up to the surface."

"Come with us," Hoshiko said, looping one of Professor Amari's arms over his shoulders. Theo tossed Rylla his can of pheromone spray and took Amari's other arm.

"Keep trying to shut down those drones," Hoshiko said, shooting Rylla a sharp look.

"Got it," she said, knowing he really meant, *Use the drones to herd the hornets all the way to the fifth sub-floor!* She had to be sure the hornets reached the clean room, so Hoshiko could use the chaos as cover to download a copy of the Humanity department's server.

For the benefit of the security cameras, Rylla shot her can of pheromone spray at the occasional hornet, as Theo and Hoshiko hauled the semi-conscious professor to the stairwell. On the first sub-floor, Rylla got to play the part of the hero, bursting into rooms filled with screaming people and magically chasing off the hornets with her pheromone spray. The students sobbed their thanks as she led them to the now-cleared stairwell.

At the same time, her right hand drummed against her thigh — controlling the drones to whip the hornets into a frenzy and chase them to ever-lower floors. There were a lot of moving pieces to keep track of, but the plan was working. The people's gratitude when she rescued them made her swell with pride — until she remembered that she had caused the pain and terror she was saving them from. Then, just as she cleared the last students from the fourth sub-floor, something stabbed into the back of her leg.

Pain like nothing she'd ever known ripped through her muscles, pushing out every thought of what she was doing and who she was and exploding from her throat in a blood-curdling scream. Before she knew what was happening, she was writhing on the ground. Her body clenched into a fetal position of its own accord. When she gasped her next inhale, she forced herself to look back — expecting to see someone holding a blowtorch to her leg. On her right calf, where her pant leg had hitched up, an angry welt swelled.

She tried to steady her breathing and focus — there was something she was supposed to be doing here, something important — but the throbbing in her leg was so intense, she couldn't gather her thoughts. All she wanted was for the pain to stop. She would do *anything* to make the pain stop.

And then, with a surge of gratitude, she remembered there *was* something that could take away her pain. Rolling onto her back, she slipped the baggie of tam from her pocket and poured a few crystals into her mouth. Tears sprang to her eyes as relief spread through her body — easing the pain in her leg to a dull ache. All her worries, all her fears, her sense of self, even her name — melted away into the cool tile floor of the fourth sub-basement corridor.

In the air above her, shiny black-and-yellow insects whirled in fractal-shaped formations — no, coordinations — conflagrations. Sketching cryptic patterns in the light-scattered air, their wings buzzed a melody for the end times. At the edges of her vision were windows to other worlds, where people ran screaming from her fleet of tiny robots and the hornets, who only wanted to sing. "Just lie down and listen!" she wanted to tell the fleeing people. But her tongue was too far away to budge.

Someone was leaning over her, roughly shaking her shoulder. Dark hair spilled out around that face she'd always liked so much. What was a face, but hills and valleys, peaks and shadows — eyelashes like swaying palms? Such long, lovely eyelashes. Theo was shouting something at her, because he didn't understand about the fractals and the hornet music.

"Listen," she managed. "They're singing."

"Fuck, are you high right now?" Theo roared.

"Got stung," she said. "Had a lil tam, took the edge off."

"There's no hornets on the fifth sub-floor! No hornets, no panic — no panic, no way to get everyone out. There's a decidedly un-stung professor down there," he hissed. His face was so scrunched up, Rylla had to laugh. "Ugh, you're useless," he said, and he grabbed her hand, touching one of his MANIs to hers. His other hand whirred like a hummingbird.

Then yellow-on-black code filled her eyes, blurring by lightning-fast. "Whooooooo!" she cried as she tumbled into a delighted blackness, with swirling neon digits glowing all around her. A grumpy shoebill appeared and told her that a foreign user was attempting to access her system controls. "S'okay," she told the fussy old bird. "S'just Theo."

Then her vision cleared to reveal Theo's face, stern with concentration. The cleaning drone feeds were under his control now. He commandeered a window-cleaning drone to terrorize the hornets left on this floor, until they'd consolidated around it in a roiling ball of shiny, striped thoraxes. With a flick of his hand, he sent them hurtling through a ventilation duct that led down to the fifth sub-floor — the clean room — and then he was gone.

Rylla thought about following him, but when she tried to move, her swollen leg weighed a thousand pounds. On the camera feeds, she watched hornets burst into a pristine-white chamber, where someone with hairnets on their shoes and a plastic suit was fiddling with a circuit board. The person screamed — bolted for the door — and a few moments later, Theo and Hoshiko rushed inside, leaving poor professor's Amari's body slumped in the doorway.

Rylla should've offered that guy a hit of tam.

In the clean room, Theo and Hoshiko busied themselves over the humming machines, swatting at the occasional murder-hornet performatively. Rylla shivered, teeth clacking together. She should get up. Go help Theo and Hoshiko. Or maybe crawl all the way to her warm, cushy bed. But her dorm room was far away. Maybe she'd just close her eyes for a few seconds. Then she'd rally the energy to —

32

Just One More

On the ceiling above Rylla, stern-looking people raised their fists, clasped hands, or wielded sledgehammers in black, white, and red animated holoposters — many featuring scrolling text she couldn't read because they were written in Cyrillic or Chinese characters. Hoshiko's dorm room, then. Groaning, she rolled up to a seat.

Hoshiko, Theo, and Magenta were arguing in front of a holowall filled with code.

"What happened?" she asked, rubbing her throbbing temples. "Did we do the — the thingy?"

Three pairs of pissed-off eyes swiveled toward her. "We hacked the server, yes," Hoshiko said.

"No thanks to you," Magenta muttered. "What were you thinking? Going cosmic on tam, when all our asses were on the line?"

"I had to take it! I got stung," Rylla said. She pointed at Theo. "It's *his* fault that pheromone stuff didn't work!"

"It *did* work, because none of us got stung," Theo snapped. "You must've missed a spot."

The anger in his voice made her head pound. Without thinking what she was doing, she slipped the baggie of tam out of her pocket and did a swipe to take away the pain.

"You've got to be kidding me," Magenta said. The others made disgusted sounds.

Rylla froze with her finger still stuck inside her cheek. "Wha —?"

"You're flushing that. Right now."

Rylla clutched the bag against her shoulder. "No!"

But the others yelled at her, called her an addict, and the responsible part of her brain — weak as its voice had become — knew they were right. "Fine," she mumbled. Magenta followed her into Hoshiko's bathroom and supervised as Rylla reluctantly tipped the last of the glittering crystals into the water and flushed. She moved to stick the baggie back in her pocket, still glittering with tam dust, but Magenta snatched it out of her hand and dropped it in the trash.

Back in the main room, Theo filled her in on what had happened after she blacked out. Inside the clean room, Theo and Hoshiko had cranked the temperature controls for the school down to fifty degrees, triggering the hornets' return to their crate to hibernate. Then, with access to Ward 3's operational controls, Theo had looped the security feed so Hoshiko could hack the Humanity department's server and download its data unseen. When they'd gotten back to Rylla, she'd been awake but delirious. With Magenta's help, they maneuvered her back to Hoshiko's room. She'd been passed out for hours, while Wingates security interrogated the other three.

Rylla leaned forward eagerly. "So what's on the server?"

"That's not so easy to tell. Sure enough, they're using some old encryption protocols I coded back in my undergrad days to protect the server as a *whole* — and that let me get ... well, sort of like I'm in the foyer of a building, but the inner doors are locked. I can see the metadata on the door of each room — and we did find one drive called "Manifest," but it has its own internal encryption, one I can't crack."

Hoshiko chewed his bottom lip. "I can tell that this 'Manifest' is *huge,* made up of about five hundred million distinct files. Looking at older versions, we can see a lot of activity. The files get deleted, added, and edited daily, but the number always hovers around five hundred million."

"So that's all we know?" Rylla felt deflated. "The Manifest is five hundred million *somethings*?"

"I've set de-encryption software to work on it, but that'll take time — weeks, maybe months." Hoshiko rubbed a hand through his hair. "If I knew whose encryption protocols we were working with, I could crack it faster."

"Other people have access to these files right? There are people besides Watt editing them?" Magenta mused. "I bet Watt's grad students have access. Maybe I can get close to one of them."

"And I'll keep an eye on Watt's communications," Theo said. "If she contacts any cryptosecurity experts, I'll let you know who. They might be your encryption-coder."

"What should I do?" Rylla asked.

"You —" Theo shot her a withering look. "Just don't give us away. They're still investigating what happened in Ward 3. If they talk to you, make sure you've got your cover story straight. Remember: you were doing nightwork when the cleaning drones went haywire. You have no clue why. Hoshiko's convinced them that the cleaning-drone virus was a prank. Don't say anything to screw that up."

"I won't," Rylla said. Her tone was petulant, but her guts roiled with shame.

⁂

Rylla was surprised that the campus seemed back to normal the following day. In her morning classes, everyone gossiped about where they'd been when the murder hornets swarmed.

Kids who'd been stung showed off their welts like they were battle scars. There were rumors about who might've pranked the cleaning drones, but everyone assumed it was someone from the comp sci department.

Had they gotten away with it? Or would security guards haul Rylla out of class any moment? By the time her last class ended, she was barely fending off a panic attack, and she had no tam to help her relax. She rushed back to her dorm, planning to take a long, hot shower, but as soon as she stepped through the door, Kyle appeared. Watt was summoning her to appear before a committee investigating yesterday's "incident" in Ward 3.

Shit.

Watt must've figured it out — that they'd planned the murder hornet attack, that Rylla had been spying on her, that she knew about the Manifest —

"No, no, no," she moaned, balling her fists against her skull. "Stay cool. Remember your cover story." But what had it been exactly? When her brain was firing off adrenaline like this, she couldn't remember what she was and wasn't supposed to say.

Kyle preened in the middle of her cluttered desk. "You should leave now in order to arrive at your scheduled hearing in seven minutes."

Her palms broke out in a sweat. Even if she *could* keep her story straight, her body would betray her. Watt would take one look at her hyperventilating, sweating self and know she was lying. She *had* to calm down.

And there was only one sure-fire way to do that.

Her eyes flicked to Magenta's side of the room. Magenta always kept a little tam on hand, didn't they? Magenta was such a fucking hypocrite — they'd made Rylla flush her stash, but they were the one who'd given her tam in the first place!

Rylla rummaged through the makeup and crusty food-bowls on Magenta's desk, under their mattress, in their drawers, and finally — there at the back of Magenta's sock drawer, next to some handcuffs, a length of rope, a strap-on dildo and a half-full bag of weed, there was a baggie the size of a postage stamp containing a bit of glittering powder. Rylla stuck her tongue inside and licked up every last bit.

✺

Throughout the hearing, Rylla floated somewhere slightly outside herself. Interrogating her across a long, intimidating table were two professors she knew, Watt, Amari — his facial stings now shrunk to pea-sized welts — and, to her shock, Hoshiko. She had to master her face to keep from giggling when he asked if she knew who had tampered with the drones — had she accepted files from another student recently? Had she shared OGlenses with anyone? Clearly, the other professors trusted Hoshiko completely, and he'd convinced them that Rylla couldn't possibly be at fault. After all, how could a technologically-ignorant Humanity major have hacked the cleaning drones' AI code?

She was so glad she'd taken tam. Without it, she wouldn't have been able to keep a straight face, answering "no" and "I don't know" over and over. Watt narrowed her eyes at her, but asked no questions. Finally, Professor Amari dismissed her.

"I'll walk you out," Watt said. In spite of the tam, Rylla's chest tightened with dread.

In the corridor, Watt rounded on her. "I'm worried about you, Rylla, with everything going on in the Dust — it must be very hard. How's your family?"

"They're —" Rylla opened her mouth to answer, but something was blocking her throat. Watt knitted her eyebrows pityingly. Rylla swallowed hard and tried again. "My mom's job got blown up. So, uh, that's not good," she managed. "I'm really worried about her." A thought occurred to her. "Is there any way you can help her get a visa?"

Watt smiled sadly. "I'm afraid not. The government's frozen all visas to and from the Dust. But I'll ask around. See if there's anything I can do."

"Thank you," Rylla said. Watt was being so kind. She felt slightly guilty for spending the last half-hour lying to the professor's face — and the past month spying on her.

Watt cocked her head to one side. "And your brother? Have you heard from Tyler?"

Rylla shook her head "Not since J —"

An alarm rang in Rylla's brain. Hang on a wild minute. Had she ever talked about her brother to Watt? She racked her brain, but couldn't remember ever mentioning his name.

"Not since?" Watt leaned forward, expectant — and her mask slipped. The professor's eyes weren't concerned, they were *eager*. A chill went up Rylla's spine, and her gut told her not to reveal anything about her brother to Watt.

"Not since, uh, we were in Camelot." Rylla shrugged. "He's just disappeared."

"That must be hard," Watt said, with a sad smile. The mask of a concerned professor was firmly back in place.

As Rylla crossed the meadows to the Grove, she ran through the conversation with Watt in her mind. Watt had told the board members that they needed Dusty students to "secure assets" in the Dust. Did her brother have something to do with those "assets?" Did Watt know something about Tyler that she was hiding from Rylla?

The lick of tam she'd gotten off Magenta's baggie was quickly wearing off. Her nerves felt fried, her blood ached for another hit. And okay, maybe that wasn't good. Maybe Magenta was right — she'd gotten herself a teensy bit addicted. If she could just get her hands on a bit more, though, she'd cut down slowly. Stopping cold-turkey like this wasn't going to work. Not when the Manifest was right at their fingertips, and Watt was sniffing after Tyler, and Mom was out of a job, and X-Day was rocketing closer, and Jo was dead, and —

There, in the midst of the gently-swaying grasses of the meadows, she doubled over with the pain of a fresh bout of grief. How was it that just remembering that Jo was gone from the world could make her *hurt* like this? Like murder hornet venom in her bloodstream? Part of her wanted to give in to that grief, collapse in a heap here in the middle of the meadow and sob. But a bigger part of her was terrified that if she let herself fall into the gaping pit inside of her, she'd never climb out again.

Rylla could not function like this. She needed help — *chemical* help. Maybe if she came clean to Magenta about how bad she was hurting, they would hook Rylla up. But no, Magenta was still furious at Rylla about going cosmic during the clean room heist. Magenta would never give her more tam, or even a ride into Detroit. She'd heard of kids taking a hover-bus downtown, though. She called for Kyle and asked the shoebill to pull up a bus schedule.

Halfway to Detroit, Rylla realized she had no clue how to get to the Sunken Tanker or the Velvet Underground. So she got off at a stop in a bustling part of downtown, lined with bars and restaurants, where surely someone was selling what she needed. The first few clubs she tried wouldn't let her in without a 21+ ID, but as the bars thinned out and the street grew dingier, she found a dive bar that didn't have a bouncer at the door. Inside, she let a gross old dude who told her she 'reminded him of his granddaughter' buy her a drink. She asked him if he knew where she could net some tam. He pointed towards a table, where a scrounger-looking person was playing some hologame on chunky OGGles.

As Rylla approached, the dealer swiped the opacity on the OGGles clear, revealing red-rimmed, sunken eyes.

"Greetings, young one. Have you heard the word of the Vulpini?" Rylla knit her brows in confusion. "The gospel of Gaia's Legion? People are parasites, and the Legion is the cure!"

What the hell was this? Had the old guy pranked her, sending her to some ranting religious nut as a joke? Her better instincts were screaming that this whole scheme was a terrible idea. But her hunger for tam was stronger.

"Can you net me some tam?" she asked.

"Sure, little filly." The dealer peeled up a corner of their satchel, revealing piles of glittering baggies inside. It was all she could do not to snatch one and run. "But won't you stay and hear the Good Word? You'd make a fine Legionnaire. And the best part of Gaia's Legion? Recruits get all the tam we can eat!" The dealer grinned, showing off ranks of rotten teeth and black gums.

"Just one bag," Rylla mumbled. She wasn't far gone enough to join this creep's cult — appealing as the promise of unlimited tam was. She swiped away a chunk of the money in her work/study account, in exchange for a stamp-sized bag of twenty crystals. She immediately stuck one on her tongue, then floated out of the bar on a cloud of crystallized air.

✾

A few weeks later, Rylla was sitting in Humanity seminar, when suddenly all eyes turned to her. "Rylla ... *Rylla?*" Professor Watt repeated in frustration. Rylla wasn't sure what the professor wanted, because she'd been too busy counting down the minutes until class ended to pay attention. There was another art showcase at the Velvet Underground tonight. She fingered the half-empty baggie in her pocket. The money in her work/study account was nearly gone, but surely she could net some tam off her new friends there — she just had to make it through this last class of the day.

She arranged her face into an innocent smile. "Yes, Professor?"

"We're ready for your presentation."

This moment would have sent the old Rylla spiraling into panic, but her crystalline bubble of tam protected her from stressing out — over *anything*.

"Of course." She rewound through fuzzy memories of the last half-hour, recalling bits of her classmates' presentations, which she'd only half-listened to. Magenta had argued that for their next field trip, they should embed with an experimental art collective in Detroit. Ynez thought they should embed with the wealthy upper crust who influenced city politics. And Jae had talked about a new group taking over the drug trade downtown. Called "Gaia's Legion," they were a cross between a crime syndicate and an eco-terrorist cult. Rylla's attention had snagged on the name — hadn't her first tam dealer mentioned Gaia's Legion? Hadn't they said people who joined the Legion could have all the tam they wanted?

The others had given slick presentations with facts, figures, and holographics. Rylla had nothing ready — she'd forgotten about this deadline. But tam made her confident. If she was charming enough, she could fool Professor Watt into thinking she had prepared.

"My presentation's the same as Jae's," she said. "We should embed with this Gaia's Legion."

Magenta shook their head and snorted with derision.

"I mean it! They're tam dealers, right? And lots of people use tam to deal with Gotterdammerungangst. It is actually *very effective*." Rylla said, patting the table with splayed fingertips "So, that's what we should explore."

"Rylla," Jae said sternly. "You realize that we all know you're high on tam *right now.*"

She had not known that.

"You're slurring your words, and your eyes are all red," Ynez said. "It's sad."

"Okay," Rylla said, her cheeks burning. "Okay, maybe I am? Maybe I'm just getting a jump-start on research."

"It's not research if you just *are* a tammie!" Magenta shouted. Rylla flinched back from the onslaught, her tam-induced calm slipping away. Magenta turned to Watt. "I'm so sorry, professor. This is my fault. I took her into the city a few months ago, and —"

"Y-yeah, you do tam too!" Rylla wagged a finger at Magenta desperately. "So what's the big deal?"

"I do it *once in a while*? I have this thing called *boundaries*?" Magenta said. "You, on the other hand, take one crystal and hand over all your willpower. I've never seen someone get so addicted so fast."

"It's been hard to watch," Ynez said, nodding.

"That scene in The Grove?" Jae snorted derisively.

"Wait — what?" Rylla asked, a bottomless feeling spreading in her gut. "What are you talking about?"

"You don't remember?" Jae asked. "It was *yesterday.* That bioengineer you hang out with? Dragon guy? You screamed at him, *'Mind your own business, Dr. Frankenstein.'*"

"Then you tripped over a chair." Magenta snorted a laugh. "And that short person with the curly hair? She asked if you were okay, and you were like" — they imitated Rylla's slurred, shouting voice — "*Go play with your robots and leave me alone!*"

Rylla had no memory of what they were describing, but it sounded like she'd gotten in a fight with her best friends. She felt dizzied by the revelation, and dangerously sober.

Watt watched her closely.

"You knew I was on tam, Professor?"

"I've suspected since the inquiry into the Ward 3 incident," Watt said. "You seemed ... *scattered,* and since then, you've failed to attend six of your classes. There was the scene in The Grove. The incident in the Jet Stream."

Responding to Rylla's baffled look, Magenta explained. "You passed out in a pod, and some Bio majors carried you back to our dorm."

"Why didn't you say something? Try to stop me?" Rylla asked, voice thick with hurt.

"It's true we have a no-drugs policy on campus, but the rules for Humanity majors are *flexible.*" Watt shot a look at Magenta. "For you to learn about humans, you need leeway to make human mistakes. And few things are more human than burying your sorrows in intoxication." Watt frowned. "And I'm your professor, not your mother."

At the word "mother," Rylla felt a surge of self-disgust. She had always loathed Amaryllis for wasting money on tam and shirking her parental responsibilities for a party. Now Rylla knew she was no different.

"Have you learned anything from this experience?" Watt asked.

Rylla nodded slowly.

"Good. As punishment, I want five thousand words about exactly what that is." Watt's voice dropped and turned danger-ous. "And if you relapse, if you miss another class, if I catch a whiff of a rumor that you are using again, you will lose your scholarship and your place at this school — is that clear?"

Rylla nodded again, not trusting herself to speak.

"As for the rest of you —" Watt's glare swept around the room. "If Rylla relapses, it reflects poorly on all of you, and you will all fail this seminar."

Rylla's classmates cried in outrage.

"That's not fair!" Ynez snarled.

"That'll put us back graduating a year!" Magenta cried.

"What can your seminar hope to accomplish if you don't take care of each other?" Watt snapped, looking hard at

Magenta. "You want to be leaders? Lead Rylla out of this trouble. Or is that too much for you?" The others shifted awkwardly in their seats.

Magenta sighed and held out a hand. "You won't be needing that baggie in your pocket then." Rylla recoiled. How had they known? "You've been fingering it for the last hour." Reluctantly, Rylla pulled the bag from her pocket and dropped it in Magenta's palm.

"Now, there's still the matter of our upcoming field trip." Watt stroked her chin. "Rylla, I don't think it's good idea for you to embed in Detroit right now. Certainly not with a group of drug dealers."

Rylla had never felt more miserable and humiliated — and that was saying a lot for a girl who'd become famous for a vid called *Ass is Hope*. She'd come close to losing her place at this school — but as scary as that thought was, the thought of sobriety, a life without tam stretching endlessly into the future, seemed even more terrifying.

Suddenly, a face sprang to Rylla's mind — a sober face in a crowd of drunken, drugged-out people. And that serene, ageless nun hadn't seemed bored by sobriety, but calm and content in a way Rylla had never quite encountered.

"Wait!" she cried out. "I have an idea ..." Her MANI-clad fingers drummed on the table as she searched the OGnet.

Flicking a hand, she sent a hologram into the middle of the conference table. Nestled between two abandoned factories was a lush garden and an odd temple, like a log cabin made from old telephone poles. Instead of wood carvings, there were sculptures assembled from bits of plastic. Mosaics of flattened soda cans patterned the courtyard.

"The Wastrels?" Ynez wrinkled her nose. "You want to be *one* with your *waste?*"

"I met this Wastrel nun, Sister Fun Guy. She was nice, and they're all sober — it'd be like rehab!" She poked the marquee with her MANI and read aloud the text that appeared, hoping Watt would give her credit for this on-the-fly presentation. *"Do you feel weighed down with cares and fears? It's because you are carrying your waste on your back, and you have not tended to it. Wastrels tend to our waste, as lovingly as we tend to our garden."*

"What does 'tending to your waste' even *mean*?" Magenta asked, grimacing.

"I'm not sure," Rylla said, confidence flagging. What *was* she signing up for? "But that's why we should go, right? To learn."

Jae narrowed his eyes at the holographic temple. "I've heard they're a bit like Buddhists mixed with scroungers? It's not the *worst* religion."

Watt frowned and scrolled through the information. "We haven't studied a religious sect this year." She arched an eyebrow at Rylla. "But I'm not sure I trust you to embed so close to your old tam associates."

"A lot of people turn to religion to deal with Gotterdammerungangst, right?" Rylla said. "These people — they've made a garden in this ugly place. And Sister Fun Guy, she was like — totally peaceful, in a world where everyone else is drowning in fear. I want to know how she does it."

Watt pressed her lips together in a frown. Rylla held the profesor's gaze, trying to convey that her interest in the Wastrels was genuine. Finally, Watt said, "Okay."

Everyone erupted in groans. "But she got to pick the last field trip!" Magenta shouted.

Watt waved her hands to silence them. "Calm down. I was also swayed by Jae's presentation — the three of you will investigate this Gaia's Legion. Figure out how they pushed out the other crime syndicates so quickly. Try to get close to their leader — this one they call 'The Vulpini.'" She turned to Rylla. "But that's not for you. You're going to *become one with your waste*."

33

A Whole Lot of World

As Watt dismissed their seminar, Rylla was already calculating how many minutes until the next hoverbus to Detroit. Her seminar-mates were right — her tam use had gotten way out of hand. But she needed to score one last bag, so she could wean herself off slowly. Maybe she'd get two bags, just to be safe.

But as she reached the doorway, a hand clamped on her shoulder. "No you don't," Magenta said, jerking her back. "We're not letting you out of our sight."

"What?" Rylla said, wide-eyed. "You can trust me! I'll never touch the stuff again."

"You'd be more believable if you could stop staring at this." Magenta patted their front shirt-pocket where they'd stashed Rylla's confiscated baggie. "Now go sit over there, and shut up while we figure out what to do with you."

Ynez, Magenta, and Jae argued while Rylla slumped in a chair, wondering if the fifth-floor windows opened. It had been three hours since her last hit of tam, and her skin was starting to itch. She hid her throbbing head in her arms and tried to tune out the others' conversation — something about the gradual extinction of cold turkeys.

The sun sank below the horizon and the sky turned the color of a bruise. After what felt like an eternity of arguing, her classmates told her to get up. She thought about bolting for the door — if she ran, she could still catch the last bus to the city. But as she stood, her legs buckled. Jae caught her around the waist and looped her arm over his shoulder.

"She's already sick?" Magenta sounded almost impressed. "Her habit was worse than I thought."

Rylla was vaguely aware of Jae and Magenta steering her out of the building, across the quad, and into a Jet Stream pod. By the time Jae dumped her on her bed, back in her dorm, she was shivering with fever.

"I've got it from here," Magenta said. After kicking off platform boots, they sat on the foot of her bed. "Get ready," they said quietly. "This is going to be the worst night of your life."

They put an old black-and-white flatvid on the holowall. "Flatvids are better for the nausea." It was a historical drama set in the Joseon era, with lots of trees in the background and pretty clothes. The king had just confessed his forbidden love for a soldier when the nausea kicked in. Rylla spent the next few hours curled around the toilet. Magenta scratched her back half-heartedly while doing nightwork on their OGlenses. "You have an addictive personality. You cannot handle your drugs. You need to know this about yourself," they said. Beneath their prickliness, Rylla realized, Magenta had actually been worried. About *her*.

The next morning, when she awoke, everything hurt — her skin, bones, every muscle, even her *teeth*. She was wondering how she was ever going to climb out of bed, let alone make it to class, when Ynez appeared in the doorway. Beside her, to Rylla's abject humiliation, was her Neuropsychosociology professor, Dr. Nelson Hernandez.

"She's all yours," Magenta told Ynez.

Rylla forced herself to sit up in bed, but that was all the greeting she could muster. Ynez pulled out Rylla's desk chair and brushed some crumbs off the seat before sitting. Dr. Hernandez perched gingerly on the edge of Magenta's rumpled bed.

"I hear you've developed a tam addiction," he said. "Tell me when this all started."

The last thing she wanted was to have an impromptu therapy session with Dr. Hernandez and Ynez. "I have class," she groaned, hoping they'd leave her alone.

Ynez and Dr. Hernandez looked at each other and smirked — like they knew perfectly well she wasn't making it to the shower, let alone to class today. "We have a few hours before your next class," Ynez said. "Just talk to Dr. Hernandez."

"Can we wait until my blood stops hurting?" Rylla said, clutching her head.

"I can give you something to help with that," Dr. Hernandez said.

"Something?" she asked, mouth flooding with saliva. "Like tam?

"No. But I can give you something to relieve the withdrawal symptoms. Get you up and about." He arched a defined eyebrow. "But first, I need to understand what happened. When did you first start using?"

Rylla sighed, resigning herself to the humiliation. "I went to this club with Magenta, and Tyler called me and —" Tears stung her eyes. She made a brief effort to fight them off, rubbing them away with the heel of her palm, but quickly gave up. She had no dignity left to preserve. She slumped back on her pillow, tears streaming towards her ears. "He told me Jo died."

"Who's Jo?"

She told him — about Jo and their garden, how they'd loved her brother and softened his rough edges. How mornings after sleep-overs, she'd danced with them to twentieth-century pop songs while cooking breakfast. She talked about the horrible way they'd died. Dr. Hernandez steered her to talk about X-Day, her fears for her family, and Alastair's betrayal in

Camelot — which, as much as she tried to forget it, was still messing with her head. She described the panic attack she'd had near Crystal Lake. She got so lost in the sound of her own voice that she *almost* told them about spying on Professor Watt, but caught herself at the last second. A sudden panic spread in her chest, realizing she'd revealed so much of herself to someone who was practically a stranger.

"What's your assessment?" Dr. Hernandez asked Ynez, like Rylla was a piece of nightwork.

"Generalized anxiety disorder," Ynez said. "Gotterdammerungangst and acute personal trauma. She started microdosing tam to self-medicate and fell into addiction."

"Very good," Dr. Hernandez pronounced. "What would you prescribe?"

"Seraclorazine, 500mg, to take as needed at the onset of panic attacks. For the withdrawal symptoms — Tamadone, starting at 200mg and decreasing over the course of a month."

"Excellent!" Dr. Hernandez beamed. "And it so happens, I brought samples with me." He dug into his shoulder bag, where Rylla heard the rattling of pill bottles.

"Ynez is authorized to prescribe me drugs?" Rylla asked.

Dr. Hernandez pulled out a couple pill bottles. "Ynez excels at psychopharmacology and is doing an independent study with me. She prescribed exactly as I would have." He explained that Rylla should take Seraclorazine to calm down if she got the breathless feeling again. It wasn't as strong as tam, but it would ease her nerves, and it wasn't addictive.

Ynez brought her a glass of water, and she swallowed the pills. Within moments, the Tamadone eased her aches and pains, but it didn't quite slake her thirst for the real thing.

Dr. Hernandez slipped out of the room and closed the door behind him, but Ynez simply crossed her legs and stared.

"So, what? You're, like, babysitting me now?" Rylla asked.

"For the next two weeks," Ynez said. "We're taking it in shifts, until we can hand you off to the Wastrels. I'll walk you between classes, and Magenta will babysit you in the evenings. Jae's got something planned for the weekend."

"Is this really necessary?"

Ynez raised an eyebrow. "You tell me."

Rylla imagined Ynez walking out and felt the urge to bolt for the bus stop. Her mouth watered at the memory of tam. Hanging her head, Rylla sighed. "Yeah, it probably is."

"I had no idea that you were going through so much stuff," Ynez said softly. "I'm so sorry about your friend Jo. And your brother, and your mom's job — all of it."

"Yeah, well, now you know why I'm not perfect like you."

Ynez snorted. "You think I'm perfect?" She pulled a small silver case from her skirt pocket and popped open the lid. Inside were the diamond-shaped, orange Seraclorazine, plus others — green, white and blue pills. "If I don't take these, I'll start pulling out my hair and washing my hands until they bleed. We all need a little psychopharmacological help sometimes. It's the end of the fucking world."

Rylla barked a laugh. Ynez smiled at her with a warmth she'd never seen before.

"Now you should really go take a shower," Ynez said. "You smell like puke."

✳

The bright flare of summer had dimmed while Rylla was high on tam. Now the flowers were fading, and the leaves were turning sunset shades of yellow and red. Rylla felt too sick and ashamed to marvel at them, however, as Ynez escorted her to her morning classes, then followed her to the Grove for lunch.

"Are you gonna sit with me too?"

Ynez shook her head. "I'm not gonna make it that easy for you." She nodded her head towards the far side of the Grove. "Go talk to your friends."

Rylla's stomach churned with dread as she loaded up her tray with food. At first, she thought she was imagining the glares and giggles, but soon it became impossible to ignore what people were whispering.

"That's the one who flipped out yesterday."

"I heard she was on drugs."

"I guess it's true what they say about Dusties."

Her blood boiled with shame. Just when her "Ass is Hope" infamy had died down, she'd given people reason to gossip about her all over again.

Tray in hand, she steeled herself and headed across the Grove to her usual table. Dae-Dae, Theo, and Azam were having an animated conversation, but abruptly fell silent as Rylla approached. Her gut twisted in knots as three stony faces turned to face her.

"I don't remember what happened," Rylla said, staring down at her tray miserably. "But I'm off tam now, and I'm so sorry. I wasn't myself."

"How do we know that wasn't your *real* self?" Dae-Dae folded her arms over her chest.

"How can we trust you've stopped using? You've told us more than once that you quit," Azam added.

Rylla searched their faces, unsure how to convince them.

"There's an app for that," Theo said. He got up from the table and leaned close to her. "May I take a hair?" She nodded, and he plucked a strand, twiddled his MANIs to pull up an app, and peered at the hair closely. "She's been clean for about ... twenty-four hours?"

"Spot-on," she said, wondering what chemistry in her hair follicle had revealed this.

"You said all we do is nightwork, and we might as well be robots," Dae-Dae said.

Theo smirked. "You called me Dr. Frankenstein. Which was actually sort of funny."

"You said your *real* friends were in Detroit, and they were cooler than us," Azam added, lips pressed in a frown.

"I was a jerk." Rylla stared down at her tray. "But those aren't my real friends. Just people I did tam with. *Y'all* are my real friends! I don't know what I would've done this year without you!"

"It's fine, Tex," Theo said. "Sit down."

"No, it's not *fine*," Dae-Dae snapped, glaring at Theo before turning again to Rylla. "Besides, it was kind of nice not having her here. We didn't have to keep slowing down and explaining our research for a *Humanity* major."

Her words socked Rylla in the gut.

"The wound is still fresh," Azam said kindly, though her eyes were distant.

Rylla knew when she wasn't wanted and turned away. She found an empty table and ate alone, her food tasting like cardboard. As she was finishing, Theo sat down beside her. Rylla's heart swelled with gratitude.

"Don't worry. Azam's already forgiven you, and Dae-Dae will get over it. She's been pissed at me loads of times, but she's no good at holding a grudge for long." He looked at her earnestly, for once in his life. "Are you back with us for good?"

"I think so," she said, hoping it was true.

"Good, because we haven't made any progress cracking the Manifest. I don't know if you remember this — because you were absolutely cosmic on tam — but after your Ward 3 inquiry, you said Watt was asking weird questions about your brother? Maybe *he* has something to do with the Manifest. Try to get her to trust you again, maybe you can weasel something out of her."

"Sure," Rylla said, feeling deflated. For a second there, she'd thought Theo had come over just to be a good friend.

For the rest of the week, Rylla dealt with the humiliation of being walked to her classes by her peers. She swallowed her shame and tried to focus on nightwork, but she still couldn't get ahold of her mom or Tyler. Her friends wouldn't sit with her in the Grove. She got cravings for tam so bad she fought the urge to kick Magenta in the shins and take off for the nearest hoverbus stop. And while the Seraclorazine helped stave off panic attacks, it didn't help her Gotterdammerungangst.

No matter what she did in Climate Modeling, she couldn't get X-Day to shift. What was the point of taking a little orange pill to feel better about living in a world careening towards extinction? That was the feeling she couldn't shake — that she, her family, all the trees and bugs and rivers on earth — were doomed, doomed, doomed.

On Saturday, she was surprised when it was Jae, not Ynez, who showed up at her dorm to take her off Magenta's hands.

"We're taking a trip today," he explained. "I want to show you something."

Rylla groaned when she saw the climbing gear poking out of the duffel slung over his shoulder. "Let me guess, you're gonna make me climb until I puke?"

"For once, would you just trust me?" he said, exasperated. "Babysitting a tam addict isn't the number one thing I want to do with my weekend, you know? But we're all trying to help you, so you don't ruin your life and get kicked out of school. The least you can do is not complain about it."

Rylla bit her lip and followed Jae to the aircraft hangar. They climbed into the same skimmer she'd taken to Wingates — the one with the pink fuzzy seats — but a student engineer she'd never met was their pilot. Rylla reeled at the memory of meeting Dae-Dae, all the hope she'd felt for her future and the world on that first skimmer ride. She missed her friend, and felt sick with the certainty she'd screwed up that relationship forever.

The countryside flashed by, Michigan's forests dissolving into the lighter green of Indiana's farms. "Can I ask where we're going?"

"West Virginia," Jae said, staring out the window as the ground swelled into rolling hills.

"To go climbing?"

He nodded.

"On a real mountain?"

He cocked his head to one side. "Something like that."

For the first time all week, Rylla felt a familiar spark in her chest, something hopeful and alive. They were going to see the Appalachian mountains! Many of the country's few remaining bird species still lived in its forests, not to mention fascinating regional insect life. She might see a tiger swallowtail, or even a Dobson fly!

But when they disembarked from the skimmer, her heart sank. They might as well have stepped onto the surface of Mars. Here, the once-rolling hills had been flattened and pounded into unnatural terraces. The only wildflife was the occasional clump of scraggly grass swaying in wind that tasted of dust.

"What the hell did we do *here*?" she asked.

"Mountaintop removal." Jae shouldered his pack, shifting under the weight of his climbing gear. "Coal corps used it to extract every last bit of coal from these mountains in the 2000's and 2010's." He took off on foot for the far end of the valley, where a cliff face soared, unnaturally sliced in half, billions of years of history writ in its jagged stripes.

"You know I was depressed enough already," Rylla said, picking her way over the uneven ground. "Did you have to bring me to the most depressing place on earth?" Jae didn't answer, so she kept talking to herself. "Even the mountains. We had to go and destroy whole-fucking-entire mountains."

When they reached the foot of the towering rock wall, Jae explained the basics of climbing without a top rope. He showed her how to activate arachnocams — little robotic spiders that crawled up into cracks in the rock, then braced their legs against the walls, so you could loop your rope through them. The rope itself was a strand of synthetic spider-silk, spooled in a box no larger than her palm.

She paid careful attention, knowing her life would soon be dangling from the arachnocam's spindly limbs. Finally, they started to climb — Jae keeping above and to the right of Rylla. Her fingers hurt immediately — the rock she gripped was so much sharper, harder, and colder than the sculpted plastic handholds of the climbing gym. When they were only twenty feet above the ground, her heart started hammering with fear. The arachnocams would catch her if she fell, but even as she repeated this to herself, she didn't believe it. At fifty feet up, her arms trembled, her fingertips lost their strength, and her leg muscles cramped. She was braced in a crack in the cliff. When she gripped the thin ledge high above, a chunk of the rock came away in her hand. She stared at it for an instant frozen in time, and then she fell.

Terror flooded her as she plunged, swung, then slammed into the rock face. Her hip exploded in pain. She was dangling from the rope — one arachnocam had been ripped from the wall, but the next one down had held.

For now.

"You okay?" Jae yelled from twenty feet above.

"No, Jae, I'm not fucking okay!" The rope dangled past a shelf, so she now twirled in midair and couldn't reach the rock face. "What do I do?"

"Swing!" he called, pointing to an outcropping of rock to her right.

"I can't!" she cried, voice twisting into a shrill scream of panic.

"You have to!" He shouted down to her. "No other way but up."

Rylla allowed herself three panicked breaths, and then she stretched out her legs, and grazed the rock face with her toes. On her second bounce, she kicked off hard, stretched out a hand — grazed the outcropping to her right with her fingertips. On her next swing, her fingers scrambled for purchase, and she caught a toehold. She took a steadying breath.

"See? Knew you could do it," Jae called.

"I hate you!" Rylla called back. "Did you know that?"

Jae chuckled, dipped his hands into his chalk bag, and reached for a crack overhead.

Rylla fell twice more on their ascent, but neither was as serious a fall as the first. Whenever she flagged, whenever she swore her muscles were spent and there was no way she could get an inch higher, Jae would call down some infuriating taunt that forced her to find her next handhold.

At last, when she could see nothing but blue sky above her, she hooked a knee over the top of the wall. Jae, already on the precipice, squatted down and helped her scramble up and over to the top of the cliff.

Panting, muscles screaming, she caught her breath, then pushed herself up to survey the view.

The scarred, destroyed landscape behind them stopped at this ridge. Ahead, forested mountains stretched to the horizon. The trees blazed with the colors of fall — green, gold and crimson, and a winding river glittered through the valley below. This was how the Appalachians must've looked two hundred years ago — or two million.

But the glimpse of paradise was slashed with death. To the north, the shattered landscape of mountaintop extraction continued, blighting the ridgeline. To the southeast, huge swaths of blackened tree stumps showed the devastation of a recent wildfire.

"So many dead trees," she muttered breathlessly.

Jae pointed at the bright swatch of forest. "Yes, but look how many are left! Tens of thousands of trees — and that's just what we can see! Over that ridge, the mountains go on and on, all the way down to Georgia."

"Tens of thousands," she repeated in a sad whisper.

"So yeah, okay, we've blown up a lot of mountains, we've killed a lot of trees. But look how much is left. There's still a lot of world left to save." His voice was urgent. The wind whipped at his hair and his clothes, and for a second she forgot that he usually annoyed the crap out of her. The valley was so beautiful, the world — vicious and scarred as it was — was so beautiful. And even he, obnoxious gym-teacher-mansplainer Jae Boudreaux, was beautiful.

"Still a lot of world left to save," Rylla repeated, tears pricking the backs of her eyes. "Is this why you brought me up here? To see this?"

"This and — did you think about tam while we were climbing?" Jae asked.

"Damn it." She grinned good-naturedly. "No, I didn't."

He laughed.

"You don't have to be all smug about it."

"It's the life-or-death thing that does it," he said. "The adrenaline, the endorphins ... there's a kind of high to climbing in the real world."

"How'd you get into all this anyway? Rock climbing?"

He sat down terrifyingly close to the edge of the cliff, feet dangling hundreds of feet above the tallest tree-tops below. "I had a, uh, *bad* childhood. My dad was a real asshole."

"Ah," Rylla said, sitting down cross-legged to one side, but leaving a few feet of solid rock between her and the abyss.

"When I was thirteen, my mom left him, and I could've gone with her and my sister, but I was real worried about him being alone. I thought he was going to kill himself. So I stayed with him."

Rylla felt a surge of guilt at Jae's loyalty — she'd leapt at the first chance to leave Amaryllis's trailer far behind.

"But it was awful, especially when he went off his meds. So I learned to escape when he got like that. I'd take my sand-bike and ride until I hit the San Jacinto mountains. I'd hike around and scramble over boulders — didn't know what I was doing.

But then I met some serious climbers, and they taught me the *ropes.*"

He waggled his eyebrows proudly, and Rylla groaned at the pun. But then his eyes grew unfocused, his voice tender. "There was this place we called 'The Grotto,' white boulders scooped out by the river into a hundred different waterfalls, tumbling down the side of the mountain. You could see clear across the valley from there — over the LA smog, all the way to the Pacific. Sometimes I'd stand under a waterfall and just scream."

He smiled wistfully at the horizon, and Rylla got a sudden, reckless urge —

She scooted to the edge of the cliff and sucked in a huge breath. "Aaaaaaaaaahhhhhhh!" She emptied all the air from her lungs. Jae laughed as the echoes rang across the valley.

"Yeah, like that," he said. He took a deep breath, and she sucked another one in too.

They screamed again, together this time, pushing out the air until there was nothing left in their lungs. Then they burst into laughter. Rylla felt emptied-out and clean and good. She had to admit, there was something about this whole climbing-and-screaming thing. There was something about Jae Boudreaux. Maybe the only two Dusties at Wingates could be friends after all.

A sloping path led into the forested valley below, and they hiked down. The air turned cool and damp as they neared the river. As they waited for the skimmer to pick them up, she turned over smooth river stones in her hand, finding some fascinating dragonfly larvae and even a salamander. As the cool water washed over her fingers, she repeated the same words over and over.

"A whole lot of world left to save."

34

The Way of the Waste

Stepping through the arched gateway to the Wastrel temple grounds was like entering another world. The gnarled limbs of fruit trees shaded the path, and on either side, blackberry vines twined among their trunks. Rylla made her way slowly through the sun-dappled orchard. After weeks of around-the-clock babysitting by her classmates, it felt incredible to be alone again, away from Wingates, exploring a new, lush place.

Finally, the trees gave way to a sunny, junkyard garden. Monastics in patchy brown robes weeded garden beds made from rusty bathtubs and old tires. Rylla approached the nearest one and asked after Sister Fun Guy.

A few minutes later, she sat in a small office off the main temple, sharing a cup of tea with the serene nun she'd met in the Sunken Tanker. Only Sister Fun Guy's hands, wrapped around the teacup, gave a hint to her true age. There, her smooth, ochre skin was speckled with age spots, her knuckles gnarled with arthritis. The shelves around them were crammed with paperbooks — the ones in English were all about gardening and botany, but there were many more with titles in Hangul on their spines. The air smelled of dust and green tea.

Sister Fun Guy blew over the top of the cup, narrowing her eyes at Rylla through the steam.

"Monastics make a life-long commitment to the Way of the Waste," she said. "Why do you wish to walk this path?"

Rylla felt a pang of guilt that she had no plans to make a life-long commitment. She was only here for a few weeks, so she could write Watt an essay on how Wastrels deal with Gotterdammerungangst. Not wanting to lie to the nun's face, she chose her words carefully. "Last time you saw me, I was high on tam. I was using it to hide from the bad things in my life, but it just made everything worse."

Sister Fun Guy nodded in understanding. "Many people use drugs to ease their suffering, only to find their suffering increases."

"But you seemed so peaceful, even sober. I guess — I want to find that peace too." Rylla meant it — or at least, the best parts of her did.

Sister Fun Guy spoke slowly, pausing to breathe between each phrase. "Our ideas are simple. You can learn them in a day, but it will take a lifetime of walking the Way to achieve enlightenment." She sipped her tea. "We do not consume any drugs. We don't engage in romantic love or sex, and we will never have children. These are not easy things for young people to give up. Are you sure you're prepared to follow the Way of the Waste?"

Rylla nodded — giving up those things for two weeks was no sweat.

"You must be willing to abandon even your ego. Are you prepared to let go of 'Rylla?'"

After all the ways she'd humiliated herself over the past year — the *Ass is Hope* video, getting tarred and feathered, becoming a drug addict, and alienating her friends — a vacation from herself sounded amazing. "Yes," she answered definitively. "I'm ready to leave Rylla behind."

"Our need for permanence is even harder to give up. Are you ready to accept that every person, place, and thing that you love will change? That the nature of the universe is change?"

Of course everything changes, Rylla thought. You grow up, your brother becomes a terrorist, he blows up your mom's job. You shave your hair. Again, she nodded.

"Finally, do you accept that you are one with everything in the universe? That you, nuclear waste, a cockroach, and a speck of dust in another galaxy, are all one and the same?"

Rylla didn't *really* get all that, but she nodded anyway.

"At least we won't have to cut much hair!" Sister Fun Guy laughed.

She took Rylla on a tour of the monastery. In the main temple, Sister Fun Guy showed Rylla their murals of wildlife, constructed from bits of trash. In the dormitory behind the temple, monastics slept on futons on tatami mat floors — it seemed the Wastrels had borrowed architecture, as well as philosophy, from Buddhism.

Past the dormitory, they left the greenery behind and headed into an industrial warehouse, where the floor was mounded with plastic garbage. Monastics sorted the trash by type and color. "This is one of our recycling facilities," Sister Fun Guy explained. "Brother Polypropylene is in charge — he's loading up the printer." A wizened monk, operating a forklift, tipped a drum of blue plastic into a massive 3-D printer that had half-printed a tiny house. Sister Fun Guy explained that the houses went to homeless Dusty refugees newly arrived in the city.

In the next warehouse, a mountain of clothes, blankets, and linens stretched to the rafters. "Your first task as an initiate will be to make your own robes and futon here. Do you know how to sew?" Rylla shook her head. "Sister Lycra will show you how."

There was another warehouse for sorting metal scraps, another for composting organic waste. In the vacant parking lots beyond, monastics used heavy machinery to sort through junked hovercars. There were greenhouses, a warehouse for smelting metal, and a reclaimed woodworking shop.

The Wastrel compound was much larger than Rylla had realized, and everywhere, monastics were turning garbage into useful objects. Rylla was starting to understand what it meant to "tend to your waste." The work looked hard and tedious, but the monastics wore restful, content expressions as they labored. And whether they were shoveling, sorting, or hauling trash, they all moved smoothly and deliberately, like they were doing yoga or tai chi.

Finally, Sister Fun Guy stopped before a small cement building. "This is where I work." Inside the building were racks of HazMat suits and an elevator. "We're going underground," the nun explained, "and you'll need to wear one of these. The Waste downstairs is particularly dangerous."

Rylla took slow, steadying breaths as she zipped into the leaded suit. The "dangerous" trash downstairs must be radioactive if they were wearing these, and she hoped she wouldn't suffer another panic attic like she had at Crystal Lake.

Beneath the earth, the elevator doors opened on a dimly-lit cavern, filled with long rows of bookcases. As Rylla stepped closer, she could see that the shelves held, not books, but piles of dirt, and growing out of them were thousands of species of mushrooms.

"Oh," Rylla whispered to herself. "Not Fun Guy. *Fungi.*"

"Fungi are amazing beings," Sister Fungi explained, leading Rylla between two bookcases. They passed simple brown toadstools, red spotted toadstools, and bright purple puffballs. They passed fungus that grew like stacks of dinner plates, and fungus that glowed in the dark. Each shelf bore a tag that read, "Lead, 20,300 PPM" or "8-tetrachlorodibenzo-para-dioxin, 1,753 ppm."

"What do these labels mean?" Rylla asked.

"Toxicity descriptions," Sister Fungi explained. "All the dirt here is contaminated. Fungi are excellent for cleaning toxic soil." Sister Fungi caressed a green spotted mushroom lovingly with her lead-gloved hand. "The fungi suck poisons into their bodies and store them inertly. They teach us of the impermanence of all things — even toxic waste!" She laughed.

Sister Fungi led her to the far end of the subterranean cavern, through a sterilization chamber, and into a brightly lit laboratory, as high-tech as anything at Wingates.

"Here we help the fungi to be better soil cleaners."

"When you say you 'help,' you mean —"

"We modify their DNA to make them more effective," Sister Fungi said, beaming.

"You're bioengineers?" Rylla gaped. "You're making mods!"

"Why not?" Sister Fungi said, holding up a finger. "Remember, the nature of the universe is change. Bioengineering simply helps the fungi to change *faster*."

Sister Fungi lifted the lid off a crate of brown, wrinkly mushrooms. "This fungus has been engineered to grow on soils contaminated with uranium. They are headed for a place in Siberia where nuclear waste was dumped a long time ago. Nothing has grown there for a hundred years, and if we had not created this fungus, nothing would have grown there for tens of thousands of years more." Sister Fungi sighed and shook her head sadly. "But these fungi can pull that radioactive material out of the soil. After a few years cleaning the site with these mushrooms, certain kinds of grass will be able to grow. Wildlife may return in as little as a decade!"

It was a hopeful story. Still, Rylla eyed the mods warily, worried about the unintended consequences of radioactive mushrooms.

A bell sounded three times, piped into the underground lab through a speaker. "That is the call to meditation," Sister Fungi said. "Come."

Soon Rylla was back in the main temple, amid hundreds of other Wastrels in worn brown robes. She felt out of place in her t-shirt and jeans, but everyone smiled kindly as they took seats on small cushions.

An ancient monk atop a raised platform directed them to focus on their breathing as the bell chimed again. Like everything else here, the bell was patchy, made of hundreds of rings of different-colored metals, stacked together. But when an initiate struck it, a clear note rang out.

As the sound faded, Rylla expected something to happen, but everyone around her just sat.

And sat.

Was this meditation? Keeping her head still, Rylla peered around the room at the other monastics. They all wore serene expressions, the gentle rise and fall of their chests the only movement in the hall. After a few minutes, Rylla's hip started throbbing painfully. She wanted to shift her weight, but no one else was moving a muscle. Then a hair fell obnoxiously into her face and her nose started to itch.

Was she allowed to scratch it? And how much time had passed? Ten minutes? Twenty? An hour? How much longer was she expected to just *sit* here? Embedding here had been a terrible mistake. Magenta, Jae, and Ynez were probably partying in some club with those Gaia's Legion dealers, cosmic on tam, while she was stuck here, sitting in torturous stillness, stone-cold sober.

The meditation continued for what felt like hours. At long last, the man on the podium cleared his voice and began to speak. Rylla started to stretch — she couldn't wait to get out of the stuffy temple, now reeking of unwashed armpits. But instead of dismissing them, the monk began lecturing on the Way of the Waste. Like Sister Fungi, he spoke slowly, breathing deeply between his words. Rylla's joints screamed and she wanted to yell, *Spit it out, old man!*

He talked for a long time about life cycles in nature, and she was mostly zoned out in fantasies about stretching her back, until something he said caught her attention.

"So when someone dies, do not grieve. They are still with you. Every atom of them remains. All the plastic they have

consumed remains. Truly, there is no birth and no death —
only cycles of waste."

The fuck was he talking about? She thought of Jo, singing
to African violets, sharing water rations with Pothos vines,
dancing beside her at a Cicada Circus show. Jo would never do
those things again, and of course she was sad about it. Maybe
their atoms were still swirling around the atmosphere, but Jo
was gone in all the ways that mattered.

As everyone finally rose from their mats, Rylla wiped the
tears off her cheeks.

"It looks like you had a powerful experience," Sister Fungi
said.

Rylla let the nun believe the meditation had moved her in
some profound way, and that her tears weren't of grief and
anger.

By the end of her first week, Rylla fell into the rhythm of life in
the monastery. Under the tutelage of Sister Lycra, she had
sewn herself a set of patchy brown robes. To an outsider, she
would have looked indistinguishable from the other monastics,
except for the anxiety that, if she was not careful, still crept up
on her. She'd find herself clenching her jaw, shoulders drawn
up to her ears, caught in a spiral of worrying about Tyler or the
Manifest. When she got like that, she'd sneak a Seraclorazine
from the bottle she kept in a pocket of her robes. But with each
passing day, she needed the pills less and less.

Every morning, she arose at dawn in the stuffy room she
shared with five other initiates. They washed, shaved their
heads to the skin, and ate a simple meal in the dining room,
seated on the floor around long, low tables. Each day after
morning meditation, Rylla went to a different job site. She was
supposed to find the waste that "called to her." Initiates were

often given the most tedious and smelly work. Sometimes she got to use OGGLes to complete a job, but otherwise, she wasn't allowed her OGlenses, as they'd distract her from "contemplating waste." After a few days, she stopped swiping at nothing — trying to pull up apps that wouldn't appear — and discovered there was something restful about just *being* in the real world, without the OGnet at her fingertips 24/7.

Even meditation wasn't so painful anymore, and sometimes the lectures gave her a feeling of deep clarity. When a nun lectured on the Way of the Waste's most sacred commandment — do nothing to increase the suffering of others — Rylla remembered the murder hornets and the plot to break into Ward 3. She and her friends had caused *a lot* of suffering that day. She'd been on tam all the time back then, numbing the part of her brain that worried — including the part that worried about ethics. They'd justified their plan, saying, "What if Watt and the board were planning something evil? Wouldn't a few bug bites be worth it to find out?" But Rylla remembered the gunshot-blast feeling of the hornet sting. Surely, if they'd thought a bit harder, they could've come up with a plan that wouldn't have caused that kind of pain in so many people. Now, the shame of what they'd done made her cringe. But she couldn't change the past. All she could do was vow not to use other people so callously in the future.

In her second week, she earned her Wastrel name at the receiving yard, where a steady stream of garbage trucks dumped the city's waste. That day, Rylla was assigned to drive the backhoe, using a vintage set of OGGles and Gluvs to control the big shoveling arm. Her job was to scoop the garbage and move it to the back of the yard, so more trucks could dump their loads. Driving the backhoe made her feel powerful. She'd been keeping her aggressive, noisy emotions bottled up since she arrived, and the backhoe let her take them out on trash. She was having so much fun, she missed the call to afternoon meditation. When Sister Rebar flagged her down, she begged the nun to let her drive the backhoe the next day.

"I think we've found your name, *Novice Backhoe*," said Sister Rebar.

"That suits her perfectly," Brother Aluminum agreed.

Rylla's chest swelled with pride to have been named after such a powerful machine. Maybe it meant they'd let her drive the backhoe forever. But later that night, wide-awake on her cot, it hit her. *Back ... Hoe ...* Just as she had mistaken Sister Fungi's name, an outsider might mistake *her* name in an embarrassing way. First thing the next day, she requested a name change, but Sister Fungi thought she should keep it — as a good exercise in letting go of her ego.

Her last week with the wastrels coincided with the pumpkin harvest, and by then, Novice Backhoe had almost forgotten that she was a Wingates student. When she did remember, she felt guilty for deceiving her fellow initiates. There really was *something* to this way of life. She felt calmer than she could ever remember. She didn't need her Seraclorazine anymore. And just as she had in Camelot, she started toying with the idea of staying on a field trip forever. It had been a terrible idea to give up her scholarship for Alastair — a dude she'd known less than a month. But leaving school to achieve enlightenment? That was legitimate.

Sister Fungi had coached her to imagine her mind as a river and, using this new strategy, Rylla began enjoying meditation. When a thought popped to the surface, like, "I wonder what Theo looks like shirtless?" or "In fifty years, the Dust will cover the entire continental United States," she pictured those thoughts as little ducks floating by. She waved to them, then watched them go.

An outsider looking at Novice Backhoe would see the same serene half-smile on her face that the other Wastrels wore, rendering her almost unrecognizable from her former self.

Which might've been why he gawked at her for a few, long minutes, cocking his head to one side in concentration.

Novice Backhoe was working at the farmer's market that morning, selling the excess produce grown in the monastery's gardens. She spotted him staring as she was stacking cartons of sweet peas, her mind calm as a lake on a windless morning.

"Rylla?" he asked tentatively.

It was like someone dropped a nuclear bomb in that peaceful lake in her mind.

It was Alastair.

35

The Born-Again Knight

Breathe in, she thought, *breathe out,* using her Wastrel training to calm the conflicted emotions raging in her chest..

"You're a nun now?" Alastair asked with an amused smile. "Another Wingates field trip I take it?"

"Shhhh," she hissed, inclining her head at Sister Melon Rind. But the nun, perhaps perceiving Rylla's need for a private conversation, headed to their truck for more vegetables.

"It's cruel, you know, to make people think you're with them to stay, when all along you're planning on leaving." He watched Sister Melon Rind until she disappeared into the back of the truck. Then he grabbed Rylla's hand. "I left Camelot. The very next day. I went south and saw the clear-cut trees with my own eyes. I'm so sorry. I never should have doubted you."

She sagged against the string bean crates. She hadn't realized how badly she'd needed to hear that from him. "Thank you." She breathed, pulling her hand back from his grasp. "But why are you here? How did you find me?"

"Find you? No, this is a total coincidence. Man, life is nuts sometimes!" He tossed his brass curls to one side. It felt like just yesterday she'd buried her face in that hair. But it had been months, and in that time he'd changed — he was thinner and *dirtier*. His eyes darted manically. Had they always done that, or was she only now noticing it after her time with the Wastrels?

"After leaving Camelot, I was so depressed. I'd *believed* in what we were doing there, you know?"

She knew exactly what he meant. "But how'd you end up here?"

"I found Gaia's Legion," Alastair said, eyes wide. "They're *actually* doing what Camelot only pretended to do."

Alastair had fallen in with the drug-dealing eco-cult? She was tempted to ask if he'd seen Jae, Magenta, and Ynez lately, but didn't want to blow her friends' cover.

"I've never heard of them," she lied.

Alastair smiled. "You'd love us. I mean, the Wastrels are fine — it's nice they recycle and all, but they're not going to save the world."

"And Gaia's Legion is?" Her tone came out very sarcastic for a Wastrel.

"The Vulpini has a plan to save the planet from the human parasite. His ideas are like —" Alastair mimed his head exploding.

Sister Melon Rind returned, bearing a crate of blackberries. "I should get back —"

"Come see me!" Alastair pleaded. "I'll tell you more about the Vulpini. You'd really dig his message."

She made a noncommittal noise, but Alastair gave her the address where he was staying. "Just to talk," he assured her, winking. "I know you Wastrels have *rules*."

As he walked away, the memory of his muscled body, slick with sweat, filled her mind, and she had to breathe deeply to rid herself of the image. She tried to picture her attraction to him as just another duck in the river of her consciousness. But the duck bobbed on the surface obstinately, refusing to be carried away by the current. What was all this meditation for, if a single wink from an ex-boyfriend could unravel her? Now she was angry, so she tried to picture her anger as another duck — no, a big goose. She sent the goose to drown the duck of attraction. Soon the waters of her mind were roiling with fighting waterfowl.

"Do you need to sit down?" Sister Melon Rind asked. Novice Backhoe had just slammed a crate of lettuce beside their stall. Apologizing, she went back to their truck to meditate in the shade. Alastair had betrayed her. Clearly, he had joined a cult — but still she could not shake her desire even as she recognized how *dirty* he had looked.

And that night, lying awake on her futon, she realized that she'd memorized the address he'd given her.

Brother PVC gave a lecture that evening on "enlightened consumption," and Novice Backhoe fought off intrusive memories of Alastair as she struggled to pay attention. Everything monastics consumed should help them follow the Way, Brother PVC explained. By only eating fruits and vegetables grown in their gardens, they knew their food did no violence. By making their own clothes, they knew their garb did no violence. But, he warned, they also must guard against psychic violence. The books they read should be enlightened, never violent or sexual. The music they sang should be peaceful, not loud or emotional. He stared pointedly at Sister Fungi as he said this.

After dinner that evening, Novice Backhoe sought out Sister Fungi near the beehives.

"Have you come to enjoy the crisp, fall air?"

Novice Backhoe inhaled deeply. "Lovely. But actually I wanted to ask you about the lecture."

Sister Fungi laughed. "You noticed some of the comments were directed at me?"

"I met you at a smash band concert. But Brother PVC said we're not supposed to listen to loud, emotional music, and smash is definitely —"

"Believe it or not, we monastics don't always agree on interpretations of the Way of the Waste," Sister Fungi said.

"So what do you think?"

"I think ... it is so hard to be a young person these days. So much is dying and fading away. Even very young children are aware of this. It causes them a great deal of suffering." Sister Fungi brushed a hand over white flowers, releasing a sweet scent. "When young people take that suffering and put it into music — what a beautiful transformation! I don't feel *violent* listening to smash, I feel the young people's pain. By feeling it together, we heal one other."

"I think I know what you mean. At a great smash show, you lose track of yourself — you lose your ego!"

"Exactly," Sister Fungi said. "Everyone at a show becomes a great beast. The drums are the heartbeat, the guitar the pulsing blood, and the singer our voice, howling at the moon." She flushed. "I feel so close to enlightenment in those moments. It's even better than sitting meditation!"

"For what it's worth, I think the Buddha would go to a smash show with you."

"There's a great lineup at The Sunken Tanker this Friday," the nun said, grinning. "Would you go with me?"

What would it be like to return to the Tanker now, skinbald, robed, and sober? Novice Backhoe would have to face all those people she used to party with. She'd be in a place where scoring tam was as easy as breathing. "I'm not sure I'm ready," she said. "Too much temptation."

"That sounds wise." Sister Fungi nodded serenely. But for the first time, Rylla thought she saw a flash of disappointment cross the nun's face.

Sorting micro-plastics was easily Novice Backhoe's most tedious assignment yet. She wore a pair of Gluvs so old they were actual *gloves* made of thick nylon fabric. Heavy OGGles labeled the type of each sliver of plastic her eyes focused on, so she could sort them for recycling. She tried to meditate and enjoy her breathing, but the Way of the Waste felt out-of-reach today; she couldn't breathe her way out of the boredom of sorting plastic. Almost without thinking, her Gluvs whirred, and she used the OGGles to log on to her Wingates OGnet profile.

Twelve missed calls. All from her mother. She dropped the slivers of plastic in her hands.

Without bothering to check the messages, Rylla called Amaryllis. Not wanting to explain the shaved head and robes, she left her end voice-only.

Amaryllis's head appeared in the bin of shredded plastic. The bottom half of her face was covered with a gas mask, and behind her, Rylla could make out a labyrinth of walkways, linking buildings on stilts above oily water. Her mom held up a finger for "wait a minute" and hurried down a catwalk into a building. As the door pressurized behind her, she ripped off the gas mask.

"Finally. Goddamnit, Sassy, where have you been?"

"Away — for school. Mom, are you in Houston?"

"That's why I've been calling you! It's all your jackass brother's fault."

"Why are you in *Houston*?"

"His little gang — whatchamacallit — the DLA? They were hijacking trucks bringing water rations to New Braunfels. At first, folks were glad, 'cause they were giving the water away for free. But then the government said they weren't gonna ship us water no more, on account of 'terrorist activity.' Told everyone to evacuate."

"Shit, mom. I'm so sorry."

"I heard there's work in Houston. Always wanted a waterfront view." She barked a bitter laugh. "But the refineries here have these newfangled welder drones. They don't even need people like me anymore." She shook her head. "There's some low-paying gigs doing drone maintenance, so that's what I'm looking for. But there's a lot of emigrants here."

"What happens if you can't get a job?" But Rylla knew the answer already — she knew the last stop for all desperate Dusties — Emigrant City.

"Oh, I'll find something." Amaryllis sniffed and wiped her nose on the back of her hand. "Damn chemicals in the air make me allergic. Say what you will about the Dust, but at least the air's clean. Even when you're inside the airlocks here, Houston smells like a hot fart."

Amaryllis said she had to go, check out some leads on jobs. By the time she hung up the call, Rylla had made up her mind.

Once, Alastair had said he could get her mother her a visa out of the Dust. Maybe he still could.

36

Gaia's Legion

Since novices weren't exactly allowed to visit ex-boyfriends, Rylla told Sister Fungi she'd changed her mind about that show at the Sunken Tanker. The address Alastair had given was close to the venue. She'd go with the nun, slip away during the opening band, and return before the last act finished.

But her chance to sneak off came sooner than expected. They took the MagWay at rush hour, changing lines at 14th street. The platform was crammed, and Rylla simply let the crowd separate her from Sister Fungi. As the train's doors slid closed, the nun's stricken face turned to the window. Rylla gestured to say she'd take the next one. Instead, she changed into her old clothes in the station bathroom, stuffing her robes into a shoulder bag.

She had expected to find a house at the address Alastair had given her, not a derelict car factory. The sun was setting behind the enormous brick edifice, casting long shadows across a crumbling parking lot. A hundred years of overlapping graffiti covered the walls, and the thousands of small-paned windows had lost their glass long ago. It looked like a place where bad things happened. Rylla steeled herself with the memory of her mother's desperate face and slipped through the chain-link gate.

As she mounted the stairs leading to the front doors, figures materialized out of the shadows — five on the roof, two at the doors. Rylla froze. A glance behind her revealed three more figures dressed all in black, heavy rifles pointed at her head. They looked like Navy Seals, not drugged-out cultists. She held her hands up, arms trembling.

"I'm sorry. I think I'm in the wrong pla —"

"Shut up," barked one of the two masked figures by the door.

They rushed towards her, and she was too terrified to protest when one grabbed her bag and the other patted her down. Finding nothing but brown robes, they hauled her towards the doors. A hood was dropped over her head, and she fought against the panic threatening to strangle her with steadying breaths. As she was steered through corridors leading deeper and deeper into the building, she tried to memorize the turns — left, right, up three stairs, left. Finally, she was pushed onto a couch, a door slammed, and the room around her was silent.

She lost track of time in the darkness — it could have been ten minutes or two hours that she waited. She tried meditating, but her mind was a raging river that wouldn't settle.

Footsteps approached, muffled at first, then a door opened and she knew several booted people were in the room with her. Her heart raced a mile-a-minute as the hood was yanked from her head — and she sagged with relief at the familiar sight of Alastair's face.

"Sorry! What a misunderstanding," he said, leaning on one hip. "I'd told the guards to watch out for a Wastrel. 'Give her the red-carpet treatment,' I said. But when you turned up in a t-shirt," he waved a careless hand towards her figure. "They didn't recognize you."

He turned to one of the black-clad shadows in the doorway and said, "She's mine."

"Sir." The guard spun on his heel and shut the door behind him.

The high walls of the room were covered floor-to-ceiling in graffiti and posters. Grimy, mismatched couches stood against the walls. In the two corners of the room was a makeshift chemistry lab and a massive antique printing machine, churning out paper-posters.

"I'm so glad you came," Alastair said, but then he narrowed his eyes. "Why *did* you come? You're not trying to spy on me like your little friends?"

He swiped a hand, and a wall of holoscreens hummed to life. Alastair tapped something out with MANIs, and three of the screens showed familiar faces — Jae cleaning a cement floor with a push-mop. Ynez hunched over a sewing machine. And Magenta, elbow deep in a toilet, scrubbing it with a stiff brush.

"They showed up a few weeks ago, pretending to be recruits. Of course, I knew right away they were sent here by your Professor Watt." He shook his head and sighed with satisfaction. "Oh, it's been good fun giving them the run-around, assigning them to the most menial tasks I can devise. And I've kept out of sight, so they don't even know I'm here, making sure they don't learn anything useful!" He laughed mischievously, and Rylla couldn't help but smile — it *was* kind of funny to see Magenta mucking out a filthy bathroom.

"So if you're looking to pry secrets out of me, think again," he said sternly, smile fading.

"Watt doesn't know I'm here."

He arched an eyebrow. "Don't tell me you want to join us?"

"No, it's ... personal."

Alastair's smile deepened in a way that made her uncomfortable.

"Not that —" she stammered. Being alone with him again was so flustering. Taking a deep breath, she tried again. "You owe me, Alastair."

He nodded. "I do."

"You got me tarred and feathered."

"I know. I'm a bastard." He dropped onto the couch next to her.

"Once, you said you could get my mom a visa out of the Dust." She rubbed her hands together. "She's in trouble now. Can you help her?"

He leaned forward, resting his elbows on his knees. "Oh Rylla, I wish I could. Truly. But when I joined Gaia's Legion, I gave everything to the Vulpini. All my wealth, the property, the assets — I gave it all to him, to help the cause."

Alastair's words were a punch in the stomach. *You fucking clown*, she thought, though she wasn't sure if she meant Alastair or herself. How the hell could she help her mother now? Tears of desperation pricked her eyes, and not wanting Alastair to see, she sprung off the couch and moved to the far wall, inspecting the posters there.

Mother Earth Is Dying!

Join Gaia's Legion — Fight For Her Today!

"So what *is* Gaia's Legion, exactly?" she asked bitterly. "A militia?"

He laughed. "Nothing like that. We're a — a family."

"You're a cult."

"If I'm in a cult, so are you." Alastair's eyes twinkled. "The Wastrels and Gaia's Legion both believe in living in harmony with Mother Earth. We're not that different."

"Wastrels don't have machine guns."

"Look, Gaia's Legion is growing quickly, and the FBI has ... taken an interest," he said. "We wouldn't be the first activist group to be massacred by the government for the crime of giving people hope. We have to protect ourselves."

"Wastrels don't believe in violence," Rylla said. "All life is precious."

"Is that so? And what if there's a weed choking your garden, spreading so fast that all your crops will die if you don't act — don't you pull that weed?"

"We were talking about guns, I think," Rylla said, shooting him a sneer. "And human beings."

"Do you pull the weed or don't you?"

Rylla leaned in to inspect another paper-poster on the wall.

Is The Human Species A Planetary Parasite?

The Vulpini Has The Answers *THEY* Don't Want You To Hear.

Join Gaia's Legion Today!

"So who is Vulpini anyways?"

"*The* Vulpini is our teacher." He spread his arms across the back of the couch. "Vulpini is a term of respect."

"Can I meet him?"

Alastair barked a laugh. "Why, so you can run back and tell your professor?"

Rylla turned away from the part of the room with the disheveled bed, inspecting instead the high-tech equipment in the corner. She ran her finger over a dusty chemical printer, a clunkier version of the one Azam had used to print a lotus flower seed. "If you don't even know the Vulpini, how can you trust him?"

"Oh, *I* know him," Alastair said. "You could say I'm his conduit. He's busy starting Legions in cities all over the world. I meet with him and share his teachings with this commune."

"And what's so special about him?" She ran a hand over the antique printing machine, *ka-chunking* as it printed more paper-posters.

Alastair's eyes went wide and manic again. "When the Vulpini speaks, it's like the universe is speaking through him. Just being around him, you feel this ... energy. He's had a difficult life, but his suffering has brought him clarity." Alastair shook his head. "It's impossible to explain if you haven't met him."

"He's a con artist, Alastair! He scammed you out of all your money. That's what cult leaders *do.*"

"Don't Wastrels give up their earthly possessions?" he asked, unruffled. "The money I inherited from my family only ever brought me suffering. I didn't earn it. I didn't deserve it. My greedy ancestors hoarded it for generations." He shrugged. "Now it's put to a higher cause."

"Oh, machine guns are a higher cause?"

"This again," Alastair rolled his eyes with impatience. "I told you, we have to protect ourselves!"

"You're brainwashed. This Vulpini says jump, you say how high? He says give me all your money, you say, *Here you go.*"

"Don't you follow the Way of the Waste?" He got up from the couch stretched his arms overhead laconically, his tight, black, long-sleeve t-shirt tracing the curves of his sculpted arms. She couldn't help looking — and remembering what it was like to have them wrapped around her. "The Wastrels say you can't drink, so you don't drink." He strode towards her, crossing the room, grinning so his sharp canines slipped over his lips. "The Wastrels say you can't have hair, so you shave your head." He stepped close — too close — and gently ran a palm over the stubble on her head. At his touch, a cascade of electricity shot from her scalp throughout her body. She could smell him now — dirt and sweat and smoke and — *him*. She took a deep breath to steady herself.

"The Wastrels say you can't fuck," he purred in her ear. "So you don't fuck?"

She was a recovering tam addict, and he ran a drug cartel. He'd gotten suckered out of his money now by not one, but *two* deeply creepy cults. He'd sold her out to a medieval mob. Alastair Canterbury was ten thousand red flags wrapped in a bad idea. But he was also the first person she'd ever kissed. Ever slept with. The only one who'd ever said he loved her.

Before Rylla knew what was happening, her body took over. It told her willpower to *shut up* and told the Way of the Waste to go enlighten itself. Then she was reaching her arms around Alastair's neck and pulling him close. Their kisses were not sweet or gentle, his stubble rough against her skin. His hips ground her into the ancient printing machine. He lifted her up — she wrapped her legs around his waist — and then he was carrying her towards the bed, their lips never separating. As they crashed onto the bed, her conscious mind wondered how long it'd been since he'd washed these sheets, and whether or not he'd picked them out of a dumpster somewhere. But her body told her brain to stuff it, because Alastair had just stripped off his shirt, revealing the freckled, muscled torso she remembered so well. He grabbed a condom from a pile of them beside the bed — she refused to think too hard about that — and then he was ready.

A few minutes later, both of them were panting and slick with sweat, Rylla feeling a bit disappointed. Alastair pulled a small baggie of pink crystals from under the bed and waved it midair. Rylla's body was still in charge, her brain riding in the back seat, so she put a crystal on her tongue before her willpower could stop her. Instantly, her senses sharpened, and her body flooded with pleasure. She suddenly understood that her weeks with the Wastrels had been an utter waste of time. All those hours in sitting meditation, trying to enjoy the present moment, when a single hit of tam worked a thousand times better! Tam *was* enlightenment. Tam was the best thing on this good earth, and Alastair's body was the next best thing. And here, in this filthy bed, she was exactly where she was meant to be. She rolled over, straddling Alastair, and soon he was ready again.

37

The Cicada

The sunlight was sharp as the serrated cockroach leg, inches away from her face on the grimy pillow. Rylla sat up and the room whirled. Her head pounded to the familiar beat of tam withdrawal.

She groaned. This was not what she had intended. Alastair snored next to her, his skin looking sallow in the harsh morning light. How could she have slept with him, after he betrayed her in Camelot? How could she have done tam, after struggling for a month to get clean?

Everything hurt, and now she felt the tug of addiction, stronger than ever before. The bag of tam lay open on an overturned crate beside the bed. One teeny crystal would be enough to take away the pain. But if she took one crystal, she'd stay in bed cuddling with Alastair. And then, later, when it wore off, she'd do another. She would stay with him, and be his cult-wife. She'd never return to Wingates.

The faces of her friends crashed into her mind, alongside a surge of guilt and regret. Magenta, Ynez, and Jae had spent weeks babysitting her through the worst of her tam withdrawal, giving up their free evenings and weekends for her.

Dae-Dae was still mad at her for the hurtful things she'd said last time she was cosmic, but Azam and Theo had given her another chance. Professor Watt had given her one last chance too. And for some inexplicable reason, the professor still saw something special — or at least *useful* — in Rylla.

But it was the memory of her mother's face, tam-addled, stumbling home from Lucky's at dawn, slurring her love for Rylla and Tyler while burning a batch of pancakes — that finally steeled her resolve. As a child, Rylla had sworn she would never be so pathetic. She wasn't going to become a tammie, and she wasn't going to throw her life away for Alastair-fucking-Canterbury.

She climbed out of bed and picked up her scattered clothes. As she was buttoning up her jeans, she felt Alastair's eyes on her.

"Stay with me."

"No," she said. "This was a bad idea."

"Join us. Join the Legion. We're making a difference."

"No, thank you," she said, finding her bag and slinging it over her shoulder.

"I love you, Rylla."

He was sitting on the bed, the blanket on his lap. The sunlight framed his curly hair in a fuzzy halo. He was cute, and it was tempting to believe him, but he didn't mean it. She understood that now. He just didn't want her to leave.

"You're bad for me, Alastair. I have to go." She headed towards the door.

"Wait!" He jumped out of bed, unashamed of his nakedness. "I can't let you go wandering out there. Since you won't join us —" He picked up the black hood from the couch.

"You're seriously going to make me wear that?"

He nodded, grimacing apologetically. "Let me get dressed, and I'll walk you out. But before you go —" He crossed to the lab and fished around in a desk drawer.

"I found this, and it reminded me of you." He held out a necklace. The pendant was a silver cicada, about half the length of her thumb. "Aren't they your favorite? Cicadas, I mean."

She was touched that he'd remembered that detail from their conversation, that night they'd first gone riding together outside of Camelot. The night of their first kiss.

"Will you wear it and think of me?" he asked, pressing his forehead to hers.

She pulled away but looped the necklace over her head and tucked it in her shirt. "I'll wear it and remember who we *were*," she said. *And it'll remind me to never be that naïve again.*

A guard with an assault rifle appeared in the doorway then, and Alastair dropped the hood over her head.

✺

On the MagWay ride back to the temple, Rylla thought up stories to explain her absence — I got lost, I got mugged, I took the wrong train — but face-to-face with Sister Fungi, the truth poured out of her. Sister Fungi said that all monastics make mistakes, that the Way of the Waste is never a straight line, and it's normal to occasionally get lost. Still, Rylla could tell she'd lost the nun's respect. Worse, she'd made Sister Fungi suffer — a sleepless night searching for Rylla, reporting her missing to the police.

Life at the temple wasn't the same after that. During sitting meditation, her mind was a churning river of regret. Now, beneath the placid smiles of the other monastics, she spotted anxiety, dread, boredom — and some very judgmental looks. There were a few monastics, like Sister Fungi, who still seemed to radiate true inner peace. But she understood now that it would take decades for her to achieve that level of enlightenment. And she didn't have that kind of patience.

She missed the bustling Grove and the challenge of her classes. She missed Dae-Dae's zeal, and sleuthing with Theo, and even Magenta's teasing. The day of her departure, she explained to Sister Fungi that she had figured out monastic life was just not for her. Sister Fungi wished Rylla well, encouraged her to keep meditating daily, and seemed almost relieved as Rylla left the temple for the last time.

38

Specks in a Void

Fall had edged towards winter while Rylla was with the Wastrels. On the walk from the hoverbus stop to her dorm, she crossed the quad, crunching fallen leaves beneath her feet. She shivered in her T-shirt and made a mental note to dig out her Wingates-issued sweaters.

"Rylla!" called a familiar voice, and she spotted Azam waving at her from across the quad. Theo gave a head nod in recognition, but Dae-Dae stared pointedly at the ground. She was still mad, then. With a sinking feeling of regret, Rylla crossed over to their group.

"Oh, this is ridiculous," Theo blurted to Dae-Dae. "We know you've missed the hell out of Rylla. You keep trying to get us to read *fiction*, so we'll be 'better conversationalists.'"

Dae-Dae met Rylla's eyes then, and they held each other's gaze. At first Dae-Dae's look was stony, and Rylla tried to communicate how sorry she was with her eyes. The muscles in Dae-Dae's face softened — maybe it was working. Then the corner of Dae-Dae's mouth twitched, so Rylla raised an eyebrow in question. Dae-Dae sighed loudly. Rylla smiled back tentatively. At last, Dae-Dae's lips curled into a smile, and she said, "All right, all right! I missed you!" And then they were hugging, rocking side-to-side on the path.

Theo and Azam looked on, utterly bemused.

"I'm so sorry," Rylla cried. "I don't think you're a night-work robot! You're tons of fun!"

"I know you're sorry," Dae-Dae said. "I was trying to punish you. But ack!" She broke from the embrace to look up at Rylla. "I have so much to tell you! Huge breakthrough with the Phireflys. We cracked the problem of scalability!"

"That's great!" Rylla said. She was bursting with gratitude at this reunion, but she had no clue what Dae-Dae was talking about.

"The solution was so simple — *specialize* the Phireflys. Our Recycler Phireflys deconstruct polymers, our Gardener Molecules gather elements from them to print seeds — like Azam's lotus seed. And get this — some *replicate!* Queen Phireflys utilize liberated elements to print *more* Phireflys —"

"Whoa, clean!"

"The idea is for a swarm of Phireflys to spread over a landfill, break down all the garbage, and plant a prairie in their wake."

"*Dae-Dae,*" Azam hissed sternly. "All that is classified, remember? Ward 7?"

"Oh, Rylla doesn't understand us when we talk about engineering anyways," she said dismissively, and Azam shrugged.

Linking her arm through Rylla's, Dae-Dae steered her towards the Grove. The other three picked up a conversation they'd been having about Theo's research into the RID devices — something about biocybernetics. Dae-Dae was right, 90% of what they said about their research was incomprehensible to Rylla. But she didn't mind. Arm-in-arm with her friend, she was filled with nothing but glowing gratitude.

In the Grove, Rylla could hardly find the time to take bites of her food, as Dae-Dae and Azam peppered her with questions about her time with the Wastrels. Theo remained tight-lipped, until she described Sister Fungi's mycology lab, and he scoffed derisively. "I bet they're still using CRISPR for gene splicing. How quaint."

"Ignore him," Azam said. "He just hates anything to do with religion."

Azam had a centeredness that reminded Rylla of Sister Fungi. She was often quiet, not because she was shy, but because she listened and considered things carefully.

Rylla ran a hand over her scalp, dusted with a day's worth of peach fuzz. "The Wastrels, we — *they* shave their heads so they don't focus on physical appearance. Is something like that — is it — why you —?" Rylla wasn't sure if there was a polite way to ask her question.

Azam smiled wryly. "You want to ask why I wear a hijab?"

Rylla blushed.

"They always gotta ask," Azam said with a sigh. "No, it's not quite the same. Obviously, I care about my appearance. This lipstick wasn't cheap!" Azam smiled, her lips cobalt blue with gold shimmer — perfectly matched to her silk head scarf. "I never wore hijab back in Iran. For a long time there, women were *forced* to wear it, so now if you do, it's like, very old-fashioned? But when I came to Wingates, I was so homesick. And one day, I wanted to put it on. It made me feel connected to my mother and grandmother."

"So it's not religious then?" Rylla asked.

"I wouldn't say that. I *am* a Muslim woman, though not in the same way my mother is. She's very literal about religion and I'm — well — a scientist. A very gay, Muslim scientist. But these things aren't contradictions for me."

Theo folded his arms and snorted.

"I don't believe in the *super*natural," she said. "But I don't have to. The *natural* is enough. I study the building blocks of the universe. You know what's wild about atoms? They're mostly empty space." She gestured to the trees and tables surrounding them. "If the Grove was an atom, the nucleus would be one grain of dirt, there in the center. The rest — empty space. And the protons making up that nucleus? They're made up of quarks, which are mostly — what? Empty space!"

Azam placed her hand on Rylla's wrist. "When I touch your arm, the electrical fields of your atoms repel the electrical fields of my atoms. Some form bonds or swap electrons. Parts of you become parts of me. We're both just clouds of specks, dancing near each other in a void!"

"And out there," she gestured to the dusky sky above the dome, where the first stars were beginning to appear. "Our Earth is just a speck in a galaxy, that's a speck in a universe, that could be a speck in some greater pattern. Our human world is a tiny sliver of the scales of existence. What if God is the spaces between things? What if all the stars are like quarks in the proton of a higher being we can't fathom?" Her voice was breathless. "This is what I meditate on when I pray. When I remember to pray, that is. I'm not religious about it or anything," she laughed.

"Whoa, that's deep," Dae-Dae said. "You never told me any of that before."

"You never asked."

"My parents are atheists." Dae-Dae shrugged. "I worry it's, like, not polite to ask about religion."

"And you, Rylla? Are you a devoted Wastrel now?" Theo asked contemptuously. "Should I save up my trash for you to worship?"

"Some of the more woo-woo stuff I didn't get," Rylla said. "But learning to meditate was good. It helps me. And some of their ideas — like about interconnectedness? It's a lot like what you were saying, Azam."

"You want to know my earliest memory?" Theo scowled, leaning towards her. "I was sitting on the toilet, shitting my guts out. My mom was rubbing an egg on my stomach and praying in tongues." He laughed derisively. "I believed in her bullshit back then — believed there was a 'demon' in my belly. Finally, she called her pastor to pray over me. He's one of these Apocalypse-Gospel con men, but he took one look and told her to take me to the hospital. Turned out I had a *C. difficile* infection and I was dying of dehydration." He shook his head angrily, staring down at the table. "To this day, she says it was 'God's plan' — that the pastor arrived just in time to save me. It was doctors and an IV drip that saved me!"

"I'm sorry that happened to you," Azam said. "But every religion isn't like that."

Theo rolled his eyes.

"See? This is why I don't talk to you about my faith," Azam said. "Ignore him, Rylla. *I* want to hear more about the Wastrels."

In Humanity seminar, Jae, Magenta, and Ynez looked bedraggled and exhausted from the past three weeks. Ynez had deep bags under her eyes. Jae had sprouted a shaggy beard. And Magenta had gotten those cool twig-like hair extensions, but they looked matted and mossy. Rylla bit her cheek to keep from laughing as they described their difficulties infiltrating the eco-cult.

"They made us sleep on filthy cots, with the far-gone tammies who were only there for the drugs," Ynez said. "We didn't learn anything about what the Legion is planning."

"I scrubbed bathrooms for three freaking weeks, and I didn't even meet anyone who's laid eyes on this Vulpini guy," Magenta said. "I'm starting to think he's a hologram."

"The only useful information I learned came from other drug syndicates," Jae said. "Until a few months ago, the Tusks sold lollylolly and heroin. El Polvo ran tam and weed. And the Jusikoesea sold XD17. Everyone respected everyone else's turf.

But then Gaia's Legion got big and started selling everything to everyone."

"How'd that go over?" Watt asked.

"The other gangs went to war with them, but they were outgunned. Gaia's Legion is outfitted like an army. And they keep stealing members from the other gangs. They set you up with a place to live, three square meals, and a steady supply of whatever drugs you like. It's attractive to a lot of desperate people."

"They must cut the drugs with something that affects the speech center of your brain," Ynez said. "Because all the Legionnaires we met wouldn't talk to us — about *anything!*"

Finally, Rylla couldn't hold in her amusement anymore, and a laugh escaped from her lips. "Sorry, it's — I don't think they're drugging people into silence."

"What would you know about it?" Magenta asked.

"They weren't talking to you, because they'd been *ordered* not to. Because the head of the Detroit chapter of Gaia's Legion knew you were spying on them the whole time." The others looked baffled, and Rylla relished the feeling of knowing something they didn't. "Because the head of the Detroit Chapter of Gaia's Legion is Alastair Canterbury."

The others burst into a chaos of questions, but Professor Watt regarded Rylla with an amused smile. Rylla explained her run-in with Alastair, keeping most of the details private. Her classmates certainly didn't need to know about their hookup, or the tam, or the cicada necklace hanging under her shirt.

"Typical, that Alastair would fall for the next reductionist ontology telling him how to live his life," Magenta mumbled.

"If the Legion thinks humans are parasites, should we be worried about a mass-suicide event?" Ynez asked.

"They *say* they just want to change how people live," Jac said. "Stop human behavior that harms the planet."

"The Wastrels preach the same thing," Rylla said. "But they're not militant about it. I think Gaia's Legion plans to *force* people to change."

"It sounds to me like your field trip has failed," Watt said, capturing Ynez, Magenta, and Jae in her glare. "You still don't know what the Legion has planned or who the Vulpini is. And a drugged-up army stockpiling weapons, with a radical, anti-human ideology is *very* concerning. You need to gather more intelligence."

"How can we?" Magenta blurted. "Alastair will sabotage our every move."

Watt smiled. "What a perfect opportunity for you to practice deep undercover research. Prosthetic faces, altered biometrics, digital espionage — what a wonderful challenge for you all!"

"And we need to learn to do this *deep undercover research* because —?" Rylla trailed off, but Watt didn't supply an answer. She just held Rylla's gaze, eyes twinkling inscrutably.

As the class got up to leave, the cicada pendant bumped against Rylla's breastbone. This assignment would mean spending more time around Alastair. Dread tightened in her chest, as she wondered if she'd be able to resist his charms — or his seemingly endless supply of tam.

39

The Fall

In the gloom of the Climate Lab, Rylla chewed her cicada pendant in frustration, staring at the glowing, dead Earth turning before her. By the end of November, she'd tested out of most of her classes, but in Jae's class and Climate Modeling, she was stuck. Nothing she tried moved X-Day back significantly. And Jae was probably keeping her in his class just to torture her.

The pendant tasted cold and metallic on her tongue, and suddenly she remembered Alastair's room where he'd given it to her — and the poster on his wall. *The Human Species is a Virus.*

What if 'The Vulpini' was right? What would happen if she wiped out that virus? Heart pounding, her MANIs whirred, and she removed all the humans from her Earth. She re-ran the X-Day calculation. It *did* take a bit longer for everything to die. Without humans burning fossil fuels and damaging habitats, life on Earth gained another few hundred years to live. But without people doing something to stop it, the Earth kept warming, deserts kept spreading, and carbon kept building up in the atmosphere until all land-based life went extinct.

Professor Pupala crossed the room and stood in front of her, hands on his hips. "What are you doing?"

"Just seeing what happens to the planet without people."

"No, no, no," he said. "You haven't accounted for power plants, sewage treatment plants, and nuclear reactors. If all the people were to suddenly "disappear" like you've modeled, then the power to these facilities gets cut — they explode and melt down, starting toxic fires, leaking radioactive waste, thousands of them, all over the world." His hands blurred as he tweaked the parameters of Rylla's model, then re-ran the X-Day calculation. Rylla watched in horror as the globe lit up with explosions, wildfires, and the atmosphere filled with radiation. The X-Day calculation read: <50 Years.

"You see? The only future is one we create."

Rylla saved that simulation in her modeling app. If she ever ran into Alastair again, she would show it to him. Maybe that would free him from the Vulpini's brainwashing.

Late one night in early December, she was in Hoshiko's room, and for once they weren't meeting about the Manifest. What would be the point? They'd gotten no closer to figuring out what its 500 million *somethings* were. Instead, Hoshiko was teaching Rylla how to upload spyware for her upcoming field trip to Gaia's Legion.

"It's a lot like the program Theo created to hack Professor Watt's holowall," Hoshiko explained, tucking his hair behind both ears. "Only *I* wrote it, so naturally it's more sophisticated and undetectable. It'll let you to monitor all of Alastair's communication with this 'Vulpini' guy." He narrowed his eyes at Rylla. "You sure you know how to install it, or do we need to go over it one more time?"

"No, no I got it. I'm just worried about how long it'll take to break through his security system. I'll have to be alone in his room for at least ten minutes."

"But he trusts you, right?" Hoshiko said. "That's why Watt's having you go in as yourself, unlike Magenta and those other two. By the way, Magenta showed me their prosthetic face for the trip — it's unreal what the art department can do. Looks better than plastic surgery."

Rylla chewed her bottom lip, only half-listening. "Yeah ... I think Alastair trusts me. At least he used to, and I can probably get him to trust me again."

"Sounds kind of dangerous though, huh? You said these 'Legionnaires' are, like, armed to the teeth."

"I mean, yeah," Rylla said, stomach churning with doubt. "But if I can find out what this 'Vulpini' is planning to do with his army of guns and drugs — if I can save Alastair from his brainwashing — then it's worth it, right?"

"I guess." Hoshiko folded his arms. "Still, it's kind of low, isn't it? Even for Watt. Making you cozy up to your ex-boyfriend for a mission? Making you bait for a cult leader? That's a wild 'assignment.'"

Being described as "bait" spiked her anxiety, and she fumbled at her collar for her latest fidget — the cicada pendant, which she liked to run back and forth on its chain. But her fingers found nothing. The chain must've snapped earlier in the day.

Maybe it was for the best. If she was going to survive this mission, she needed to steel her emotions and stamp out any lingering trace of feelings she held for Alastair. She'd be a stone-cold spy, lying and manipulating people, because that's what Humanity majors *did*.

"What's the matter?" Hoshiko asked, knitting his brows in concern.

"Nothing," Rylla said. "I lost something, but I don't need it anymore."

On Thursday evenings, Professor Pupala held "office hours," working on his own research while he ignored the few students who showed up to work on their models. Rylla was the only student in the lab that evening, the blue-brown globe of her climate model spinning between her knees.

She had programmed her humans to be on their best behavior. They had replaced all plastics with plant-based alternatives. They were planting forests and sucking carbon out of the atmosphere as fast as they could. Not one person on her planet ate a bite of meat or dairy or burned so much as a drop of fossil fuels.

But it still wasn't enough.

Her X-Day calculation hovered around 800 years. She'd slowed down doomsday considerably, but ultimately, her model Earth was heating up faster than humans could fix it. She tried to alter the app's default settings for agriculture. The wastrels had grown food densely — different species all jumbled together. These "food forests" were supposed to be a better carbon sink than the app's default mega-farms. But she couldn't quite recreate their system in the modeling program.

"This is getting painful to watch." Professor Pupala stood above her, his bag slung over one shoulder. "I don't think I've ever had a student take this long to pass my class. And fiddling with the ag metrics won't even make a dent."

Rylla slumped forward, head in her hands. "Can't you at least give me a hint?"

He sighed. "The assignment was to prevent X-Day, right?"

"I know that," Rylla said.

"Then why are you trying so hard to accomplish another objective?"

"I'm not! I'm doing everything I can think of to stop X-Day."

"Are you?" He pulled up a summary of her resource usage. "1.75 billion acres set aside for crop production? 200 million cubic kilometers of water a day for human activity?"

"According to the app, I *have* to set that much aside!"

"Why?"

"That's how much water and farmland people need ..." Rylla's voice trailed off as dread crawled up her throat.

"That's how much *9 billion* people need to survive," he said.

The simple, monstrous solution to X-Day finally dawned on her. She wasn't supposed to save — she *couldn't* save — all 9 billion people. She only needed to save enough people to do the work of restoring the climate.

Heart hammering in her throat, she turned to her model and slashed the number of acres used for crop production, turning them over to carbon reclamation forests. She felt like a mass murderer as her global human population dropped from 9 billion people to 6 billion. She re-ran the X-Day calculation.

1,735 years.

She kept going, turning more and more of the arable land left on Earth from farmland to forest. Freeing up freshwater resources, turning entire cities over to wilderness, calculating X-Day for smaller and smaller human populations.

5 billion people. 5,396 years.

3 billion people. 11,424 years.

1 billion people. 49,001 years.

And then a number popped into her mind. A number that Theo and Hoshiko and Magenta had been obsessing over for months. Stomach twisting with dread, she calculated what X-Day would be if there were only 500 million people left on Earth.

Calculating ... calculating ...

Rylla held her breath. An error sign popped up. *X-Day cannot be calculated within the given parameters.*

She swiped her MANI to clear the message and looked up at Professor Pupala, who was smiling down at her sadly.

"Congratulations," he said. "You pass." He turned to walk from the lab.

"Wait!" she called. "There has to be another way."

He shrugged but didn't turn around. "Maybe," he said. "Be sure to tell me if you find it."

Icy clarity swept over her as he disappeared down the hall. With trembling fingers, she pulled the bottle of Seraclorazine from her pocket. Only one pill left. She swallowed it dry, hoping it'd be enough to get her through the night.

When her breathing finally steadied, she texted Theo, Magenta, and Hoshiko.

I know what the Manifest is.

40

Five Hundred Million

"This place is an infosec nightmare," Hoshiko pronounced, as he and Theo dashed between each of the holo-generators in the Climate Modeling lab, installing ProfBlock on all of them. Finally, he straightened up from fiddling with Professor Pupala's control panel. "Go ahead."

Rylla pulled up her climate model and showed them what she'd discovered. "Look — when I drop the human population to five hundred million, the system can't calculate X-Day! And there were five hundred million items on the Manifest. It can't be a coincidence!"

The three others looked puzzled.

"Yes, it can." Theo folded his arms. "Your model is just that — a *model*. Every student has a different one, which would return a different max population to avoid X-Day. I remember this assignment. I think my model could only sustain, like ... two hundred million humans."

Hoshiko's eyes glazed and his MANIs whirred. "I still have my saved file from this class ... here it is ... in my model, Earth could support 1 billion humans and still avoid X-Day."

"Mine was 2.1 billion," Magenta said.

Rylla sagged. "But five hundred million is still *between* all those numbers." She tapped a finger against her lips. "What if I'm right? What if I just happened to nail the right number? And the Manifest is a list of the people who will survive ... who will be *allowed* to survive? Oh god," Rylla said, holding a hand to her mouth. "What if Wingates is planning to wipe out everyone else? The other 8.5 billion humans? Some kind of — of purge?"

Silence fell as the others considered her words. Magenta was scowling furiously. Hoshiko chewed his lip. And all the blood drained from Theo's face.

But a moment later, he laughed, shaking his head. "No way. You're too paranoid. Wingates is *good,* remember? They're trying to *save* humanity, not wipe them out."

Magenta scratched their scalp under their twig-like extensions. "I don't share your faith in the goodness of Wingates," they said. "But I agree it's unlikely *Rylla* has stumbled upon the exactly-correct climate model."

Rylla shot eye-daggers at her roommate.

"We do need to crack that Manifest though," Magenta said, ignoring the look.

"I've been thinking I might find a clue to cracking the encryption by searching Watt's OGnet history, using a modified version of the program I developed for Rylla's field trip," Hoshiko offered. "But I'll need access to her holowall again."

"I'll go with you," Magenta said. "It's late and the building should be empty. Now's as good a time as any."

The two of them headed out of the lab, leaving Rylla and Theo alone. He stood, gripping the back of a chair with white knuckles, staring into space.

"If you're so sure I'm wrong, why do you look so worried?" she asked.

He startled like he'd forgotten she was in the room, but then a familiar, slow smile spread across his face — a mask sliding over his true feelings. "Maybe I'm nervous about being alone with you. I don't think we've had the chance — not since our *ruse* in the Humanity building."

The memory of Theo pinning her against Watt's holowall sent heat racing across the skin of her chest, entirely without her permission.

"It's funny when you blush. You go red all over," he laughed.

A different kind of heat spread through her then, and her words came out sharp as razors. "Ha-ha," she said drily. "It's funny, huh? Flirting with me?" She stood up to lock eyes with him, forgetting how much taller he was. It occurred to her that she was angry with him for exactly what she was planning to do to Alastair — faking feelings to manipulate someone — but she shoved the thought away. That was different, that was necessary to save the world from a dangerous cult. Theo just messed with her for fun. "This is all a game to you, isn't it?"

"It's no game," Theo said flatly, his smile falling. "I flirt with you because I *like* you."

She gaped at him in stunned silence, searching his face for signs of a lie. "If that's true, then why haven't you, like, *done* something?"

"Why haven't you?" he shot back. "Did you want me to shove you up against a wall and kiss you without your permission, like in some twentieth-century flatvid? I'm not going to get expelled for a consent violation." He folded his arms and stared unseeing towards the back wall. "And besides, I could never tell if we were flirting or fighting ..."

That was a familiar feeling. "But wait —" she stammered. "So — just to be clear — you *do* want to kiss me?"

"Hell," he said, raking his hair back with his hands. "I want to do a lot more than that."

For once in his life, he was being earnest. She'd been fighting her feelings for Theo since the day they'd met. Because that was the day he'd taken her on a wild jet stream ride and nearly gotten them attacked by 'Sentinel.' Because her gut — and her friends — had told her that he couldn't be trusted, that he'd crush her heart if she ever handed it over to him.

But as dangerous as Theo had seemed back then, it was nothing compared to how dangerous her world had become. And Theo was brilliant and cunning, and spied on professors without getting caught. Being *special* to someone like that — it might make her feel safe in the world again.

And besides, he was so fucking pretty.

She couldn't help smiling, then. He arched an eyebrow in question. As an answer, she reached up and dug her fingers into his thick knot of hair, pulling him close. His forehead rested against hers. Their breath came hot and fast. She stretched up on tiptoe, lips parting, closed her eyes —

And a *boom* shook the walls of the climate modeling lab. Rylla and Theo broke apart and shared one baffled look before the lights went dark. A siren screamed, the floor shuddered, and the ward sunk into the earth.

Of all the times for a cataclysm drill.

ATTENTION! THIS IS NOT A DRILL! the announcement blared. *FOLLOW THE LIGHTPATHS TO THE NEAREST DESIGNATED SHELTER AND SEAL THE DOOR. REPEAT. FOLLOW THE LIGHT —*

Ghostly hazard lights blinked on, and arrows appeared on the floor, leading out of the climate lab. They exchanged a worried glance, then took off after the lights, bursting into the corridor. Together they ran down the hallway, ducking into a small office. Theo pulled the door shut behind them, and a holoscreen appeared on the inner surface.

ARMED INTRUDER ALERT!

PRESS TO SEAL DOOR

Theo stuck his head into the corridor one last time, scanning for other students, then pressed his hand to the glowing screen. There was a loud *KA-CHUNK*, and a sheet of metal slid over the door. The holoscreen warned them to stay silent and leave the lights off. Then it too winked off, and they were doused in darkness.

A minute later, the floor finally stopped rumbling, meaning the whole school was now deep underground. She fumbled in her pocket for her Seraclorazine, then remembered she'd taken her last dose. Shakily, she sank to a cross-legged seat.

"You okay?" Theo whispered. She heard him doing something by the door. The holoscreen glowed to life, filled with code. One of his hands was pressed to the screen, the other tapped against the wall.

"We're supposed to be silent," she whispered, "and keep the lights off!"

"Oh please, we're sealed up in six inches of steel. Someone could press their ear to the door, and they wouldn't hear anything."

He meant to be comforting, but the thought of being trapped inside a metal box sent her heart rate spiking again.

The code vanished, and the holoscreen showed a top-down security feed of the corridor outside. "I don't know about you," he said, "but I want to find out what the hell is going on."

Another *boom!* rent the air. They heard a series of pops — not in their corridor, but nearby.

"Gunfire," Theo said. His MANIs blurred and the holoscreen divided itself into smaller and smaller boxes as he hacked into cameras all over the school. The first dozen corridors they saw were empty, but then he pulled up a view of a Jet Stream platform.

A nightmare crawled out of one of the tunnels. Its segmented body was ten feet tall and filled the tube. It's six legs moved with vicious coordination as it snapped serrated front mandibles. It looked like a mutant larval Megaloptera, except the plating on its abdomen reflected the light, like metal. It *was* metal. The monster scanned the Jet Stream platform with a sweeping grid of red lasers, then disappeared down another tunnel.

"What the hell is that?" Rylla breathed.

"If I had to pull a name out of the air," Theo said, "I'd guess *that's* a Sentinel."

Another monstrous metal insect appeared on the platform and slipped into the same tunnel. Then another, and another.

"They're headed for Ward 7. But I can't hack those systems." He swiped a hand and Hoshiko and Magenta's faces appeared in a corner of the holoscreen, crouched in Watt's office. "Hoshiko, can you get access to any of the holoscreens in Ward 7?"

Hoshiko shook his head. "No way. That ward runs on its own internal server. I don't have an access point."

"Shame we don't have a floorbot to send there," Rylla muttered.

"Genius!" Theo cried. His MANIs blurred, and moments later, dozens of flying and skittering cleaning drones emerged on the video feed of the Jet Stream platform, then headed down the tunnel to Ward 7.

Theo filled the holoscreen with the cleaning drones' feeds. At first, all were black, as they sped through the darkened jet stream tunnels. But then a pinpoint of light appeared, and the sounds of gunshots grew louder.

The drones emerged into a war zone. Many were shot immediately, their feeds glitching and going dark. But enough survived to send glimpses of the battle. A group of black-clad commandos were unloading machine guns into the Sentinels, but the hail of bullets barely slowed the robotic monsters. Rylla screamed as one of the Sentinels grabbed a commando with its prehensile mandibles and sliced the person in half.

"Look where the wall's busted," Theo said, tapping one of the feeds of a corridor choked with plaster dust. "That's where they must have tunneled in."

"Who are they?"

"No clue. If I had to guess? Siberians. Or Saudis. But honestly, there's no end to the people who want to steal Wingates research."

"Is that why they're here?"

"Why else break into Ward 7?"

Soon all the cleaning drones had been shot dead, except for one SpiderBot, skittering over drywall rubble. Theo expanded its view to fill the holoscreen. "Let's hope this one's a survivor," he said, breathless as he steered the SpiderBot between the crashing legs of a Sentinel. It dodged some running soldiers, ducked into a side-corridor, and emerged in a part of Ward 7 that was relatively quiet. The SpiderBot clambered over the corpse of a commando. Rylla averted her eyes, but Theo steered the drone with a single-minded purpose, whispering, "No, no, no." At the end of the hallway, an airlock door had been blasted off its hinges. Scuttling over twisted metal, the bot inched inside.

Theo bared his teeth at the screen, where three people in white HazMat suits stood with hands raised over their heads. A dozen black-clad commandos trained guns on them. Theo turned up the volume as loud as it went, but they couldn't make out voices over the sound of gunfire. When the bot's camera refocused, a flash of pink silk appeared behind the visor of one of the HazMat suits, and Rylla leaned in for a closer look. She thought she could make out curly, bronze hair behind the other hood — someone so short, the suit bunched at their wrists and ankles ...

"Oh god. It's Dae-Dae and Azam, isn't it?" she choked out.

The commando in front shouted and waved his gun. The third person in a HazMat suit took a step forward, stretching out a placating hand.

"That's Professor Morris," Theo said in a tight voice. "He's their research supervisor."

Gunshots. The professor's body jerked then crumpled to the floor. Dae-Dae and Azam grabbed each other, screaming. Red bloomed across the front of Professor Morris's white suit and spread in a dark pool beneath him. Rylla squeezed her eyes shut, whispering, "Let them be okay, please let them be okay."

"They're cooperating," Theo said matter-of-factly. "Dae-Dae and Azam — they're handing over the Phireflys." His lip curled into a sneer. "I'm going to kill them all."

But the reality was, Theo and Rylla were powerless to do anything but watch. A second later, they couldn't even do that, because one of the commandoes noticed the SpiderBot and leveled his gun at it. One last burst of sound, and they were plunged back into darkness.

After a long silence, Theo said, "You were right."

"About what?" Rylla whispered.

"The day we met. We were in The Grove and there was that cataclysm drill. Afterwards, we were talking about what would be the end of Wingates. Dae-Dae said it would be one of my mod viruses, and I said bacteria farts."

Rylla nodded, even though he couldn't see her in the total darkness.

"But you said, nah. It'll be people. People with guns." He fell silent, and they listened to the gunfire popping somewhere in the subterranean distance. "You were right."

Another explosion shook the floors.

"I used to think the entire Humanity department was a waste of space. But you're smart about *people* in a way I just don't get." He sucked in a long breath. "I guess that's important."

Theo had never sounded so earnest, and that scared her. The explosions and gunfire were possibly — no, definitely — coming closer. *Breathing in, I focus on the present moment.* She took a long steadying breath, falling back on her Wastrel training. *Breathing out, I embrace the waste of this moment.*

The popping sounds were close now — somewhere in the Climate building. What if Dae-Dae and Azam were already dead? What if she only had minutes to live? Despite her efforts, her breathing grew strangled.

"You're meditating, aren't you?" Theo said. "Will you teach me? I have to sit criss-cross applesauce, right?" She heard him shifting beside her.

Rylla snorted. "*You* want to learn to mediate? I thought you hated anything spiritual."

Another barrage of gunfire rang out — the closest one yet.

"I've changed my ways. Teach me, O Enlightened One."

She rolled her eyes. Of course, he was making fun of her, but at least teaching him to meditate would distract her from the explosions.

"Okay, first try to make your breaths deep and slow."

He took an absurdly deep breath and then whooshed it out in one forced exhalation. "Not like that!" She guessed where his shoulder was and pushed him a little. "I said *slow*."

"Okay, okay," he whispered. "Serious breathing." In between the blares of the alarm, she heard his in-breath and out-breath fall into rhythm with her own.

"Now, try to focus on this present moment. Don't get lost thinking about the past. Don't worry about the future."

"Like that someone might blast through that door and —"

"Exactly," Rylla said. "Don't think about that. Focus on how, in this moment, you're alive, and that's amazing. You can breathe in and out, and that's amazing."

"I'm with Rylla McCracken, and that's amazing."

Her breath caught in her throat.

"It'd be a real shame —" Theo whispered.

"What?"

"— if we died without finishing that kiss."

Bone-rattling blasts sounded outside their door. Theo's hand found hers, and she gripped his long fingers tightly.

A scuffling, then a metallic click. The blast shield slid into the wall, admitting a sliver of purple light at the doorframe. Then the door hissed open, and they stared into the gaping maw of a Sentinel.

41

Suspect

Time crystallized, and Rylla took in every detail of the monster before her in torturous slow-motion — every reflection of the Sentinel's spotlight on the curved plates of its thoracic armor, and the terrible serrated mandibles as they spread wide to slice her in half. She squeezed her eyes shut against the glare, gripping Theo's hand tight, preparing be ripped apart. But when nothing happened, she hazarded another peek. The sentinel's lower jaw unhinged, revealing a ramp leading into its body — a well-lit chamber, with white, padded seats. The belly of the beast looked like a Jet Stream pod.

"Sassparylla McCracken and Theodor Reyes?" came a disembodied voice. "For your safety, please board the Sentinel."

Theo and Rylla shared a baffled look, disentangled their hands, and mounted the ramp leading into the giant robot. As soon as they sat down, the Sentinel's mouth snapped shut and it began to move. Rylla grabbed the edges of her seat to keep from being bucked off by the undulating motion. Through windshields shaped like compound eyes, they watched Ward 4 blur by, until they plunged into the Jet stream tunnels. In the darkness, Rylla clung to her seat, and tried not to throw up from the parabolic motion. This was nothing like riding a horse.

The sentinel finally stopped in a vast, industrial chamber with perforated metal floors and exposed ductwork overhead. A half dozen other Sentinels crouched along the walls, darkened and still, bearing bullet holes and gouges from the recent battle. As Theo and Rylla disembarked through the Sentinel's maw, she realized they weren't alone. Dae-Dae knelt in a corner by a door, rocking back and forth, while Azam rubbed her back. Dae-Dae hadn't looked up, but Azam acknowledged them with a confused nod.

"They're okay," Rylla said, hand flying to her chest in gratitude. She started towards them, but then a door flew open and General Dorne charged in, surrounded by soldiers in the black and grey camouflage of urban warfare.

"I gave orders for her to be *secured*!" Dorne thundered.

"Who are you —" Rylla managed, before she realized that the soldiers were coming directly for *her*. They grabbed her roughly under the armpits.

"Hey!" Theo shouted. "What the hell?" Rylla locked eyes with Theo and Azam, but Dae-Dae continued staring at the floor, rocking.

"That's Rylla McCracken! She's a student here," Azam cried, one arm outstretched in outrage. But Dorne didn't deign to respond, and the soldiers pulled Rylla towards another set of doors. Considering the massive guns strapped to their backs, she stumbled along with them. But as the doors closed behind her, leaving her alone with the soldiers, she forced herself to speak. "What — why'd you — where are you taking me?"

"We're not authorized to answer your questions," one said severely. They steered her through a labyrinth of rough, industrial corridors, dimly lit by bare bulbs. Exposed wires and ducts ran overhead, and some portions had no walls or flooring — just exposed dirt tunnels. She'd assumed the Sentinel had taken them to Ward 7, but this looked nothing like the pristine white walls and orderly labs she'd seen on the cleaning drones' feeds. This was someplace else entirely.

Finally, the soldiers reached a steel door, shoved her into a featureless cell, and slammed it shut behind her.

The walls and floor were cement, and there was no furniture except for a toilet in one corner.

Where the hell *was* she? And why? Had Watt found out they'd been spying on her? Did this have something to do with Tyler and whatever he was up to in the Dust?

She couldn't breathe. She sank to all fours, panting for breath, wondering if they'd sucked the air out of the room to kill her. *No, this is just a panic attack.* She dug the empty bottle of Seraclorazine out of her pocket and ran her tongue around the edges, where a little orange powder remained. It didn't help. Was anyone ever going to come back and *explain* themselves, or had she been thrown in here to be forgotten about, left to die, like in the oubliette in *Castle of Mystery*?

Her heart beat painfully fast. She sat on the floor cross-legged and tried to sink into meditation. Her shuddering breaths slowed, but she could not get the panicked questions playing in her mind to stop. What was this place — some underground army base, even more top-secret than Ward 7? Why had the Sentinel brought her and Theo, Dae-Dae and Azam here? And why had Dorne singled out Rylla to be isolated from the others?

She tried to access her OGlenses, but they weren't working. She felt around the walls pointlessly, as if this was a sim with a secret trap door. Finally, after what could have been twenty minutes or hours, the door opened and General Dorne stepped inside, followed by Professor Watt. Rylla looked to Watt for reassurance, but the Professor's face was as stony as the General's.

"When was your last contact with the Vulpini?" the General bellowed.

"What —? I — I've never met the Vulpini," Rylla stammered. If Dorne was asking about the Vulpini, that must mean the intruders were from Gaia's Legion.

"Oh, but you have," Watt said, matter-of-factly. "And we think you know exactly who he is."

Rylla's mind scrambled to catch up. "Not … not Alastair?"

Watt nodded.

Rylla shook her head furiously. "No, no — he just *meets* with the Vulpini, but he's not —"

"He is," Watt said, folding her arms. "Now how have you been communicating with him since you left Camelot?"

"I haven't! I told you about that time I ran into him at the farmer's market," Rylla said, pressing her palms to her forehead. "And then I met with him at his headquarters, but I haven't been communicating with him."

"I find that hard to believe," Watt said icily, "given that he followed you here, to Michigan, just a few days after your field trip to Camelot ended."

"He didn't follow me! He — he said that was a coincidence." But as soon as the words left her mouth, Rylla realized how naïve she sounded. Of course their run-in at the farmer's market wasn't a coincidence. What kind of cult leader did his own shopping at a farmer's market, anyways?

"Bullshit," Dorne snarled. "You've been feeding him critical information about Wingates — the location of Ward 7, our internal security protocols, your friends' research —"

"I didn't! I swear, I —" Tears stood out in Rylla's eyes. How *had* Alastair known about Ward 7? How had he known to target *her* friends' research in particular? And was this some sick revenge plot for her refusal to stay in Camelot?

"What I want to know is *why*," Watt said. "Why betray your school? Are you convinced *humans are parasites*? Or was it for the drugs? Or just because your *boyfriend* asked?"

The derision in her voice made Rylla want to curl up in a ball and disappear. "I didn't betray Wingates," she cried, tears streaming down her cheeks. "I don't know how he did this!"

Watt searched her face for a long time, and Rylla held her gaze defiantly.

"It *is* possible she was an unwitting accomplice," Watt muttered to Dorne.

"Sure, it's *possible*," Dorne said, but her gaze remained skeptical.

"But you freely admit you did meet with Alastair at his headquarters last month?" When Rylla nodded, Watt stepped closer. "We need to know everything that transpired at that meeting."

"Everything?" Rylla asked miserably.

"Any small detail might help us recover what's been stolen," Watt said. "Many lives are at stake, Rylla."

She groaned and turned her back on them to stare at the wall. She couldn't bear to look at Professor Watt as she recounted her hookup with Alastair. Watt wanted to know every word of their conversation, every bit of lab equipment in his room, even the composition of the filth on his sheets. She was hoping to gloss over the actual sex, but —

"Did he inseminate you?" Dorne interrupted.

"What?" Rylla's cheeks burned. She glanced to Watt for help.

Watt raised an eyebrow as she turned to Dorne. "You think it could have been *in* his ejaculate?"

"We know he has a sophisticated understanding of nanotech."

"Answer the question, Rylla," Watt ordered. "Did he ejac —"

"No, no!" Rylla said, *really* wanting them to stop using that word. "We used condoms."

"Did he ever inject you with something? Say, a hypodermic needle?"

"What? No!"

"The bug could have been in a beverage," Watt mused. "Did you consume anything while with him?"

"Just — just a little tam," Rylla said, reluctantly offering this last detail.

"Oh, Rylla." Watt's look of utter disappointment made Rylla want to dissolve.

"It could have been in the tam," Dorne mused.

"Wait —" Rylla said. "What was that about a bug?"

"A microscopic recording device. He may have installed one in or on your body. One that would have allowed him to gather data on the school without your knowledge."

"But there *was* a bug! He gave me a necklace — a cicada pendant."

The General's eyes went wide, and she and Watt shared a meaningful glance. "Where is it now?"

"I don't know. I lost it, about a week ago."

To Rylla's surprise, Watt chuckled. "An actual bug." The professor shook her head. "He's very literal, this Vulpini. I bet that's it."

Rylla described the necklace in detail. The last time she could remember having it was before playing a sim — she'd tucked it into her e-mag suit before she'd entered the arena.

"We can review the security footage," Dorne said.

"Better yet, program the sensor sweeps."

"We'll find it." Dorne waved a MANI, the door *clicked* unlocked, and she disappeared through it.

"I still don't understand," Rylla moaned, leaning against the wall. "It's only been what — five months since we left Camelot? How did Alastair start a cult and raise an army in that amount of time?"

"Alastair Canterbury has more personal wealth than most *countries,*" Watt sighed. "Gaia's Legion had about a dozen members when he showed up, calling himself The Vulpini. He poured billions into their operation and built himself an army. Sure, he gives recruits housing, food, drugs — but even more powerfully, he gives them a *purpose.* He's charismatic, your Alastair. Under different circumstances, he'd have made a fine Humanity major ..." Watt trailed off in thought.

Rylla wiped at the wetness on her cheeks. "Do you believe me? That I didn't know what he was up to?"

Watt sighed. "If Dorne finds this bug? Perhaps. Mostly because I've seen no evidence that you have either the cunning or foresight needed to pull off an operation like this."

Rylla recoiled. For a wild, reckless moment, she wanted to shout, "Oh yeah? If I'm so useless, how come I've been spying on you all year without your noticing?"

But that wouldn't help her situation. She looked at the floor. "I'm so sorry."

"Tell that to the dead," Watt said, leaving Rylla alone again.

She sank to the floor and gave in to tears of self-pity and shame. On a continuous loop, her mind replayed the death of Professor Morris and the Legionnaires torn in half — *my fault, all my fault.* What was going to happen to her? Expulsion was the least of her worries now. Would she be tried in a military court? Jailed for treason? Executed? If what she'd suspected about the Manifest were true, Watt wouldn't hesitate to knock off a single student who stood in the way of her plans. She probably deserved to die anyways. *All my fault.*

Eventually, contact with the cold cement numbed Rylla's side, and she rolled to a seat. Without a clock or windows, it was impossible to gauge the passage of time, but she guessed that hours had passed. The stabbing pains in her gut got steadily worse. With horror, she realized the pains *weren't* just emotional. As if things weren't awful enough, she'd started her period.

"Hello?" she said to the ceiling, picking herself up off the floor. Maybe there was a camera up there somewhere. She scanned the smooth cement surface again, looking for even a small indication of an opening, a lens, a speaker — anything. "Please, I need my cup?" she called. She hammered on the door, but no one came. If she didn't do something soon, she was going to bleed through her pants. There was toilet paper stacked beside the toilet. She wadded some into a makeshift pad and stuck it in her underwear.

Then she slumped to a cross-legged seat against the wall, hugging her aching middle. But the absurdity of getting her period at a moment like this had shaken her out of despair. "Some ibuprofen would be nice!" she shouted at the ceiling. "Or Seraclorazine! Tam, if you've got it." She didn't think anyone was listening, but she didn't care. It felt good to shout.

"I didn't mean any harm you know! Maybe it is my fault, but it's not my *fault*-fault. It's fucking Alastair's fault!" she yelled. "I didn't start a creepy cult, did I? I didn't raise an army, and stalk my ex-girlfriend, and kill people!" A satisfying anger pumped through her veins. "So I'm a sucker for insect jewelry? Shoot me!"

At that moment, the door opened and General Dorne entered, flanked by two soldiers. Rylla's heart clenched — had they come to grant her last request?

One of the soldiers carried a clear box, and something inside buzzed like a murder hornet. It was her cicada pendant, come to life, its wings thrashing against the sides of its prison.

"Is this the necklace?" the general asked.

Rylla nodded.

"Neutralize it." The soldier saluted and disappeared down the corridor.

"All right, McCracken," the General said grudgingly. "Your story checks out. If it were up to me, you'd stay locked up until the Legion is dust. But Watt has decided we need your help."

42

Stolen

General Dorne led Rylla through the maze of tunnels to a cavernous, octagonal war room, bustling with soldiers in black and gray. Holoscreens lined the walls, showing live feeds from cities around the world. At the center of the room, a holomap of Wingates rotated slowly, its network of underground buildings and tunnels sprawling like an ancient oak's root system. Rylla hurried across the room, dodging soldiers, to keep up with Dorne. The general passed through a doorway into a simple conference room, where Watt and her friends were waiting.

All her friends.

Rylla understood why Dae-Dae and Azam were here — Alastair had stolen their research. But why Theo and Tavia? Why Jae, Ynez, and Magenta?

"Hey," Rylla said in a small voice, dropping into a chair. Some nodded in greeting, but Dae-Dae stared fixedly at the table, and Theo wouldn't meet her eyes.

"Let us begin," Dorne said. "At 2100 hours last night, a group of heavily armed persons from the plants'-rights group, Gaia's Legion, tunneled into Ward 7, disabling our substrate security measures."

354

A hologram of the cicada pendant appeared in the center of the table. "The Legion gained intel on our facility from this drone, given to Sassparylla McCracken by the leader of Gaia's Legion — Alastair Canterbury."

"Always struck me as more of a sidekick than a cult leader," Jae mumbled. Theo shook his head like he was disgusted. Magenta repeated "Sassparylla?" in a dumbfounded tone, like Rylla's full name was the most shocking bit of information Dorne had revealed.

Rylla's face burned with shame.

"They only knew what to look for because some of you around this table discussed *classified* research in front of Rylla," Professor Watt said pointedly. "They stole thousands of prototypes from Project Phirefly. Professor Morris tried to stop them, but he was —"

"Shot," Dae-Dae whispered. "After that, I helped them. I shouldn't have, but I was so scared." Tears filled her eyes. When she spoke again, her voice was desperate. "The Phireflys — they're terribly dangerous! We have to get them back."

Professor Watt's eyes clouded over. "Nelson, we need you in here with the cocktails," she muttered.

Watt wanted them to *drink* at a time like this?

General Dorne ignored Dae-Dae's outburst. "Their second target was Theodor Reyes and Tavia Johnson's RID project."

"Jog my memory," Magenta said, picking at a bracelet. "What was RID exactly? Something about cows?"

"Retroviral Implantation Devices," Theo said between clenched teeth. "Nanorobotic chemical printers, powered by the charge in human blood. Once injected, a RID can be remotely triggered to print a retrovirus to alter the organism's DNA."

No wonder he was so angry. His research had been stolen and he blamed Rylla for it.

"I'm so sorry," Rylla mumbled. "This is all my fault." Theo's eyebrows shot up as he nodded in agreement, but he still wouldn't meet her eyes.

"No, it's *my* fault," Dae-Dae sobbed. "I never should've talked about my research in front of Rylla. And I'm the one who handed over the Phireflys!"

"I also blame myself," Ynez's lips tightened into a line. "Vulpini is Latin for 'fox,' and in Camelot, the fox was on Alastair's coat of arms. It's so obvious, it's like he *wanted* us to figure it out. But we've spent the past few months researching the Legion, and somehow I never put two and two together."

"Enough," Watt said. "Now is not the time to parcel out blame."

The door opened and Dr. Hernandez entered holding a small silver case.

"Nelson, thank you for joining us," Watt said. "Gaia's Legion has stolen some very dangerous nanotechnology, and each of you have a role to play if we're to recover it." She looked around sternly. "So I need you all calm and collected."

Dr. Hernandez placed his case on the table. "Pathocine for this one?" he asked, raising an arched eyebrow at Dae-Dae's tear-stained face.

"Those two," Watt pointed at Dae-Dae and Azam. "Stims for the rest, I think."

Hernandez clicked open the case to reveal a collection of vials and syringes. "You've experienced great trauma," he told Dae-Dae and Azam, filling a syringe with clear liquid. "And when you return from this mission, you can take all the time you need to heal." He knelt down. "But right now, you have a job to do, so I'm going to give you something to help you focus."

Dae-Dae sniffed and wiped her nose on her sleeve. "Okay."

Dr. Hernandez injected her. Dae-Dae took a few deep breaths and her body visibly relaxed. She spoke in an oddly flat voice, "It's like not having emotions at all."

"Such clarity," Azam said after her prick, in the same monotone.

"You've all had a sleepless night," Watt said. "But there's no time to rest. Dr. Hernandez will give the rest of you something to help you stay sharp."

Rylla didn't know if she trusted Hernandez to pump her full of god-knows-what. What if it was addictive like tam? But Magenta offered up their arm without protest. And after getting pricked, they let out a long breath. "That is a *clean* high."

"The side effects can be intense," Hernandez said, pricking Ynez and Jae in turn. "Contact me if you experience dizziness, nausea, or an urge to commit cannibalism."

Theo simply shivered and said, "Effective."

Rylla reluctantly pulled up her sleeve. As Dr. Hernandez punctured her arm, icy liquid spread from the pinprick, dissolving all her aches and leaving her mind crystal-clear.

"Do you happen to have any Seraclorazine on you?" she whispered. Feeling a cramp twist in her gut, she added, "and maybe some ibuprofen?" He said he'd see what he could do.

The stims had given Rylla courage to speak her mind. "You said we each have a role to play," she told Watt, "but aren't we a little out of our league here? The army's involved, people have died! This isn't a time for a field trip. We're just a bunch of teenagers!"

"The Vulpini, as you know, is also a teenager," Watt answered. "And due to your *personal* relationship, you may be uniquely able to reach him." She turned to Theo, Tavia, Dae-Dae, and Azam. "You four developed this research, and we need your help to ensure we recover every trace of it." She turned to Jae, Ynez, and Magenta, "And you three have been studying Gaia's Legion for months. The knowledge you've gained may be invaluable in devising a plan to recover this research."

"Hasn't the army been spying on Gaia's Legion? Surely you have better agents than us," Ynez said to Dorne.

"We have run into, ah, *difficulties,*" Dorne cleared her throat, "penetrating the legion's command structure."

"Well, I feel that," Magenta said, slapping the table. "We didn't get past scrubbing toilets."

"*Her* agents got hooked on drugs and switched allegiances to the Vulpini." Watt said stonily, ignoring the way Dorne's jaw clenched.

"Compared to that, I guess we didn't do so badly on that field trip after all?" Jae said, arching an eyebrow at Watt.

She pursed her lips at him and changed the subject. "We're waiting on one more student, who we'll need to hack into the Legion's internal communications. Professor Amari assures me he's better than anyone on faculty at cracking security encryptions — ah, here he is." The door opened and Hoshiko stepped through. Rylla had to bite her cheek to keep from bursting into laughter. Watt was putting all her faith in Hoshiko, the guy who'd been spying on her for months, who'd architected ProfBlock! Watt had always seemed like she had all the answers. But it dawned on Rylla that Watt and Dorne had no plan here — no idea how to recover the stolen tech. And they were looking to Rylla and her friends for guidance.

"So — what *is* the plan?" Theo asked, echoing Rylla's thoughts.

"We'd like your help figuring that out." Watt answered honestly, swiping her MANIs to display satellite footage of a forest clearing, where black-clad commandoes emerged from a tunnel and boarded a camouflaged skimmer. "Several Legionnaires escaped with the stolen research at 0100 hours. We've tracked their craft to Chicago, where the Vulpini is currently holed up."

"I suggest we send a targeted drone strike to their location," Dorne said. "Destroy the Legionnaires and the stolen research."

"No!" Rylla's hand flew to her heart. As horrible as Alastair was, the thought of him getting blown up made her feel like she was breaking apart.

Hoshiko shook his head. "Destroying their base will destroy their records of digital communication. If I were this

Alastair chump, I would've already sent the stolen research to all my high-ranking Legionnaires."

Theo scowled. "Then any of them could chemically print new Phireflys or RIDs."

"That is very bad," Dae-Dae said, in that strangely flat tone.

"So we have to hack into their servers, find out where the information has been shared, hunt it down, and destroy every last digital trace," Hoshiko said.

"How do we do that?" Dorne demanded.

"I've been thinking on that —" He chewed his lip. "I've found that the weakest point in most organizations is their wearable tech — OGGles, OGlenses, MANIs — the security on the hardware of those devices is pitiful compared to what you'd find on a holowall or a server."

Rylla remembered the times Hoshiko and Theo had commandeered her OGlenses, scrambling her vision with code.

"But it's hard for hackers to exploit those weaknesses, because you have to *physically* tap into the nanotech — meaning, like, tackle the person and rip off their eyewear to get to the hardware. Most hackers are more hands-off."

"Those Legionnaires have a lot of firepower," Ynez said. "For the record? I am not *tackling* anyone."

"You wouldn't have to." Theo leaned forward excitedly. "We could use a drone of some kind — a tiny one. Say, a nanorobot that could land on their devices, infiltrate the hardware —"

Dae-Dae tilted her head to one side. "You're talking about using Phireflys."

Hoshiko turned to her. "Could we adapt a Phirefly to land on wearable tech — say a set of MANIs — drill into its internal nanochip, and upload a hacking protocol?"

"Of course," Dae-Dae said, knitting her brows. "But they stole our prototypes."

"Can't you just print more?" Dorne asked.

"Have you *seen* the labs in Ward 7? They trashed them." Dae-Dae shook her head. "It'll take me a few days to program another 3D printer, but — wait!" Her hand flew to her front pocket. "My pets!" Her MANIs blurred, and a small cloud of grey specks streamed out of her pocket — the original Phireflys. "These older-gen models could do it!"

"Okay, so we fly some Phireflys into their base, land them on Alastair's MANI's, upload the hacking protocol — and *then* drone strike the hell out of them?" Dorne asked.

"You can't just kill him!" Rylla shouted, flinging her hands out. "What about due process and shit? Right to a fair trial?"

"Actually, Gaia's Legion has been classified as a terrorist organization." Ynez held up a hand to Rylla's furious glare. "So I'm not saying we should! But that we *can*, legally speaking, just kill them."

Jae shook his head, "I don't care what the government says, everyone deserves a fair trial. And we should to talk to them, find out what they're planning!"

"Is it really a big mystery?" Magenta cried. "Their whole thing is *humanity is a parasite*, and Dae-Dae said these Phireflys could be super-dangerous. They're going to try to wipe us out! We need to wipe *them* out first."

"No, I don't believe it," Rylla said, shaking her head. "Alastair isn't capable of mass murder. There's no way —"

"Oh, please." Magenta cut her off. "Your little *opinion* of your cult-boyfriend is not a consideration here."

"Surely, though," Watt interrupted, "we should avoid needless violence?" She shot Magenta a stern look, then turned to Dorne, "And don't you agree that interrogating the Legion's top leadership would be worthwhile?" The general grunted reluctantly.

"There's another problem with your plan," Dae-Dae said. "These older-gen Phireflys have tiny batteries and limited comm range. We can't just "fly one" all the way to Chicago. We'll have to release them *in* the room with the Legionnaires you want to hack."

"Which means we'll need someone who can get close to Alastair," Magenta said.

All the heads in the room turned towards Rylla.

"I — look — trust me, I want to help," Rylla stammered, "but I don't know the first thing about all this tech! I can't work the Phireflys."

"If you can smuggle me into their base, I can steer them," Dae-Dae said. "While you get close to Alastair and ... distract him."

"No! That's way too dangerous," Jae said, pinching the bridge of his nose. "How are you going to get Rylla out of there once the hack is complete? What happens if their security systems catch the upload?"

"What if ..." Theo started, a slow smile spreading over his face. "What if we use RID?"

Tavia's jaw dropped, and Watt glared at him.

"Hear me out. Like Dae-Dae, I have some earlier prototypes that Alastair failed to steal. So, we use some of the Phireflys to hack the Legionnaires' MANIs, like Hoshiko said. But *some* Phireflys get loaded with RID instead. We land them on the Legionnaire's skin and inject them with RID."

"And how exactly is some cow-sterilizing implant going to help us?" Magenta asked, arching an eyebrow.

"RID can be used to deliver a *variety* of gene therapies," Theo said. Watt shot him another sharp look, as if to say, *careful*. He gave her a tiny nod. "We can use them to cure cancers in cows, sterilize them — or *tranquilize* them. So if we inject the Legionnaires with RID, then trigger RID to print a sedative —" He snapped his fingers. "The Legionnaires pass out, and Dorne's soldiers charge in."

"How do you know this is safe?" Ynez asked. "Have you completed any animal trials?"

"Fucking Humanity majors," Theo clawed his fingers through his hair in frustration. "You don't grasp what's at stake here. We need to reclaim every bit of information — in their databases and their *brains* — before they spread this research any further."

"Tavia, as Theo's advisor, do you approve of this idea?" Watt asked.

Tavia pursed her lips. "Normally? Hell no, you don't experiment on humans before an animal trial. But this is an extenuating circumstance. And the biotech for sedation is basic. But you'll need to adjust the dosage for each Legionnaire based on their biostats."

Watt nodded, which Theo took as approval of his plan.

"I'll infiltrate the Legion Headquarters with Rylla instead of Dae-Dae then," Theo said. Turning to Dae-Dae, he added, "I can establish a remote link to you and Hoshiko — so you can stay at a safe distance, steer the Phireflys, and hack their OGnet systems remotely." He turned back to the group. "Meanwhile, I'll oversee the RID implantation, sedating the Legionnaires. And Rylla, you'll — you know — *distract* him."

"Right. You'll need intel on the layout of their headquarters," Watt said.

"Send me the address," Ynez said. "I'll look up the building archives." Her MANIs were already drumming against the table. Jae and Magenta started talking about plans to draw as many Legionnaires out of the base as possible. Tavia and Dae-Dae commandeered one half of the conference table for a nanorobotics lab — soldiers materialized with the equipment they needed — and they got to work modifying some of the Phireflys to inject Theo's old RID prototypes.

But just as the plan started to come together, the door to the conference room flew open, and a soldier summoned Dorne into the war room.

Watt followed the general out, and after a moment, Rylla and her friends hurried through the door to see what was happening.

Now all the holowalls showed different views of the same city block, where a tall building was *dissolving*.

"No," Dae-Dae breathed.

General Dorne flicked her MANI and a news anchor unmuted. "I'm here in Logan Square, in downtown Chicago, where moments ago, an apartment building started to ... well, *disappear*." She turned to a wild-eyed man, wrapped in a foil emergency blanket. "Sir, can you tell us what happened?"

"They were crawling all over me! Eating the walls, the floor, even my clothes!"

"Only the synthetic materials," Dae-Dae breathed.

"They're some kinda bugs!" the man went on. "I was on the first floor, so I got out in time. The folks higher up —" His voice faltered and he pulled the foil tight around his shoulders.

Behind him, a tendril of gray cloud rose from the dissolving building and settled on another roof, vanishing everything it touched. The onlooking crowds screamed and ran. The reporter ducked beneath her arms as a dark hail fell around her.

"It's raining something — dirt? I think it's raining dirt! And — ow!"

"— and seeds," Dae-Dae said, in that eerily flat tone. "They're turning Chicago into a garden. And with a city's worth of polymers to absorb, they'll grow exponentially. The more they eat, the more Phireflys the Queens will make ..."

"Is there any way to stop them?" Dorne demanded.

Dae-Dae frowned for long moments, then snapped her fingers. "I hadn't finished the waterproofing —"

"Get the Chicago Fire Department," Dorne bellowed. "And every fireship in a two-hundred-mile radius!" At the sound of Dorne's voice, half a dozen soldiers in the war room broke into a run.

"Hate to interrupt," Magenta said, eyes glazed. "But this is blowing up on Joinly —" They swiped a hand, sending a vid to the closest holowall, where armed black-clad commandoes charged the lobby of some luxury skyscraper.

"Where is this?" Dorne asked.

"875 North Michigan Ave. The old Hancock Building."

"There's an orbital shuttle pad on the roof of the Hancock," Ynez said. "Maybe they're trying to escape the city that way?"

"Or they're trying to get it airborne?" Theo said slowly. He and Dae-Dae shared a look.

"Low orbit dispersal," Dae-Dae said. "That would spread it *very* effectively."

"Fuck," Hoshiko said.

"Fuck is right — that's them — that's the Legion!" Theo bellowed. He turned to Dorne. "There's no more time. You have to get us to that shuttle pad now!"

Dorne looked to Watt and the professor nodded. Theo barked orders, and Dorne's soldiers *listened*. As Rylla was herded towards the exit, her breath hitched in her chest. Where the hell was Dr. Hernandez with that Seraclorazine? She couldn't do this. She wasn't a soldier or a spy. She was a terrified kid who was perilously close to bleeding through her pants.

"Wait!" she shouted. "I need —" Dorne's head whipped around, and Rylla froze, grasping for the words. She needed so many things. A vat of Seraclorazine, and a time machine, and so many questions answered. But with everyone's eyes on her, she asked for the one thing that felt most pressing of all. "— I need a tampon."

43

Swarm

Ynez placed two paper-wrapped tampons in Rylla's hand, and then a military escort rushed them to an underground aircraft hangar. Thankfully, the military shuttle had a bathroom, and Rylla was able to take care of her period situation in private. She emerged with relief that one problem, at least, had been solved. But the feeling only lasted a second.

An officer thrust a bodysuit at her. "Put this on." Major Gwiazdjowski was barrel-chested, with pitted skin and a mouth like a knife-slash. He introduced himself and tossed another bodysuit to Theo.

The fabric felt slimy and stretchy as Rylla struggled to get it on over her jeans.

"This is dragon skin, isn't it?" Theo asked, zipping it up to his neck. "Bulletproof."

"To a point," the major said. "Each impact weakens its resistance, so don't go getting caught in a hail of bullets."

Rylla thought she might puke at the thought. As soon as she zipped it up, the major started strapping things to her utility belt.

"Gas mask, med kit, grappling hook with spider silk, arachnocams." At least she knew how to use the climbing gear, thanks to Jae. "These boots have built-in e-mags. Kick the heel to turn them on, and they'll hold your full body weight."

He shoved a helmet on her head, then held up a shoulder harness. "Your weapons —"

"No," Rylla said, shaking her head. Her voice came out tinny through the helmet's respirator. "I've never shot a gun."

He pulled one of the pistols from the holster. "This is the safety. Switch it off. Aim," he lifted his arm in demonstration. "Shoot."

The memory of Professor Morris's body jerking back and crumpling, lifeless, to the floor flashed through her mind. "No," she said again. If there was one thing the Wastrels were dead-clear on, it was that nothing — *nothing* — was worth taking a human life. "Aren't I supposed to like, seduce Alastair or something? So Theo can land Phireflys on him? How's it gonna look if I come in guns blazing?"

"My orders are to outfit you —"

"This outfit is great, thanks," Rylla said. "But I'm not taking the guns."

Theo snorted, slipping into his own gun harness. He looked like a skinnier version of the other soldiers, and he slouched as he tied his hair back.

Tavia, Dae-Dae, and Hoshiko hunched in a corner of the shuttle, eyes glazed, MANIs blurring as they finished last-minute modifications on the Phireflys, some of which would hack the Legionnaire's wearable tech, and some of which would inject RIDs to sedate the Legionnaires. The three of them would stay behind and work remotely while Theo and Rylla landed on the shuttle pad.

"You need to hurry," the Major told them. "ETA in seven minutes."

"Shit," Dae-Dae breathed, and her hand movements accelerated. She and Hoshiko conversed in snatches of code-speak Rylla couldn't begin to understand. Finally Dae-Dae grinned, swiped a hand, and her vision focused on Rylla. Standing, she pulled a small white object from the front-pocket of her jumpsuit. A smile spreading over her face, she tucked the object into a pouch on Rylla's belt. It was another tampon.

"What —?"

Dae-Dae snorted a giggle. "Your outburst back there gave me an idea for how to store the Phireflys safely, in case the Legionnaires search you. Who would deprive someone of their tampon, right? So the Phireflys are all *in there* — and see, here's the hole they can fly out of."

In spite of her mortal terror and embarrassment, Rylla had to laugh.

"I'm sending you an app for releasing the Phireflys. The motion to release them has to be subtle." Dae-Dae held up her hand and swiped her thumb across the base of her ring finger. "It's the motion you'd use to twist a ring on your ring finger. Got it?"

Rylla imitated the motion and Dae-Dae nodded.

"Now don't do that again until you see the whites of Alastair's eyes. The app will launch a few Phireflys at a time. Release as many as you can, but don't let them out all at once or the Legionnaires might notice."

Light flooded the cabin as they burst from the treeline, out over the vast brown waters of Lake Michigan. The Chicago skyline, a jagged edge on the horizon, was *churning*.

"Oh god," Dae-Dae breathed.

The Phirefly swarm looked like a many-limbed beast stretching over the city, dissolving everything it touched. Fleets of fireships battled the swarm with water cannons. Everywhere the water touched, clouds of Phireflys fell to the earth. But there were not nearly enough fireships, and the swarm grew larger with every devoured building.

"Strap in!" the pilot called over her shoulder. "Things are about to get hairy!"

Rylla dropped into a seat and fumbled with the complicated straps of the harness. When she looked up again, her breath caught, because now they were close enough to see the *people*. In places where the Phireflys had cut off the upper floors of a building, people were jumping. Tears blurred Rylla's vision of bodies falling through a rain of black soil. In the streets below, crowds stampeded and scattered, barely visible through the haze of concrete dust.

The numbing refrain started up again in her mind. *My fault, all my fault.*

As they reached the tallest skyscrapers downtown, the chaos subsided somewhat. The Phireflys were sparing most of these few blocks — probably because this was where Gaia's Legion was holed up.

"That's it!" The pilot pointed to a sheer black tower, criss-crossed with steel X's. Two large antennae reared up from the top like devil's horns. Twisting her MANIs, the pilot dodged a plume of the swarm.

"Shit, the roof is closed!" the pilot bellowed. A dome of retractable glass panels covered the launch pad. A commando standing atop the dome was pointing something at them, something that exploded in a burst of fire, then spiraled closer. "Oh fuck," the pilot whispered. She twisted her hands and flew them into a barrel-roll. Rylla screamed, clenching the harness-straps as the world scrambled, waiting for an explosion to end it all —

But then they were straightening out. "They've got fucking rocket launchers up there," the pilot breathed. "I'll set you down as close as I can to the building. You'll have to get up to the launch pad from the ground floor."

It seemed impossible that the pilot would find a place to land between the fallen chunks of building, plumes of dust, and throngs of stampeding people, but finally the shuttle touched down, a block away from the Hancock building.

Then the shuttle doors opened, and soldiers spilled out. Rylla looked back at Dae-Dae, Tavia, and Hoshiko who'd be staying behind, supporting Theo remotely.

Tavia wished her luck, clapping her on the shoulder. "Give 'em hell," Hoshiko said.

"I'm so sorry," Dae-Dae choked, a sudden flash of emotion slipping past the mind-numbing drugs. Then it was gone.

Rylla hugged her friend tightly, never wanting to let go. But then Theo cleared his throat. He touched two fingers to his head in salute to them all and jumped out the shuttle door after the other soldiers, vanishing into the haze smothering the streets. Screams tore through the air. The earth trembled as somewhere, another severed building crashed to the ground.

Rylla braced herself in the doorway, working up the nerve to follow him into that chaos, but her legs refused to move.

Someone grabbed her shoulder and hurled her out of the shuttle. The major. Now that she was moving, inertia carried her forward until she caught up to Theo. As long as she didn't lose him in the swirling dust, everything would be fine.

HALT

The directive from the major appeared in glowing letters in Rylla's field of vision. Theo pressed his back to the wall of the nearest building, and she copied him. Ahead of them, several soldiers broke off in different directions. The major followed the soldiers around the corner of the building.

Gunfire exploded from that direction — overlapping volleys of assault weapons fire. Rylla squeezed her eyes shut, willing it to stop. But when it finally did, she only felt worse. Now all she could hear was the blood hammering in her ears. What if all the soldiers had been killed? What if she and Theo were now stranded in a dissolving city?

After a few long, terrible minutes, the major re-appeared and signaled for them to move. They followed him around the corner of a tall marble fronted skyscraper.

Bodies of Legionnaires littered the sidewalks, obscured by a thick layer of dust and fallen soil. She had never seen dead bodies before — not in real life — and bile rose in the back of her throat.

MOVE, her lenses commanded, and she ran — past the corpses, towards the soldiers stationed on either side of the skyscraper's shattered doors. They hurtled inside. The rest of the soldiers charged across the bullet-riddled marble floors toward a bank of elevators. Two soldiers pried the doors open — but then they were running again towards Rylla, waving at everyone to get back.

TAKE COVER

Where?! At the last instant, Rylla copied the other soldiers and dove for the floor, covering her head with her hands.

An incredible *crash!* resounded through the marble floor. Rylla peeked through her fingers. A cloud of dust bloomed outwards from the rubble that used to be the elevator bank. Someone on the floors above must have cut the cables on the elevator cab, sending it crashing to the first floor.

The soldiers charged towards the debris, and Theo and Rylla followed. The Major leaned out into the ruined elevator shaft and shot something up into the darkness. Spidersilk unspooled as the hydraulic hook rocketed upwards and attached to something high in the empty shaft. He shot twice more, so that three spidersilk ropes dangled down from the cavernous space. He clipped Rylla's belt to one line and motioned for her to grip a handle wrapped around the spidersilk.

HANG ON

Then Rylla was rocketing up into the elevator shaft. She tried to count the sets of doors whipping by, but soon the light from the ground floor no longer reached her, and she hurtled up in total blackness. Her eardrums tightened, then popped, as she flew.

Then, with a jolt, she stopped, twirling slowly in the darkness, too terrified to move. A metallic groan sounded above her head.

A whoosh of air to her left and right told her that the major and Theo had arrived at her sides. The major turned on his helmet light. Above their heads, twisted steel girders stretched over the elevator shaft like fingers — fingers barely holding back a mountain of rubble from the collapsed stories above.

The metallic groaning seemed to vibrate down the length of Rylla's spidersilk rope, into her fingers, and settle like dread in her core.

"They've blocked the way up," the major said. "Try not to move or that mess'll fall on our heads." Gently, he reached out and caught a beam beside the nearest set of elevator doors. He pulled himself close and stuck his e-mag boots to the steel surface of the beam. Then, taking a crowbar from his belt, he pried open the elevator doors.

"Ladies first," Theo whispered, staring nervously at the groaning debris above them.

Rylla was too terrified to argue. She reached for the major's outstretched hand and he caught her wrist and pulled. The momentum swung her through the open elevator doors. At the apex of her swing, she released the clip on her belt and collapsed to the floor, her legs trembling with exertion and fear.

She found herself in a bright, glass-walled office space, looking out over the dissolving city.

Still in the elevator shaft, Theo couldn't reach the major's outstretched hand. "Swing," the major commanded. Theo pumped his legs until he was able to kick off the back wall. He arced through the open doorway, landing beside Rylla, still on his feet.

Rylla had felt the first tremor as Theo passed through the elevator doors. She had started to tune out the booms of falling buildings, but this one was different. Her head whipped towards the windows, where an enormous, black skyscraper was crashing in on itself. As it fell, the billowing cloud of dust it created darkened the sky to twilight. The Hancock building shuddered beneath Rylla's feet, then swayed sickeningly, as the neighboring tower crashed to the streets below.

When the building finally stilled, and she was sure it wasn't going to collapse on them, Rylla looked back towards the elevator doors. Theo sat on his knees, staring at the empty shaft in horror.

"The major —?"

"When that tower fell, it — it shook loose some of the rubble in the shaft. The Major —" He met Rylla's eyes and shook his head.

The major was dead.

44

Heroes

Theo pulled off his helmet and peered into the elevator shaft. "A lot of the debris fell, but the way up is still blocked."

Rylla sunk to the floor. Another death. Another corpse laid on her conscience. How many more would she be forced to bear? Theo didn't seem to care about the death of Major … Gronski? Glodowsky? Oh god, he'd died saving her, and she didn't even remember his name.

"I never wanted any of this," she moaned, pulling off her own helmet. "I just wanted to ride horses!"

Theo ignored her. "This is the 88th floor — I should be able to hole up here and be in range of the roof. I'll set up the comm link to Hoshiko and Dae-Dae, and I can trigger the RID devices from down here. But *you* still have to get up 12 more floors to the launch pad." He looked around frantically. "Stairs. There have to be stairs." He took off through the maze of desks and glass-walled conference rooms.

"I didn't want to be a hero," Rylla whispered, hugging her face to her knees. "I just wanted to go to *college*."

"Here!" Theo called. He ducked through a door, but instantly reappeared. "Never mind. They've blocked the stairwell too."

She squeezed her eyes shut, hoping to wake up from this nightmare.

"For fuck's sake, Rylla!" Theo cried, grabbing her shoulders. "Get it together! We have to figure out how to get you to the launch pad."

"You just said it — there's no way up," she groaned.

"Well, help me figure something out! I mean, hell, this is all your fault!"

She recoiled as if burned. It was what she'd been telling herself ever since she learned about the pendant, but hearing it from Theo's lips felt unfair. Heat rose in her cheeks.

"No," she said through clenched teeth, wrenching free from his grip. "It is *not* all my fault. I hooked up with an asshole. Okay. I wore his little necklace. Okay. But I didn't start a cult! I didn't steal a bunch of research! I didn't invent machines that can do fucking *that*!" She pointed outside the window, where a fireship ducked and weaved a grasping plume of Phireflys. "And I didn't invent some creepy, cow-sterilizing implant!"

Theo took a step back, the blood draining from his face.

"What?" she demanded, noting the sudden change in his expression. "What did I say? There's something awful about your research you're not telling me, isn't there?"

Theo sank to the floor, resting his wrists on his knees. "Shit, you're right. Blaming you is easy, but *I'm* the one who —" He covered his face with his hands and moaned. "Rylla, it's so much worse than you understand!"

"What is?"

"Haven't you figured it out?" Theo looked up again, and now his cheeks were streaked with tears. "Remember when I said RID can print *a variety* of gene therapies? What I meant is — RID can print *any* gene therapy. If an animal has RID in its body, I can print a retrovirus to alter that animal's DNA *however I want.* I can put it to sleep, sure. I can cure cancer, sure. Or — *or* I can make it sprout a hundred tumors, go bald, even make it … *unviable."*

He raised his eyebrows at this last word, and she didn't have to ask what he meant. A sickening realization came over her. "And it's not just cows, is it? You're gonna use RID on Alastair, to print a sedative …"

"All mammal DNA is pretty similar."

"Oh my god," Rylla said, pressing a hand to her heart. "You think Alastair stole RID because he wants to make us all *unviable*?"

Theo barked a bitter laugh. "Not him. Or maybe him too — I don't know if he actually understands what he's stolen. But don't you get what I'm saying? Why were we developing RID at all? I didn't bother to *really* ask that question until you brought us to the climate lab."

Rylla squeezed her eyes shut, scrambling to put the pieces together. "When I told you my theory about the Manifest?"

"I didn't want to accept it at first, but what if you're right?"

All the hairs on her body stood on end. "You mean, what if Watt wanted you to develop RID for — for some kind of *purge*?"

"Let's say that the only way to save life on earth — or at least, the way *they* want to save it — is to reduce the global human population drastically."

"But the population *has* been decreasing since the 50s. Wildfires, hurricanes, droughts, floods, pandemics — they've killed millions. And — hang on a second — who's *they*?"

"Do you really have to ask? The Tom Waltrips of the world. Board members. Rich fucks who've holed up in their climate bunkers while the rest of us roasted. What if they've decided us poors aren't dying off fast enough for their climate models?"

"But you really think they're planning genocide?" Rylla asked breathlessly.

Theo gave her a pitying look. "You study human history in that major of yours, don't you? Genocide is *distinctly* human. You don't think the end of the world is going to bring it out in the rich and powerful?" He didn't wait for an answer, his eyes wide and frantic. "But how to accomplish it? A genocide that would be orders of magnitude larger than what the Nazis or Siberians or even the European colonials ever managed? Walling off the undesirables, like they've done in the Dust, or poisoning them with pollution — that's been going on in the US for a century, but it works too slowly." His voice was acid. "Death camps like the Nazis used are costly and tend to inspire armed resistance. The Siberians tried out a bioengineered plague in '63, and we all know how that backfired. Viruses are too unpredictable — it's impossible to control the mutations."

"But RID is a machine," Rylla said, beginning to understand. "You can implant the device in *exactly* who you want."

"Code it to kill *exactly* who you want. And you can make it look like cancer or the flu or — whatever you want."

"And you could spare *exactly* 500 million people. The 'right' people."

He ran a hand over his face and groaned. "I never should have created RID, but — you have to understand — the science was just *sitting there*. My professors were so excited, and I got full access to Ward 7, and ..." His voice trailed off as, outside the window, a fireship spiraled to the earth as it was devoured by Phireflys.

"The RID prototypes Alastair stole are designed to implant when *inhaled*, and he stole millions of them."

"Um," Rylla frowned, holding up a finger. "Why did you create millions, if they were *prototypes*?"

"See, now there's another great question I should've asked when my professor ordered them!" He pressed his fists into his skull and took a deep, ragged breath. "The point is, if Alastair disperses the prototypes at low orbit, he can spread them all over the country. Everybody who inhales one will be vulnerable. Their DNA could be *hacked,* by anyone with basic coding and bioengineering skills.”

OGnet trolls with the power to rewrite their enemies’ DNA? Rylla shuddered.

“And once this technology is out there like that? Implanted into millions of people? There’s no putting that cat back in the bag. People will find out about it. And soon every country and syndicate and terrorist group in the world will develop their own versions of RID. The whole world will be like — like a Wild West of DNA-hacking biocybernetic warfare.”

“Fuck,” Rylla breathed. “Okay, so *first* we have to stop Alastair. And then deal with Watt and the board?”

He nodded.

Rylla paced to the window and pressed a hand to its cold surface. She stared down at the dizzying, 88-floor drop to street level, where the Phireflys were devouring the last smoking remains of the doomed fireship.

“I know how to get to the roof,” she groaned, turning to extend a hand to Theo. “Give me your gun.”

45

Post-Mortem

Rylla was wholly unprepared for that first gunshot. The blast was so painfully loud that afterwards, all she could hear was ringing. She'd held the gun one-handed, and the recoil had nearly sent it flying out of her hand. But the bullet was only embedded in the thick glass. Firing a gun was so much more terrifying and violent than it seemed in holovids. She braced herself to try again, holding the gun with both hands this time, flinching against the noise. It took three bullets for the glass to shatter into tiny crystals.

Icy December wind whipped through the window's jagged opening, tossing papers off desks throughout the office. She peered out over the opening, fighting her body's urge to run from the edge.

She hooked an arachnocam to her spidersilk rope, and the little robotic spider scuttled up the wall and wedged itself against a support beam running along the ceiling. Jae was going to be insufferable when he found out that his climbing lessons had come in handy.

Hugging the shattered window frame and cursing her shit luck, Rylla inched out over the drop into nothingness, glass crunching beneath her boots. Then she kicked on the e-Mags in her heels and attached her boots to the steel window frame outside.

With the wind screaming in her ears, she forced a trembling hand to her belt, pulled out another arachnocam, and threaded it successfully. It scuttled up the wall, wedging itself above the next pane of glass. Cautiously, she tested her weight on the spidersilk. It held. She hit the back of her left boot to turn off the e-mag, hitched her leg as high as she could. Turned the e-mag on. Turned off her right boot. Stepped her right foot up. Found a crack for her fingers, and hoisted herself a little higher.

A few stories up, her bones felt iced over. She clung to a crack in the sheer edifice, a thousand feet above the streets below, and pulled another arachnocam from her belt with fingers stiff inside her dragonskin gloves.

Shit! She fumbled her grip, and the arachnocam's tiny, robotic legs flailed as it twirled into the abyss. Her stomach lurched. *Don't think about falling. Don't think about the city dissolving. Don't think, just move.*

The wind wrapped around her like an ice giant's hand trying to rip her off the wall. Only her e-mag boots kept her tethered to its surface. There were no more crashing skyscrapers now, as the Phireflys had devoured all the other buildings downtown. Only a few clouds of Phireflys remained, chasing the last fireships as the main body of the swarm spread towards the suburbs, growing larger all the time. The John Hancock building stood untouched, a lone obelisk in a sea of swirling black dirt. Alastair must still be inside, controlling them. *Don't think about the dead. Just climb.*

The cold tightened her muscles and made her period cramps worse. Sometimes the pain got so intense, she had to stop, concentrating on breathing and clinging to the side of the building until the spasm passed. The dust-choked sky was shrouded in a twilight gloom, even though it couldn't be past early afternoon. How much time had passed while she and

Theo were freaking out on the 88th floor? How long had she been climbing? How long before Alastair launched the cloud seeders? When her mind ran away like this, the strength left her fingertips and she was sure she would fall.

Everything okay? Theo texted her every time she stayed still too long. She didn't know how he was monitoring her movement, but it made her feel less alone. She didn't waste the energy typing back — her continued movement was her answer.

You got this, Texas.

Finally, muscles screaming with exhaustion, she clung below the 100th floor, peeking through the windows above. A massive dome of retractable glass panels enclosed the cloud-seeder launch pad. Inside, Legionnaires — some in camo, some in lab coats — swarmed over a dozen small airships — the cloud seeders. She ducked out of sight, bracing against the window ledge of the floor below.

What now? she thought. *What fucking now?* She'd brought the gun to shoot her way inside the 100th floor, but she was no commando. If she fired the gun, she was sure to catch a "hail of bullets" from the Legionnaires inside — and like the major had said, even dragonskin couldn't protect her from that.

She couldn't stay here forever though. She'd freeze to death, or the charge on her boots would fail, and eventually she'd fall. She'd have to shoot her way in, here on the 99th floor and hope for the best.

What are you waiting for?

She started to type a snarky reply, when she realized the message wasn't from Theo. "Sender unknown," it said. What the hell? Had their comm link been hacked?

Her MANIs twitched stiffly. Who's this? she typed, afraid she already knew.

Look up.

Once again, she climbed up to the base of the 100th floor. There, pressing his nose against the glass dome, Alastair waved down at her.

All the death and destruction she had witnessed reared up in her mind, and rage spread through her bloodstream. But she took a deep breath and reminded herself of her mission. Forcing her frozen lips into a smile, she waved back. He was being flippant? She could be flippant too.

`Kind of chilly out here. Think I could come in?`

He called something over his shoulder.

The window beneath her exploded outwards. Two sets of hands reached up and pulled her down onto the carpet of the 99th floor. Someone took her gun, ripped off her helmet, and rifled through the pouches on her belt. Thankfully, they didn't take the tampon-turned-Phirefly case. The legionnaires hauled her to her feet, then marched her up a stairwell to the 100th floor.

She blinked hard, adjusting to the bright lights of the orbital hangar. From here, cloud seeders launched into low earth orbit, releasing chemicals to ensure that enough rain fell over the Great Lakes to maintain the watershed. The Legionnaires in lab coats didn't spare her a glance as they loaded the ships with Theo's terrifying technology. But a dozen Legionnaires kept their assault rifles trained on Rylla. She knew she should be afraid, but her body was so relieved to be out of the cold that it was hard to feel anything but grateful for the warmth and the solid floor beneath her feet.

Alastair strode towards her, wearing what looked like a dragonskin suit of his own. "This is the assassin General Dorne sends for me? No offense, Rylla, but I think she could've done better. You don't seem the cold-blooded killer type."

Rylla stretched her thumb towards her ring finger and swiped. She hoped that a grey speck was now heading towards Alastair, but she wouldn't risk a look.

Why wasn't Theo texting anything? Had Alastair discovered their plans when he hacked her comm link? Was everything already ruined? Was Theo captured, like her, or worse —?

She swallowed the panic rising in her throat. She would carry out her role, and hope Theo was still in control of the Phireflys. If all else failed, maybe she could *talk* Alastair down from his genocidal plans.

"I'm not here to kill you," she said. "I just came to talk."

Alastair considered her, chewing on his lip, shoulders hunched. She'd never noticed how much fear he held in his body. "You're too late to change my mind," he said. "We launch in a few minutes. RID will be seeded into the atmosphere all over this continent."

Rylla made a show of massaging her hands, releasing a dozen more Phireflys. From her belt, a dozen grey specks flew out and disappeared. She fought off her smile — so someone *was* steering those Phireflys. Soon — if all went according to plan — Hoshiko would be hacking Gaia's Legion's OGnet systems while Theo ensured the Legionnaires snored.

"I'm glad you're here, Rylla, to witness this. None of it would have been possible without you." She looked out the wall of windows at a dust storm of swirling black earth, where a city of millions had stood hours before. She wanted to scream, hurl the most vicious insults she could think of, but she was on a mission. She had to keep him talking.

"Why are you doing this?" she asked, twisting her imaginary ring.

"You opened my eyes, Rylla. You showed me that humans, left to their own devices, will continue selfishly destroying the earth until all life is wiped out."

"I never said that," she hissed between clenched teeth. "And I certainly never told you to start a cult! Or dissolve Chicago!" *Twist.*

Alastair scratched the back of his neck. "The Phireflys have proved, uh, a bit harder to control than I anticipated. They weren't supposed to eat people! I mean, they don't —"

"No, they just dissolve the buildings beneath their feet," Rylla snarled. *Twist.*

He looked out at the dissolved city. "There were ... unintended consequences. It's all I can do at this point to keep them away from this building." Panic flashed across his face. Some of the armed Legionnaires shifted uncomfortably — they hadn't signed up for this either. Maybe she could use that.

"But we had to use the Phireflys as a distraction, don't you see?" Alastair recovered his charming smile and guru-voice. "We had to get to these cloud seeders."

"So you can release RID? How many millions more do you mean to wipe out?" *Twist.*

"The loss of a species is ... regrettable," Alastair nodded. "But a small price to pay for the survival of life itself!" His eyes went wide and manic again. "For over a hundred years, we've known we were killing the planet. And what's changed? Nothing." He pounded a fist into his hand. "Humans will eat and eat, until they've eaten up all life on earth, and then they'll eat each other," he spoke with conviction, and the other Legionnaires watched him adoringly. There was something off about them — eyes dilated. Jaws endlessly working. They were all on stims.

Then again, so was she.

A white, bearded Legionnaire approached Alastair with a bow. "The payloads are installed, Vulpini. We're ready to launch."

"Wait!" Rylla needed to buy Theo and Hoshiko more time. "I — I have to show you something!" She pointed at a nearby holoprojector. "Can I use this? Just let me show you one thing — it's just a .wrld file, not a virus or anything. Then — then I won't stand in your way."

Alastair arched an eyebrow at another Legionnaire who leaned in close and whispered something into Alastair's ear. "— Not linked to our comms —" was all she caught.

Alastair nodded, gesturing for her to proceed. She synced her OGlenses to the holoprojector and pulled up her saved X-

Day calculation — the one where she'd suddenly killed off all the humans on earth. The holoprojector glowed, and her model planet twirled in the center of the room.

"If you release this virus and wipe out humanity, you'll only speed up X-Day! Life on Earth won't even survive another half-century." She ran the program. From the perspective of orbit, little mushroom clouds bloomed, tiny fires flashed as power plants exploded, e-mag containment fields failed and radiation clouds spread over the rapidly-desertifying Earth. "See? If you wipe out every human, no one will tend to the nuclear facilities —"

Alastair's eyebrows knit together. "What are you talking about? RID sterilizes cows! COWS, Rylla. The cattle industry is killing the planet, and we have to stop it! People will never stop eating meat on their own. Our only chance is to make the whole world vegan!" He shot her a pained expression. "What exactly did you think I was going to do?"

Rylla scoffed. "What about all that shit you're always saying? *Humans are parasites! They must be stopped!*"

"Yeah, *stopped.* Controlled, but not exterminated! What kind of monster do you think I am?"

Rylla flung an exasperated hand towards the windows and the destroyed city beyond.

"I *told* you I didn't realize the Phireflys would get so out of hand!" He looked through the windows where, miles away, the outskirts of the city were no longer dissolving. The swarm had utterly vanished. Alastair rounded on her. "What the hell did you do?" he roared.

She held up her hands innocently, trying to keep the smile from her face. If the Phireflys had disappeared, then the plan was working! Hoshiko must've hacked their systems and shut down the Phirefly swarm. Now she just had to keep stalling long enough for the RID sedatives to kick in.

"Launch the seeders!" Alastair bellowed.

"No!" she cried. If the cloud seeders launched, then RID would be spread all over the country. Everyone's DNA would be one disgruntled hacker away from becoming unviable.

The glass panes overhead began to retract, sliding back into the floor. The cloud seeders' engines hummed to life, and she flinched, expecting them to rocket into the sky at any moment —

But nothing happened.

"Vulpini, sir, our — our flight apps aren't responding."

She fought her grin. Hoshiko must have gotten to those too.

Alastair let out a deranged chuckle. "Always trying to be the hero, Rylla, but as usual you've fucked everything up." When he turned back to his Legionnaires, his voice came out shrill and desperate. "We can't have all these cows running around, don't you see? We have to save the planet!"

"This wasn't the way to do it," she said, disgusted. "And I don't think *I'm* the one with a hero complex."

Moving almost reluctantly, he pulled the gun from his hip holster. Her heart caught in her throat — Alastair wouldn't shoot her, would he? But his eyes had the same icy look as when he'd turned her over to the mob in Camelot. What the hell was taking Theo so long? Why hadn't the Legionnaires passed out yet? She must have released a hundred Phireflys by now! Maybe Theo was compromised. Or maybe his sedative didn't work.

Time stood still as Alastair leveled the barrel of the gun at her face. She swiped frantically at her ring finger.

"You think *I'm* a monster?" he laughed bitterly. "I was happy in Camelot, before you came and ruined everything."

"I was happy with you too — truly," she said, in her most placating voice. "But when I learned that place was built on the suffering of others, I — I couldn't stay there and pretend like I didn't know the truth. And I didn't leave you, Alastair. I got exiled, remember? Because you *told* on me!"

"Because you'd already decided to go!" he spat. "And you did it again, in Detroit. You left me. Like everyone else." His gun arm dropped to his side, and she sagged with relief.

He seemed ridiculous suddenly, in his dragonskin suit, strapped with guns and gadgets. A kid playing at bad guys and superheroes. The Legionnaire at his side cast a sideways glance. "Sir, the cloud seeders won't respond. What are your orders?"

He ignored them, looking out over the ruined city. "If you'd just stayed, none of this would've happened."

"Don't you dare," she said, fighting to keep the rage out of her voice. He still held the gun in his hands. "Do not put this on me. I didn't want to be your girlfriend, so what? You destroy a city?" Her anger was getting the better of her. "Is this all a fucking temper tantrum?"

Alastair turned, a sneer contorting his face. But she never found out what he was going to say, because in that moment, he dropped.

Everyone dropped.

Like puppets whose strings had been cut. Like gravity had reached up and slammed them to the earth. Every one of the guards at the windows. Every one of the Legionnaires scrambling at the shuttle engines — they all fell in the same instant. Their bodies lay in horrible, contorted shapes. Eyes open, mouths slack.

Even as she ran to Alastair, she knew.

He had died before he hit the floor.

Pressing two fingers to his neck, feeling no pulse, feeling his skin rapidly stiffen and cool, that was what finally broke her. All the death, all the terror of the day flooded over her, and she gave in to choking sobs. She wanted her mom — or rather, her idea of a mom, someone who would've loved her and protected her from getting wrapped up in this kind of world-shattering mess. She wanted Tyler — the way he used to be, turning mannequins into teachers just to make her smile.

She wanted his gentler, sweeter half, Jo. She wanted to unlive the last year and go home.

After a while, footsteps sounded behind her.

Theo was crossing the hangar, flanked by a half-dozen people in white HazMat suits.

"Rylla," he smiled hugely, spreading his hands low.

"What the hell, Theo?" She stood and backed away.

"You did so good," he said. His face bore no trace of the panic and tears from earlier. He looked triumphant.

"You were supposed to sedate him, not kill him!" She took another step back. Her foot brushed against something heavy and soft. The outstretched arm of a fallen Legionnaire. "You killed all of them!"

"Well, RID *is* experimental," he said, cocking his head to one side. "It seems I've overshot the dosage. We never did an animal trial, you know."

But something in his voice, in his manner, screamed that he was lying. She knew him well enough for that now. Her voice shook as she struggled to form words. "How do I know you didn't *mean* to kill them?"

"Look, I'll explain everything back in the shuttle. But right now we need to clean this place up."

"Clean?" Rylla shrieked. "Is that what you call —" She shook her head, swallowing the vomit in her throat. "You didn't have to do this! He didn't even know what RID *was*."

The soldiers "cleaned" with terrible efficiency, zipping bodies into black vinyl bags, while the HazMat suits swarmed over the cloud seeders. Who the hell were the HazMat people? And why did it seem like Theo was in charge here?

"Come back to the shuttle," he said.

"Or what?" She skirted another body. "Oh god, did you infect me too?" She rubbed her arms frantically. "Is a RID inside me? Are you gonna make me unviable?"

"I'm so sorry," he said, "but you're hysterical, and we have to be able to work." He gestured to two soldiers.

Rylla ran for the edge of the dome, but the soldiers were faster. They dropped her easily, slamming her onto her side. A sharp pain exploded in her chest where she crashed into the floor. Theo leaned over her, tenderly brushing the hair from the spot where her neck met her shoulder. For a wild moment, she thought he was going to kiss her there, but then he plunged a syringe into her muscle.

No longer able to hold her head upright, Rylla's gaze rolled towards the windows. Far below, people moved through a desert of glittering, black dust. The dust billowed up, obscuring the edges of her vision, and then the world went dark.

46

GPTT

Rylla passed a heavy hand back and forth through the horizontal bars of moonlight that fell across her face. The movement stirred dust motes hanging in the air, and they swirled — hundreds of glittering specks moving in tandem, reminding her of something —

Her brain swerved, avoiding the memory. How long had she been here in the hospital ward, staring at this drop-tile ceiling, white walls, and that painting of a sailboat? She had no real memories of the time that had passed — just blurred images of the nurse coming and going, a shower, trips to the bathroom. Her period had ended a while back, so it had been at least a week.

Sucking air in through her teeth, she clutched her side as she pushed up to a seat. A stabbing pain reminded her of her broken rib. It had fractured when the soldiers tackled her to the floor of the orbital shuttle pad. But the memory of that awful moment slipped away whenever she tried to focus on it.

"You awake?" came a sluggish voice to her left. In the bed beside her, bright eyes, a lazy smile, and a mass of curls. Dae-Dae.

Rylla's tongue felt too big for her mouth and she scanned the nearby tables for a glass of water. "Why're you up?"

"You were screaming in your sleep again," Dae-Dae said.

"Oh ... sorry." She looked around the ward. Eight beds. Six were empty. "Where'd everyone go?"

"You don't remember? Azam and Theo and them got to go home two days ago. But we had to stay 'cause we're the most traumatized." Dae-Dae's smile didn't reach her eyes.

"Oh." A smear of ugly memories flashed through her mind. Bodies, cold, climbing. But everything was disjointed — like the lingering images of a bad dream. "Wait, why though?"

Dae-Dae rolled onto her back and stared at the ceiling. Her words came out slow and slurred. "'Member the Phireflys? I invented 'em. They killed three hundred eighty-five thousand, two-hundred seventeen people." Tears leaked from the corners of her eyes. "And you saw your boyfriend die. That's what you're usually screaming about in your sleep. *Alastairrrr! Alastairrrr!*"

Hearing his name was like a bucket of ice water to her brain. She squeezed her eyes shut, but that didn't stop the images. Alastair pointing a gun in her face. Alastair slamming to the ground. Alastair's corpse in her arms.

Beep beep beeeeeep! A small grey box strapped to Rylla's wrist sounded an alarm. A tube snaked from it, disappearing under the skin of her hand. She felt a flush of cold pleasure spreading through her bloodstream from that spot.

"What's this thing?"

"Your psycho-ka-something-or-other. Every time you get upset, it gives you the stuff. Calm-down juice."

The calm-down juice unspooled her muscles one by one. She leaned back on her pillow to enjoy the sensation, but a tiny, nagging voice in her head was saying, *Something's wrong.* There were things she was supposed to remember.

And then she pictured Theo, smiling triumphantly over Alastair's corpse, stretching a hand towards her. She saw him hunched over on the floor of an office, sobbing, eyes wide with terror. Theo. What had he told her then? It was getting harder and harder to think, and she felt herself slipping back to sleep.

No —

She fought to keep her eyelids open. Once, she'd promised herself she would never again use drugs to hide from painful thoughts. She wasn't going to break that promise. Grasping the grey box strapped to her wrist, she pulled. The tube snaked out from under her skin, followed by a long needle and a bead of blood.

BEEEEEEEEEP!

She shoved the box under her pillow to quiet it.

Dae-Dae snorted, covering her mouth with a hand. "You weren't supposed to do that!"

Rylla fought off the drug in her system, shaking her head and slapping her forehead to clear her mind. "We can't just stay high forever. We need to *remember*."

"Remember?" Dae-Dae snorted. "Even high off my ass, I can't forget I killed three hundred eighty-five thousa —"

The nurse appeared in the doorway. "Sounds like your pschokinetic monitor fell out," she said cheerily, coming towards Rylla. "Let me help you —"

"No!" Rylla shrank back. "I don't want your calm-down juice anymore!"

"Yeah!" Dae-Dae said, bursting into stoned giggles. She pulled the psycho-ka-whatever from her own hand. "No more calm-down juice!"

"Girls, please!" the nurse said.

"We're not girls!" Dae-Dae cried. "We're mass murderers!" And she flung the device at the nurse, who held up her arms as she dodged it.

Rylla laughed and threw her own psycho-ka-thingy, which clattered to the floor harmlessly.

"Well," the nurse sniffed, "Dr. Hernandez will hear about this." And she fled the room. Rylla and Dae-Dae looked at each other and burst into giggles. But after a moment, Rylla froze.

"What?" Dae-Dae asked.

"Dr. Hernandez — he's in the Humanity department."

"Yeah? So?"

"So? So the Manifest, remember? And RID! And — and the *purge*! Don't you see? That's why they're keeping us drugged. We know too much. They're trying to scramble our memories, or brainwash us or — Shit, Dae-Dae, we've got to get out of here!"

With one hand holding her broken rib, she slid off the bed and hobbled towards the door.

"I literally have no clue what you're talking about," Dae-Dae said, still giggling.

Right. Rylla and Theo had never told Dae-Dae about their spying. Maybe that meant she'd be safe from Watt and Hernandez.

Rylla reached the door. It was locked. She wasn't wearing MANIs or OGlenses, so she couldn't try hacking the door panel. She gripped the edge where it met the wall and tugged. Searing pain shot through her ribs. It wouldn't budge. She was trapped.

But the door slid open of its own accord, revealing Dr. Hernandez and Professor Watt, standing shoulder to shoulder, blocking the room's only exit.

Rylla backed up. Her eyes cast around for something she could use to fight them. Pillows, clipboards, the psycho-ka-thingys? Ridiculous — Dr. Hernandez surely had some kind of tranquilizer up his sleeve. Maybe she could make a run for it, but she wouldn't get far barefoot, in a hospital gown, with a broken rib.

Watt took a step forward, and Rylla flinched backwards, towards the window. Would it open? What story were they on? Could she jump?

"I know you know about the Manifest," Watt said, matter-of-factly. To Rylla's baffled look, she pointed towards a black orb set in the wall near the ceiling — a holophasic field generator. Of course, they'd been monitoring Rylla and Dae-

Dae this whole time. "You must have a lot of questions, and I'm here to answer all of them."

Rylla eyed Watt warily. The professor wasn't wearing one of her usual geometric-patterned suits, but a hooded sweat-shirt over pajama pants. It was hard to feel mortally afraid of someone dressed like that.

"No more drugs?" Rylla asked.

"No more drugs," Watt promised.

She was curious about what Watt had to say, and she didn't seem to have much choice in hearing it. "Fine," she said. "Let's talk."

"Um, excuse me?" Dae-Dae said, still perched on the edge of her bed. "Does someone want to tell me what's going on?"

Watt and Hernandez decided that Dae-Dae had heard enough that she should be included. They brought in some chairs from the hallway, and Rylla eased herself back on her bed, holding her side. The pain meds were wearing off and each breath hurt worse than the last.

"Why have you been drugging us?" she asked first.

"The treatment is called Graduated Psychopharmaco-logical Trauma Therapy," Professor Hernandez explained. "GPTT helps you process a trauma gradually, preventing a psychotic break. Wingates has invested a lot in you. We don't want to see you lose your minds over this incident."

Rylla scowled. The word 'incident' was woefully incapable of encompassing the death and mayhem she'd seen in Chicago.

"But if the two of you are ready to move to the next stage of treatment, then we can discontinue the drugs. Next question?"

"What *exactly* is the Manifest?" Rylla asked.

"Oh, but I think you already know," Watt smiled slowly. "Six months ago, you used a floorbot to spy on me and General Dorne, and you heard us mention something called the Manifest. At the time I told you never to spy on me again or you would face expulsion, do you remember that?"

Rylla nodded warily.

"But you kept spying on me, didn't you?"

Shit, how did she know? Had ProfBlock failed them? Or was Watt just guessing? In that case, maybe Rylla could still weasel out of this. "I don't know what you're talking about."

"Cut the act, Rylla. Your dragonskin suits were equipped with holorecorders, of course. When the senior staff and I reviewed the footage from Chicago, we heard every word of your very, uhh, *imaginative* conversation about the Manifest with Mr. Reyes. We know the two of you have been hacking classified Humanity department data."

"What? Why didn't you guys tell me about this?" Dae-Dae blurted, sounding more hurt than shocked.

"Theo said you weren't the rule-breaking type." Rylla shrugged apologetically. "And that you always told your parents everything."

"Okay … fair," Dae-Dae said, slumping. "I guess I did tattle on him a lot when we were younger. But that was a long time ago!"

"So what, then?" Rylla asked Watt bitterly. "Are you gonna expel us?"

"No, Rylla. My threat to you was a kind of test — one you passed. It's important that Humanity majors relentlessly pursue the truth, even at risk to themselves." She smiled, but Rylla remained wary, certain this was another of the professor's mind games.

"And so, you and Theo learned about the Manifest — five hundred million names, of the most influential people in the world — top minds, world leaders, and powerful figures."

Hang on. Had they ever figured out who was on the Manifest? Rylla couldn't remember — maybe the drugs had scrambled her memories. But no, she was sure of it. Watt was telling her more than they'd figured out on their own.

"And then you and Theo learned that leading climate scientists believe five hundred million to be the largest human population that the Earth can sustain in order to avert X-Day."

This, too, seemed wrong. They'd based their guess about the Manifest only on Rylla's climate model. They'd had no clue that "leading climate scientists" agreed with her. And was that even true? She hadn't come across that research in Climate Modeling.

"So you put two and two together." Watt raised her eyebrows. "And you let your imaginations run away with you." She shook her head. "Did you really think I was planning to — to *execute* eight and a half billion people?" Dr. Hernandez chuckled and Watt joined in. Wearing their pajamas, it was true, the professors didn't look like evil masterminds. They looked like overworked teachers. Rylla started to feel silly for suspecting them of plotting genocide.

"So you're not planning a … purge?" she asked, wanting it to be true.

"No," Watt said, smiling ruefully.

"Then what's the Manifest?"

"A contingency plan. Every government on Earth has them. If nuclear weapons are launched at the US, there's a plan for which officials will be sent to which secure, underground bunkers. Wingates has simply been working on integrating those plans across the globe." She shook her head. "We haven't studied geopolitics much this year, so you can't appreciate how close the Siberian Empire and the U.S. are to war over the Great Lakes. Our contingency plan involves working with other countries to rapidly build nuclear shelters — Wingates itself is one of them." Watt sighed. "Sadly, we don't have the capacity to send everyone in the world underground. But we *can* save — well, I bet you can guess how many people we're hoping to be able to save?"

"Five hundred million?"

"Exactly. And we *do* have to be selective of who we save. People with critical knowledge for rebuilding society and restoring the planet — top scientists, doctors, leaders ..."

Rylla flashed back to a conversation in their first Humanity seminar. There are twenty people, but only enough water to save ten. *Who should you save?* It wasn't some abstract philosophical question. It was a terribly real problem the professor grappled with every day.

Watt leaned forward, bracing her elbows on her knees. "None of this is top-secret information, Rylla. All third-year Humanity majors work on the Manifest — researching individuals and suggesting who should be included. If you'd waited a few years, I would have *assigned* you to work on the Manifest, without you needing to sneak around hacking into my OGlenses."

That last word struck a discordant note in Rylla's mind. They hadn't hacked Watt's OGlenses — they'd hacked her *holowall.* And Watt kept talking about her and Theo. *Just* her and Theo. The professor hadn't mentioned Hoshiko or Magenta at all. Watt still didn't know they were involved, because she and Theo hadn't mentioned them at the top of the Hancock building.

The professor's smile was as serene as ever, her eyes like two chips of black stone. Rylla wanted to believe Watt — believe that Wingates was a force for good in the world. She wanted to go back to worrying about nightwork and crushes. But she could never fully trust the professor again. It might be useful, though, if Watt thought Rylla believed her completely. Safer, too.

"So the Manifest has nothing to do with RID?" Rylla asked, forcing a smile.

"No," Watt said.

Rylla sighed, as if relieved.

"Wait, what does the Manifest have to do with RID?" Dae-Dae asked.

"It doesn't," Watt said, looking out the window, where the sky was rosy with the burgeoning dawn. "But there are some things it would be helpful for you to see for yourselves."

47

The Future We Create

Rylla and Dae-Dae crossed the aircraft hangar towards a cluster of familiar faces. Jae and Hoshiko leaned against a skimmer. Ynez and Tavia were deep in conversation. Magenta rested an elbow on Azam's shoulder, and the two talked together, intimately. That was odd — had Azam and Magenta even met each other before the Legionnaires' break-in? What was going on there?

Everyone looked grim and about ten years older than the last time she'd seen them. But she didn't see the one face she was dreading.

Spotting their approach, Azam broke away from Magenta and ran toward them. She pulled first Dae-Dae and then Rylla into a hug.

"I've been so worried about you. They wouldn't let us visit while you were in the 'sensitive phase' of your recovery," she said, tracing air quotes.

"Glad you're back on your feet, roomie," Magenta said to Rylla as they snaked an arm around Azam's shoulders. "Although, I admit, the privacy has been nice." Azam blushed deeply and gave Magenta a little shove. Rylla's head spun —

how had these two gotten together? Magenta was so brash and spontaneous, while Azam was always thoughtful and deliberate. She couldn't tell if they made no sense together, or if they were a perfect match.

Tavia approached, and when Dae-Dae turned to her, she pulled her friend in and held her to her chest for a long time. She spoke softly and comfortingly into Dae-Dae's hair.

"I heard about you scaling the top twelve stories of the Hancock building?" Jae said, walking up, arms folded. "I *told* you climbing was useful."

"I knew you were going to say 'I told you so.'" Rylla said, rolling her eyes.

"I guess this means you pass my class."

"Oh, that's all I had to do?" she said, voice flying up into a shrill register. "Scale the outside of a skyscraper during a nanobot swarm — *in winter*? Why didn't you just say so!"

Jae grinned insufferably.

"Professor —" everyone called out as Watt approached the skimmer.

"I know you have questions, and I'll answer everything once we're en route," Watt said, holding up her hands.

"Wait — where's Theo?" Rylla asked.

"I'm afraid Mr. Reyes won't be joining us." Watt paused on the gangway up to the aircraft. "He has left Wingates."

"WHAT?" Dae-Dae shouted and Azam placed a consoling hand on her arm. "How could he leave? Without saying goodbye?"

The bottom had dropped out of Rylla's stomach, but she arranged her face into a neutral expression. She didn't want Watt to know how much this revelation shook her.

"I'm sorry," Watt said to Dae-Dae. "I know Theo was like a brother to you."

"Are you going to tell us where we're going?" Magenta demanded, as they followed the professor into the aircraft.

"To see the aftermath of your actions," Watt said enigmatically. Magenta scoffed, throwing their hands in the air in exasperation, then dropped into a seat next to Azam.

"I hope you have better answers than that about what happened in Chicago," Jae said, taking the seat beside Rylla. "I thought the plan was to sedate the Legionnaires. Not kill them!"

"You made us accessories to murder," Hoshiko growled, as he pulled the skimmer's door shut behind him.

"The way they *dropped* like that," Azam shuddered, hugging her arms.

"And how about you explain why the hell Wingates was developing something like RID in the first place?" Magenta said.

"I'll answer your questions, but if you all talk at once, I can't explain," Watt said, crossing one leg over the other. She signaled to the pilot in the cockpit, and with a gentle lurch, the skimmer rose into the air and sped for the opening of the hangar.

Watt turned back to the group. "For those of you in my seminar, do you recall Mr. Reyes's proposal for developing RID?"

They nodded.

"You viewed the sales-pitch part of his presentation, promising to sterilize the worlds' cows on command. But buried in the technical specs was a far more sinister proposal. He mentioned that this technology, once developed, could be adapted to any mammal. He mentioned that sterilization was only the beginning of RID's capabilities — eventually, we could develop retroviral gene therapies to cure any illness — or induce them. We could even make an organism's DNA *unviable.*"

"Why would you fund something so dangerous?" Jae shouted. "And — and —"

"— evil?" Rylla suggested. Hearing all her friends voice her own questions had fueled her outrage and given her the courage to confront Watt directly.

"Have you ever heard of the principle of multiple discovery?" Watt asked, unrattled.

The Humanity majors shook their heads, but Azam spoke softly. "It's the idea that most scientific breakthroughs are inevitable, isn't it? Several people tend to invent the same thing around the same time?"

"Correct," Watt said. "Algebra, the telephone, hologenerators — all were invented simultaneously, by people on different parts of the globe. Once scientific understanding reaches a certain point, the next step forward becomes obvious."

"Theo happened to be friends with engineers whose research made RID seem like an obvious step forward," she continued. "He borrowed ideas from your nanotechnology, Dae-Dae, your chemical printing, Azam, your biocybernetics, Tavia." Watt looked at each in turn, then shot Rylla an amused smile. "And he told me once that it was your insatiable appetite for cheese, Rylla, that gave him the idea to use this technology to control global cow populations."

Rylla grimaced with embarrassment.

"Now, if a mere undergraduate student, albeit a brilliant one, could come up with RID on his own, well —" Watt spread her hands wide.

"Then other people would have come up with it too," Rylla said, beginning to understand Watt's point. "Multiple discovery."

Watt nodded. "During the twentieth century, both sides in the Second World War were racing to develop the technology for nuclear weapons. The Nazis, along with the other Axis powers, wanted to use nuclear weaponry to conquer the world and exterminate non-white races. Luckily, the United States developed their bomb first."

"It wasn't *lucky* for Hiroshima and Nagasaki," Hoshiko sneered. "The allies used nuclear bombs to wipe out two cities. They killed hundreds of thousands of innocent civilians."

"Whether or not it was ethical for the allies to use the bomb —"

"It was *not!*" Hoshiko interrupted.

"Agreed," Watt gave a conciliatory nod, but continued making her point. "But had the Axis developed the bomb first, they likely would have used it far more ruthlessly."

"I bet those scientists who invented the bomb felt horrible," Dae-Dae muttered.

"Some did. Oppenheimer and Einstein expressed regrets later in life."

"Sorry, history is not my best subject," Dae-Dae said. "What does this Nazi stuff have to do with Theo's research?"

"She's saying it's inevitable that something *like* RID would get invented," Ynez said. "The science was sitting there — anybody could put together the pieces and create a nanomolecular retroviral printer."

Rylla clutched her head. Every time she closed her eyes, she saw Alastair's lifeless body drop to the floor, tall buildings crashing to the earth. When she spoke, her voice shuddered with rage. "Just because *someone* was going to invent it, doesn't make it right that *we* did."

"Imagine if the Siberian empire developed RID first. Imagine if they managed to seed it throughout the population." Watt paused to let them picture the horrifying prospect. "If the Siberian Emperor could kill off the entire U.S. population with a flick of his MANIs, do you think he would hesitate to do so? With all the water in the Great Lakes just sitting here for the taking?"

"So?" Jae cried. "If the U.S. uses it to wipe out the Siberians, is that any better?"

"We developed RID to learn how to defend against such attacks," Watt said. "I assure you, we have no intention of using it as a weapon." She shot Rylla a meaningful look.

"But you already have," Rylla said, unimpressed. "The first chance you got. You used RID to murder the Legionnaires."

"Surely you understand why it was vital to recover this research?" Watt leaned forward, bracing her hands on her knees. "That meant wiping out every trace of Theo's research — digitally and ... personally. Over the past week, Dorne's operatives have been tracking down and eliminating everyone who had access to the RID files."

"*Eliminating*," Rylla said with disgust. "Say what you mean. You're *killing* them." It felt like everything she thought she knew about the world was crumbling to dust around her. "Theo never meant to sedate the Legionnaires, did he? He killed them on purpose. And we helped him."

"Theo, better than anyone, understood the terrible destructive power of RID, and he was willing to do whatever it took to protect people from it," Watt said.

"... protect them from his *own* creation," Jae said.

"Fucking hell," Magenta breathed, staring at their hands. "Are we infected? Are there little bots under my skin right now?"

"None of you are implanted with RID," Watt assured them.

"How can we trust you?" Ynez asked.

Watt shrugged. "That's a decision you'll each have to make for yourselves. We're working on anti-RID implants, which will be distributed to all Wingates students as soon as they're ready. Until then, we have to hope this research hasn't fallen into the wrong hands." She turned a pleading gaze to Rylla. "And if you hear from Theo, please, tell him to return to Wingates. He has the wrong idea — about so many things."

Watt was referring to the Manifest, of course. Rylla gave the professor an *I'm-on-your-side* nod. But the truth was, she didn't know who she could trust anymore. Watt had kept terrible secrets from her. But so had Theo.

The skimmer slowed, the blurred landscape resolving into dead trees and the ruins of fallen buildings. They passed a long line of humming pylons, stretching into the sky. She recognized this place.

"Why are we at Crystal Lake?" Rylla asked, exchanging a glance with Hoshiko, who shrugged.

"A little demonstration," Watt said. "Of the powerful good Wingates — and all of you — have made possible."

"There she goes with the vague-ass, mysterious-as-hell answers again," Magenta mumbled to Azam. Rylla snorted a derisive chuckle.

Watt opened a storage hatch stocked with HazMat suits, and once everyone was suited-up, they disembarked at the edge of the radioactive landfill. A team of scientists in HazMat suits raised their hands in greeting as Professor Watt and the students gathered outside the skimmer. But one scientist pressed their palms together and bowed. There was something familiar in the way they moved — slowly, deliberately. But it couldn't be —

Rylla squinted through the visor of her HazMat suit. "Sister Fungi?"

"Rylla!" The nun spread her arms wide. "I am so glad you are here to witness this wonderful day for the Way of the Waste!" She turned to Watt. "We're ready to begin, professor."

"Go ahead," Watt said, nodding. At the professor's signal, the scientists dispersed around the radioactive mound of earth. Watt turned to address the group of students.

"The Wingates School for the Future was founded to ensure that humanity *has* a future," she began. "At a time when the Earth seemed doomed to death and extinction, our founders dared to dream of a brighter tomorrow. You represent the best and brightest students from around the globe, coming together to create a better world."

Rylla wanted to believe the Professor's words were true, but her faith in Wingates was haunted now by too many ghosts. When she'd first arrived at the school, she'd dreamed of learning how to save her river, and she'd been proud to be a part of the school's lofty mission. But whatever Watt said, the university didn't exist for the "best and brightest" — it existed for the rich and powerful. If their mission was, in fact, to create a better world, that world had to be one that benefited the Board of Wingates.

"This work is not always easy," Watt continued. "Powerful technologies may be used to sustain life — or destroy it. But we must not fear scientific discovery just because it might be misused."

Behind Professor Watt, a spider-like drone bearing a cylindrical container on its back crawled up the slope of the landfill.

"Designing the future takes a great deal of courage. The courage to try, though you may fail. The courage to create, though your creations may be used against you. The courage to try again, even when things have gone terribly wrong."

The spider-drone stopped. The lid split open, and a cloud of gray specks swarmed out.

"Wait a second. Wh — what is this —" Dae-Dae held out a hand, her eyes darting between the swelling swarm and Watt's face. Rylla stumbled backwards, remembering another cloud of gray that devoured a city, killing hundreds of thousands.

"No, no, no!" Beside her, Dae-Dae screamed as she fell to her knees in the grass, covering her head with her arms. Panic flooded Rylla's body and she tensed to run.

"COURAGE!" Watt bellowed. "Have the courage to watch your brilliance in action." Dae-Dae dropped her arms and unsteadily got to her feet.

The Phirefly cloud hovered in midair, its borders shifting like a murmuration of starlings, while the drone drilled a hole deep into the surface of the landfill. When it extracted its drilling arm, the Phireflys swarmed into the hole.

The surface of the landfill rippled like gelatin, and then the sod crumpled inward, into a thousand shallow sinkholes.

"We recovered incredible data from the Phireflys in Chicago," Watt told Dae-Dae. "Over the last few weeks, your team has used that data to strengthen their safeguards. These

Phireflys won't rampage like the ones in Chicago. And they've been water-proofed."

"Are you nuts?" Rylla shouted. "That was our only defense against them!"

"The Phireflys can be disabled with acidic foam if things get out of hand. That's what's in those," Watt gestured towards a half dozen large canon-like spigots pointed at the hill. "Waterproofing was necessary, though, if they're going to clean dead water. The Phireflys have the potential to clean trillions of gallons of water trapped in polluted sites like these. It's a breakthrough that could push back X-Day by a hundred years."

"Wait," Dae-Dae said, still watching the collapsing hill with the eyes of a cornered animal. "Isn't Crystal Lake radioactive? The Phireflys can't clean radioactive waste — just plastics."

"That's where our spores come in," Sister Fungi said, beaming.

"When Rylla told our seminar about the Wastrel's fungal nuclear waste mitigation, I sent a bioengineering team to work with Sister Fungi," Watt explained. "They've developed fungi designed to clean Crystal Lake. And your Phireflys have been calibrated to chemically print those spores."

As she concluded, the Phireflys streamed out of the ground and back into their canister. The top of the landfill was now pitted and cratered, a few inches shorter than it had been.

"The first treatment is finished," Sister Fungi cried, clapping her hands with more exuberance than Rylla had seen in her before. "Now, we wait for the mushrooms to grow."

"Then what?" Hoshiko asked wryly. "You have radioactive mushrooms?"

"Fungi incorporate the radioactive matter in a more stable form. Much easier to store safely than radioactive water or soil. We will collect them, store them in thick cement containers, then repeat the process until the soil and water are clean."

"So how long until Crystal Lake is a *crystal lake* again?" Jae asked.

"We estimate eight to nine," Sister Fungi said.

"— Hundred years? Thousand years?" Dae-Dae asked.

"Months," Watt said.

Some of the students whistled. Even Rylla was swayed. The Phirefly swarm in Chicago was the most terrifying thing she had ever seen. But if they could do this ... if they could clean dead water sites in a matter of months — that would save millions of lives.

"You are not responsible for what happened in Chicago, do you understand that?" Watt knelt before Dae-Dae. "None of you are. The loss of life was tragic. Place the blame for that on Gaia's Legion. Place it on me, if you must." She smiled at Rylla. "But not on yourselves."

Sister Fungi bowed deeply before Dae-Dae. "Your Phireflys have the power to transform so much waste. I'm honored to meet their creator."

Dae-Dae returned the bow in stunned silence.

Watt stood and smoothed her HazMat suit as if it was her usual brightly-patterned pantsuit. "Right," she said, turning briskly for the skimmer. "We have one more stop."

Rylla hugged Sister Fungi goodbye, their HazMat suits crinkling between them. If Sister Fungi was working with Professor Watt, maybe the professor wasn't evil. Rylla trusted the nun's judgment more than her own. And all of Watt's explanations, taken together, were starting to make a lot of sense.

Aboard the skimmer, Dae-Dae sat straighter, like a weight had lifted from her shoulders.

"I think you may be ready to plug back into the world," Watt said, eyeing Rylla. She produced a small OGLens case from her pocket and handed it to Rylla.

Magenta's hand flew to their mouth. "She doesn't know, does she?"

Watt's glare was enough to silence them.

Rylla felt a stab of dread. In the last few days, she'd been so drugged-up, she hadn't spared a thought for her family. What had happened in the wider world?

"Go ahead," Watt said, nodding at the OGLens case.

She had 23 messages, mostly from her mother. In the first, Amaryllis shouted, "Where are you? Call me! Have you seen the news?!" Breath coming fast, she pulled up one of the big news sites, and bubbles filled her vision, blotting out the skimmer. Talking heads shouted at one other, and the headlines glowed red:

CIVIL WAR!

DUST NATION THREATENS NUKE ATTACK

CONGRESS DECLARES WAR ON DUST NATION

The screaming headlines registered only peripherally, though, because she couldn't look away from the face glaring out of the central bubble. He had furious, pale eyes, a scraggly blonde beard, and a grown-out mohawk flopping over one eye. His shouts were muted, but above his face a banner read, *Dusty Dictator Declares War on Lush States.*

The *Dusty Dictator* was Tyler McCracken.

This had to be some kind of prank. Some test, by Watt and Hernandez, to see if they could break her brain once and for all. There was no way Tyler — who'd only ever yelled at her when she used the last of his dry shampoo — had organized a scrounger army, formed a new nation, and declared war on the Lush States. And what the hell was he wearing? In that midnight blue coat with epaulets and an absurd number of buttons, he looked more like a pirate or a circus ringleader than the head of an army.

He was *Tyler* — couldn't they see that? He was only twenty-two! How could anyone take him seriously? But if the headlines were true, his scrounger army had taken control of multiple nuclear weapons stockpiles, and it seemed the U. S. government took that *very* seriously.

Rylla unmuted the talking heads. She was used to news anchors spouting hate towards Dusties, but she'd never heard anything like this. One woman said that all Dusties were spies, and they should be locked up in camps. Another man said they should be deported back to the Dust — even those who'd been living in Lush States since they were born. A third was calling on President Kraft to strike first — nuke the hell out of the entire Dust Nation.

With trembling hands, she swiped her MANIs to clear her vision. Inside the skimmer, everyone watched her silently, like she was a bomb about to go off.

"You okay?" Jae mouthed. Rylla tried to speak, but no words came out. She shook her head, fighting back tears.

The skimmer had stopped on a long, curving beach of white sand, stretching to either horizon. Rylla was too stunned by what she'd just seen to wonder where they were.

"Let's give her some space," Watt said, as the door slid open. Everyone filed out, casting worried glances back at Rylla. Watt squeezed Rylla's shoulder as she disembarked. "Take all the time you need."

Alone in the aircraft, Rylla pulled up her messages again. She clung to a wild hope that there'd be a message from Tyler in there — one that would explain everything. He'd been framed, somehow. It was all a misunderstanding.

And sure enough, she had a message from an unlisted caller. But when she swiped it open, the haggard, filthy face that filled her vision wasn't her brother's.

It was Theo.

48

The Catalyst

"I'm guessing you're pretty angry right now." Rylla snarled in agreement at Theo's holographic face. "I'm betting Watt's told you that I killed the Legionnaires on purpose, and I am sorry it came to that. I'm sorry about Alastair."

"Fuck you," Rylla hissed. Did he think his "apology" made up for lying to her and using her to murder her ex-boyfriend?

"But don't let Watt turn you against me," he pleaded. "And don't believe whatever bullshit she's told you to explain away the Manifest."

"Why should I listen to anything you have to say?" Rylla asked aloud. The holovid was only a recording, but Theo responded as if he could hear her.

"I know you won't believe, though, so — just watch this. And listen close, because this message will delete when it's done. I can't risk Watt getting hold of it and tracing it to me."

Theo vanished. Suddenly she was in the center of a domed room, lined with arched windows looking out on a snow-covered pine forest, ringed by tall mountains. Somewhere north, then. She was surrounded by a conference table — the holovid must've been recorded from its hacked hologenerator.

Around the table, a dozen people shouted over one another — grotesquely youthful people, with hydraulically enhanced movements. Kaylee Jaxx was there, and Tom Waltrip, and a bunch of other artificially preserved, ancient people she'd never seen before. The Board of Wingates. And all of them were furiously shouting at a slight woman at the head of the table in a brightly-patterned, flowing pantsuit.

When their clamor died down, Watt tipped her chin and spoke. "Yes, we've experienced a setback. And if you call for my resignation?" She spread her hands wide. "So be it."

"Yes, our security was breached, but we are working rapidly to address these vulnerabilities. Yes, the Phirefly swarm was … regrettable … but we've recovered valuable data from that event." Watt paced before the angry board members. "And yes, RID briefly fell into the hands of a hostile terrorist group, but the recovery mission was a complete success. What's more, we were able to perform a live test on human subjects." Watt sounded almost giddy. "And RID worked beautifully."

Bile surged up the back of Rylla's throat. Watt thought Alastair's death was *beautiful?*

"Quit trying to spin this, Alexandra," Tom Waltrip bellowed. "Isn't it true that the inventor of RID has left Wingates and turned against you?"

"Regrettably, yes. Mr. Reyes left Wingates after destroying all digital records and prototypes of RID."

"And what if he uses it against us?" someone demanded.

"We are developing defenses against RID implants which should be ready soon. In the meantime, I don't believe he will use RID to kill again, or he already would have. After all, I'm still here." She smiled ruefully. "And his research supervisors believe they can recreate RID in a matter of months — at which time, we'll be closer than ever to achieving our goals."

"Speaking of our *goals*." Sergei's voice dripped with derision. "Didn't he figure them out? Him and the girl — the cult leader's girlfriend?"

"McCracken," Watt said, nodding. Rylla's blood turned to ice at the mention of her name. "Unfortunately, she learned about the Manifest too soon after completing the climate modeling course, and she put the pieces together. She and Reyes both learned too much too soon. That's why we lost him. I still have hope we can win McCracken over to our plans."

"McCracken — this is the *Ass is Hope* girl, right?" Kaylee Jaxx blurted. "How many times do I have to say that we don't need Dusty filth on our Manifest? That song wasn't even *good.*"

Watt placed her hands on the table and leaned in, speaking with barely-restrained anger. "McCracken is one of our most valuable assets, Jaxx. Her brother now leads the Dust Nation. She's Reyes's closest confidant, and our best chance of recovering him. I want her on our side."

"You've demonstrated you have no control over your students." Waltrip scowled as he turned to the other board members. "How can we trust you to clean up this mess?"

Watt leveled a glare and waited for Waltrip's gaze to return to her. "I'll remind you, Thomas, that my students may be the brightest minds on the planet, but they're teenagers. As you know *quite* well, teens can be reckless, impulsive, obstinate. If any of you think you can do this job better than me, by all means," she waved a hand graciously, "I'd love to go back to teaching the ancient philosophers."

The board fell silent under the weight of Watt's smirk.

The vid ended. Theo's face filled Rylla's vision once again.

"I hope that settled any doubts you might have that Watt is the good guy here," Theo said. "I'm working with some new people on a way to stop Watt and the Board. And we think you were *exactly* right about the Manifest. We've looked at the coding of Wingates' climate modeling app. We've found that no matter what kind of Earth you build — even if you set up a totally lush, pre-industrial world — the app is rigged for a climate catastrophe, which can only be averted if you kill off most of the humans. It's designed to convince you that genocide is necessary. And I don't need to remind you that every student at Wingates is required to pass that course."

Rylla closed her eyes, stomach churning with the memory of her last day in Climate Modeling. She'd tried to change the agricultural settings to make farming more carbon-efficient — to replicate how the Wastrels had grown food — but the app wouldn't let her. That was when Professor Pupala had swooped in and finally showed her the app's horrific solution. He'd convinced her that there weren't enough resources on Earth to sustain humanity. Was it all a lie? Red-hot rage sped through her bloodstream.

"If I know you, which I do," Theo interrupted the memory, "I'm guessing right now you either want to charge up to Watt and confront her, *or* you're gonna run away from this. Eat a golfball of tam and move to Siberia or something."

"I am not!" Rylla cried, forgetting momentarily that she was talking to a recorded hologram.

"But I need you to stay at Wingates, Rylla. We need to understand who exactly is behind this plot and stay one step ahead of them. Convince Watt you're on her side. Keep working with Hoshiko to crack the encryption on the Manifest — you can trust him. And get me the names on that list."

When the recording ended, Theo vanished and, as promised, the file disappeared from her messages. Staring at her empty inbox, she wondered if what she'd seen was real, or if she was losing her mind. Damn it, Theo *did* know her after all. Half of her wanted to scream at Watt, and the other half wanted to run until her legs gave out. The absurdity of being so predictable made her want to burst into hysterical laughter.

Could she even trust Theo? That video of the board meeting was damning, but she knew better than anyone that vids could be faked. And Theo had lied about so many things — the sedative, for one. He'd murdered Alastair and invented a DNA-hacking device that could wipe out humanity. Did she really want to be his ally?

But what was the alternative — helping Watt enact her plans? The professor had always believed in her, mentored her, given her endless chances to prove herself. Then again, Watt might be planning global genocide.

Rylla needed air. Holding her aching rib, she climbed out of the skimmer onto the white sandy beach of Lake Michigan. Wind blew off the lake, and she hugged herself to keep warm. Beyond the dunes, a carpet of black dirt stretched for miles in every direction. Occasional slabs of concrete and chunks of buildings rose up from the barren plain. And in the center stood a single, intact tower, crisscrossed by steel X's.

The John Hancock building was all that was left of downtown Chicago.

With her back to the lone skyscraper, Professor Watt delivered another rousing speech about their bravery in stopping Gaia's Legion. Dae-Dae sat on the sand, staring up at the obelisk with tears in her eyes. Azam and Tavia stood behind her, each with a hand on one of her shoulders.

"And now we must continue our work," Watt shouted over the wind whipping in from the lake. "Wingates will work with the Army Corps of Engineers to rebuild Chicago. We have the opportunity to design a brand-new kind of city. A city unburdened from history. A city of the future."

She waved at the vast expanse. "New Chicago will be the greatest feat of engineering ever undertaken." She smiled at the three young women huddled together in friendship. "And I can't think of any engineers I'd rather have working on that team."

"A brand-new city?" Tavia said cautiously. "We could optimize the city's water and electrical systems for peak efficiency."

"We could engineer *living* building materials." Azam said.

"If the Phireflys helped with construction," Dae-Dae said, "if we were *very* careful of course, we could rebuild in record time and with a neutral carbon footprint." Her tears had dried, and her eyes shone excitement for the first time in weeks.

"The Humanity Department, under my direction, will work closely with the engineers," Professor Watt said. "Ensuring New Chicago is not just a technological marvel, but a wonderful place to live. Every feature of its design will encourage community, safety, and joy."

"Is that where we come in?" Magenta asked.

Watt shook her head. "No. You will not be working on New Chicago."

"Why not?" Jae asked suspiciously.

"You did well in your first year of study. You've all matured a great deal and learned to work as a team," Watt said. "So I hope you're ready for a rather advanced assignment for a group of second-years."

"And what's that?" Rylla demanded, squaring her shoulders.

Watt met her gaze and smiled sadly. "You're going to stop this Civil War."

Acknowledgments

To all the beta readers who provided feedback on early drafts of this book—Hannah Roberts, Kyna Byrd, Nathan Kingery-Gallagher, Sydney Olson, Kevin Chen, Sarah Assenmacher Honore, Glen Deakin, Darby Cupid, and Aiden Feltkamp — you saw this novel when it was a messy behemoth and helped me find a coherent plot!

Thanks to Kerstin Wolf, the agent who fell in love with Rylla's story, gave me a foothold in the publishing world, and taught me so much about plotting and tension — no soggy middles!

Thank you Mariah Nichols, for taking this book out on sub, and finding it a great home at Stelliform Press.

To Selena Middleton, the most assiduous editor I have ever had the immense privilege to work with — thank you for pushing me to breathe life into every scene and to dig deeper into characters' minds than I manage with my own! Thanks also go to Kristen Shaw for her exacting proofreader's eye. Thank you to Isip Xin for this gorgeous cover design.

Thank you, Ramona, who exploded into this world and became the most glorious catalyst for me to quit my teaching job and write this novel. The first draft of this book was all written in snatches while you were napping. Thank you for those peaceful stolen half-hours when I was able to write and for changing my life in the most beautiful way.

Thank you, Lane, for rooting for me through the highs and lows of publishing and for being Team Edward (Teach) for life.

And finally, Ike. How can I envision this book or any part of my life without you? Thank you for believing in my dreams and making it possible for me to chase them. You're the best alpha reader, BFF, co-parent, stand partner, and spouse in the world.

About the Author

Sim Kern lives under a live oak tree frequented by screech owls, near a whole bunch of chemical refineries in Houston, Texas. *Depart, Depart!* (2020), their quiet horror novella about ghosts and hurricanes, made the Honor List for the Otherwise Award and received a starred review from Publisher's Weekly. They have two books out in 2022—this book, plus a clifi short story collection, *Real Sugar is Hard to Find*.

As a journalist, they mostly report on petrochemical polluters and drag space billionaires. Sim is one of the hosts of the Climate Fiction Book Club on YouTube and Instagram, and they tweet @sim_kern.

Also by Sim Kern:

Depart, Depart!

Real Sugar is Hard to Find

Coming in 2023:

The Free People's Village

Rules for the Reckoning (the sequel to *Seeds for the Swarm*)

I. Drill

"It's really bad today, Miles. Like, I'm having a hard time standing up straight," Rylla lied, clutching her abdomen for dramatic effect.

"Can't you just take a pain reliever?" Miles whispered, rubbing his mustache. It had filled in over the past year, redder than the shaved gold fuzz that ended in a rattail at the nape of his neck. He cast a sidelong glance at the rest of his "squadron" — two dozen Dusty teenagers wearing ill-fitting, stolen army camos which they'd doodled on with permanent marker. A few of them stretched half-assedly under the big AC vent in front of the sealed hangar doors. Miles had said they were going on a suited run through the Dust today, and that was a special kind of hell Rylla just didn't feel like facing.

"I already took some ibuprofen, twice the max dose, but I'm still in a world of hurt over here. And you know I don't fuck with anything stronger."

"Didn't this just happen a week ago?" he hissed.

"Ah!" Rylla grimaced as if from a sharp, sudden pain, and bent at the waist. "I think it was two weeks, but you know, stress can make them irregular. And this whole brink-of-nuclear-war thing is *very* stressful."

"None of the other recruits have this kind of problem." He covered his mouth with his hand. "And half of them have uteruses. Can't you just power through?"

"It's my heavy day, Miles," Rylla said apologetically, already backing away. "So it's not just bloody, but *chunky*, you know —"

"Eugh, don't tell me —"

"I'll just hang out here till you get back, all right?"

"Fine." Miles pinched the bridge of his nose, looking defeated. Rylla almost pitied him. "Go over there and study the new command structure Tyler sent out. Maybe you can explain it to me later. He keeps changing things up every few days ..."

Miles's words dissolved into grumbles, as Rylla hoisted herself up into the open door of a heavily graffitied helicopter and stretched out in the pilot's seat, feeling delighted at escaping the miserable run through the desert. All around the aircraft hangar, other squads of recruits were clumped together, prepping for their runs. Some of the squads were attempting to do push-ups, but half of them were doing "kiddie" pushups on their knees, and a few lay on their backs staring at the ceiling.

"Why isn't Rylla going with us? *Again*," demanded a familiar voice. Tobi paused with one leg inside a cooling suit. As usual, Tobi's hair was pulled up into two afro-puffs and she wore a baby pacifier on a string around her neck. Tiny, neon-pink heart tattoos decorated her dark brown skin along the line of her cheekbones. In spite of this baby-punk style, though, Rylla was slightly terrified of her sixteen-year-old bunkmate. Then again, Rylla was slightly terrified of most people.

"Rylla's doing a special project for me. Don't worry about it," Miles explained.

"She faked having cramps again, didn't she?" Tobi said flatly, slinging an arm into her thermal exchange shirt.

"I don't get why *any* of us have to do this," Rainbow grumbled. He'd gotten the nickname for the bald stripes of pale skin shaved horizontally into his tightly-curled hair. "I thought y'all were *supposed* to be scroungers. This place used to be a party!"

"Yeah, well thanks to all that *partying*, y'all fucked up tens of millions of dollars of military equipment." Miles counted off on his fingers as he listed off each travesty. "— trashed dozens of vehicles, blew up the west barracks, killing sixty-three of your comrades. Oh yeah, and thanks to a prank-gone-wrong, we were like *seconds* away from accidentally nuking Cincinnati. So, yeah." Miles threw his hands in the air in exasperation. "General McCracken has decided to put an end to the partying and instill some discipline around here." Despite his raised voice, he sounded more like an exhausted teacher's assistant than a drill sergeant.

"Aren't we just becoming like *them* though? Like all the Lushie, Capitalist, imperialist, militaristic assholes that we're supposed to be rebelling against?" Rainbow's voice was slow and slurred. He always smoked Lolly before climbing out of his bunk in the morning. "This was supposed to be the dawning of a new world, but like, we're just doing pushups? Because you said so?"

Miles rubbed his temples and looked to Rylla for help, but she just frowned and shrugged. Miles and Rylla had been friends as kids, but as a teen he'd joined a scrounger gang, groups of scavengers who survived the Dust by whatever means necessary. Since Rylla and Miles had gone their separate ways, Rylla's brother, Tyler, had unified all the scrounger gangs in the Dust, forming the Dust Liberation Army, with Miles at his side. After the DLA had declared independence from the Lush states, thousands of bored teenagers and jobless twenty-somethings had started showing up to DLA HQ to join their ranks. For the first few weeks, the old Fort Sam Houston had been more like a music-festival-gone-wrong than an army base, with recruits partying, getting in fights, and trashing equipment. Now the leaders of the scrounger gangs were doing their best to whip everyone into shape, but Rylla had no idea how anyone could turn this rabble into anything like a real army, least of all Miles Walker.

"Look, you get two gallons of water a day here, right? Plus food and a bed to sleep on. For the Dust that's a pretty good deal. Tyl — I mean, General McCracken — says we kella run this morning, so we kella run! If anyone doesn't like it, go the fuck home," Miles said.

"Whatever," Tobi said, zipping the cooling suit up to her neck, which made her arms and legs look puffy, like Marshie the Marshmallow from that hologame franchise. "But you still play favorites. Just 'cause Rylla's the General's sister, doesn't mean she shouldn't have to work out."

"She don't get special treatment 'cause of that," Rainbow chuckled. "It's cause Sarge looooves —"

"All right, shut up!" Miles bellowed, finally sounding like a real drill sergeant. He cast a nervous glance at Rylla who stared out the copter's window, pretending she hadn't heard. "I want you suited up in thirty seconds or I'm adding 2K to our run. It's already 110 degrees outside, and it's only getting hotter, so let's go, go, GO!"

Rylla bit her lip to keep from laughing as Miles's dozen recruits finished pulling on their cooling suits and headed towards the thermalock at a reluctant jog. A tiny bit of guilt needled her for lying and abandoning her fellow recruits. But what for? She wasn't here because she'd signed up to be a soldier in Tyler's army. Professor Watt had sent her here to get close to her brother, in order to stop the impending civil war between the Dust and Lush states. For the last few weeks, she'd let Miles Walker boss her around, and she'd hardly caught a glimpse of her older brother. It was time to try something else. Besides, she loathed running with a passion, ever since Jae Boudreaux had made her run till she puked in his Orienteering class freshman year.

From the cockpit of the vandalized attack helicopter, she could survey the whole hangar — the squads of recruits warming up for their runs, a group of mechanics trying to repair damage to a military skimmer. The skimmer had probably crashed when someone totally inept had tried to fly the massive hovercraft. Amid all this bustling activity, there was a good chance that she might see Tyler and get a chance to talk to him. She couldn't bear the thought of checking in with her Humanity seminar, only to tell them that yet another week had gone by without her even speaking to her brother.

Leaving 50% of her vision cleared, she swiped a hand to pull up her schoolwork. As if stopping civil war wasn't enough for one human being, Professor Watt still expected Rylla to maintain a full course load via remote learning. Thanks to her brother's new zeal for military discipline, Rylla had barely had time this week to catch up on the recorded lectures for Intro to Artificial Intelligence. Figuring she had at least two hours before her squad got back from their run, she settled into the chair as a holographic Professor Amari paced across the helicopter's dashboard, explaining the differences between iterative and recursive algorithms. She fought off sleep, but it was a losing battle.

Just as her eyelids were getting irresistibly heavy, a blur of determined movement crossed the hangar in front of her. A clump of DLA soldiers passed through the thermalock and were moving toward the damaged skimmer at a brisk pace. At the center of the half-dozen people was a tall, blonde white guy, wearing an Air Force dress uniform jacket with the sleeves torn off and embroidered patches of thirty different scrounger gangs stuck all over it. The sight of her brother made a lump of hurt and nostalgia rise in the back of her throat, but she swallowed it down with grim determination.

Rylla swung herself down from the helicopter and jogged to catch up to her big brother, the "Dusty Dictator," the General of the Dust Liberation Army, leader of the parched half of the United States — Tyler McCracken. This time, she wasn't going to let him blow her off. She summoned the image of Magenta, in their seminar's last virtual check-in, saying,

"You've been with the DLA a month and haven't even managed to *talk* to him yet?" Rylla willed herself to be as forceful as Magenta always was.

"Tyler!" she yelled as she approached. The DLA soldiers clumped around him whipped their heads to her direction. She recognized the dark-skinned guy with the thick black beard as Dante — a scrounger she'd met last year, before her whole life had changed. The others were unfamiliar faces, scowling at her, but she wouldn't be intimidated so easily. "I need to talk to you."

"Why aren't you with your squad?" Tyler asked flatly. Rylla squared her shoulders, steeling herself against the emotionless welcome. The last few times she'd approached him, she'd been too hurt by his dismissal to insist on an audience. Not today.

"Half an hour, that's all I need. I've been trying to tell you —" She dropped her voice to a whisper. "I have privileged information that relates to the security of the entire DLA!"

"Just because you go to a Lush state college doesn't make you an intranational spy, Rylla," Tyler said, turning away. "You want to help the DLA? Be a good recruit. Quit giving Miles a hard time and set a good example for your squad. Now I'm busy." He waved to one of the other soldiers, urging him to continue talking.

Rylla fought off the ache surging in her gut, pounding it into another shape — into an anger that heated her cheeks. She had to try another tactic—get under his skin somehow. "Okay, maybe I'm *not* an intranational spy, but I've got a ton of privileged information on you, Tyler *Boseefus* McCracken."

Tyler's face muscles twitched at the sound of his middle name. Good. Rylla stifled a smile. "Now I can keep that privileged info private, or I can start telling folks what I caught you doing at Schlitterbahn that one time? In the lifeguard hut? With the CPR dummy —"

Tyler lunged at Rylla to clap a hand over her mouth, but she dodged out of the way, cackling. Dante boomed out a laugh and some of the other scroungers-turned-soldiers stifled smiles.

Tyler's lips disappeared he had them pressed so tightly.

"And that's just the tip of the iceberg," Rylla said, dancing away from another of Tyler's lunges. "It's not gonna be good for morale when I tell folks about that one time when you were eleven, when mom had to take you to the hospital because —"

"All right, fuck," Tyler yelled, dropping his arms. He met Rylla's eyes and there was so much annoyance there, but maybe — just maybe — there was also the hint of a smile.

She remembered teasing him like this once, when he was first dating Jo. Despite his cold brush-offs over the past few weeks, maybe he'd been missing her too.

"Thirty minutes. You can have exactly one half-hour to tell me whatever it is you think is so important."

"In private," Rylla said, folding her arms.

Tyler lifted his hands to the hangar ceiling and let them drop, as if a little sister was the most exasperating of all his world-leader problems. "Sure. In private."

✦

Tyler sat on the twin bed in the corner of the plain, cinderblock room, while she pulled a cheap rolling chair out from under the desk. Tyler had claimed a simple room in the officer's barracks, among the rest of his most trusted scroungers, rather than moving into one of the fancy, plantation-style General's mansions on post. She hoped that decision meant that all this sudden power hadn't completely ruined his head.

"Well thank you, your dictatorship-highness-sir, for sparing me some of your precious time, at long last."

"Twenty-nine minutes left. This really how you want to use them?" Tyler asked, unamused.

"How are you?" she asked, seriously.

He shook his head ruefully. "We don't have time for that either, Rylla. Just tell me what it is that's so urgent."

"It's urgent to me to know how my only sibling in the world is doing!" she said.

"I'm doing how the movement is doing, okay? Ever since Jo died —" Tyler's voice hitched, but then he swallowed, and his eyes turned to steel. "The DLA is making allies, shoring up our borders and influence. We're unifying the scroungers and turning these recruits into something like soldiers. The Lushy politicians in Philadelphia are still arguing about what to do with us. But whether or not they attack, something's got to give, because our water reserves are dwindling, and they're running out of oil and plastics. That's all common knowledge. That's how I'm doing. Now what do you *want*?"

"Okay, so you know that college I used to go to — Wingates? Well the thing is, I *still* go there. Like me being here, it's all an assignment. Me and four of my seminar-mates, get this —" Rylla barked a laugh at the absurdity of what she was about to say. "We've been *assigned* to stop this civil war between the Dust and Lush States."

Tyler's face looked incredulous and annoyed, but he didn't interrupt.

"And the thing is, Wingates is *powerful*, like they have connections and resources you wouldn't believe. They have a military base under the school, and they're developing all this future tech —"

"I'm somewhat familiar with Wingates, and what it does," Tyler cut in, holding up a hand. "I have my own intelligence network now."

Rylla couldn't tell if he really did know about Wingates or if he was bluffing. "Okay, cool — so you know that their Humanity majors, like, fuck with world powers? To learn stuff about … leadership, I guess?" Rylla trailed off, staring out the window at heat lines rippling above the unrelenting dust. Far-off, a line of figures in puffy, camo cooling suits were stumble-jogging over a dune. All the terrible secrets she'd learned about

Wingates last year came crashing into her mind. Worst of all, she'd discovered that the Board of billionaires were planning a purge of most of the billions of people on Earth, using nanotechnology developed by her friend Theo. It had horrified Rylla to stay on as a student after that revelation, pretending like everything was fine. But after fleeing Wingates with his research, Theo had begged Rylla to do just that. To stay at Wingates, working to stop the Board's genocidal plan from within. Still, it made her skin crawl to say to Tyler, "I still *am* a Wingates Humanity major."

"That's just great," Tyler said, sarcastically. "You know that makes me feel really good about the fact that you've had access to this entire base for a month."

"But I'm on your side, Tyler," Rylla said, turning back to him and pressing her hands between her knees. "And I have friends in key places. My roommate, Magenta, has infiltrated the U.S. Army as an undercover Captain. Their company is stationed at the Wall, right outside Emigrant City on the Louisiana border. My friend Jae Boudreaux is the creator of *The New Dust News* — that Dark Net site that's been giving you a ton of sympathetic press. And Ynez Espinoza is working as an aide to a Senator in Philadelphia. She's got the ear of the Senate Majority Leader! We all want to work together to help you. To stop this war!"

Tyler shook his head at the ground and chuckled darkly. "For all your college-smarts, you're pretty dense, Rylla. If our goal was to avoid war, why do you think we raised an army? Why do you think we took over military bases and declared independence if we wanted to *avoid* war?"

"Right, right — I know!" Rylla interrupted. "Because you care about the Dust. Because you think folks here have a right to water, and political representation in Philadelphia. I get that. But I'm saying, maybe there's a way to get those concessions *bloodlessly*. Use my contacts in the military, and the media, and the government to your advantage! Sway public favor your way, and we can get justice for the Dust without going to war and wrecking the entire fucking world with nuclear fallout."

Tyler was biting his cuticles viciously — an old habit that hit Rylla with a wave of bittersweet nostalgia. He always used to do that when Amaryllis was drunk, and they were having to walk on eggshells to avoid getting screamed at. Looking at him now, part of her still saw that scared, chubby-cheeked eight-year-old hiding behind his golden beard and harsh, skeletal features. He wasn't eating enough.

"They're not going to nuke us," he said, spitting a bit of skin on the carpet. "Mutually assured destruction. We actually have a few dozen more nukes than they do. And we have a lot less to lose. Hence, the stalemate."

"Okay — still, you admitted, this stalemate can't go on forever. You need Lush state water, and food rations. And they need their precious oil and plastics."

Tyler coughed a bitter laugh. "Yeah, after the West became Dust, the Lush states didn't want all the pollution from the oil and gas industry poisoning their precious watersheds anymore. So they moved all the toxic refineries and chemical plants out here. And look how that's bit them in the ass."

"I know all that." Rylla shrugged off her annoyance at the unnecessary history lesson.

Tyler stared in Rylla's direction without seeing her. "You were always such an idealist. Always talking about how when you grew up, you were going to go to college, and make the river 'back the way it was.' But there's no putting the world 'back the way it was,' Rylla. Even if I could, I wouldn't. Everything's been too unjust and broken and cruel for too long." He folded his hands together and pressed them against his lips. "No, the world is changing — it needs to change. A reckoning is coming, and it will not be bloodless. You're either with me, or you're standing in my way."

Find More Books by Sim Kern at Stelliform Press

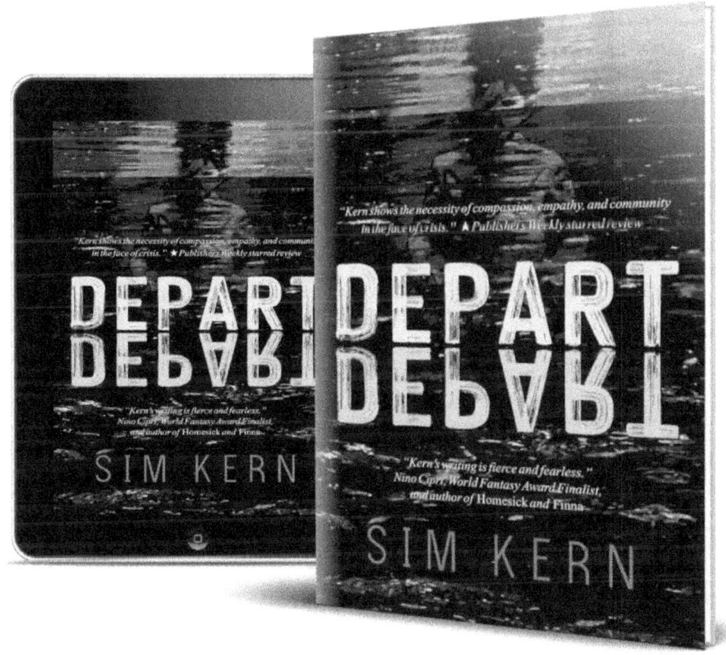

Sim Kern's Otherwise Award Honor Listed novella *Depart, Depart!* is the "fierce and fearless" queer climate ghost story you need. Find *Depart, Depart!* wherever books are sold. Digital books are always on sale at www.stelliform.press.

NOW AVAILABLE

A collection of stories for reluctant witches, sugar smugglers, and soil thieves.

Android Press
www.android-press.com

Earth-focused fiction. Stellar stories.
Stelliform.press.

Stelliform Press is shaping conversations about nature and our place within it. We invite you to join the conversation by leaving a comment or review on your favorite social media platform. Find us on the web at www.stelliform.press and on Twitter, Instagram and Facebook @StelliformPress.